Elise.

Elise.

MELANIE MARTINS

Melanie Martins

VAN DEN BOSCH SERIES

BOOK THREE

Melanie Martins, LLC
www.melaniemartins.com

First published in the United States by Melanie Martins, LLC in 2023.

ISBSN ebook 979-8-9861626-3-8

ISBN Paperback 979-8-9861626-4-5

Printed and bound by CPI Group (UK) Ltd, Croydon, CR0 4YY

This is a 1st Edition.

DISCLAIMER

This novel is a work of fiction written in American-English and is intended for mature audiences. Names, characters, places, and incidents are either the product of the author's imagination or used fictitiously. Any resemblance to actual persons, living or dead, is entirely coincidental. This novel contains strong and explicit language, graphic sexuality, and other sensitive content that may be disturbing for some readers.

To all of you, my dear readers.
Thank you.

READING ORDER

While you don't need to have read the Blossom in Winter series to start this book, you do need to have read the first two books of the Van den Bosch series:

Blossom in Winter series (Petra & Alex's story)

1. Blossom in Winter
2. Lured into Love
3. Lured into Lies
4. Defying Eternity
5. Happily Ever After: Part 1, 2, 3, and 4

Van den Bosch series

1. Roxanne.
2. Andries.
3. Elise. (You are here)
4. Dan.
5. Julia.
6. Sebastian.
7. Hannah.
8. Johan.

PROLOGUE

V.D.B. estate, September 15, 2019
Dan

I can feel the breeze through the holes in my sweater; it's crispy and the smell of leaves pinwheeling down from the trees around the Van den Bosch estate overwhelms me. Had I been standing still, I might have even caught a chill, but as I move across the terrace opposite Andries, he's actually pushing me hard enough that I'm breaking a sweat.

Despite being outside, the only thing that can be heard is our loud breaths, footsteps, and the occasional blades colliding. Andries might be smiling, but there is always this edge of seriousness to him that permeates everything he does—including the playful fencing match the two of us are currently engaged in. I can see it in the line of concentration between his eyebrows and the exhales of frustration when I best him.

"Fuck," Andries mutters under his breath as I win against him once again.

"That wasn't too bad," I tease, walking slowly back toward him. "You even made me sweat a bit."

Losing against me isn't out of the ordinary for my friend. After all, I'm five years older and have much more experience in fencing than him. All in all, it's a beautiful day to have a few playful matches outside. The sun is shining and there aren't any obligations looming over my shoulders.

Andries's mom, Julia, is sipping coffee at the terrace dining table, caught between reading what seems to be paperwork and watching the two of us.

"Let's start again," Andries says, his excitement matching his expression as he puts himself in position.

"Very well." I do the same, but when he's about to strike, he pauses mid-move, holding up his hand to tell me to halt, but I playfully poke him with the foil anyway. He scowls, one of his most common expressions, and waves me away.

"Knock it off," he grumbles, turning fully to the railing overlooking the rest of the property as if something caught his attention. Their estate is massive; green rolling hills give way to wild forests full of fauna that are rarely seen on the more manicured estates about these parts.

Curious, I follow him to the railing and meet where his gaze is locked, foil hanging limply in my hand. I can see two figures emerging from the forest; one, the hulking frame of Sebastian Van den Bosch, and the other, more slight and willowy. She carries the same "I own the world" strut that Andries has been perfecting over the years, albeit unconsciously.

Another Van den Bosch, then.

As they get closer, it's clear that it's Sebastian and a young woman, and both are holding dispatched pheasants by the feet in one hand with shotguns slung over the shoulders.

"Who is it, dear?" Julia asks.

"Dad and Elise are back from hunting," Andries replies, shivering as he says so. I know all about the story of Andries balking during his first hunt when he was only twelve years old and the way it traumatized him, so I keep my mouth shut. At least it's only birds they're bringing back.

The second name that rolls off his lips catches my attention, though.

Elise.

I know very little about her. All I know is that she's the second oldest of the children, just under Andries. I've only ever caught fleeting glances of her running through the halls of the Van den Bosch manor, dark blonde hair escaping some prissy style in rebellious little ringlets. Even when I join the family on their summer vacations, they'd always have an excuse for why their eldest daughter wasn't around. Apparently, Elise preferred to spend her summers at equestrian camps instead of lounging on beaches. Part of me respected that, but the other part of me wondered how she could so easily give up that time with her family. The mysterious sister is a teen, after all, so it wasn't odd that her decisions made little sense.

Andries raises his hand to wave at them, and they each raise a hand back in greeting. Both father and daughter are dressed in olive green hunting gear, their leather boots fastened above the pants. I know Sebastian well, so my attention is stuck on Elise. I feel my interest pique as she gets closer. She looks like Julia, which comes as no surprise, but her hair is darker at the roots and her finely boned features have that almost sulky, overcast vibe about them. Andries has this as well, but with him it makes him look pouty and like the tortured poet he so longs to be, Elise looks sharp and focused.

The hunting gear doesn't give me much more information about her body, and for that, I'm thankful. Running through the math in my head, I determine that Elise is entirely too young for me to take any sort of interest in. I sneak a guilty look at Andries, but thankfully, he's paying me no mind.

"We'll be right up!" Sebastian booms once the pair is directly beneath us. Andries gives him a thumbs up in response and turns back to me.

"Ready to pick up where we left off?"

"You mean me defeating you in one fell swoop?" I quip, and Andries rolls his eyes. It's a startlingly immature gesture that makes me laugh. Sometimes I forget just how young he really is. He might be only sixteen, but he's already got the height that will follow him into adulthood. Standing well over six feet, and in his bulky sweater, I can't see the narrowness of his shoulders that gives away his youth, along with the softness still present in his face. Once he comes fully into adulthood, poor broody Andries will undoubtedly be a lady killer, whether he likes it or not.

"En garde," Andries says to get my mind back on track, assuming the position. With a smirk, I do the same, and our fencing commences.

Eventually, Elise and Sebastian make their way out onto the terrace. Sebastian leans down to kiss Julia while Elise strips off the green hunting jacket, festooned with numerous buttons and pockets, moving to hang it on the back of one of the chairs. Underneath she wears a skin-tight moisture wicking athletic shirt, a long sleeve, and a mock turtleneck over the top. I shouldn't be distracted. I don't want to be distracted, but damn... I'm still a man.

My brain knows she's young. Younger than Andries by a year, I believe, and the knowledge helps to keep my more debauched thoughts at bay. I have enough of a leash on myself that whatever I'm feeling toward that young lady leans heavily on fascination. Because she is, undoubtedly, fascinating.

Muscle memory keeps me on even ground with Andries, but I manage to turn him around so his back is to his family and I can see everyone now in my line of vision seated at the table. Elise has her chair leaned back, balanced on the back two legs, watching me just as intently as the two adults she's sitting with. Where Andries always has that touch of sadness about him, his sister has smugness. Her gaze tells me she isn't impressed by the show, but the novelty of it is enough to keep her engaged for the moment.

It's just a friendly match between Andries and me, but I'm well aware the five years I have over him put me at an advantage. It's why I don't mind zoning out a little bit; we're using blunted blades anyway. His sister is holding her hands up now and pulling off a pair of supple leather gloves finger by finger, tossing them on the table in front of her and then wiggling her bare hands to stretch them out. There's a spot of pheasant blood on her white sleeve, and it causes something primal to stir deep inside me. She's a huntress— Artemis, trapped in some nobleman's daughter.

I wish I could just stop this game and introduce myself to her. But, of course, that would be totally inappropriate. I'm twenty-one, after all. And while Julia and Sebastian don't have any problem having me around as their son's best friend, I'm fairly sure they'd be less enthusiastic if I displayed any kind of interest, even platonically, toward their precious daughter.

Three years…

If I'm counting correctly, I could befriend her in three years when she reaches adulthood. Until then, I'm going to try to get to know her as much as possible through her brother. It'd either show me how uninteresting she really is or give me a prime advantage if I really did want to pursue her years down the line.

I try to put all my focus back on the match, but I'm more distracted than I want to admit. My mind is busy and floating away from me, and Andries is getting annoyed with how slow the match is going. I'm ready to just call it a day and be finished, but when Elise stands and moves to go inside, stretching her arms over her head and displaying just an inch or so of midriff, I falter completely.

In an instant, Andries is on me harder than before, and I feel the blunted tip of his foil poking me in the chest. Stunned, I look down at it in disbelief. He had never bested me before. Ever.

Julia and Sebastian clap, but Elise is long gone back into the house by the time Andries pulls the foil away from my pectoral. I start to congratulate him, but his expression is stiff and angry.

"Can I talk to you for a sec?" he hisses between his teeth, jerking his head toward the railing where we could get a little privacy away from his parents.

Shrugging, I carefully sit my foil on the ground and follow him farther from our small audience. There is a muscle working in Andries's jaw and a vein pulsing on his forehead.

"Are you alright?" I ask hesitantly.

His lips are pressed in a straight line and his eyes are staring right through me like he's trying to read my deepest thoughts. He doesn't answer, though. Instead, he just bluntly asks, "Were you checking out my sister?"

Oh shit. I've been busted. "No! Of course not!"

He scoffs. "Yeah, right. I've seen that look before. She's fifteen, you pervert!"

"I swear I wasn't!" I protest, wishing I could tell him that yes, I was appreciating Elise's beauty, but I know better than to be interested in a fifteen-year-old in that way. I'd table whatever feelings I might have until she was of age, but I think that statement would make him even angrier.

"I'd better not catch you looking at her like that ever again," he says, raising the foil still in his hand to point at my heart. I know it's a practice blade, but it still sends a shiver up my spine, especially since his expression is deadly serious. "Or I will make sure to cut you into pieces."

I chuckle at what can only be a joke. "Andries, what the fuck?" I step forward, putting my gloved hand on the top of the blade and pushing it away from me. "You're acting crazy. I'd never do anything with your sister."

"Am I?" He doesn't raise the blade again but gives one step forward until we're standing too close for comfort. A threatening gesture, and even if Andries has height, he has to know that he could never take me in a real fight, him and his still young bones. "I've never won against you," he continues. "And the only reason I did it now is because you were checking her out."

"Andries, my friend." I lay my hands on his shoulders, my tone more comforting. "Man to man, this behavior is out of line. Even if I was ogling her, which I wasn't, all it'd take is one respectful word from you, and I would back off. I would hope you'd trust me enough for that, but all of this makes me think otherwise."

His expression falters, but he doesn't relent, shrugging my hands off him. "Very well, then promise me right here you'll never do anything with her."

"I swear," I tell him solemnly, even if I feel unhappy about it. We could cross that bridge years from now if it came down to it.

Andries doesn't seem satisfied though, and his eyebrows raise suspiciously. "You swear on your honor?" he presses, a frown wiped across his face.

"On my what?" I repeat, my eyes widening in shock at his question. "Are you serious?"

"Yes! I'll never talk to you again if you try to compromise her."

"*Compromise* her?" I guffaw. This guy is crazy! "How can you be so old school!? She's a person, not an object that can be ruined or *compromised*."

"Dan! She's my sister," Andries reminds me, his tone coming across more authoritative than I ever expected. He then exhales heavily and runs a hand through his too-long hair. He's trying a longer look, and it doesn't suit him the way he thinks it does. "We are best friends, but she is my sister. She's family. Get it?"

Well, if in a few years I end up marrying her, I'll be family too, I find myself thinking.

I want to shake my head and give him a piece of my mind, but I'm just a guest at his estate and decide against it.

"Now, are you going to swear on your honor or not?"

"Fine." I sigh, resigned, as I hold up my right hand. It's all for show, but whatever will calm him down in the moment. "I, Dan O'Brian, swear on my honor that I'll never try to *compromise* your beloved sister," I mutter, hoping my sarcasm isn't too noticeable. "Good enough?"

My friend's face changes immediately, going from tense to jovial. "Great!" He claps me on the shoulder. "As long as you keep your word, we can remain friends."

I'm beyond shocked at how protective he is of his sister. Even when thinking of the future, after she reaches adulthood. Doesn't he think I'm good enough for her? Since I remain quiet, he starts leading me toward the table. "Now let's go and have some tea with my parents. They're serving blooming tea, your favorite."

THREE YEARS LATER...

CHAPTER 1

Amsterdam, April 18, 2022
Dan

Yamazato is packed as always, but it's not a problem for me to get us a table tucked in a corner with some semblance of privacy. It's amazing what a couple of folded bills handed to the host will do for the wait time.

Elise looks as if she's wound tight, her shoulders stiff and her lips in a straight line. Whatever she and Sebastian talked about has clearly given her a lot to think about, and even though I'm nosy about how everything went down, I need to get her guard down before she'll let out the more valuable information.

I grab the arm of a passing server, who scowls until he hears me say, "A bottle of your finest sake, please."

Seeing the flashing euro signs that could come from taking care of me, the server immediately nods with a polite smile. "Right away, sir."

Elise and I settle in, her interlacing her fingers and looking around without a word while the host hands me a menu and lays the one for Elise beside her.

Menu in hand, I take a moment to savor the fact it's just the two of us here. There's no Andries, no Jessica, just us.

After all, it's not often that I have the opportunity to take the ice queen of the Van den Bosch family out for a one-on-one dinner.

"Comfortable?" I ask.

Her eyes snap back toward mine. "Yes, why wouldn't I be?"

Ha! I'd forgotten the ice queen is also a mean bitch.

"Oh, it just looks like it must be uncomfortable to sit with that stick up your ass."

She wrinkles her nose in distaste, scoffing. "Shut up, Dan."

"Then relax. This isn't an interrogation, just a dinner with a treasured friend."

She snorts at "treasured" but I can see her letting go of at least a little bit of the stress she must be feeling.

The server returns with a green, transparent bottle of sake and bowl-shaped cups, and when I tell him I'll take care of the serving myself, he nods, ready to depart from our table.

"Wait," Elise says before he can do so. "A bottle of still water for me, please."

I can't help but let out a quick chuckle at her statement; if she thinks the sake is only for me, she's very mistaken.

Once we are left alone, she takes the bottle of sake first, tilting it so she can look at the label as if she's reading it.

"Can you read Japanese?" I ask, surprised.

"Some. Barely." She turns the bottle at me, her lips twisting into a smug smirk as she asks, "Are you trying to get me drunk?"

"No, I'm just trying to thaw you out a little bit, so I'm not having dinner with an ice sculpture. Here, let me pour for us."

With Elise, I've learned to speak in absolutes, because if she has a choice in something, there is no turning her away from her path. Reluctantly, she hands me the sake and I open it, filling our cups with a shot before setting it down. "Ready?"

She looks like she wants to protest, but when she watches me pick my own cup up and hold it to my lips, she takes it as a challenge and lifts her own. "Fine. Yes, I'm ready."

I close my eyes and tip the cup back and the sake fills my mouth like liquid fire, turning smooth as it flows down my throat and warms my belly from the inside out. When I open my eyes again to ask Elise how hers was, it's just in time for me to see her throat work as she drinks, her lips wet with the liquor. For one-second, it's irresistibly seductive, but then she coughs, barely raising her hand in time to cover her mouth and grimaces.

"Oh, hell," she laments through small coughs, which only makes me laugh.

"Another!" I proclaim, even as she's still getting herself under control, and while she tries to wave me away, she can't form whole sentences quite yet, and her cup is full before she can stop me.

As I pause with the rim of the cup on my lips, I smirk. "Try to keep up, little girl."

I know she's cursing me in her mind, but Elise will never let me best her in any way, so as I take my shot I see her do the same, this time followed by a full-bodied shiver and an eye roll.

I pick the bottle up to pour a third, but this time she snakes an arm out and snags it, sitting it decidedly on her side of the table. "Absolutely not."

I ignore the rough, sultry sound of her abused throat. "Okay... for now."

Before I can proceed, though, the server stops by our table holding the much-awaited bottle of Acqua Panna and two glasses. Once he fills hers, Elise wastes no time in giving a long gulp. We take this moment to order food and when the server departs from our table again, a small smirk emerges on my lips at what I have in mind. "Let's hear about this mysterious meeting then, if we aren't going to get drunk first."

There is an obvious red flush to her cheekbones, telling me that the little lightweight might not be completely drunk, but she's definitely feeling those two shots. She parts her lips to speak, pauses as if she's deciding her words, and starts again. "It was nothing, Dan. I swear," she repeats the same broken record like she did in the car, to which I give her a frown in annoyance.

"Fine." She sighs, knowing fully well there's no way to escape this conversation. "It was just about how my brother is a moron and how we need to break him and Roxanne up to teach him a lesson. The usual stuff."

Fuck. I knew it. "God, that man is obsessed. I don't know why he's even so concerned about what his son is doing when he has you, the perfect heir."

Elise preens. "I know, right?" she says, a muffled chuckle escaping her lips. "Having Andries not only spurn his offer but also get married to a former escort is just a bridge too far away for him."

I nod, a few questions forming in my head. "You think he knows that Andries is never going to change his mind about taking the job?"

She doesn't answer immediately. Elise is too calculated for that. Instead, she takes a sip of her water, pondering her words carefully. "My impression is that Dad considers Andries young and foolish, and is still holding out some hope, but he's already shifted gears to prepare me as his successor." She pauses for a beat before her eyes meet mine again. "I think at this point, he just wants to punish Andries for his reckless behavior."

"Fuck. How dreadful," I blurt out, deadpan, before I lean forward, resting my forearms on the table and lowering my voice. "Do you know exactly what your dad intends to do?"

A few beats of silence ensue, my eyes locking on hers as if I could read the answer in her gaze.

Elise blinks twice, cutting eye contact, and her lips twitching with uncertainty, before she finally says, "Dad will never tell me what his actual plan is, but I do know he wants to make sure that wedding doesn't happen—which is totally fucked up."

Yeah, right… I'd bet a thousand bucks that both Elise and Sebastian are scheming together. But, of course, Elise knows what to say.

Just then, the server comes by, dropping off our meals. For me, two intricate sushi rolls topped with ruby-red roe for one roll and tempura crab on the other—decadent and not traditional in any way at all, but delicious nonetheless. Elise, unsurprisingly, has ordered simple nigiri with fatty slices of pink salmon and bright red tuna. She carefully fills a small dish with soy sauce and breaks apart her chopsticks, rubbing them together.

While she's already engrossed with her food, I can't help but ruminate over her last words. "What do you think he's planning, then? I guess there's no way we'd be lucky enough to persuade him to leave Andries alone."

"Ha." Elise delicately picks up a piece of nigiri, dipping it in her sauce before popping it in her mouth, chewing, and swallowing before continuing. "Definitely not. I've narrowed it down to a few things. I think the best-case scenario in his mind is dragging Andries away from Roxanne and back into the fold, and having both of us take over the company in a decade or so as co-CEOs. Even though we both know I'd be doing all the work and Andries would be staring out a window being broody."

Despite her humorous tone, I can't help but see the disappointment in her gaze. "That's not fair to you, though."

"Of course it isn't, but life isn't fair." Her tone comes off as more gloomy than she had aimed for, signaling to me it struck a nerve. She then straightens her posture, regaining her usual confidence. "What I find more likely is the second option; making me CEO when he retires and painting Andries as some philanthropist to the media, doing charitable work, but having no actual title at the company. That would still involve him ditching Roxanne, though, which we know will never happen. Who knows how this will actually go down?"

We eat in silence for a few minutes as I think over what she's told me. There's still the glowing issue of Elise being tasked with breaking Andries and his fiancée up that she so carefully avoided talking about. Oh well, I'm not shy.

"Do you plan on following commands and splitting the happy couple up for daddy dearest?"

"I…" she breathes out, obviously twisted up inside about it. While I thought she'd snap something back at me, to my astonishment, she just looks confused, as if lost for words. "I sort of have to try, don't I? If I don't at least put some effort into it, Dad will never consider me."

"Don't do that, Elise," I tell her, voice low and serious as I lean forward. She looks up at me in surprise, no doubt at the lack of levity. "You'll just be making things even more distant than they already are between your family and your brother."

She heaves a sigh, her gaze dropping for a moment. "I know that. It's just that I don't see much of an option."

"Support your brother," I say right away. "Love him when he feels abandoned by the rest of the household, and be part of his engagement. Part of his life. He's your brother, after all, and I truly think he'd do the same for you. Look how far he went for his love for Roxanne. Andries doesn't let the people he cares about down."

"You're right." She sighs, mulling over what I just told her. "I know you are, but I feel like I'm being torn in two. This whole engagement thing caught my dad so off guard that it's gonna take a few days for him to digest it."

"Speaking of the engagement," I begin cautiously, still not over the fact that my best friend is already engaged. "Did you try and persuade your dad to come to the party like Andries asked?"

She shakes her head as she finishes eating one of her nigiri. "There's no way in hell that our parents will attend, so I didn't even bother...not with how pissed off Dad is already. Andries will have to get used to the idea that I'll be the only one of the family attending it."

My face falls a little in disappointment at Sebastian's behavior. What parents would refuse to attend their child's engagement party?

"So you're going to attend as the spy of the family or something?" I ask, chuckling at the idea, but Elise stares at me without an ounce of a smile.

"Kind of," she says, causing my eyebrows to inch up in surprise. I wait a few more seconds to see if she will develop her answer, but when Elise resumes eating, it's clear that she doesn't want to elaborate on it anymore, so I drop the subject. It's enough that I know she doesn't want to sabotage Andries and Roxie, which gives me room to work with.

I let her lead the conversation away from her brother and father after that, simply enjoying the food and her company. I don't want to press her too hard and make her reluctant to spend time with me, so I make sure to make the rest of the evening lighthearted and enjoyable for her. She's beautiful when she laughs, and even when she scowls at me, her nose wrinkles. I pour us a few more shots, and by the fourth, she isn't hacking it up. The only sign that it's affecting her is her watering eyes.

Spending the entire night at this table with Elise doesn't sound like a bad idea, but the hours continue to pass, and I know I've got to let her go. Once I finish paying, I escort her outside, arm in arm, her steps a little heavier than usual because of the sake. I'd driven us to dinner and four shots of sake over a few hours don't affect me any, but I see Elise stopping by the sidewalk when I'm about to go to the driver's seat.

"Don't you want a ride?" I ask her.

"No, don't worry. I booked an Uber before we left."

Her announcement causes a slight pang in my heart. "I can give you a ride home. I'm okay," I offer somewhat hopefully, but she shakes her head.

"That's fine, really, but thank you for dinner. It's just what I needed after such a rough day."

To my surprise, she approaches me, opening her arms. I gather her into a hug instinctively, and her face rests below my chin, fitting so perfectly in my embrace. I can smell her floral perfume and the sweet scent of her skin, and it makes me dizzy. I've never been this close to her before, and holding her warm body makes all those feelings I've been trying to tamp down swirl out of the depths of my mind. Elise is gorgeous, strong-willed, and keeping her firmly in the friend zone is driving me crazy. I expect it always will, and I'll just have to learn to live with it.

Just as she snuggles her face into my shoulder, my phone goes off shrilly in my pocket, causing us both to jump back. Jaw clenched in annoyance, I pull it out and see that it's Jessica letting me know that she's arrived at my place and already let herself in. I curse under my breath, tucking the phone back into my pocket. I had completely forgotten about her coming over tonight.

One look at her tipsy, bright face and Elise makes me think that it's probably a good thing Jessica is waiting for me. She'll be a good distraction if nothing else. The thought makes me feel guilty because Jessica deserves to be more than just a distraction, but as of right now, I have zero interest in commitment, and I'm not about to shackle myself to someone just to make them feel better.

I take one last glance at the eldest Van den Bosch daughter, feeling melancholy but not letting it show on the outside. "Just text me when you get home, okay?"

Elise huffs in annoyance but gives a quick nod. "Yes, yes, I'll let you know I'm safe or whatever."

When she spots a car stopping by the sidewalk, she looks down at her phone and gives a few steps back. "Well, I'm leaving... my ride's here."

I wish I could hug her again, but instead, I just offer a soft smile. "Have a good night, El."

***

Back at my townhouse, Jessica isn't anywhere to be found inside, but then I spot the light coming from the terrace of my bedroom, and I can't help but wonder if she's already made herself comfortable on the loungers. When I pull open the door to join her outside, I'm immediately hit with the pungent smell of the marijuana she must have taken out of my bedside table. I'm a bit annoyed that she helped herself, but she looks so good in her leggings and cropped top, her hair curling down her breasts, that it's easy to forgive her.

Without a word, I lie next to her on the lounger, and she passes me the joint without even glancing my way. It's always this way between us—casual to the point of it being almost strange—but it suits me well. I take the joint and hit it, the heady smoke filling my lungs and staying there while I hold my breath before releasing it to curl up into the dark sky.

I pass it back to Jessica, who is all too happy to wrap her lips around it. Her eyes are lidded and heavy, and while I would usually be thinking filthy things at this point in the night with her, my mind is still elsewhere. I want to talk about it, I realize, but I certainly can't talk about my inconvenient feelings toward Elise with Jessica, so I tell her the next best thing I can think of, desperate to at least get some things off my chest.

After exhaling my second hit, I say, "My best friend is getting married."

Jessica looks at me quickly. "Andries? Is he marrying that woman we all met in Ghent?"

I don't mention that I knew her long before Ghent and just nod. "Yeah, Andries and Roxanne." I turn my head slightly to check her face. "Isn't that crazy?"

"Yes, very crazy, actually." She shakes her head, her gaze returning to the sky. "He's so young! I can't believe he'd be making a commitment like that at such a young age."

"Me either," I agree. "But once Andries sets his mind on something, there is no stopping him."

Jessica says something about hoping Andries knows what he's getting into, but I'm distracted by my phone going off.

I touch the screen to wake it up, reading the message preview from Elise and smiling to myself.

Elise: *I'm back at my place, Mr. Annoying.*

CHAPTER 2

Amsterdam, April 19, 2022
Dan

My best friend is finally back and I couldn't be more excited to see him again. Andries is waiting for me at one of the cafes on campus, just like we had agreed. He'd decided to sit on the patio for the unseasonably warm day, his long legs spread out and his posture relaxed. It's an odd state for the usually churlish Andries, but I'm glad for it.

"What's up, man?" I ask as I reach the table, and Andries stands to greet me with an affectionate handshake and shoulder pat.

"Just waiting for you, my consistently late friend," he answers, his face beaming with joy.

"You know I'd never stand you up," I joke, taking my seat and ordering a cappuccino when the server stops by to check on us.

"Yeah, lucky me," Andries quips, and I can't help but laugh. He's never so easygoing!

As I look at him more closely, he's got a nice color on his cheeks, and a very unusually cheerful demeanor. "So, how is it going, Mr. Commitment? Do you love being shackled down to one woman for all time during the prime of your life?"

"Adore it, actually," he drawls. "Looking back, I'm even more sure that I made the right choice in proposing. It was the most enjoyable trip of my life."

I shake my head, trying hard not to chuckle. "Paris is overrated. You must be more sheltered than I thought."

"It's not about Paris, Dan. It's because Roxie was with me. Even if we had never left the suite, it'd have been perfect."

I grimace exaggeratedly. "Gross. Moving on from your sex fest in France, how are things going with the two of you? Are you still living in separate places?"

The server walks over, putting my cappuccino in front of my place setting, while Andries takes a sip of his espresso to cover his frown. Did I hit a nerve with my question or what? "Actually, I've been living with Roxanne for a while now. Her penthouse is amazing. And I don't want to spend any night without her, so it just makes sense."

My eyes widen in surprise and I can't help but wonder why he never told me about it before. "Your parents must be apoplectic." I chuckle, taking a swig of my cappuccino and reaching for one of the scones in the middle of the table. "Oh, uh, speaking of your overly stuffy family, I talked to Elise last night." I don't mention that by talk, I actually mean "had dinner and drinks with."

This seems to be enough to give him pause. "For someone who doesn't like my nosy sister, you spend an awful amount of time with her," he points out, his tone suspicious, but I wave him off.

"Only because the both of us have to keep an eye on you. Honestly, you should be thankful, because Elise would be able to meddle in your affairs quite a bit more if I wasn't there to buffer her enthusiasm."

Andries raises his eyebrows. "Actually, yeah, that is true. So what did she have to say?"

With his interest piqued, I take this moment to lean back in my chair, reveling in it. "You're so lucky to have a friend like me, you know? She had a meeting with your dad yesterday that had quite a bit to do with your engagement."

Andries throws his croissant on his plate, suddenly annoyed. "Of course it fucking did. I'd be fine with him never speaking to me again If it meant he'd get over this obsession he has with me. And now he's continually dragging Elise into it."

For some reason, I feel slightly defensive at his statement. "Hey, she apparently doesn't want to be a part of it, but he doesn't give her much choice."

"She might not want to be involved in messing with my engagement, but she certainly wants to be involved in the company and take over Dad's position once he retires." He picks up his cup, clutching it but not drinking. "How far she'll go to get what she wants is yet to be seen."

"I hate to admit it, but you're right." In fact, I did hate to agree. I don't want to think that Elise would go to such huge lengths to advance in her career, but even if I had some out-of-place affection for her, I wasn't a fool. I know that she's capable of anything, including—if her dad insists —trying to break the engagement between her brother and Roxanne. She was definitely not the biggest fan of the former escort, even on a normal basis, and her distaste for the whole affair might just be enough to push her over the edge and into doing her father's bidding.

"It doesn't matter, anyway. My sister can pull whatever tricks she wants. Nothing in this world could change my mind about marrying Roxanne." Andries meets my eyes, and in his gaze is such a tremendous love for his fiancée that it makes my heart hurt. What must it be like to feel so strongly about someone that you'd have no doubts about moving heaven and earth for them?

I lean forward, resting my forearms on the table, and lowering my voice, I say, "You know, after your breakup, I never thought you would get back together and get engaged so quickly."

"Me either," he admits, a small smile forming at the corner of his lips. "But she is the only thing that makes life worth it."

I try to picture myself in his situation, completely smitten and dedicated to one person. It seems like an impossible feat… like something I could never do. Even though I'm five years older than him, the simple thought of marrying someone and waking up to her every morning makes me feel nothing but emptiness. I try to picture Jessica, which has been my longest hookup so far, but it feels just as wrong. That is, until Jessica's face flickers and then, lying next to me in my imagination, is Elise, her face bare of any artifice and beautiful beyond measure. With her there, there is no emptiness. There is something else… something massive and indescribable.

No. No. And fuck no! I can't think like that. I shouldn't, especially sitting next to her fucking brother. What's wrong with me?

"I'm genuinely happy for you," I tell him, shutting down all my previous thoughts. "I'm happy I could be part of this with you, and that you didn't give up when it felt difficult."

His smile keeps growing until it displays perfectly aligned white teeth. "I hope to return the favor one day."

"Mm, that's unlikely." I try to sound amused, but in the back of my mind I'm thinking, *I never will have that connection with someone, since the only person I could imagine being with for that long you made me swear off forever.*

Brushing away the grudging feeling I'm starting to have for my best friend, I change the subject, desperate to get Elise off my mind.

"Anyway…what's the plan for the engagement party?"

Andries exhales, running a hand through his hair. "Hell if I know. Traditionally we'd have it at my estate, but with my parents being so stubborn about the whole thing…"

"Just have it at my parents' then," I tell him with a shrug. "You're family. It makes sense."

Andries looks dumbstruck for a moment. "Dan…I couldn't do that to your parents! I don't want to bother them with my controversial engagement."

"Nonsense," I interpose, before finishing my cappuccino. "You're my best friend. Plus, they seem to think you're a good influence on me or something." Given the frown forming between his brows, I decide to be more persuasive and say, "When I told them about your engagement they even offered the place up for whatever you might need." It's totally made up, but I'm confident they wouldn't mind hosting the engagement on the big patio of their townhouse. They have always loved Andries like a son of their own.

He looks at me speculatively; after all, he must feel some disappointment that it isn't something he'll get to share with his own family on the home estate, but we both know he will probably be more comfortable at my parents' instead. Roxanne will be more relaxed there, for sure. I can't imagine the tension she must be feeling, so maybe this offer will make things a little easier for the couple.

After a moment, Andries nods. "Okay, sure. That sounds like a great option. If you are sure your parents really meant it, then of course."

"Great," I answer simply. "Do you have any date in mind?"

"Mm… How does May twenty-first sound to you?"

I shoot a text out to my parents and confirm that the date isn't a problem, and once I have an affirmative, Andries calls Roxanne and we set the whole thing in stone.

Being able to remove a burden from my friend's life makes me happy, and feel a little less guilty for how much I'm juggling trying to balance both his friendship and the time I'm spending with Elise. As far as Andries knows, I'm only hanging out with his sister to spy on her, but little does he know I have much more selfish reasons.

We finish our snack and Andries stands, stepping around the table to shake my hand and pull me into a hug. "Seriously, Dan, thank you for everything."

"It's nothing," I assure him, welcoming his embrace. "I love to throw a good party."

He chuckles, before putting a hand on my back. "That's true. Needless to say, you're now officially my best man."

"I wasn't expecting anything less," I tease.

"Well, I've got to get back to school. I have class in ten minutes." We start walking on the sidewalk so he can retrieve his bike. "By the way, do you have any plans this Saturday? It's Roxanne's birthday and we're having dinner with her family. Would you like to join us?"

I don't have any plans, actually, but with how melancholic Andries's grand romance makes me feel I almost want to turn the invitation down. It sounds like it'll be a wonderful time, but I don't want to show up alone if everyone is going to bring their significant other.

"Can I bring a plus one?"

Andries seems taken aback by my question but then considers it for a second. "Sure, I don't see why not. See you Saturday, then?"

"See you Saturday."

CHAPTER 3

Amsterdam, April 19, 2022
Elise

It's warmer than it should be this early in the year, but I'm not complaining, having chosen to break out a pair of white pants to go with my light blue cotton shirt. Spring is beautiful in Amsterdam, but there's no arguing that my outfit is better suited for summer, when my pale complexion would bloom in pale freckles no matter how many layers of sunscreen I apply. If I had time, it'd be the perfect day to ride my horse, but with class all day long, I'll have to settle for pestering my brother on campus instead.

It's funny that I still think of it that way. So much is at stake with Andries and his idiotic engagement, but in my heart, he's still my annoying older brother who is constantly brooding and dramatic. It gives me a pang of nostalgia, and I wish I could go back in time to when we were kids and our arguments weren't about anything serious—like who got the last piece of cake at a garden party; not like today, when we're arguing literally about the future of our family.

Ugh. It's stressing me out. A lot. Which is why I've decided to surprise my brother after his class today and shift a little bit of that stress onto him.

Truthfully, I want to see how he is. Maybe even apologize for how things have been between us. It all depends on how he receives me.

I adjust my bag on my shoulders, checking the time on my watch as I wait in the hallway for the few last tedious minutes before his class lets out. Finally, I hear the sound of people shuffling papers and clicking laptops closed inside the lecture hall, and then students begin to file out.

I perk up, searching for my brother in the crowd, but he finds me first. He looks exasperated when he first sees me, but after an eye roll he comes in my direction, and I instantly smile brightly.

"Look who's here," I say early, despite the seriousness on his face when he laid eyes on me. "Have time for a bit of a walk between classes?"

"With you?" he asks, sounding suspicious.

"Duh, of course with me. I was thinking we probably had some things to talk about."

"That's an understatement," he grumbles, but he's already leading the way out onto the concourse. His back is to me but he's walking slowly enough that I don't lose track.

I hurry to reach his side, soaking in the moment of just having his company for a time without any strings attached. But we can't be quiet forever and I must talk to him about the more serious things that have been on my mind.

I'm going to apologize to my brother. I have to. After all, no matter who he is marrying, we're still family, and being as estranged from him as our parents currently are isn't something I want for us. With Roxanne, Patricia, and Karl all coming between us, there were a lot of issues to bridge. With that in mind, I decide that I might as well start.

"Sooo… how was Paris? Did you enjoy it?"

The happiness at the memory of his trip flickers across his face, but he closes it off quickly, not wanting to share it with me. I can't exactly blame him. Taking the trip was idiotic, just like trying to make a life with an escort is idiotic, but my brother will never be one to admit that he is wrong.

"It was wonderful," he says, keeping it simple. "It felt like a new chapter of our lives started when Roxanne became my fiancée."

I try hard not to puff at the word *fiancée*. "…That's nice."

He snorts. "You don't have to pretend to be interested."

"I am, though!" I protest as we walk side by side. "I'm interested in your life, what you've been doing…you just know how I feel about that woman."

"Elise," Andries's voice is icy, and he shoots me a glare. "The moment you say something negative about my fiancée, I'm leaving."

"I wasn't trying to," I interpose straight away. "It was just my opinion, nothing more."

Andries shakes his head in disbelief. "Yeah, right…"

"Hey," I say quietly, but it gets his attention, nonetheless. "I want to say I'm sorry for the fight we got in last time. Now, before you get all smug, I think you're somewhat at fault too, but I don't want all of that to make you think that I hate you or something."

"Don't you?" he replies, sounding genuinely surprised, and he even stops in his tracks to face me. "Everyone else at home does. There's a reason why I'm disowned after all."

I flinch, but he isn't wrong. At least not when it comes to Mom and Dad, who refuse to have anything to do with Andries's relationship. My brother is so loyal to Roxanne that there is no way he'd consider attending family functions alone and just leaving her behind. They are a single unit now. There isn't really any other way to put it but "disowned."

"That's a harsh way to put it," I hedge, and we resume sauntering on the concourse of the campus. "They're really pissed off though, I won't sugarcoat it. Especially Pops."

"You know what's funny," he says, the hurt evident in his voice even if he won't acknowledge it. "No one outside of the house really seems to care, family-wise. I won't say names, but multiple other family members have encouraged me to be with Roxie, and Oma is entirely supportive, somewhat surprisingly."

I frown, turning my head to look up at him. "What do you mean? How do you know she isn't just being polite?"

"Because she agreed to let us have the wedding on her property."

Andries drops this little tidbit of information like a bomb, and my step falters. I knew they were engaged, but not that they were already in the wedding planning stage of it all. That bothers me so much that I let the information about Oma being supportive fall to the wayside and focus on the time frame.

"Isn't it a little early to be choosing venues and all that?" I manage to choke out.

"Not at all," Andries says with confidence. "We're planning for August, when the weather is good."

My steps falter immediately and I can't help but let my mouth hang open. "*This* August!?"

"See, I knew you'd behave this way, Elise," he scoffs. "Yes, this August. There's no point in waiting. I don't have any illusions that the idea of the relationship will become more bearable for our parents over time, so it is what it is. I want to be her husband, and she wants to be my wife. The sooner the better."

I want to snap back at him and make him wake up once and for all from his naiveté, but alas, I didn't come here to start another argument, so instead, I just swallow the curses I have for him and say, "Don't you want to live as an engaged couple for a while? That's what most people do. To make sure they're compatible or whatever."

"We are already living together. We are very compatible."

Flustered, I sputter, "You've been living together for a month or so, that's not enough."

"It's more than enough." Andries snorts. "Anyway, yes, we're getting married this August, toward the end of the month. It will be a small ceremony with just friends and… family. What family will be able to stomach attending, that is."

His tone becomes sarcastic toward the end of his statement, and I can see why. I just don't ever think he will be able to convince our parents to go to his wedding to an older ex-escort. It'll be a scandal that they want no part of.

Am I okay being a part of it, though?

"I mean… if you're sure," I offer, unable to take the disappointment out of my tone. "And happy."

"Happier than I've ever been, if I'm being honest." He's been on guard with me this entire time, I know him well enough to pick that out, but when he talks about Roxanne, it's like he can't help but melt a little. It almost makes me feel guilty for hating them together so much. *Almost.*

"You know I just worry…" I sigh. "I know as the oldest sibling you're supposed to be the worried one, but I can't help it. On paper, there is so much that can go wrong, and I don't want to see you hurt. You'd want the same for me, right? If I ended up with someone you didn't approve of."

To my astonishment, my brother just chuckles at the idea. "We all know you'll end up with the perfect nobleman handpicked by Mom and Dad, marry him, and then slowly ruin his life while never allowing him to leave. So I probably won't have to worry about that."

I huff, offended, but my brother only laughs. I check the time, realizing that I don't have long until my next class, and exhale slowly, tilting my head back and looking toward the sky. I didn't cover nearly as much in this talk as I wanted to, but it's a good start, and he doesn't seem like he's ready to chase me away anytime soon. Leaving our interaction here is fine.

"I've got to go," I tell him, sounding like an apology. "I'd like to talk again soon, though, if you have time for me."

His face softens, and he nods. "Of course. If you're willing to be amiable, I am too."

We both do a sort of shuffle, not knowing whether to just walk away or hug first, but when I turn to go and head to class, Andries stops me. "Elise?"

"Yes?"

"I…" He seems hesitant, running a hand on his hair as he ponders whether to continue or not. His behavior gives me pause, and I frown observing him. "Roxanne and I are having an engagement party on May twenty-first, and, um, I'd love it if you attended."

What! They have already a date for the party?

Shocked, it takes me a moment to respond. "Um, maybe, I think I can do that. Where are you hosting it, exactly?"

"At the O'Brian's," he answers, screening my face to pick up my reaction.

My shock is quick to turn to fury, but I keep it pushed down inside of me, not wanting Andries to see how much that little bit of information is affecting me. "Oh, really? Okay, um, well, just let me check my schedule."

Andries apparently doesn't pick up on my overly cheery tone, simply raising a hand to bid goodbye as I pivot and start stomping to class. I have to pace my breathing, clenching and unclenching my fists as I go.

How dare Dan do this!?

After we had just spoken all about my brother and his ill-fated engagement. He must have left me behind and agreed to throw the party within less than twelve hours!

I can barely pay attention during class, sitting behind my open laptop screen and not absorbing any of the lesson. Tapping my fingers on the desk, I count the minutes until I'm free and confront Dan about his betrayal.

Once I'm finally released, I find the quietest corner I can and make the phone call, one of my feet tapping an angry staccato against the marble floor. He answers, sounding annoyed and rushed.

"Elise, I'm a little busy right now, can I call you later?"

"Come to campus," I snap right away. "We need to talk."

Dan releases a frustrated groan. "I can't do that. I'm at my parents' place anyway, and like I said, I'm busy."

"I don't really care how busy you think you are, this is more important than—"

"Bye, Elise!" he interrupts, and then the line goes dead.

Fuck! I growl in frustration, feeling my blood pressure rising. The fact that he had the audacity to hang up on me only adds to how angry I already was, and now I'm positive there's no way I can wait until Dan's schedule opens up enough to give me a few minutes of his precious time.

He did say he was at his family's house, and I just happen to know where that is. Surely, it's out of line to barge into the O'Brian's without being invited, but Dan had already decided that there wasn't going to be any honor between him and me.

Before I can change my mind and err on the side of civility, I book the Uber, letting out a long breath once I do.

No one hangs up on Elise Van den Bosch. Ever.

* * *

Tucked away behind the city's canals, lies one of the most beautiful grand houses downtown—the one of Jake and Caroline O'Brian. My brother used to come here often after his fencing classes, and eventually, started to invite me over too.

I step out of the car and into the open air, gazing up at the tall historic façade that stands just a few steps from me. It's undoubtedly a lovely home, intricately detailed with pale gray stone, but it's the secret gardens in the backyard that are the real crowning jewel.

Without time for second guesses, I walk up to the front doors and press the bell for a long moment. Enough that when I stop, there's already someone on the other side opening it for me.

"Hi," I greet, putting on my most prim and proper tone as my eyes lay on the butler of the family. "I'm here to see Dan. He told me he was here."

The old man doesn't seem to recognize me and checks me out from top to bottom without shame. "And you are?"

"Elise Van den Bosch."

"Oh, of course." Almost as if by magic, the old man switches expressions, from smug to friendly and I can even see the semblance of a smile tugging at his lips. Then he steps aside, his hand gesturing for me to come in. "This way please, Ms. Van den Bosch."

I step inside, my chin high, and my eyes already taking in the sumptuous hallway while he leads the way. I've only been here once or twice before, but I do remember what a scenic place the seemingly endless house is.

Reaching outside, I fill my lungs with the floral scent that permeates the gardens.

Here in the backyard, the grass is emerald green and wild, filled with different plants and floral species. It also features a large stone patio dotted with gas-powered fire pits that are filled with multicolored fire glass, each surrounded by sumptuous outdoor couches and seats. On the edge of the property, nearly out of sight, there is a small orchard of fruit trees, and when the summer is at its peak, you can smell them on the breeze. Standing on the stone patio, I catch a quick glimpse of Dan, flanked by an older man and woman, who both have notebooks and they are dutifully writing in. It's rude showing up unannounced, and even more so to barge onto his family's property after such a terrible phone call, but the idea of the element of surprise is pulling at me hard.

The small group hasn't seen me yet, and I take extra joy to observe them attentively from where I stand. Dan looks thoughtful, one hand on his chin and the other pointing at a certain place on the lawn, to which his companions nod and continue writing. He doesn't look stressed, or even upset, but he is serious. Maybe more so than I've ever seen him.

I partly expected that I'd cease to be angry once I saw my tentative friend in person, but that is just insulting the case. Seeing him so wrapped up in whatever he is doing, not even giving me a second thought when I'd been fuming about him the whole Uber ride is infuriating.

Because of this, when the butler announces me, I don't change my pace, just continue advancing with my hands fisted at my sides. Finally, Dan looks in my direction, a bevy of emotions crossing his handsome face. First is shock, next is annoyance, and then eventually, begrudging amusement.

"Elise," he all but purrs as I come into earshot. "What a... surprise to see you here."

I shrug one shoulder and flip my hair. "You've told Andries hundreds of times that your door is always open for him, and as the current reluctant liaison for the Van den Bosch family, I figured I could be the stand-in."

"Of course. You're always welcome, as well." His words sound honest, but his face says otherwise. "So what do I owe the pleasure, then?"

I ignore his question. "Are you going to introduce me to these two?"

Almost like he forgot they existed, Dan quickly looks at the man and the woman next to him, his expression sheepish. "Ah, sorry. This is Fran and Harold. They're here to help me plan your brother's engagement party."

It's like I hear the words in slow motion, all the anger that had slowly faded before coming back with a vengeance. I nod to the party planners tightly, snapping out a hand to grab Dan's bicep. He jolts, looking down at my hand and then back at my face.

"Can I speak to you in private?" I say through my clenched teeth.

"Um, okay." His eyes go from my face to the two party planners. "You two can finish touring the property and just send me the final plans and cost later, alright?"

I resist the urge to grab him by the ear and pull him along behind me like a bad child, instead letting him lead me over to a small ornamental garden full of roses with a tinkling fountain in the middle featuring the stone figure of a little girl pouring a watering can. I want to kick it.

"I can't believe you came all the way out here just to yell at me!" Dan says incredulously.

"I haven't even started," I snap.

"Oh, but I can tell by your face that you're working up to it. What are you doing here?"

I step closer to him, having to tilt my head back to look into his face because of the extra height he has over me. "In what world could you possibly have thought that throwing an engagement party for my brother would be a good idea, especially without even telling me first?" I hiss.

"The world in which I am a grown man who makes my own decisions, and the world in which Andries is my best friend, not you."

His words sting for some reason that I can't pinpoint. "I've told you how much I dread him marrying Roxanne, and now here you are participating in the fast-tracking of that doomed event. I've had zero time to try and convince Dad and Mom to attend, and until I spoke to my brother, I didn't even know the party was already being planned! Dad is going to have a conniption fit." I blow out a breath. "You could have at least consulted me first."

"But why?" Dan holds his hands out, motioning to the property around him. "This is my place and your brother's engagement. Why would I consult you at all? Have you thought that maybe Andries isn't even sure that he wants you at his engagement party? You certainly haven't been the picture of caring sisterhood for him."

The stinging feeling gets worse, but I refuse to acknowledge the hurt his words are building in me. "I'll have you know that not only did Andries and I talk today, but he also invited me to the engagement party."

He smirks and shakes his head. "Sometimes I forget how young you are. If you're trying to regain your brother's trust, it's going to take a lot more than just attending this party, El. Trust me on that."

"How can I trust you about anything now?" The corners of my eyes are burning, and I blink rapidly to avoid any budding tears. "I thought you were someone I could commiserate with. Now I know you're just a backstabbing asshole."

"Elise," Dan replies, voice soft and slightly hurt. "I've been your brother's best friend for so long. I don't know what you expect from me. You and the rest of his family pretty much left him high and dry when it came out that he was in love with Roxanne, and now he's basically planning a wedding with me and a few distant relatives. This isn't about you. Stop being selfish."

The decision to storm away is so instant that I don't even register it until I've pivoted and am all but rushing back to the main road, Dan yelling my name behind me but making no moves to chase after me.

There's no point talking to him any further about it. Dan simply doesn't understand. He has no idea what it's like to play second best to Andries even when he is off fucking around with a hooker and basically giving the entire family the middle finger. My older brother is disinterested in the family legacy, while I am running myself into exhaustion working and going to school to be the best heir possible, but everyone is still pampering and catering to him. It's not fair, and it never will be.

I reach the end of Dan's driveway, and in the middle of booking another Uber, the screen flashes with my father calling, as if he could sense me thinking about him and all the ways he and everyone else puts me in second place. I swallow hard, once again pushing those feelings down, down, down, and answer.

"Hey, Dad," I say, aiming to have a joyful tone that doesn't give him any hint of my current state.

"Hello, dear. I was wondering if your brother has returned to school?"

I grimace. Like everything else, it's all about Andries. "Yes, but I'm not with him. I talked to him earlier, though."

Dad lets out a breath of relief. "At least he's not squandering his education, then. What did he have to say?"

"That he's having an engagement party on May twenty-first at the O'Brian's house." I conveniently leave out the fact that I'm currently at said house.

"What!" he bellows, and I hear him struggle to get his temper under control for a moment before continuing. "He's really doing everything he can to shame me. It's unbelievable. Are you invited to this party?"

"Well, for now, yes. We'll see as we get closer to the date if he really does send me an invite. Are you and Mom going?"

"Ha. Your brother hasn't said anything about it to your mother or me yet, but even if he does, there is no way I intend to go to that shit show."

I don't know what to say to that, so I murmur a vague agreement. My news has Dad distracted, so he doesn't say anything else on the subject, no doubt ready to get off the phone and fume privately.

"Thanks for the information, El. I'll see you in the office tomorrow."

"Okay, Dad. I love—" I try to say, but before I can get the words out, the line has gone dead.

CHAPTER 4

Amsterdam, April 23, 2022
Dan

I like to think I'm not a completely shallow man, but there is no denying that Jessica is hotter than sin. That, and her relatively easy-going nature are the reasons I'm with her more often than not, which explains why she's the closest thing I've had to a real relationship in years.

Not that we're in a relationship. Just… close. Sort of.

It's times like these, though, that her attractiveness and all the little intricacies that go into perfecting it grate on my nerves. We have less than twenty minutes to be at the restaurant for Roxanne's birthday, and Jessica is tediously checking her lipstick for the fiftieth time in the mirror hanging by my front door.

"Babe," I groan. "We have to go. I don't want them waiting on us."

"If you hadn't insisted on that little rendezvous over the bathroom counter with me then I wouldn't be rushing," she tells me primly, smacking her lips one last time and straightening up. "Alright. I'm ready."

She isn't wrong... I had hiked her little black dress over her ass and had my way with her less than an hour ago, but I'm not going to take the blame. She was nearly done with her makeup at that point, anyway.

The truth is, I'm fond of Jessica, but there is this divide between the two of us that I don't think will ever fully connect. It's why I'm sure we'll never progress beyond the point we are now, but because I'm not exactly looking for romance, I don't mind. Jessica is lovely, kind, and a tiger in bed. I like her, but I don't think I will ever love her.

Tonight, though, that's irrelevant. Another perk to Jess is that she looks amazing on my arm, and is the perfect date to any function, especially when I don't want to attract any attention from other nosy women that may be in the know about my wealth. On the off chance someone does catch my eye, I sometimes tell Jessica, and she will lure them in with me and we will both enjoy her together.

Tonight she's radiant, and my hope is that her shine will help dull the emptiness that is yawning inside of me whenever I see Roxie and Andries together. My soul seems to know I'm missing something, even if my brain and my dick don't want to admit it.

We take my Audi, Jessica folding her long, bare legs onto the leather seat. "Do you think we can order a bottle of champagne?" she asks absentmindedly. "I've been craving it ever since we had a few glasses at that one restaurant downtown that we ate at."

"Maybe. We'll let the birthday girl have first pick on the drinks though, I think."

"Oh, of course!" I watch her nibble her lip before sighing. "Dan, I like Roxanne, but I feel like she doesn't like me very much. Are you sure it's alright that I'm coming?"

"The last time you spoke to her in depth was when she was still lying about her job to Andries, so it's no wonder she was on guard then. Now, if she's standoffish, it's probably because Andries's family is being exceptionally difficult. It's nothing to do with you."

"Okay. I just don't want to make things more awkward for you."

"Trust me, Jess, it would be weirder if I was going alone." I reach over and lay a hand on her leg between shifting gears. "You're my security for tonight."

She giggles and relaxes. I'm not lying to her, either. Jessica won't be protecting me from any real danger, but having her there will be a balm on my heart in the face of the saccharine sweet love between my best friend and his future wife. At least I will know I'm not going home alone or sleeping in an empty bed, even if the woman with me is just an enchanting placeholder.

***

Roxanne's restaurant of choice is a bit out of town in Amstelveen, and by the time we arrive, I'm starving. Aan de Poel on the lakeshore is breathtaking at sunset, and I hear Jessica gasp quietly when she steps out of the car to see the orange and red sky reflecting off the water.

I take her hand, interlacing our fingers as we walk inside and out onto the patio. It's no surprise Andries has booked the best table in the place; a long rectangular table for ten, giving us plenty of room to stretch out and not be crowded by one another, is placed right along the edge of the patio. Beyond our table, the land sweeps gently downward and into the water, giving us an unobstructed view.

Everyone else has already arrived, but it seems they're all just settling in themselves, and I'm relieved we aren't obnoxiously late. Andries rises, shaking my hand and pulling me into a hug, and then I move to Roxanne, kissing both of her cheeks and telling her happy birthday.

There's an obvious difference in Roxie; a peace that she hadn't carried before, like all the pieces of her life have finally settled into place. She introduces Jessica and me to the other guests at the table—Lili, her sister, and Lili's boyfriend, Robin, Yao, her mother, and a younger woman with shockingly red hair named Poppy, who she tells me is her personal assistant.

Jessica gets hung up on Roxanne, taking both of her hands. "Congratulations on your engagement!" she says, beaming. "How exciting! It's such a whirlwind romance."

I catch Yao and Lili looking at each other in amused agreement with Jessica's statement. Roxie smiles kindly at my date. "Thank you, Jessica, and thanks for coming to my birthday dinner."

It's then Jessica gets a glimpse at the ring on Roxanne's hand, pulling said hand up to get a closer look at the gemstone. "What a wonderful ring, oh my goodness, have you seen it, Dan?"

"I have, yes. But don't go getting ideas," I laugh stiffly, not enjoying the change of topic, but Jessica just rolls her eyes, and after a little more small talk, everyone sits down. I sneak a glimpse at Roxanne's ring... it truly is stunning, and it makes me wonder what ring my future potential bride might like.

An image of a rose-gold circlet with a single glittering diamond pops into my mind, placed delicately on the ring finger of someone with nude polished nails. I follow the wrist up the mystery woman's arm in my daydream, but when the face of a certain Van den Bosch daughter begins to take shape, I shake my head to dispel the thought.

"Are you okay?" Jessica whispers at my side.

"Yeah, just a bug," I lie.

When Andries had described Roxanne's family to me, I had trouble imagining where he would fit into the equation. The wealthy, aloof poet didn't seem like the type to integrate into a family like Roxanne's, but it was clear that I had been mistaken. Andries's love and adoration of Roxanne easily garnered him the approval of the Feng family, and it's wonderful to see. With his own family turning their noses up at the whole ordeal, I feel better knowing that at least one side of their union will be peaceful and joyous. Yao and Lili talk to him like they've known him forever, and seeing it makes me incredibly happy for my friend.

But them being on the edge of that happiness is exactly what I'd feared accepting this invitation. I'm extraordinarily jealous of them. It isn't Andries and Roxanne's obviously passionate love for each other, but the way they've overcome such obstacles just to be in each other's lives. Being with each other was simply important enough that they were both willing to uproot their lives for a chance at happiness.

I feel that chasm of loneliness opening up inside me, and I reach under the table to Jessica, running my hand up and down her leg just to have a stitch of human connection. Her expression is warm and welcoming, and it helps a little. Not enough to make it go away, but enough that I can breathe again.

Conversation flows as naturally and abundantly as the wine, and by the time the food arrives, we are all relaxed and glowing from the alcohol. Jessica has her glass of champagne, and while I'm craving something a little heavier, I happily share the bottle with her. Something makes me feel like doting on my hookup tonight, and I indulge that desire.

The Feng sisters are both similar and completely different, Lili the more controlled, less fiery version of Roxanne, but I don't doubt that she is the epitome of still waters running deep. Yao is quieter still, but when her daughters get her going, she becomes just as lively as anyone else at the table. Lili's boyfriend, like Andries, struggles to get a word in edgewise with the Feng women. That part of the relationship is one that I don't envy.

Poppy is winding down a story about her first day working with Roxie and how intimidated she was when Roxie herself taps her fork on her glass to get all of our attention. We quiet, turning our attention to her as she rises from her seat.

"Now that we've all had some fun, I have an announcement to make! You all already know that Andries and I are engaged," she says, showing her ring causing the table to laugh, "so rest assured I won't be bothering you with that." The table falls silent, holding their breath with anticipation. "But I have something else, work-wise to announce; since I've turned the page as an agency owner,

I've been working on a memoir, and just yesterday I signed with a literary agent."

Lili and Yao are thrilled, hugging Roxanne, and patting her cheeks, and Andries's content grin lets me know that he is already privy to everything Roxanne's revealing. I wait until the congratulations have died down and for Roxanne to be seated again to speak.

"A memoir, huh? Any certain focus?" I ask, my interest piqued.

"My time in the sex industry," she says without thinking twice. "Starting from when I was an escort to my life as an agency owner." Roxanne sighs, stirring her drink with her straw as she speaks. "I've met so many people along the way that I'll never forget and are worth mentioning. Girls that just needed to feed their families, others that were trying to escape abusive households, and everything else in between. It will portray a raw reality of what life is like for those who go down that path."

I raise my eyebrows. "That's quite the undertaking."

She nods. "It is, but it's time somebody shines the light on what escorting in Amsterdam is really like. The good and the bad of it."

I look to my friend, who I know doesn't love the subject of Roxanne's days as an escort, but to my surprise, he looks proud of her.

"Have you been using the services of our resident poet and writer extraordinaire, Andries?" I tease, causing him to scowl.

Roxie grins. "No, but he introduced me to an agent that he discovered through his author friend, Paul. Apparently, this book will be the first of its kind and there are already a few publishing houses interested in the project."

I feel a small thrill of nerves run through me at that statement, a picture forming in my mind of what that could mean. "Wow, that's an incredible achievement for sure. Good for you."

She laughs, but it sounds slightly anxious. "I didn't think I was able to be nervous about anything anymore, but when my agent started talking about national signing tours and marketing campaigns, I actually felt scared. But it pushed me to be even better and to write something that really meant something to me. I actually added on a large portion in the second part of the book talking all about sex worker rights in Amsterdam and how the power needs to go back to the sex worker and not the consumer."

"Does that happen a lot? Clients having better rights than the escorts?" Jessica asks at my side, trying to join the conversation.

"Absolutely. In Germany, for instance, clients can get a refund for even the smallest inconvenience, even if the sex act lasted the allotted amount of time. Courts usually side with the consumer and that needs to change. Sex workers are more vulnerable than any other type of service providers, and I think that people need to realize that they aren't just dolls to be played with: They're living, breathing people that deserve proper protections and rights."

"You're so right," Jessica says, her voice of quiet awe.

I have to admit, I'm pretty impressed that Roxanne managed to come up with all of this in such a short amount of time. From the way she's talking about the whole thing, she and Andries must have brainstormed the idea for the memoir while together in France.

"It's incredible you've put so much thought and planning into this already. Did this all come about when the two of you were in Paris?"

She shakes her head. "No. Actually, I got the idea when I was having lunch with my sister quite some time before Paris, but being with Andries helped me condense my ideas down into something worthwhile."

I'm not even part of the Van den Bosch family, and the idea of the eldest son's wife releasing a memoir about the inner workings of high-end escorting has me a little stressed, too. Of course, she found an agent in record time. That book is going to be like a bomb going off when she publishes it.

"Surely you're going to use a pen name?" I ask hopefully, but I should have known better. This is Roxanne, of course, and she does nothing by half measures.

"Of course not!" Roxie exclaims. "Why would I want to hide my identity?"

Andries reaches over and lays his hand over hers, squeezing. "It's something she should be proud of. The agent has been talking to some publishers already, so if we're lucky it won't take too long to get the ball rolling."

This topic of conversation is, without a doubt, the most interesting one of the night, and Roxanne regales us with snippets of the stories she plans to tell, much to everyone's delight. Her mother does look a little uncomfortable with all the escort talk, but she keeps a brave face and doesn't protest.

Had Roxanne been engaged to anyone other than Andries, this book would be fantastic news. It's a noble cause that morally I completely agree with. Things get complicated, though, when you mix in the reputations of old money families. I wonder if Roxanne even knows the chaos she's going to cause with this. At the same time, I feel bad for wanting to tell her to reconsider. Everything she's saying about escort rights and the dark underbelly of the whole business is completely correct.

Dinner winds down, and the happy couple orders another bottle of champagne. Andries is especially demanding about the after-dinner confections, and once the flutes of champagne have been all filled and distributed among the guests, I notice another server walking in and bringing something else over. Andries had the kitchen craft a special, pale green mochi princess cake for his fiancée, topped with a delicate sugar rose on the top and long, elegant lit candles that bathe Roxie's face in firelight.

We sing to her, and she blows out the thirty-six candles, laughing like a little kid as she does so. Everyone has just started to enjoy their treats and the accompanying fresh, crispy champagne when I feel my phone vibrating in my pocket. Frowning, I pull it out and look at the screen. It's Elise.

I silence the call, hoping to ignore her altogether, but she calls a second, and then a third time, at which point I know I can't escape.

"Pardon me, I'll be right back. I just have to take this call," I tell the table, standing and walking briskly into the building and back outside at the front of the restaurant.

Elise has texted me after my multiple ignored calls, asking: *How is the birthday dinner going?*

Shocked, I look around, but see no one.

Dan: *How did you find out about the birthday party?*

Elise: *I know everything, Dan.*

Flustered by her response, I give up and call her. When she picks up, I ask her, "What do you want, El? Besides being nosy."

"Considering you've been lying to me I figured the best way to find out the truth of what is going on is to keep tabs on everything. Anyway, how exactly is dinner going?"

I wish she could see how hard I'm rolling my eyes. "It's great, Elise," I tell her sarcastically. "We just had cake. Can I go now?"

"And Roxanne? How is she doing?" she insists. "No baby announcement or anything that would cause my dad to have a heart attack?"

I'm sure she's just fishing for information for her dad at this point but I find myself unable to lie to her.

I flick my eyes over the space around me, making sure that none of the other party guests have followed me. I can't help but feel some lingering guilt about how harsh I had been with Elise when she stormed onto my parents' property the other day, and that little remainder of emotion makes me want to do something to make up for hurting her. While I had only intended on shutting her down so she would drop her complaints and let Andries have his engagement party in peace, I can't help but think that maybe I took it too far.

There is one tidbit of information that I can give Elise that I know she will find fascinating. I just hope it doesn't come back to bite me in the ass.

"Well, not a baby but… Roxanne announced to the table that she's going to publish a memoir about her time as an escort. It's apparently going to be incredibly detailed."

Elise makes a choked sound and then gives an incredulous laugh. "But she's going to use a pen name, right?"

"Nope. She's going to publish it as Roxanne Feng and even go on a book signing tour."

It's clear she's flabbergasted, even over the phone, and when Elise finally gains the ability to speak again, she sounds shell-shocked. "You know what this means, right? What it's going to do to our family?"

Unfortunately, I do know, and it makes me feel ridiculously conflicted. At this point, Roxanne is just a secondary character in the Karl Townsend scandal. If she releases this book, though, she'll be catapulted into the limelight and become the main character, whether she likes it or not.

With this memoir, Roxanne and Andries's relationship will feed the news cycle to no end.

CHAPTER 5

Amsterdam, April 25, 2022
Elise

I toss and turn all night after Dan revealed that info about Roxanne's memoir to me. It makes me feel sick, especially since I'm so on the fence about where I stand with everyone. I want Dad to think I'm the perfect fit for the job…in fact, I crave it, but then again I still want my brother in my life, and throwing his future wife to the wolves would assure that he never spoke to me again.

So what do I do? I want it all and I can't have it, but as of right now, it feels impossible to choose.

I spend Sunday in my flat, between getting my homework ready for school and ruminating about what to do next.

Monday is a work day, which is a blessing and a curse. It means I can't mope around campus all day, conflicted about my next course of action, but it also means I'm basically lying to Dad the entire time we are at the office together. He'd expect me to tell him immediately about things like

Roxanne's memoir, and every minute that passes that I hide the information just makes me look worse and worse.

My thoughts are still all tied up in knots when I make it to the office, my hair pulled back in a slick bun to hide how unkempt it really is and only the bare minimum amount of makeup gracing my face.

I greet everyone, walk toward the open layout, and when I'm finally about to reach my desk, the office secretary walks over and informs me that there is a PR meeting starting in less than thirty minutes that I'm expected to attend. Groaning, I continue to my small office space, setting my bags down and sinking into my chair.

A PR meeting first thing in the morning. What an awful way to start the day…

In my emails is the message explaining the PR meeting, and what will be discussed. I skim through it a few times, knowing that I never really get the chance to talk anyway since I'm just an intern. But if everything goes right, I'll eventually be the CEO, so I need to be beside my dad for all the important events like this and get familiar with the key players at the company. The best way to learn is by doing, apparently.

I've got about twenty minutes left, so I flee to the break room, down a shot of espresso, check my face in the mirror, and at that point it's time.

"Elise," I hear my dad's deep baritone voice from the break-room door. "Are you ready for the meeting?"

I'm fairly surprised to see him here, but I just discreetly pull a mint from the ceramic dish near the espresso machine, pop it into my mouth, and nod. "Yes. Let's go."

Dad is in a rather good mood this morning, all things considered, which makes me want to keep the memoir secret to myself even more.

"How was your weekend, darling?" he asks as we walk together down the hallway. "Did you have some fun?"

"It was alright," I reply with a shrug. "Just stayed at home, chilling and doing some homework. And you?"

"Good." We walk beside each other, the boardroom located just a few more steps in front of us. "I spent the weekend with your mom. Took her on a little hiking trip to get some fresh air."

"Oh, Mom went hiking? That's a first."

"It is… but we both need to exercise more. She actually rather enjoyed it."

He's chatty and jovial with me, and I glow from parental approval. It wasn't just that I was the best suited of my dad's children to take over for him, I was also the one who enjoyed being around him the most.

While the main portion of the office is all sleek metal and has huge, clear windows, the meeting room we walk into feels more intimate, even if it's larger than it appears. The room is dominated by a long, dark oak table that is shiny from decades of use, no doubt another piece carried over from when my grandfather ran the company. A relic and reminder of time and successes gone by. Pieces like this are all over the headquarters in unexpected places: a red lamp with gold filigree on my Dad's desk, a heavy framed painting in the hallway leading to the restroom, a priceless Persian rug on my dad's office floor, and more. I think it helps Dad stay connected to the past.

Modern leather chairs surround the table, but the detailing is the same color oak as the table, pulling the place together. There's a huge projection screen on one end of the room and a bottle of chilled water in front of each chair.

Dad takes his seat and I take the one next to him as we watch and greet the people that filter in. Across from Dad, the Director of Public Relations, Greg, sits after he and my dad shake hands. The other office higher-ups find their seats, and once everyone is settled in, the meeting begins.

"Very well, good morning everyone. I hope the weekend has been rather pleasant for you all," my dad begins, before giving a glance down at his paperwork. "As you know, the subject of today's meeting is the upcoming annual shareholders meeting for Van den Bosch industries that will be hosted at The Taets Art and Event Park, next Monday…" While my dad speaks, Greg's assistant passes out trial scripts of topics and things to avoid talking about when we attend. I skim it, noting that there is nothing out of the ordinary that would make me nervous. I should be able to handle my portion of the shareholder's meeting with no problems.

Just as I begin to feel comfortable with everything on the horizon, the meeting room door opens, a shaft of bright light cutting across the floor and table and dimming the slide that is currently being projected on the screen.

When my eyes adjust, I'm shocked to see that it's none other than Karl himself and his assistant that have interrupted, Karl looking both harried and apologetic.

"Sorry for the delay," he says, giving the room a quick wave. "I was on the phone with my lawyer hammering out some details and he tends to be very long-winded. I'm sure you are all familiar."

People in the room murmur in amused agreement as Karl moves to find his own seat. I blink a few times to make sure that I'm not hallucinating, because Karl Townsend was supposed to be in jail right now. How he is walking free—free enough to attend a PR meeting—is beyond me. I watch him, goggle-eyed, before turning to Dad and whispering, "What is he doing here?"

He sends me a sharp look, but some of the younger board members at the table are clearly feeling similar, looking both mildly alarmed and uncomfortable at Karl's entrance. After a quick scan of the room, Dad sighs, and whispers back, "I guess I have to address this, then."

He clears his throat to get everyone's attention, and when he has it, begins to explain why Karl has suddenly reappeared when he was supposed to be absent. What disturbs me most, though, is how so many of the attendees just accepted his return without even a question. This man has been accused of heinous things. Shouldn't everyone want some more perspective on everything before just blindly welcoming him home?

"Karl won't be taking leave like we expected and will be in the office like normal. His lawyer filed an appeal on his case, so his sentence has been suspended until it's been reviewed, which means everything is above board and perfectly legal. I expect no one to allow idle gossip about Mr. Townsend's case to affect work or their professional relationship with Karl. If all goes well, our colleague will simply have to pay the ten thousand euro fine and there will be no prison time. Again, let me reiterate, after this we won't speak of the case in the office at all, and Mr. Townsend will be treated with respect."

Everyone, including the few that had looked hesitant in the beginning, nodded and seemed satisfied. I can't keep the surprise off my face that we are just going to sweep this under the rug, but I'm obviously in the minority, considering how the friendly conversation with Karl commences as soon as Dad finishes his spiel.

Greg shrugs and finishes his presentation, taking his seat once he clears the screen. Dad looks down at me afterward, and the pride in his smile sends me reeling. It looks as if he's happy I'm here with him, even at this boring, mundane meeting, and at that moment I feel impulsive.

"I've got some news," I tell him, his attention piqued, and he raises his eyebrows.

"Oh? For the meeting, not just me?" Dad asks.

I look anxiously at Karl, wishing I could just send him away. Knowing that he might play a big part in Roxanne's memoir makes things even more awkward, but I don't have a choice. Plus, it isn't like I care what he thinks. I just wish I wasn't the one informing Dad of it.

I nod, and Dad gets the table's attention again. Everyone is getting restless, ready to leave and move on with their day, but I'm confident this will keep them engaged once they realize what I'm revealing.

"Roxanne Feng will be releasing a tell-all memoir that is already garnering attention in a lot of publishing houses, and it'll be about her time as an escort and madam."

Everyone in the room seems taken aback by the news, including Dad. I explain everything in as much detail as I can. Once Dan had spilled the secret to me, he had become more tight-lipped than I'd have preferred, but I still knew enough to hopefully give the company time to do damage control.

When I get into how detailed the book will be, the PR Director, Greg, holds up a hand to stop me.

"Do you know if this memoir will use real names and information, or will she use pseudonyms to protect her former clients' identities?" he asks.

All eyes shift slowly to Karl, who looks uneasy, but stoic.

"As far as I know, she's *not* using a pen name for herself, but I don't know about pseudonyms for anyone else. I'm not sure about any other details at the moment…"

Greg looks ill, but Dad is clearly pissed. "I'm sure she'll hire that tabloid trash reporter Kenneth to do one of his famous sensationalist interviews, too."

I lace my fingers on the table in front of me, hating that I don't have anything else to give. "I'm not sure…"

"Just try and see if you can get some inside information on whether she'll be using pseudonyms or not. Hopefully, she will, just to avoid potential lawsuits, but that woman never seems to do anything the easy or smart way, so who knows."

Nodding, I tell Dad, "I'll try my best to find out."

"Quickly," he adds, voice tight.

Once the meeting is over, Dad walks me to my desk, looking grim. Still, even if I feel a bit guilty, I'm glad that I have tried my best to help him and the company.

"You did well," he tells me as we reach the entrance to the open layout. "Knowing about Feng's book is going to give us a great head-start on spinning our version of the story first if she decides to call Karl out."

I shuffle my feet, feeling weird about the subject, but having no choice but to speak about my concerns. "Dad... don't you think other employees here may have utilized Roxanne's escort service?"

"It's a possibility, but indulging in those services is perfectly legal, so I'm not concerned too much about that. Karl, on the other hand—"

"I wanted to ask you about that, too," I say, cutting him off. "I get that he's awaiting appeal, but did I understand correctly that he will be coming to the shareholders' meeting?"

"Yes," Dad confirms. "He is legally allowed to live his life normally at this time, and he has a great relationship with a lot of those shareholders. They expect to see him there."

"Don't you think it might look bad for the company, though? To have him there when he's basically in limbo on whether he's going to prison or not?"

He pats me on the cheek before I can swat his hand away, not wanting to be babied in front of my coworkers. "Don't worry about it, dear. It will be fine. Just do your part to get some more info about this book, okay?"

"Okay..." I give him a plastic smile, feeling genuinely relieved when he heads back to his own office, and I can have a second to myself.

I slink back to my desk and consider texting Dan to let him know what just happened, but he'd probably be pissed off, and that would just be another mess for me to have to deal with, so instead, I open my emails and get to work on my actual duties for the day.

It's less than thirty minutes before I'm interrupted again, this time by the assistant I had seen Karl arrive with, a slight, nervous looking young man with thick glasses.

"Hi, um, Ms. Van den Bosch?"

"Yes?"

"Mr. Townsend would like to see you in his office if you have the time."

The idea gives me pause, and I can't help the shiver of apprehension that runs through me. Patricia was my friend… maybe not the closest friend I've ever had, but it was still important for me to be there for her when she needed me. What Karl did made me anxious to be left alone in his office with him, especially when I seem to be the same type of girl that he was so clearly attracted to. Attracted enough to risk jail time for it.

But Karl had never had a single bad complaint from someone here at Van den Bosch industries, and for all intents and purposes has been the perfect employee. So despite how I feel toward the man, I give his assistant a tight nod and follow him to his office.

The older man's office is minimally decorated, but what he does have is expensive and well-maintained. He looks up from his paperwork and smiles at me as I enter, waving a hand at the plush chair sitting across from his desk. I sit, smoothing my pants and waiting for him to speak.

"Thank you for coming, Elise. I realize we have never talked on our own, and I wanted to rectify that."

"Alright," I reply noncommittally, not sure what he wants me to say.

"I also wanted to express my gratitude for letting us all know about Roxanne Feng's memoir coming out. It will be a big help for us to not be blindsided by such a thing."

"You talk about her like you barely know her," I comment, tilting my head to the side.

Karl sighs, tapping the pen in his hand against his chin as he speaks. "At one time I'd have considered Roxanne someone that I cared for deeply. A trusted friend, even. But she has shown her true colors so... yes, I feel like I barely know her anymore."

"From what she says, you got yourself into this legal trouble, and she didn't have anything to do with it besides assigning a certain girl to you for that night. Patricia."

I expect Karl to look angry, offended, or maybe even uncomfortable, but he simply shrugs. "I don't deny that. Roxanne wasn't responsible for anything except trusting an incredibly inexperienced girl to do her job."

"But didn't you specifically request inexperienced?" I query, keeping my tone level and curious instead of the disgust that I can feel roiling in my belly.

"Yes and no. Physically inexperienced in one certain way, but Patricia was both physically and mentally naïve. I do want to apologize for hurting her, Elise, since I know she was your friend, but she and I both made mistakes that night."

"I..." I look away from his face, my thoughts racing. "I've heard different versions of the story and I'd rather not get into it right now if we don't have to. This is a professional environment after all."

"Agreed. But just remember, I'm not the monster you think I am." Karl's voice is low and serious. I wish I could trust that he is genuine, but there is just no way.

"Regardless of all that, I actually called you in here to tell you how impressed I am with your loyalty to the company. Not many people would do what you did in that boardroom this morning. You're a rare breed, Elise, and I'm more than happy to help you reach your goals now that I know what type of woman you are."

I fold my hands in my lap and lean forward. "What goals? I'm not sure what you're talking about."

His lips twist into a smile. "Everyone knows Sebastian is going to retire in a decade or so, and who will replace him is still a big mystery. I know you want to be his first choice when the day comes, and I can help you make that possible."

All of my nervousness is long gone, and I actually laugh at this, thinking about how a publicly disgraced figure is supposed to help me achieve my dreams, but when he looks at me in confusion, I simply say, "Well, I appreciate it. Is there anything else?"

Karl seems to almost be taking my measure as he looks at me, but after a few long moments, he shakes his head. "No, I think that's it."

More than ready to be back at my desk working on my own things, I quickly stand and turn to go. It isn't until my hand is on the doorknob that I hear Karl stand and begin to approach me. "Elise?"

I pause, suppressing a groan as I pivot to face him. "Yes?"

He's right in front of me now, and he lays a large hand on my shoulder. "Your dad makes a lot of promises, but that doesn't mean he'll keep them."

"I think he's going to appoint me as his successor no matter what, so I don't have too much to worry about."

Karl looks almost sad when he responds. "I'm sure you don't, but I just want you to keep your guard up. Make sure when it comes to the promise he made you, he'll have no choice but to actually go through with it."

With a jolt, I know that Karl knows more than he's letting on. I don't want to even consider that Dad is dragging me along through this internship for nothing. If that's true, then Karl is on whatever games my father is playing with me. I shiver, but nod at him, shrugging my shoulder so his hand falls away.

"Thanks for the advice. I really do appreciate it."

He smiles, and in a flash, I forget what a worm he really is.

"Anytime."

CHAPTER 6

Amsterdam, April 26, 2022
Elise

After the stressful workday yesterday, I returned home, had a quick dinner, and quickly passed out for the night. There was too much going on in my brain and I didn't want to sit and dwell on it all. I needed rest, and then I could make my decisions with a fresh outlook.

Unfortunately, even though today is my day off, someone seems to want to speak to me and they happen to be an early riser. Still deep in slumber, it takes a few consecutive calls for me to realize that my phone is buzzing on my bedside table. Delirious, I sit up, blowing my hair out of my face and answering the phone without even checking who it is.

"Elise!" my brother exclaims immediately. "Have you read the paper this morning?"

"Read the paper? For one, I'm not seventy years old. Two, no, I'm still in bed. What's going on?"

"Karl has appealed his sentence and is back working at Dad's company!"

I wince, holding the phone against my shoulder with my chin and rubbing my temples. "Uh, yeah. Actually, I already knew that. He showed up when I was there yesterday."

Andries swears a string of curses. "I don't want you around him, El. That guy is a fucking creep."

"Don't be ridiculous," I huff, head shaking. "It's a completely professional environment."

"Maybe. But Karl is unpredictable. You need to convince Dad to fire him or it's going to become a huge problem for us all."

I nibble my bottom lip in thought. There is no way in hell Dad is going to fire Karl, but letting Andries know that is going to be delicate work. He isn't going to want to hear it, but I have to make him understand that it's just the way of things.

"Dad isn't going to fire Karl," I say, keeping my tone even. "It's impossible, and asking me to make it happen isn't really fair."

My brother just scoffs in return. "Everyone knows you are Dad's golden child. He'll probably do anything you ask."

I almost laugh at how untrue that statement is. Our father is going to such extreme lengths to bring his son back into the fold, all the while I wait in the background. "Andries, I said it's impossible. Senior management loves Karl, and he's going to make an appearance at the shareholders' meeting too. They'll never get rid of him with all that coming up."

"You won't even try?" he asks, incredulous.

"No, I won't. I'm not going to waste my time and make myself look bad during an internship that I really value."

When my brother speaks again, the sneer in his voice is all too obvious. "I can't tell you how disturbing it is to hear that you're going to side with the company. You're just rolling over and going with whatever management sees fit."

"Look, what he did to Patricia was horrible, but at the office, there have never been any complaints against him. He's always respectful, he brings a lot of business to the company, and he's one of the key players. From the company's point of view, we'd rather help his image than fire him." I try to explain myself, but my brother is having none of it. The minute I close my mouth he starts up again.

"You've been working there for a month or so and look at you, defending a convicted rapist." He laughs cruelly. "I should have known you'd be quick to switch sides. And here I had more hope for you than that."

I gasp, hurt. "Andries, what an awful–"

"Have you even seen Patricia lately? Maybe you should check on your friends from time to time. I guess you're probably too busy defending Karl."

"I'm not even defending him! You're just—" but before I can even get the sentence out, Andries hangs up, and the line is dead.

It hurts. It really, really does, and there isn't anything I can do about it. Once again, it feels like there is no right answer, but everyone still blames everything on me no matter what I choose.

I want to cry... maybe pull my blanket back over my head and stay here for the day, but what Andries said about

Patricia is one kernel of truth in his vast misunderstanding of the situation. I haven't seen Patricia in some time, and that makes me feel awful. I've been so busy juggling my internship with college that I haven't set any time aside to check on her since she did that interview.

With nothing else to do for the day, and the negativity driving me hard, I take a deep breath and pivot until my feet hit the floor. I will go see my friend and check on her well-being. Then, Andries can shove all his foolish opinions up his ass.

* * *

The plan to see Patricia had started out with the best of intentions, but when I found myself standing outside her empty dorm room, everything started to go downhill.

Seeing her old dorm empty frightened me at first, worrying about what might have happened to her. No one in her hall seemed to know where she had gone, but I could sense relief in some of them. It must have been stressful and distracting for normal university students to live with someone like Patricia, who had spent a significant amount of time in the news.

It's a huge relief when she answers my call, sounding much more upbeat than she has in months. Patricia seems thrilled to hear from me and rattles off an address for her new residence. It surprises me so much that I have her repeat it a second time, but I had heard right initially: Patricia was living in a condo in the best part of the city, near where Andries had lived when he first moved to

Amsterdam. Head spinning, I write the address down and promise that I'll head over shortly.

On the way there, I try to figure out exactly how she could afford such a place with basically no income. She hadn't taken the plea deal, so there was no way she had such disposable income…right? Maybe roommates?

Now though, as I take the elevator up to her top-floor apartment, it's becoming clear to me that there is something else going on here. This is not the type of place where residents have roommates or some sort of government stipend provided to pay her rent. Patricia has been attending university on a scholarship and government grant program and was one of the poorest people I knew at the school. I've never judged her for it, but it was clear at times that she resented me and other students for coming from old money, even if we never excluded her or treated her differently.

A shiver of uneasiness runs up my spine, and on a whim, I take my phone out of my pocket and turn the audio recording on. Better safe than sorry.

When I knock on the door, Patricia doesn't answer. Instead, it's an older woman in gray maid's clothing, and she leads me to Patricia's bedroom. I can barely fathom the apartment that I'm being led through; everything is brand new, looking like it's only recently been delivered. There is no sense of personal style or things that would lead me to identify the place as Patricia's, just expensive and luxurious surroundings.

Once we reach the bedroom, the maid knocks politely before opening the door. Lounging on a chaise in a silk robe, sipping a cosmopolitan while another woman tends to her toenails, is Patricia. She looks so out of place that it's surreal.

"Elise!" she nearly squeals. "It's so good to see you! Can I have my chef/mixologist make you a cocktail?"

"Oh, uh, no thank you." *Chef/mixologist, what the heck?* I think incredulously. Something odd is definitely going on here and I'm determined to get to the bottom of it. I pat myself on the back mentally for turning on my phone recording, because Patricia is definitely in the mood to talk.

"Okay! Just let me know if you change your mind. I think you're the first guest I've had here, so tell me if I do anything incorrectly," she giggles. "I'm new to this kind of life, unlike you."

Feeling awkward, I grin and shrug. "No... you're doing great... but how come no one knew that you moved out here?"

She waves a hand in the air. "Everyone was so rude and judgmental when everything was going on with Karl that I simply decided to disappear without telling any of them. Of course, you helped me through everything, so I was more than happy to see you."

The difference in the girl in front of me is staggering. Patricia has always been sort of gloomy and quiet, but now she's bubbly and almost glowing. "I'm just glad to see that you're doing well," I tell her, walking toward her. "But I have to say, this place sort of caught me off guard. How in the world did you snag an apartment like this?"

There is a glint in her eyes when she responds like she has a secret she's dying to tell. "I can't disclose that, Elise. I'm sorry."

I move to sit on the edge of her bed, leaning forward and all but whispering like we're telling secrets. "Oh, come on now, you can tell me. I can keep a secret."

The pedicurist finishes her work, packing her things up and leaving while Patricia contemplates the risk of telling me whatever mystery she's harboring. Her reaction to the question all but proves she got a windfall from some less-than-scrupulous means, and I have to know where it came from. The coincidences are just too striking to dismiss. How did she deny the deal Karl offered but still find money like this?

Clapping her hands in front of her, Patricia finally says, "Okay, okay! I'll tell you, but you can't tell a soul. I promised that I'd keep it on the down low. You're not going to believe what I'm about to tell you, though." Patricia looks around the room like there might be someone else there with us, patiently waiting to discover her secrets, before she sits up straight. "I got the money from your brother."

My brain short-circuits for a second. "Pardon?"

"Your brother!" she repeats, reveling in my astonishment. "You know how adamant he was about me pressing charges on Karl… well, when I told him I was going to take the deal because of how badly I needed the money, he offered to match the amount. When I called my lawyer and told him that I had changed my mind on taking the deal, he said he could probably get me substantially more."

"If your lawyer could get you more, why did you take money from my brother then?"

"When I told Andries what my lawyer said, he said he would still match the payout. I asked for double, and he accepted! Elise…" she lowers her voice to nearly a whisper, and I hope my phone microphone is sensitive enough to pick it up. "He gave me a hundred thousand euros to go to court against Karl, and that money completely changed my life. I feel happy for the first time in what seems like forever."

I'm dumbstruck by the news. Dad is going to have a heart attack when he hears this. "He paid you a hundred thousand euros just to follow through with the court case?"

"Oh, well, no… the court case *and* the interview with Kenneth. But he paid for my lawyers, too. Honestly, I don't know what I would have done without Andries. He's a saint."

I sit back on the bed, head spinning. "Patricia, if it's not too late, I think I'll take that cocktail."

* * *

Dressed casually and looking like I've just seen a ghost, I rush into the headquarters and straight back to the meeting room where Dad is waiting for me. He looks concerned when he sees me, standing up and pulling my chair out so I can sink down into it. The two cocktails I had drank with Patricia combined with how seriously her news is affecting me have me feeling like I'm falling apart, and apparently it's evident on my face.

"Are you okay, dear?" Dad asks, pushing my seat in for me before taking his again.

"Fine. It's just… well… I've got some news, and if I hadn't heard it for myself, I'd have never believed it."

"You're worrying me," he says, a finger tapping on the oak desk. "Let's hear it."

Instead of saying anything else, I simply pull out my phone, and begin to play the audio.

By the end of it, Dad's face is tomato-red, and I know he's feeling murderous. "This is unbelievable. The most shameful thing our family has ever been through." He pushes himself out of his seat, hanging his head and taking a few deep breaths before announcing, "I'm going to speak to our PR director. Just stay here until I'm done, alright?"

With a small nod, I say, "Um, okay."

It takes a long time. Longer than I would have thought, but I don't feel comfortable getting up, or even touching my phone until he returns. What I have revealed is the epitome of a bombshell, and I don't want to even give off a hint of possibly tampering with anything.

Finally, Dad returns with Greg, the PR director, in tow. Both men look grim and serious, and I sit up quickly when they enter the room, back ramrod straight.

Greg sits across from me, putting his fingertips together and sighing. "Look, Elise, I know that you didn't want to speak at the shareholders' meeting, but this new revelation makes me think that we'd all benefit from you having a more active role."

My stomach drops. I know that, in the future, I will be more responsible for things like speaking engagements, but this is only my first few months with the company. The idea of speaking at the shareholders' meeting with people that have been involved with the company for years... even decades... is daunting.

"Greg, I really don't—"

"Elise," Dad interposes, stopping me in the middle of my sentence. "We want you to tell the truth about everything you just showed us. It will take so much heat off of Karl and the company as a whole. It will prove that the only reason that Patricia went forward was because of money, not because she felt like she was a true victim."

He's right, I know that he's right, but I also know that it will be the end of any hope I have of fixing things between my brother and me if he gets to know what I did.

"Will the media be there?" I ask immediately.

"Of course," Greg answers with pride in his tone. "That speech will catch their attention and help the company's and Karl's reputations very smoothly."

"Oh gosh, I don't know..."

"Dear," Dad insists, his hand lying on top of mine. "I'd be very grateful if you did this for us."

Fuck! If the media broadcasts my speech there's no way my brother won't get to know about it. I have to choose between him and the company, and in this moment, I just can't make the call, so to escape I straighten my shoulders and nod.

"Okay. I'll do it."

CHAPTER 7

Amsterdam, April 26, 2022
Dan

Here, alone in the darkness of my bedroom with Jessica I can lose myself for some time, and what a delicious distraction it is. She writhes under my hands, breathing in sighs and sounds of pleasure in the brief moments that my mouth separates from hers.

Jessica's clever hands unbutton my shirt, sliding it down my arms before skating her palms over my bare chest. I break out in goosebumps, letting her press me backward onto the bed until she's straddling me, grinding herself against me.

"I've missed this," she purrs, between kisses. "You've been so busy, I feel like you never have time for me anymore."

I grab her hips, pulling her down harder. "I'm here with you now, though, can't you tell?"

She grins wickedly, feeling my hard length underneath her body. "I can."

I push my hands up her shirt, but right before I can go any further there is a hesitant knock at the door.

"Mr. O'Brian?" my maid says from outside the room.

"Whaaaat?" I groan.

"Ms. Van den Bosch is downstairs in the foyer demanding to speak with you. I tried to tell her you were… otherwise busy, but she wouldn't leave. What would you like me to do?"

What a shit show. Jessica, hot and needy on top of me, and Elise, my secret obsession, both vying for my attention at the same time. My body screams for me to stay here in the soft bed with the equally soft woman on top of me, but my heart is pulling me in another direction. What if Elise is in some sort of trouble? What if she needs me?

"Don't go," Jessica moans, doing some swirling motion with her hips that nearly makes me go cross-eyed. "You're always with Elise. This is my time."

"Jess." I pull her down to gently kiss her lips, already knowing what decision I'm going to make. "She's my best friend's sister. I have to help her if she needs it."

"But I need you!" she whines. "I need you so bad, Dan."

I curse, indulging myself in one more deep, searing kiss before I begin to extricate myself. Jessica gives up the needy act, letting her arms fall to her sides on the bed with an annoyed huff. While I button my shirt, she crosses her arms and rolls so that her back is toward me.

"I'll be quick," I promise. "Just wait here for me."

"I'll think about it," she grumbles.

Elise is waiting for me in the foyer, standing so stiffly it looks like she's made of glass that's ready to shatter. Dressed in designer jeans and a pale blue shirt, I don't think she's come here from work, but I guess whatever she has to tell me just can't wait any longer.

"What's up with you coming over uninvited?" I ask, causing her to whip around and see me descending the stairs.

"Never-mind that," she replies dismissively. "Do you have a few minutes? I have to talk to you."

"Not really, but you've sort of forced my hand by coming here and refusing to leave." I cross my arms, trying to look aloof, when in reality I'm worried. Elise is full of nervous energy, the corners of her mouth turned down in a frown, and I wish I was free to do everything in my power to fix her problems. Right now, though, all I can do is listen.

Elise doesn't wait for me to offer her a seat, instead walking the short steps into my sunken living room and sitting on a white chaise lounge. I follow, thinking that sitting means we're going to be here longer than expected, and Jessica is going to be pissed. But there's no way around it.

Taking a deep breath, Elise starts off the conversation by revealing the most shocking part of her story right up front. "Andries paid Patricia off. A hundred thousand euros."

My thoughts shudder to a stop before coming back online. "What exactly do you mean?"

"So I guess he went to see her right before she was supposed to sign the agreement to drop the charges against Karl. Andries was upset by that and told her he'd match whatever Karl was willing to pay her. When her lawyer told her she could probably get more, Andries said he would match that, too, and then she haggled with him! They agreed on a hundred thousand euros, and now she's living like a princess in a condo downtown."

I can barely believe what I'm hearing, but Elise has no reason to lie. "Holy shit, that's a lot to think about. You need to keep this quiet until we figure out what to do."

She crosses her ankles and looks away from me, a clear sign that she's uncomfortable, and my stomach sinks. "Well, about that…"

I take one deep breath and let it out. Then I do it again until I feel centered enough to ask, "What exactly did you do?"

"I already told my dad," she admits, regret dripping in her tone. "He brought the whole PR team in on it, and now they want me to reveal everything at the annual shareholders meeting. They all think it will help clear Karl's name and allow him to continue working at the company…"

Rage whips through me like fire. "Why in the hell is Sebastian so dead set on protecting that bastard!? He's one man and it seems like your father would move heaven and Earth to keep him around."

"I don't really understand it either, except that he's a really important part of the company and Dad's afraid that if they lose Karl, all the shareholders that have a good relationship with him will be pissed. Plus, Karl brings in a crazy amount of business."

"That's a pathetic excuse."

"He actually pulled me into his office and told me that he can easily see me as the next CEO and wants to help me get there. I get why so many people go easy on him, even with the rumors of what he did. He's a charismatic man."

"Again, not really an excuse," I continue, failing miserably to keep my tone even. "What Andries did is insane, no doubt, but your dad protecting Karl isn't exactly great, either." I pause, piecing together everything she's just told me. "Obviously you aren't going to speak at that event, right? You can't just throw your brother under the bus and expect him not to cut you off from his life."

"I don't want to, at all," she concedes. "The idea of doing that to Andries makes me sick."

I'm relieved she isn't going to torch her still vulnerable relationship with her brother. "Then what do you need my help for? It seems like you've already made up your mind."

Elise bites her lip. "I didn't say that."

I groan. "Please tell me you're joking."

"Look, morally and emotionally I don't want to do this thing. It makes me feel gross inside. But this is my future and my career we're talking about, and let's be real, my brother can't offer me a job with the same standings as Dad. I have to think about myself sometimes…" Her face falls just slightly. "Someone has to."

I feel a thread of guilt, and the urge to sit beside her and draw her into my arms, but all of this is much too serious for silly daydreaming. "He'll never forgive you."

"Unless…" She looks up at me through those dark lashes. "You speak to him right after my speech and tell him I didn't have any other choice."

This fucking girl… she's trying to manipulate me, and it's all so clear, but I just can't be as angry at her as I should. Still, her request leaves me flabbergasted, and I shake my head rapidly. "Oh no, no, no, Elise. You aren't going to get me wrapped up in this Van den Bosch shit show."

"But Dan!" she protests, sitting forward as she pleads. "Pops will be so disappointed in me, and I've just started gaining his trust and favor. I can't fathom just starting at the beginning again." To my horror, I see tears in her eyes. "Please, Dan."

Fuck. Fuck. Elise has my emotions in such a chokehold that I could almost just fall at her feet and tell her whatever she wants is hers if I can provide it. Thank God she and I aren't the same age, because if we had been, Elise would have both ruled and ruined my life. Now, it's just the ruin I'm worried about.

"You know I can't do that. Andries is my best friend, and I'd be outright lying to him. That's the biggest problem with what you're asking me to do because it's perfectly within your power to say no and not speak."

"You don't get it!" She throws her hands in the air. "Andries has already made his choices and is ready to start his life independently! But my life goal is to take over Dad's role at the company, and it's so close I can taste it. I'd be his successor before I'm thirty! Karl told me that Dad plans to retire in a decade or so. I can't fuck things up now."

"A job is not a good enough reason to fuck over your family like that."

"But Dad is my family too... and the company is his life's work and I want it to be mine."

I scrub my face with my hands, overcome with uncertainty about what to do. It should be an easy decision... but she isn't lying about being the second child and how much harder that has been for her. She really is gambling her future on all of this. But Andries's reputation...

I don't think things can get any worse until I hear bare feet on the stairs, and there, wearing my cashmere robe barely tied, one naked leg completely on display, is Jessica. She stands at the top of the small stairs leading into the living room, arms crossed.

Elise blanches, before turning beet red and turning her entire body away from Jessica, murmuring some apology about disturbing us. The two women are on good terms, but my increasing attention toward Elise has put Jess on edge, and it's all too clear on the way she's looking at her now.

"When are you coming back to the bedroom?" Jessica demands. "You told me you wouldn't take too long. It's been fifteen minutes already."

I sneak a glance over at the embarrassed Elise, but beyond how awkward she must feel right now, I know she's still torn up inside about everything with her brother. Torn up and utterly confused, I'm sure. Of all the people in her life that she came to, she chose me, and even if she's manipulating me somewhat, I know she's only risking it because she trusts me not to do her wrong.

I'm either about to make an enormous mistake or a brilliant move. I'm not sure which, but my cock is pretty sure it's the mistake.

"Jess—Elise and I are dealing with something about her brother and it's more important than I thought. Why don't you head home, and I'll call you?"

Her mouth falls open, and she glares at the other woman. "We were seconds away from having sex and you're sending me away so you can talk about family drama with your best friend's sister!? It isn't even your family, Dan!"

Any other time, Elise would fight fire with fire, but it's been a long day for her and when Jess raises her voice, she flinches. That's the final straw for me, and my burgeoning annoyance snaps into anger.

"Jess, I'll call you later and we can get together then, but I need you to respect my space for the moment."

Without another word, she turns in a huff, robe billowing out behind her, and then she's gone back to the second floor. Not wanting to see her again, and needing space from Elise, too, I stand and leave the room, even after I hear a small, "Dan, wait," from her.

Tina, my maid, is wiping down the marble kitchen counters when I find her. After requesting my favorite hibiscus blossom tea, I flee to the patio, annoyed that I have to hide in my own house. I sometimes wonder whether women are even worth it.

When Tina brings the tea service out on a jade tray, setting it on the table beside me, I tell her to send Elise out here if she's still in the house. The maid laughs, telling me that yes, Ms. Van den Bosch is still in the house, and seems to have made herself comfortable.

It isn't long until Elise joins me, settling herself on one of the overstuffed outdoor chairs. Without speaking, we both watch as the tea bulb blooms in the clear teapot, the green-brown leaves unfurling to reveal the red hibiscus flower, small curls of color emanating from it all, and darkening the steaming water. Once the flower is fully revealed, it looks almost alive, petals dancing in the water gently as I lift the teapot to pour. Elise takes the offered cup graciously, inhaling the aroma, and my heart skips a beat. Like the hibiscus flower wrapped in dried leaves, she is also something stunning, who is just beginning to show her true colors to the world.

I saw her first, though, and the potential she had. If only it wasn't for that asinine promise I made to her brother to leave her alone for eternity.

"I'd never tried this tea before until I went with you to the Astoria," she admits, enchanted by the whole presentation.

"Sometimes, it's the quiet moments, like blooming tea or a barrel-aged scotch that are the best parts of life."

Looking thoughtful, she nods, taking a sip of the tea and sighing as she sits back in her chair. "That's a good philosophy."

She isn't looking at me, but I take the time to search her face anyway. "You don't have many quiet moments, do you?"

She laughs softly. "No. Maybe I will when I'm older."

We keep quiet as we drink our respective teas for a little longer, but I know I can't avoid finishing our talk forever. Out here, in the fresh air, I feel like I can think. I'm not trapped, and I feel like that makes me smarter, which is why I have such a brilliant idea to make things even between Elise and me.

And, if I'm being honest with myself, take Elise on a date without it actually being a date. The perfect loophole.

"This is an enormous favor you're asking me, El, and one that could very easily backfire. Hence, it's a favor that needs to be paid back upfront."

"Paid upfront?" she echoes.

"If you want me to convince your brother that you, poor, unloved Elise, didn't have any choice but to give that speech at the meeting, then you need to do something for me first."

She blushes, and I don't correct the dirty thoughts she might be having. "And that is?"

"My parents and I are invited to a charity dinner hosted by my dad's biggest client, Pieter van Vollenhoven, and I'd like you to join me."

She blinks owlishly, surprised. "Me?"

"No, I meant the Pope. Yes, you! You seem out of sorts, my dear."

Elise scowls, and it almost seems like she wants to stick her tongue out at me, but resists. "Why wouldn't you take Jessica with you?"

"I'm meeting a member of the royal family and you want me to bring my fuck buddy?" I chuckle. "No. Jess is lovely for normal outings, but you're part of a noble family. It will be much better for my image."

She huffs. "So you're using me for your image?"

I take a long drink of my tea, the aromatics filling my senses. "Well, in a way, aren't you doing the same? Using me to save your image with your brother?"

"Hmm…" Elise swirls the tea as she thinks, tapping her fingernails on the glass. "Okay, I'll do it. It will be good PR for me, anyway. When is it?"

I grin wickedly. "This Saturday."

"What!?" Elise is irritated, which only adds to my amusement.

"I'll pick you up at seven, little ice queen. Make sure you dress to impress."

She's silent for a long time then, simply drinking and scowling, but eventually she says, "You should know by now I always impress."

CHAPTER 8

It sounds idiotic, but pulling up to Elise's apartment makes me feel like I'm taking her to an American prom like you see in the movies. We've never been on a date, and if Andries has his way, we never will, so this night is a special thing for me to hold close to my heart. That doesn't excuse how nervous I am, though, or how hard my heart is beating.

I've been with countless women, and consider myself a great lover. Beautiful women don't make me nervous, unless they are Elise Van den Bosch, apparently.

When I arrive outside of her place, she texts me letting me know the door is unlocked and to let myself in. I want to scold her for taking such a risk, but when she descends the stairs like an angel from heaven, all of my thoughts dissipate like petals on the wind.

Elise is... everything. I'm so royally fucked, tempting myself with having her by my side all night. How will I keep my wits about me?

She's wearing rose gold silk that fits her body and curves to perfection, the sweetheart neckline showing the swell of her breasts just enough that it makes my mouth go dry. It's sleeveless, flaring out only minutely below her knees. The dress is simple enough to almost be considered understated, but the woman wearing it elevates the garment to a whole new level.

And then, because fate somehow thinks I need another thing to obsess over all night, she steps a certain way down the stairs and one long, glistening leg peeks out from a slit in her skirt.

I'm a dead man.

I'm finally able to look at her face and the way her long hair is curled softly and caught in a delicate matching rose gold clip. Her lush lips are a dusky rose, and a part of me is furious thinking about smudging that lipstick off her mouth with my own.

When I realize Elise has been standing directly in front of me, silently, for at least a solid minute, I feel like sinking into the ground with embarrassment. I feel like a teenager again.

"Did you lose your tongue, or what?" she teases, and my mind is so scattered that I don't even know what retort I give. All I know is that she loops her arm with mine and lets me lead her out to the car.

"You look nice, too," she offers once we're in the vehicle. I'd gone simple, my black suit tailored close to my body, the only flash of color the vintage opal cufflinks at my wrists.

"Thanks," I tell her, trying to keep my tone even. "But I don't think anyone is even going to realize I'm there tonight."

"What? Why not?"

"Because you'll be beside me."

Elise takes the compliment happily, smiling and leaning back in the leather seat as we flow through the city. I belatedly wonder if I should have hired a limo for the night, but having Elise this close to me in the car is a reward in its own right.

Once we arrive at the gala, a valet takes the car as I hold out my hand for my date. This event is rather large, and the red carpet and paparazzi lining said carpet make it apparent that this isn't some small fundraising event: This is the big times.

As I'd guessed, Elise is perfectly familiar with all of it, and she smiles brilliantly at the cameras as we pass. There is a photo opportunity right before we enter the hall where the gala is being held, and like everyone else, we stop and let our images be captured. It feels unreal, having Elise next to me with everything going on. It's almost like we're more than just casual friends.

When she goes first inside, I notice that the back of her dress is plunging dangerously low. I can't help heaving a long sigh as I try to focus somewhere else.

Inside, lights are low, and soft string music comes from the small group of musicians in the corner of the hall. The ceilings are stupendously high, painted with beautiful motifs that are more difficult to see in the sparse lighting, looking more like splashes of color than anything else. The night is young, so not many couples are dancing, maybe waiting for the buzz of champagne to kick in so their inhibitions fall to the wayside.

It's assigned seating, so Elise and I find our table where my parents are already seated. I hadn't warned them that I was bringing her, but considering how much my parents adore her, I knew it wouldn't be a problem.

As expected, my mom jumps up from her seat when she sees us, ignoring me completely to rush over to Elise, taking her hands and gushing over how beautiful she looks. Dad stands too, shaking my hand in greeting before patting my shoulder.

"Interesting choice in plus ones," he comments, watching his wife and my guest get reacquainted.

"She and I have been hanging out a lot more now that Andries is too busy for me," I tell him smoothly, not wanting my dad to know anything about the drama going on.

Luckily, Dad buys it, nodding. "Yes, it is a strange time when your friends start to settle down and you're still single. I remember those days..." he trails off. "She does look lovely tonight though. Good choice for a guest, son."

Once Mom and Elise settle down, we get seated, my parents catching up with Elise and me about everything under the sun. It's nice to be with them... it always is, really. I've been lucky. Because our family doesn't have generational wealth, there are none of the strings attached like Elise and the Van Den Bosches have. We basically had a blank slate to start with.

I might be drinking and talking, but everything in me is focused on my faux date. I know Elise is nervous about the social aspect of becoming CEO of Van den Bosch industries, but she mingles so effortlessly, and carries herself with such grace, that I doubt there will truly be any issues for her.

I could watch her for hours; just seeing the way her mouth moves when she talks, or the way she crinkles her nose when she laughs. It's all intoxicating, but this is an event with hundreds of people, and being smitten isn't going to get me out of fulfilling my own social obligations.

Eventually, we all stand and make our way around the hall, chatting with other small groups of people and making introductions. This fundraising gala is being hosted by Pieter van Vollenhoven for the Victim Support Fund. The elderly royal spots my father from across the room, and when he waves us over we all follow.

"Mr. and Mrs. O'Brian, so glad you could make it," he tells us, shaking my father's hand and kissing my mother's. Pieter is very old, but he holds himself tall and seems to take joy in holding gatherings like this. They're usually for such a good cause that there is no way I can complain.

"Also young Mr. O'Brian. How are you, son? You're looking well." He squints down at Elise. "And what a beautiful guest you have brought!"

Elise smiles that million-watt smile as I go to introduce her. "Pieter, this is Elise Van den Bosch, second child of–"

"Sebastian and Julia Van den Bosch. Yes, yes, I know, Daniel."

Elise's eyebrows shoot up in surprise. "I didn't think you'd know who I was."

"Only a fool would forget the granddaughter of Lady Margaret," Pieter chuckles.

Elise clasps her hands together happily. "That's right! How funny that you knew me because of Oma Margaret.

That usually isn't the first connection people associate me with."

"Ah, young lady, I knew your grandmother well." There's a twinkle in his eye, which makes me wonder how well exactly.

Pieter isn't the only one with a trick up his sleeve, though. Elise moves a step closer to the old man and while graciously touching his arm, she says, "Then, from my grandmother and I both, happy birthday Mr. van Vollenhoven."

The old man blinks a few times before laughing, looking as happy as I'd ever seen him. "You know you're the first person to tell me that since we arrived, Ms. Elise. Clearly, the focus is supposed to be on my charity, but you've warmed an old man's heart by knowing that."

I'm in awe, and my parents are too, looking at each other and shrugging. "I had no idea," Mom hisses under her breath, and I nod in agreement. Neither had I.

Elise is a powerhouse of a socialite, and she attracts them like moths to a flame. Pieter stays to talk with us for an excessively long time, charmed by my date, but as soon as we bid him farewell there is always someone else in front of us, ready to be introduced.

For as boring as these galas usually are, I'm having a great time. It feels so natural being here with Elise, and it gives me forbidden thoughts about how simple it would be to take our relationship to the next level. Having her by my side feels right… like she completes me in some way.

We make our way back to the table as food is served, and the moment I have her even somewhat alone I ask, "How in the hell did you know Pieter's birthday?"

"Oh, you know, this little thing called Google." She slides me a glance. "I'm not an idiot, you know."

"I guess you had to prepare yourself to be the belle of the ball, huh?" I quip as dinner is being passed out. "How many proposals for your hand in marriage do you think your dad is going to receive tomorrow morning? All these middle-aged businessmen are tripping over themselves to talk to you."

"Just like you," she says primly, cutting into her fish.

"I'm not tripping over myself to talk to you," I hiss, before taking a sip of my wine. My parents must be eavesdropping from across the table because I see Mom giggling behind her hand.

"You aren't?" Elise asks, sounding genuinely bewildered. "My mistake, then. I thought you were just another middle-aged businessman, given how well you know them. I must have been confused."

I can't help but chuckle at her little game and decide to just play along. "You know good and well I'm in my twenties, you little—" I pretend to catch myself, covering my mouth with my hand and looking pointedly at Elise. "I apologize, I forgot there were children in the room."

She glowers at me but doesn't break her stride when it comes to the exchange of insults. "Speaking of children, shouldn't you produce an heir soon? I know when men get older, it's much harder to get a woman pregnant because he has less—"

I'm about to slap my hand over her mouth myself, but we're interrupted by a tall, slinky shape approaching the table. The new woman is tall and thin, with auburn hair and a figure-hugging green gown, holding a Cosmopolitan in one hand and a clutch in the other. She also looks vaguely familiar, but I can't place her in my mind.

"Dan O'Brian?" she asks, standing between me and another male guest. "Is that you?"

Great. It's never good news when a random woman knows my name. "Yes, that's me."

"I thought so! It's Alice, do you remember? We met at that educators' fundraiser a few years ago."

I flip through the rolodex of women in my memory, and I think I can place her, albeit hazily. No matter what, having someone like her hovering over the table where Elise is sitting next to me is bad news.

"Maybe..." I say, sounding unconvinced. "I attend so many of these things it's hard to recall."

Alice looks crestfallen but presses on. "Oh, come on now, we even danced when they played that one song—"

I shake my head. "Sorry, Alice. Maybe I had a bit too much to drink that night." I try to make it sound self-deprecating and dismissive. "Well, it's nice to see you again anyway. Have a good night."

Still, Alice apparently isn't done, and I can sense Elise getting stiffer beside me. I take a quick look at her, and her lips are pursed, eyes narrowed as she looks at Alice. Something has her clearly pissed off.

Rattling off a few utterly forgettable moments from the night I had apparently met her, Alice won't take the hint to leave, no matter how short and curt my answers become. At this point, Elise is almost vibrating with annoyance.

I refuse to let my night with her be ruined this way, and thankfully the group of musicians saves me by starting up a new song; a recognizable classical rearrangement of a popular song.

"Oh!" I exclaim, interrupting Alice. "Elise, this is your favorite song, isn't it?"

She opens her mouth to reply, but I don't have time to waste. I grab her by the arm and haul her out of her seat, telling Alice, "Sorry, my girlfriend loves this song. See you later."

I whisk Elise onto the dancefloor, pulling her into me, my hands on her waist, and after her shock eases up she rolls her eyes. "You're ridiculous."

Her comment catches me off guard, causing me to frown. "Why?"

"Really? *Girlfriend?*" she drawls.

"It was the only way to get rid of her. It worked, didn't it?"

Elise huffs. "Who was she?"

Spinning her around the dancefloor, just enough room between us to be polite, I refuse to give in to her interrogation. This is her repaying my favor, after all. "Why are you so damned nosy? I'm not your brother, miss."

"I just like to know things. Plus, if I'm actually your girlfriend for the evening, I think you owe me an explanation."

I chuckle at her little reasoning and leaning slightly closer to her ear, I whisper, "Darling, if you were my girlfriend, we wouldn't be dancing like this."

She tilts her head to the side just slightly. "How would we be dancing, then?"

Like always, when Elise is involved, all of my baser natures scream in unison to show her *exactly* what I mean, but I have to keep tonight innocent enough, or I might regret it. "I don't think it's appropriate."

This girl is stubborn though, and she never lets me forget it. "Show me," Elise demands.

Fuck it, I think, and on the next swell of music, I move closer and press her body against mine. The sizzle of electricity between us is automatic, especially when Elise releases a tiny gasp of surprise. That noise goes straight to the most scandalous parts of me. We move together like one single entity; a ship rocking on the ocean waves. Like this moment, us together like this was inevitable.

"This is how we would be dancing," I tell her, my face so close to hers that my breath stirs her hair. "*If* you were my girlfriend."

I see her eyes flutter closed, and I know she's savoring the moment just like I am, committing our dance to her memory to hold on to forever. Then, she lays her head on my shoulder, completing our connection. Seeing her do that triggers a rush of emotion in me that I've never felt before, because it means maybe, just maybe, she feels the same way I do.

Her body is soft and pliable in my arms, and I swear I can control myself, but Elise lifts her head, her nose brushing against mine, and my self-control runs away from me in a furious rush. All that's left are my desires, and at this moment, the only one I have is to kiss her.

I run my hands from her waist up her back where her dress leaves it bare, her skin like silk, and when she shivers I move in, slanting my face just enough so that when our lips meet, it will be perfect.

And, oh my God, she's moving in for the kiss too, meeting me halfway. I have to have her. I have to—

The music falls away and the lights start to come up on the dance floor. We remain in limbo for a few seconds more, but in my heart I know the moment has been ruined.

Elise jumps away first, her face flushed. She refuses to meet my gaze, pausing only briefly before fleeing back to our table. Feeling dumbstruck and defeated, I follow her, not knowing where else to go.

The rest of the night is taut and silent, the ghost of our almost kiss hovering over the table and weighing heavily on us both. I almost kissed Elise—my best friend's sister… what the fuck is wrong with me? Andries will kill me if I start to mess around with her, which of course means I'm doomed to crave this woman that I can never have like no other. Like water in the desert.

It's too much for me, talking with Elise and pretending like we didn't both almost confess our feelings in the physical sense. I excuse myself, escaping to the bar just so I can breathe a little. I order and get myself a glass of scotch, leaning against the bar and breathing slowly as I drink. If I can just have this moment alone to recharge, I'll be able to finish out the night.

What I don't expect, though, is the man sitting beside me scrolling through pictures on a tablet with his chunky camera around his neck. As he pursues them, I see one that looks just a little too familiar, and it makes my blood pressure start to rise.

"Excuse me," I tell him, and he looks up. "Can you go back two pictures?"

He does so, and to my misery, it's a perfectly framed shot of Elise and I almost kissing. We're so close together there isn't really any way to know if we actually are or not, but it's more than enough to get me in trouble if it comes out. Even worse, the man has captured the entire dance in a series of ten pictures.

"I'd like to buy the exclusivity for these pictures," I announce quickly. "Name your price."

The photographer, confused, takes a second to process. Eventually, he clears his throat and nods. "Sure. It'll be five hundred and fifty euros paid now on Tikkie."

It's highway robbery, no doubt about it, but less than other paparazzi might have charged me. I give him a tight nod. "Fine, but you'll have to email them to me first, and then I want to see you delete them and the email."

He simply shrugs, but complies, sending the pictures to the address I type in his iPad. Once the pictures have successfully landed in my mailbox, he then lets me watch him as he deletes them off his own device.

"Done," he announces, before he grabs his smartphone and starts generating a QR code for me to scan and complete the payment.

I waste no time scanning the code and the transaction is done swiftly.

"Thank you for your business," the man says with a smile before leaving my side.

I breathe a sigh of relief. At least that problem is taken care of quickly. If it had gone viral, or gotten slapped on a tabloid, I'd never live it down, and I'd lose my best friend. That's just not something I'm willing to do.

I look through the busy crowd, spotting Elise back at our table, standing and talking to some other socialites. Honestly... I'm glad to have the pictures just for myself so I can look back on this night with her and remember it all.

***

When I drop her off for the night, we're more relaxed. Almost back to normal, actually, and I consider asking her if she wants to just drive around for a while and listen to music, but decide against it. It's just that I hate to see her go.

I walk her to her apartment door, and she lets me rest my hand on her back as I do so. She walks slowly, maybe just as reluctant to have the night end as I am. Elise looks at me one more time before entering her apartment, eyes scanning my face like she's waiting on something. Should I kiss her now and make up for what we missed out on? The temptation is here, and it's so damn hard not to act on it. But no, it's a terrible idea, and even though it hurts my heart, I've got to tell her goodbye like a friend does.

"Thank you so much for the evening," I say, trying to focus on something else than her beautiful, glossy lips. "It was great."

She nods, the corner of her mouth spreading into a smile. "It was great, yeah."

We keep silent for a short instant, and before it gets too awkward, I shove my hands in my pants pocket and say, "Well, have a good one." I don't even kiss her on the cheek, keeping my lips away from her skin.

She looks disappointed but wishes me good night, before turning her back on me and pushing her door to step inside. By the time I call the elevator to go down, Elise is gone, and I'm alone again.

I head home, showering and brushing my teeth in what seems like a trance. Once in bed, I give in to temptation and open my email on my phone. Lo and behold, the photos are already in my inbox. They're all special pictures to me, but nothing compares to the one where we are nearly kissing. Looking at it, I'm full of regret. Maybe I should text her? Or send her the photo and see what her reaction is?

The photo sits in the forward email, just waiting for me to hit send, but I just can't do it. If she is actually embarrassed about what almost happened, or regrets it, it would be an asshole move to rub it in her face. If I'm being honest with myself, sending it at all is probably a mistake. There are a million reasons I shouldn't flirt with her in any way shape or form. Doesn't mean I don't want to anyway.

I agonize over what to say to her, even just over text, and I type and erase the words over and over again. Finally, I decide to just keep it short and sweet, since that would leave the least room for error or misunderstanding. Speaking from the heart, I try to tell her that the night together was very special to me, but at the very last second, I take it out and just tell her it was amazing, instead. It feels almost like I'm being cowardly, but this situation is so shaky there is no telling what the right thing to do is.

Dan: *I just got home. Thank you again for the night, El. It was amazing. X*

I don't expect her to reply until morning, but to my surprise, a text comes in from her within minutes.

My pleasure, X

CHAPTER 9

Amsterdam, May 1, 2022
Dan

I feel like I spend so much of my time being introspective sitting on my terrace that maybe I should just consider moving out here permanently.

I woke up later than usual, nearly at 11 am, but that was because I had slept so little the night before. I hate how much Elise is affecting me, and how she seems to infect my thoughts, but at the same time, I love it in a self-destructive way. I want to revel in my fantasies of us together, even if they are so bad for me.

Because of my sleeping and waking dreams about my best friend's sister keeping me up all night, I had to skip my favorite breakfast tea, and am now sipping a bitter espresso as I try to wake up. The only thing on my schedule for today is going to visit my dad to see the new Omega watch he's getting today, a new edition to its vintage collection. I prefer a newer, sleek timepiece, but I have to admit there is something the antique models have that the new ones simply lack. History, or personality maybe. It will be interesting to see if Dad will put this piece up for sale after having it restored, or if he will fall in love with it and add it to his personal collection.

Other than that there is nothing I need to do on this lazy Sunday. Maybe I could drive the Audi, my preferred cold-weather vehicle, home when I go later today and drive one of the convertibles back instead since summer is nearly here. The cherry red 1969 Jaguar with the black hood sounds like a good choice, especially since it's one of my only convertibles. If I close my eyes, I can picture a certain woman in the seat next to me, the dark blonde hair flowing behind her in a riot as I drive us along the mountainside. Maybe she reaches over and—

The fantasy is so deliciously real that I have the very real thought of throwing my phone off the terrace when it begins ringing. Frustrated, I set my espresso down and answer it.

"Hey," Andries greets me as I put the phone against my ear. "Are you free for lunch this afternoon?"

Free for lunch this afternoon? Wow! That's quite sudden for someone who's living full-time with his fiancée. Did they have an argument or something? Sounds like Andries needs urgently to talk to me. I consider lying and telling him I'm busy, but I'm starving, and the strong coffee is making my stomach burn acidly. "Yeah, actually I am. How about Gartine?"

"Sure. I'll meet you there in an hour."

I check my watch just as my stomach growls loudly. Even Andries hears it over the phone, and adds, "Actually, make it forty-five minutes."

***

After spending all night among the social elite, I'm feeling the desire to indulge in some of my finer things, and I roll up to lunch in a powder blue hound's tooth linen blazer and slacks, the white button-down shirt underneath opened to the third button. I'm overdressed, which is apparent from Andries's eye roll when I walk in, pushing the aviator sunglasses off my face and onto my head.

He's in dark denim jeans, short leather boots, and a simple white shirt, which apparently makes him think he's in any position to judge me. "You know we aren't going out on a yacht, right? This is just lunch."

"What's the point of owning all these suits if I never get a chance to wear them? Just shut up and listen to your elders, Andries," I grumble, sitting across from him. He's already ordered tea service, and the orange spice hot tea is enjoyable enough that I'm willing to play nice.

Andries has his hands folded on the table in front of him, his own teacup untouched as he watches me quietly. Finally, I give in, sitting the cup back on the saucer with a clink. "Okay, you're being weird. What's going on? Did you get into a fight with your lady or what?"

I'm half-expecting for him to nod and start opening up but to my astonishment, Andries just leans back on his chair, observing me all smug. "Don't you have something to tell me, Dan?"

I look around the room. "Is this some sort of intervention? No, I don't have anything to tell you."

"Not even that you went to a gala with my sister last night?"

I freeze, guilt washing over me until I remember that nothing truly happened between Elise and me. In fact, the charity dinner is a perfectly acceptable event to take Elise, another young businessperson looking to network, as my plus one, and I tell Andries as much.

"It was a good opportunity for her to meet some of her peers and I needed a plus one to make me look better. Elise got to network, and I showed up with the daughter of a noble family. Don't look too much into it, my friend."

"Your hand was on her hip," he counters, eyes narrowing.

I thought that he had just heard through the grapevine that Elise and I had gone together, but this gives me pause. I had purchased all the pictures of the two of us from the photographer, so how had Andries known that?

"How exactly did you get this information?" I ask suspiciously, afraid that the photographer had lied and leaked the pictures anyway, but Andries pulls out his phone and shows me a professional photo posted on an Instagram celebrity gossip account. It's Elise and I on the red carpet, posing for the camera, and yes, my hand is on her hip. But barely.

"Really, Andries, I didn't think you followed that kind of trash news."

"Actually, Patricia saw it since she follows them and sent it to me. I can't believe I had to find out third-hand that my best friend and my sister were attending an event together." His tone is annoyed, but the explanation that it had all been a business decision seems to have chilled him out somewhat. It's plausible, even half-true, but he didn't need to know the selfish reasons I invited her.

"Next time I'll give you a heads up. Promise. But if you look at some of the other pictures of the whole event, you can probably see your sister and I were seated with my parents, which should tell you that it was completely innocent."

He lets out a breath, grappling with what he thought had happened and the story I've just told him, but it all checks out and he knows it. "Fine. But remember your oath."

Our lunches come out, a beet, peach, and arugula salad for Andries and a small stack of French toast for me, and the conversation pauses so we can eat some. I'm not done with this topic, though, and Andries has landed on a sore point for me.

"You mean that ridiculous oath you forced me to do when you were just a teenager? Don't you think that it's weird how much you still care about that?" Andries looks offended, but I don't give him time to speak. "Not that I want to get with your sister," I lie, despite sounding rather honest. "But it just feels so off having it hang over us."

"I was serious about it then and I'm serious about it now," he says stubbornly.

"Whatever, Andries. I've been a good friend to you all this time and you still think the worst of me in some ways. It's not a good feeling."

He looks surprised, and then a bit sad. "It's not that I think the worst of you, it's just that you are undoubtedly a ladies' man, and I'm trying to protect my sister."

I want to talk more about this, to try and make my best friend understand that I'd never do anything to cause Elise pain, but now is not the time. Not when Andries is being ostracized from his family while also planning a wedding, so I let it go. But this isn't the last time we'll touch upon this subject, I know.

We eat in peace, talking about who I spoke to last night, but then my phone rings again.

"I swear I'm going to quit carrying this damn thing," I grumble, pulling it out. It's Jessica calling, and when I show the screen to Andries, he grins.

"Better you than me," he says.

I answer, knowing I can't avoid this conversation forever.

"Wow. After the argument we had, you go behind my back and take Elise to a gala instead of me? What the fuck is going on, Dan!"

"It was a networking thing," I explain, my tone even as I lean back on the chair. "You aren't exactly looking to network, but Elise is, so I took her. It's as simple as that."

Jessica huffs. "I don't believe that for a minute. You've been spending so much time with her and now you're taking her to events? That doesn't sound like friendly business stuff to me."

"Shit like that isn't what I want to do with you, Jess! I want to enjoy our private time together."

"Private? Since when am I no longer good enough to go out with you?" she exclaims, and I want to scream.

"I just meant I want to have fun together, not go to stuffy events." I roll my eyes, head shaking and Andries chuckles at the whole thing while taking another bite of his food.

"Listen to me, Dan, you're on the verge of losing me for good. I liked Elise when she was just a friend, but she's been making her way more and more into your life and taking my place. I'm not having it. One more fuckup, and I'm gone for good."

"Jess—" I try to say, but she's already hung up.

I groan and lay my forehead on the table, causing Andries to laugh. "Good luck with that," he says, reaching over to pat my shoulder.

"Yeah," I say, voice muffled by the table. "I'm going to need it."

***

I've managed to argue with my hookup and my best friend already today, so now I'm going home to see if maybe I can coax my parents into a screaming match just to round out the day.

Even if I were being serious, my parents are some of the calmest, most even-keeled people I know, and I'd have to commit felony arson or something to make them angry. It's why I'm headed to their house early to be around the few people in the world that won't ever cause me any drama and love me unconditionally.

I feel a rush of affection for my parents, and how wonderful they both are. Maybe I should just move back home and hide away. It would be nice, for a few days at least, until I went stir crazy.

I pull around to the back of the estate, telling the valet to clean the Audi for storage and have the Jaguar ready for me when I leave, before heading inside. My mother greets me with a kiss on both cheeks before telling me that my dad is in his workshop looking over his newest purchase.

"Will you stay for dinner?" she asks hopefully, and I'm more than happy to accept.

Dad's workshop and storage for all his collectibles take up the entire basement. Its temperature and humidity are controlled to protect the delicate fabric fibers and wood that some of the watches are crafted from.

He's standing in front of one of his worktables when I find him, cloth gloves on as he takes the watch out of an aged wooden case.

"I'm here, Dad," I tell him, not wanting to shock him into dropping the watch. "Just letting you know."

"Of course, son. Come here, come here. Look how beautiful this one is."

He isn't wrong, either. The watch is a 1908 vintage Omega World Time on a dark leather band. The face of the piece is a dark orange-brown, with names of multiple countries around the face and a painted image of the world in the center. Dad handles it gently, turning it this way and that, so I watch over his shoulder as he examines it.

Being here brings me back to what it was like when I was a kid and Dad would teach me what to look for in collectibles. I was enraptured, watching every minute little thing that he did when he would let me, and when he wouldn't, I would sit on the floor in the workshop and read or do my homework, just to be close to Dad and all the excitement.

I feel like that today, staying quiet while Dad explains everything about the watch, treating it with reverence as he does so. He looks over at me a few times and frowns.

"Dan, is something bothering you?"

I shake my head. "No, just feeling a little nostalgic and... weird, I guess."

He smiles knowingly, pulling his standalone magnifier over to look closer at the Omega. "It's that Van den Bosch girl, isn't it? Elise?"

"What?" I ask sharply. "How do you even know that?"

He shrugs one shoulder, bringing the watch closer to the magnifying glass. "Whenever you talk about her, you get reflective. No one else does that to you."

I'm suddenly concerned, not wanting my parents to know my feelings for Elise and how much they are bothering me. Not when I can't ever be with her, according to Andries, not to mention her still being seventeen. I'm trying desperately to come up with an excuse.

"There's just a lot going on between her and Andries," I explain.

"Ah, well, that makes sense. What happened between her and her brother?"

Thankfully, Dad seems to accept the excuse easily enough, probably distracted by the watch he's working on. "It's complicated. Basically, Elise has been commanded by her father to air some confidential private information about her brother at the annual shareholders' meeting tomorrow, because it will help save another employee's reputation. Andries is going to go berserk."

"Yes, I can see why he would. He'll feel betrayed." Dad looks over at me, his expression kind and understanding. "You know you shouldn't get between them, right? You're going to get burned in the end."

"I know." I sigh. "Thanks, Dad."

It's been settling over me, all day long, that I may have made a mistake taking Elise to the gala. It had been an incredible time, and the memories were worth their weight in gold, but by taking her I basically signed off on Elise trashing Andries publicly. Was a date that wasn't even really a date worth sabotaging my best friend like this?

Fuck, it wasn't, no matter how strongly I feel about Elise. I desperately need to stop this before it goes any further. Not sure what else to do, I message Elise and ask if she needs a plus one for the shareholders' meeting. When she gives me the affirmative, a plan starts to snap together in my mind.

I have to stop her from giving that speech.

CHAPTER 10

I've been sick all night, and now all morning, leaning over the porcelain toilet bowl to heave a few times but producing nothing. I don't want to go to this shareholders meeting, and it's only hours now until I can't escape my fate.

I know I'm going to ruin my relationship with my brother today. I don't even know if Dan can save it, but I have to depend on him. It's the only lifeline I have, and at least I won't be alone out there today. Dan is always a comfort to have at my side, even if he can be an asshole sometimes.

But of course, I'm also dreading seeing him. Dreading and anticipating, all at the same time, and all because of the stupid almost kiss that we had nearly shared at the charity gala. I can't believe I was so weak. Kissing Dan would have ruined *everything*.

So why, when I think about it now, do I have butterflies in my stomach?

I can't get him off my mind; not when I dress in the Chanel ivory suit I had purchased just for this occasion, not when I lightly curl my hair and pin it above the back of my neck, and not when doing my makeup in front of my lit vanity. The way he felt against me, the heaviness of his body pressing against mine, and his breath ghosting across my lips from how close he was. I blush even thinking about it, and it makes me giddy and nervous.

Still, though… at least I won't have to be alone, talking to a room full of strangers while I ruin so many parts of my life just to keep Dad and Karl happy. There will be a hand for me to hold when it's all over, the hand of a man I trust, and that's more than I really could have hoped for.

Dan arrives to get me, and there is no Cinderella moment on the stairs like there was the night of the gala. I feel grim and still a bit ill, a bottle of San Pellegrino clutched in one hand so I can try to settle my stomach.

He doesn't bother with the polite arm-in-arm loop but seems to sense how on edge I am, taking my hand and intertwining our fingers instead. "I know you feel like crap, but that suit is beautiful on you."

"It feels like a suit of armor," I admit with a frown. "Like I'm going to war."

He tugs me closer by the hand as we walk, so we're almost shoulder to shoulder. "In some ways, my dear, you are."

It's not awkward the way I thought it would be, and for better or for worse, I still feel that attraction and connection I felt with him on the dancefloor, even when he leads me to a small, bright red convertible with the top down.

"Absolutely not. It will mess my hair up."

With an exaggerated pout, he puts the top on. "You're no fun."

Once in the car, I begin to feel the dread building again, and I'm unconsciously chewing my thumbnail when I feel Dan's large, warm hand on my leg. "If you want," he tells me, "we can leave right now. I'll drive you anywhere you want to go if you want to skip this thing."

"I wish I could, honestly," I admit, heaving out a sigh. "But I'm in too deep now."

A shadow moves across his expression, but he still leaves his hand on my leg between shifting gears. It's more comfort than I probably deserve.

The meeting is being held at a conference hall inside an enormous luxury hotel, and when we enter the building, we are immediately shown where to go. My heart is pounding, and I can feel beads of sweat on the back of my neck under my hair, but I can't let it show. So, head held high, I let Dan's hand go and push the heavy double doors open to enter the conference room, where I will soon potentially make the worst decision of my entire life thus far.

Dad is there to greet me, shaking Dan's hand first before hugging me briefly. Can't show too much affection here in front of every shareholder the company has, I guess. Dan doesn't look overly thrilled with my father, but when Karl joins us and holds out a hand for Dan to shake as well, his face may as well be carved from marble for being so expressionless.

For a tense moment, Dan lets Karl's hand hang in the air, looking from the outstretched appendage to Karl's face before sneering, but finally, he takes the older man's hand in what looks like an almost painful and incredibly short handshake.

Karl flinches, flexing his hand when the handshake ends and narrowing his eyes at Dan, but Dad can sense something is off and leads him away to go talk to other guests. I breathe a sigh of relief when they're gone.

"I don't want you to be alone with him," Dan says out of the blue, his voice like ice.

"What?" I ask, bewildered at the sudden change of topic.

His tone is just above a whisper and leaning closer toward my face, he continues, "If he wants to talk in his office, leave the door open. Never travel alone together. I don't care if Patricia is a liar or not, I don't want to risk it with you."

With you, he said, like I'm something precious to him. I can't tell Dan that there are times when I might not be able to keep my promise, so I just give him a small smile. "Alright."

Dan and I are seated with the other young bloods; Dad, Karl, and the other higher-ups are all seated together. Had I been alone, it would be awful to be with all these strangers, but with Dan at my side I'm able to put aside the speech I'm about to give and talk to everyone as normally as possible, forging connections that might help me in the future.

My guest is becoming increasingly uneasy as the event goes on, watching the slides of company profits, growth, and upcoming projections as they float across the enormous projector screen over and over again. I can see how tense his jaw is, and how he fidgets in his chair. It's just minutes until

I have to take the stage, so if there is something he needs to tell me, he needs to hurry up and spit it out.

"Dan," I whisper, my mouth almost brushing his ear. "What's wrong?"

When he looks me in the eye, his eyes are so serious that it gives me pause. He takes both my hands in his, squeezing lightly and says, "Don't do this, El. I know I said I'd help you, and I'll still try, but I don't think that even a speech from God himself could make your brother okay with what you're about to do. Please don't give the speech. I care too much about you both and you just don't understand how big the divide you're about to cause really is."

Mouth agape, I don't know what to say, eyes flicking from Dad and Karl back to Dan. I find my tongue again, leaning closer to him. "You know it's too late. I can't go back now!"

"I know that you know doing this is wrong. Think about everything you'll miss out on if Andries shuts you out forever. His wedding, any children he has... everything. Make the right choice."

Feeling a lump in my throat, I'm just able to force out, "So you won't help me, then?"

"Of course, I will, but trust me when I say it isn't going to make a difference to your brother. His wrath and the way he holds grudges is worse than you know."

A future flashes through my mind; Andries marrying Roxanne and me only being able to see it in pictures and videos from friends, nieces or nephews being born and never being able to hold them. All the while, I climb the corporate ladder, but once I sit atop Van den Bosch industries, how lonely will I truly be?

I close my eyes, trying to dispel the thoughts. It's just the fear talking. I have to believe Dan will be able to pull through and solve everything. It's the only way.

Dad is on stage now, giving the opening speech and welcoming everyone. All the while, Dan doesn't let go of my hands, his gaze pleading.

"Now, everyone, I know there have been some disturbing rumors floating around about our beloved company, but today someone that I trust very much is going to speak and put all of our minds at ease. Not with more lies and hearsay, but with the truth. Ladies and gentlemen, if you'll please welcome my very own daughter, Elise Van den Bosch!"

Dan squeezes harder, shaking his head. "No, Elise, don't," he hisses, looking almost panicked. My heart is hammering, and it hurts to draw a breath. I'm so scared, but the room is clapping at my name, and eagerly waiting for me to go on stage.

"Fix this for me, Dan," I whisper, pulling my hands from his. "I have faith in you."

He breathes my name as I stand, but Dan sounds defeated, and through the din of appeases from all the shareholders and stakeholders, I climb the stairs to the stage beside my father. I'm shaking, but I put on my best daughter-of-a-noble face, tilting my chin up stubbornly, and beginning to speak.

"Good evening, everyone. As my father said..."

CHAPTER 11

Amsterdam, May 3, 2022
Dan

I wake up the next day still under the same wave of shock from the shareholders' meeting. Elise really went through with her speech, and I just sat there and watched, dumbfounded, even as the crowd around me began to whisper amongst themselves. It was a roaring success for Van den Bosch Industries, and Karl Townsend spent the rest of the night shaking hands and drinking glasses of champagne as he celebrated his newly won innocent reputation.

I've never wanted to knock someone out more in my life.

Elise looked green around the gills when she sat back down with me, and I could barely look at her. Something tells me when she got home that night, she was going to have trouble looking at herself, too.

I considered getting her drunk, but for the first time in my life, I was actually furious with the girl. Even if she made me feel lightheaded, even if she has the most perfect body I've ever seen, what she had just done to her brother was too much for me. It was beyond cruel and Machiavellian. I kept picturing Andries as the nervous, broody kid I had become best friends with, and what I let his sister do will never sit right with me.

Since I didn't sleep, I'm up at dawn and watching the news. Seeing how drawn and exhausted I look, Tina once again refuses to bring me blooming tea and instead delivers a tray with a green smoothie, espresso, and a tall glass of kombucha with a metal straw.

"Tina, I'm going to pee myself if I drink all this," I whine.

"Better that than dying where you sit, Mr. O'Brian. You look," she coughs into her hand, and I know she wants to say *like shit*, but instead she says, "unwell."

I throw a blanket over my shoulders and start working on my apparent liquid diet, scrolling through my phone absentmindedly. That is until a reel of Elise's speech starts playing on social media.

"Oh, fuck," I say out loud.

I can't watch it, so I gulp the espresso down my throat and head to the shower, hoping the heat will help ease my aching head. As usual, though, I'm shampooing my hair when I hear my phone ring.

I answer it on speaker, already knowing who it is without even having to glance at the screen.

"Andries—"

"Have you seen the fucking news, Dan? Let me read you the tagline on the screen right now." He clears his throat dramatically before saying, ""*Breaking news! Andries Van den Bosch pays victim to go against Karl Townsend*'. Sounds great for me, doesn't it? Do you want to take a guess who talked to the press, Dan?"

"I don't need to guess," I groan.

"Get to Roxanne's penthouse as soon as you can if you want to salvage our friendship at all, something tells me you know a lot more than you're letting on."

He hangs up and I step out of the shower, feeling worse than ever. He's right, I know everything and decided to stand behind his sister rather than helping my best friend. I kept Elise's plan to myself instead of telling him and all of that for a fucking gala dinner with her. Fuck. I screwed up. Big time. I dress quickly, yelling down the stairs, "Tina! Can you put that smoothie in a cup for me to take?"

The maid doesn't sound thrilled about the idea of me going out, but with a resigned note to her voice, she says, "Of course, Mr. O'Brian."

Andries is waiting for me when I get to the penthouse, looking like he's aged ten years overnight. Without a word, we go to the couch, and Andries flips on the recording he had made of the news segment. To my shock, it's Elise again, except this time she's sitting primly in a chair across from the news anchor, giving an interview about her speech the night before. She looks lovely in a shade of light taupe, but it really doesn't matter how she looks. Not with the words that are coming out of her mouth, anyway. She's wearing that face that she always has when she's talking to other professionals; an expression that reads calm, cool, and collected. She must be falling apart on the inside, though, if I know Elise at all.

Andries, on the other hand, is shattering in real time here in front of me, jumping up from his seat and pacing the floor, his hands clenched in fists. He looks pale, and the only positive I can find is that Roxanne isn't home to see him like this.

"Do you have any idea what this feels like? Dad will go to any lengths to protect Karl, even if it means ruining my life and my engagement. And for Elise to play right into his hand like that," he scoffs, head shaking in disappointment. "She knew exactly what she was doing, choosing Dad and her job over me. Tell her that I never want to see that bitch again."

I wince, but there's no arguing with him right now, not with how distressed he clearly is. I promised Elise I'd try and fix things, but from everything I'm seeing, that's an impossible endeavor.

I feel like a pit is opening up beneath my feet as I watch Andries rant and rave, and I just want to fall into it and disappear. The girl I've been obsessing over, who has occupied my every thought, has done a terrible thing that she can't take back now that the world knows. I let her get away with so much because of how much she means to me, and how much I want to please her. The guilt is almost overwhelming in its intensity, because maybe if I had tried just a little harder, I could have prevented all of this. But all I had been thinking of was getting Elise to the gala and having her on my arm all night, as if we were a real couple. I got to play pretend for a few hours, and now my best friend is suffering for it.

"You knew about it, didn't you?" The question causes my heart to skip a beat and I even stutter as I face his inquisitive gaze. "Tell me the truth, Dan, did you know about it or not?"

Fuck, fuck, and fuck! "Vaguely," I tell him, trying my best not to put myself into more trouble than I'm already in. "I knew she was giving a speech at the shareholders meeting, but I never thought it'd involve throwing you under the bus."

We keep looking into each other's eyes, Andries trying to decipher whether I'm lying or not until he just cuts eye contact and continues roaming around the living room. I let out a long sigh in relief, and give him some time to process everything.

"You know it probably wasn't her choice," I say gently, sitting on the edge of the couch. "If anyone, you should blame your dad for manipulating her. If she was forced, that's not fair to her, either."

"She's always fucking around with things she doesn't understand, and this is no different," he snaps back, his tone a sharp contrast with mine. "The only thing I can hope is that this takes some heat off Roxanne for being involved, but if I know the media, we will both just be thrown under the bus instead of just me."

He sits down heavily on the couch next to me, holding his head in his hands. I've never felt worse in my entire life.

"You should talk to your sister directly and find out the truth," I suggest, laying a hand on his shoulder to comfort him. "Maybe you're both victims here and you don't even know it. I'm sure your dad forced her to do it."

Andries leans against the back of the sofa and closes his eyes. "Elise is never a victim, a manipulative bitch, yes, but a victim never. Even if Dad pressured her to do the speech, she played some part in all this, plain and simple."

"But can you really live with yourself if you shut her out forever because of something your dad forced her into? Think about it, man."

He hesitates for a moment, thinking. "She actually texted me right before you got here and asked me to meet her on campus this afternoon. Most likely to explain herself."

"Do it!" I encourage, my tone more hopeful than I thought. "Don't let your family be pulled apart because of your father's selfishness."

Andries contemplates it and finally exhales slowly. Making a firm decision seems to bolster him some. "Okay, fine, I'll text her back later. It always helps to get to know her side of the story, but I've got no intention of forgiving her."

Seeing a chance to guide my friend back down from the storm of emotions drowning him, I wrack my brain for any other topic that might help him relax. Andries takes a long sip of his cold water and plops back on the couch when he's done, looking exhausted.

"So, uh, what are you studying in school right now?" I ask, trying to change topics, and he snorts.

"Don't pretend like you care about that."

"Come on," I cajole him. "There's always one weird class during a college semester."

Andries thinks on it before grinning, the first real one I've seen since I walked in earlier. "Okay, well, did you know that Mary Shelley was involved with Lord Byron?"

I barely know who either of those people are, but if it helps get Andries back on solid ground to talk about them, I'm more than happy to listen.

"No way," I say, playing along. "I've never heard that before. Is it true?" I have no idea if I sound convincing or not, but it's worth a shot. Thankfully, Andries likes this subject enough to just run with it.

"Scholars think so, yes. Let me pull up this paper I read on the subject, and I'll show you the passages of her diary in question."

It sounds worse than watching paint dry, but with Elise running laps in my mind and Andries ready to murder me or her or both, it's better than nothing. "Absolutely. Let's hear it."

As Andries passes me to go get his book, he grips my shoulder for just a second in an affectionate gesture. "Thanks for always coming when I call, Dan."

He shouldn't be thanking me, not with how I encouraged Elise, but what else can I do? "Anytime, man."

CHAPTER 12

Amsterdam, May 3, 2022
Elise

There is a celebratory air to the office today, and everyone seems lighter than air. Everyone except for me, of course, because I feel like absolute garbage.

Dad had called me at the crack of dawn, ecstatic that he had received a request for me to appear on the morning news and go over everything I revealed at the speech last night. A video of my speech at the shareholder meeting had gone viral, and public opinion was changing on the Karl Townsend case as fast as the crack of the whip.

Any other time, appearing on television would have been such fun, but not today, when it was just more talk about Andries and Patricia. I feel like I am digging my own grave, and no matter what anyone says, I can't stop picking up shovels of dirt. The company won't let me.

I've heard nothing from Andries, or Dan, for that matter, and their silences are almost worse than an outright angry accusation. I had planned on ignoring my brother, hoping that this will all blow over, but in a moment of weakness, I had decided to text him, asking him to meet me on campus during my lunch break. He's got to know I didn't have a choice and Dad kind of forced me to do the speech.

I remain at my desk, trying to focus on my tasks for the day, and set everything that happened to the wayside. When a notification with a new text message from my brother pops up on my screen, though, I can't help but jump in excitement. I grab the phone immediately and check the new SMS.

Andries: *Fine, let's meet during your lunch break then.*

* * *

Wanting some privacy, I have the company driver take me to campus during my break, closing the partition between the driver and where I'm sitting as soon as I get inside. Unable to stop myself, I scroll through hundreds of comments on the video of my interview, relieved that I at least look put together even if I'm falling apart on the inside.

My scrolling is interrupted by a call coming again, and my stomach drops when I see that it's Patricia. This is one outcome I knew was coming, but even if Patricia and I haven't been close in months, I still hate knowing I've hurt her. Even if she is greedy.

"You bitch!" she yells as soon as I pick up. "I tell you one single private thing and you shout it all over town the first moment that you have! I can't believe you'd do this to me!"

I hold the phone slightly away from my ear, shrinking at the sound of her voice. "I don't have any excuse, except to say that your choice to choose money over the truth has cost my family and my company greatly, and there was no other way for me to rectify those problems in any way I could."

"I didn't lie!" she says, becoming quieter. "It all happened, Elise. Karl took my virginity, and even if I liked him enough to sleep with him sober, we'll never know the truth because he got me drunk and took the choice away from me." She laughs, but it sounds sad. "The stupid thing is I probably would have slept with him anyway, that night or another, just because he was so sweet and charming, but he had to pour booze in me to seal the deal."

It feels like a slap in the face to hear the details of what happened to Patricia again. Things have gotten so mixed up between everyone and all the confusion that somehow I forgot that my friend… or ex-friend, did lose her virginity in a way that wasn't completely in her control.

"This is all so fucked up," I tell her.

"Yeah, it is, and now you've put me in the fucking news *again* and this time I'm not the victim, but a lying, conniving whore apparently. According to the comments online at least."

"Patricia–"

"No. Our friendship is over. Just for the record, it isn't my fault your brother was desperate enough to get back at Karl that he'd pay me as much as he did. That's all on Andries. You and I could have remained friends, but you just can't keep your nose out of anything, can you?" Despite her question, I keep myself silent. There's nothing else for me to say. She hangs up.

The phone call sets the tone for my meeting with my brother, as does the weather itself. It's gray outside, the clouds hanging low and fog gathering on the tops of lakes. There's a misty quality to the air that chills me, and I belatedly wish I would have brought a jacket.

Andries is waiting on the concourse, which is blessedly empty because of the weather, his hands shoved in his pockets and his face hard. I approach him, resisting the urge to appear as meek as I feel. He barely acknowledges me, only saying, "So, what do you want?"

"I just wanted to say that I didn't have a choice in what happened," I tell him immediately, putting on my sweetest and most innocent tone possible. "I was trapped, and it was the only way out. You have to understand that I have to display some sort of self-preservation sometimes. But I never wanted to hurt you."

"Well, you did, and now I'm once again the laughingstock on campus. Do you know the story everyone is weaving about this?"

I frown in confusion. "What?"

"That I fucked over Karl not because he took advantage of Patricia, but because he is Roxanne's ex. So everyone thinks I am losing my cool over my fiancée for what, the third time in the last year? When in reality, I was just trying to help someone that needed it. It's all blown up in my face now, and you lit the match."

His voice is hard like diamonds, and his posture is too. "Take the time to cool off," I say, keeping my tone even. "I understand that you're mad at me, but don't let this ruin our relationship. I want to be part of your life."

He laughs cruelly, shaking his head. "I don't think so. Don't show your face at my engagement party, either.

Consider this being me officially rescinding your invitation."

I swallow past the lump in my throat, blinking the tears out of my eyes while nodding. "Fine. I get it. But I did what I had to do and there's no way around it. You, on the other hand, are really blowing this thing out of proportion, you know?"

He turns his back on me. But before he's out of earshot, he calls behind his shoulder, "Keep telling yourself that Elise if it helps you sleep better at night."

* * *

I do basically nothing at work for the rest of the day, just answering emails about my interview and revelations at the shareholder meeting, and talking to everyone else in the office who keeps finding reasons to stop by my desk and chit chat. As expected, all those conversations eventually lead back to everything to do with my brother and Karl, at which point I just send them on the way. I'm sick to death of it.

I could almost cry in relief when the workday is over, but before I can pack up, one more figure appears in my eye-view. The one and only Karl Townsend.

"Don't worry," he starts, his demeanor friendly and approachable. "I don't want to bring it all up for the millionth time. Just wanted to say thank you and invite you out to drinks with a few clients after we leave here. You really impressed a lot of people last night and this morning."

I hesitate, thinking about Dan's warning to not be alone with Karl, but this wouldn't really be "alone" would it? Plus, I could really use a drink at this moment in time, and it will no doubt be even sweeter if I'm meeting important clients of the company.

"Fine," I tell him, draping my bag over my shoulder. "But I can't stay long."

The entire way to the bar, Karl tries to talk to me, but I keep checking my phone for messages from Dan. I'm still holding onto hope that he just hasn't had time to talk to my brother yet, and there is still a chance things could be repaired. My inbox remains empty, though. I'm starting to fear that he's changed his mind and that he might hate me just as much as my brother does, if his impassioned plea for me to not speak last night was anything to go by. The idea of Dan hating me makes my chest hurt, so I push the thought away.

Karl takes us to a low-key wine bar, where a table of older men are waiting, greeting him jovially as we enter. He introduces me with pride, and I shake hands with everyone, taking all the compliments as gracefully as I can before taking a seat.

It's impossible to forget the day I've had, but the sweet white wine and the deluge of positive feedback do bolster my confidence just a little. These are all strangers, and it isn't their approval I want, but I guess it's better than nothing.

"If you ever get bored at Van den Bosch industries, give me a call," a small, shrewd white-haired man tells me, sliding me a business card. "We always need bold talent like yours in an equity firm."

Not to be outdone, the other clients tell me what a stellar addition I'd make to their companies, too. I feel a bit like the shiny new toy on the scene, but everyone around the table insists it's because of how far I was willing to go to help my company.

Hearing it out loud like that doesn't make me proud, it makes me feel stupid. Did I really put a company over people that I love and care about?

I glance around the table, at all the faces, and think about what I want my life to be like when I reach that age. What I don't want is my business to be the only thing I have left.

When everyone orders a few more bottles to split, I excuse myself, telling them all that I have class early in the morning. In reality, I'm feeling close to tipsy from the wine, and I want to get away from all these men who barely know me. I want someone who I care about with me, a friend that always comforts me, or more.

Karl insists on walking me out while I wait on the Uber, even when I try to dissuade him multiple times.

"What would your father say if he knew I left you on the street waiting on a cab?" he asks, his tone thick with humor, and he lets out a quick chuckle which I also share. "He'd have my head, believe me."

"Karl, if you haven't been fired by now, I don't think you will ever be," I say bluntly, but with the same humor, and he barks a laugh.

"Fair enough."

Thankfully, the Uber is quick, and I don't have to make casual conversations any longer. Karl opens the door for me, and I give him a quick wave, letting out the breath I was holding once the door finally shuts and I'm alone—aside from the driver, of course.

I feel so lonely, and so starved for human affection after this terrible, long day. I call Dan, hoping beyond belief that he'd at least talk to me, or maybe even invite me over, but just like the rest of the day, he doesn't answer.

I try again. Nothing.

It's probably a stupid idea, and will no doubt end in an argument, but I'd rather argue with Dan than go home alone tonight. I tap on the glass between the front and back seat, and the driver opens it.

"Hey, sorry to be a pain, but can we actually go to a different address?" I ask.

"As long as it isn't too far away from the original, sure."

"Perfect, thank you," I tell the driver, followed by Dan's address. I hope he doesn't mind a surprise visit.

CHAPTER 13

Jessica giggles when I cover her eyes with my hands, letting me lead her out onto the patio at my house. She'd been pissed off still when I invited her over, and I could tell she was geared up for an argument as soon as she walked in the door. Luckily, I had everything planned ahead.

I let her blow off some steam, but when she finished, I calmly explained that I only took Elise to the gala to help her get some exposure. I could tell Jessica didn't quite believe me, but when I told her I had a surprise waiting for her, she softened up.

"Where are we going?" she asks suspiciously, when a fresh breeze blows her hair, revealing that we are now outside.

"You'll just have to wait and see."

I knew she would forgive me eventually, but I don't have it in me to wait. Elise has me so tied up in knots that I need the touch of a woman, and fast. It's been too long, and Jessica means something to me at this point, even if it isn't the romantic love that I know she wants from me. I don't necessarily want her out of my life, but I know I have been sort of a dick with her lately.

When we are finally standing in front of the jacuzzi I set up on the patio, I let my hands fall away. She gives a little gasp of surprise, and I smile to myself smugly.

There are candles scattered all around the jacuzzi, paired with rose petals, and a bucket of ice sitting on the side of it with two bottles of champagne chilling inside. Next to the bucket is a bowl of the ripest strawberries I could find, and they pull the seductive scene together perfectly.

"You did this for me?" she breathes.

I brush her hair off her shoulders and kiss the back of her neck. "Yes, all for you, baby. Now, let's get changed and enjoy it to the fullest. How does that sound?"

"Changed?" She wraps her arms around me, biting her lip. "Can't we just go naked instead?"

"Well, there's the maid around, not that she'll come out unexpectedly but—"

"But I didn't bring my bikini," Jess interposes before I can finish my sentence.

"You are in luck, then." My lips twist into a smile as I reach for the small shopping bag that is lying on the small table and hand it to her. "I got you a little something."

Jessica gasps in excitement as she opens the bag, and pulls from it a white bikini. She thanks me with a kiss on the lips and goes back inside to change.

Meanwhile I just take off my robe, and get myself into the hot tub, ready to relax and enjoy the evening.

Once she comes back, I can't help but smile, reveling in her beautiful figure. She looks even better than I imagined in it. She is so sexy without even trying, and when she climbs into the hot tub beside me and straddles my waist, I'm harder than steel already. God, it's been so long!

She's quick to kiss me, but I insist on having a little to drink and a few strawberries first, feeding her slowly and allowing kisses with sips and nibbles. She rolls her hips in my lap, just a preview of what we're about to do here in just a few minutes, and I groan into her mouth. I slide my hands up Jessica's body, already prepared to untie the top of her bathing suit, hungry for the taste of her skin.

I pull the strings, but just as I'm about to see my bounty, my housekeeper comes out onto the patio in a nervous rush, her hand held over her eyes.

"Tina!" I yell. "Please leave!"

"I'm so sorry, Mr. O'Brian, but there is someone here to see you in the foyer."

"Who?" I demand in an exasperated breath.

She looks quickly at Jessica, unsure, and that little look tells me everything I need to know.

Jessica picks up on what is unsaid, too, and is apoplectic. "You've got to be fucking kidding me!" She looks at me like her eyes could shoot daggers. "Either you tell her to leave now or I'm leaving and never coming back, Dan."

I sigh. "Tell her to go, Tina."

The maid nods and disappears back into the house, and I waste no time before kissing Jess again, taking her mouth with mine before she can complain anymore. She's stiff at first, but begins to relax in my arms as things start to heat up again, right before—

Right before Elise herself storms onto the patio, furious, the color high in her face. "We had a fucking agreement, Dan!"

I push Jessica off me, who falls into the water with an "oomph!" "What the fuck are you doing out here!?"

Tina rushes in behind her, looking harried. "I'm so sorry, sir, I tried to send her away, but she didn't listen!"

"Elise, I'm busy, God dammit!" I explode at her, pulse pounding in my ears. "Who the fuck do you think you are to come over uninvited?"

Elise stomps her foot like a petulant child. "I went with you to that dinner and in exchange, you promised to talk to my brother so he wouldn't kick me out of his life! Well, guess what, he's furious and I'm blacklisted both from the engagement and the fucking wedding too!"

Behind me, I hear Jessica drawing in a breath, and the last thing I want on my hands is these two fighting.

"I'll be back in just a minute, Jess," I growl, standing up and climbing out of the jacuzzi. "I'm gonna show that spoiled brat the fucking door."

Heedless of the water, I grab Elise by the wrist and drag her toward the front door, planning on throwing her out. I need this night with Jessica so badly, and I'm not about to lose out on it because Miss Elise isn't happy living with her own choices.

She struggles out of my grip as I drag her through the hallway, the front door finally in sight. "Let me go, asshole!" She rubs her wrist, glaring at me.

"Listen." I hold my hands out, while Elise just straightens herself. "I tried to talk to your brother, but just like I said, he's too pissed right now to reconsider. He needs time to cool off, and there's no guarantee he ever will. I tried to warn you, but you wouldn't listen."

"The engagement party is in three weeks, so you better make sure he's cooled off by then!" she insists, her eyes lingering down for some reason before they travel back up to my face and she adds with a smug, "You're dripping all over the floor."

"I'm well aware," I grit out between my teeth, but pause when I see her look down at the puddle slowly forming, her eyes slowly moving up my legs and fixing on my bare chest. Elise not being able to look any higher than that, and even as pissed as I am, sends a little thrill through me.

She blinks a few times before realizing what she's doing, her eyes flicking back to my face in an instant even as a blush blooms on her cheeks.

"Is Jessica going to the engagement party?" she asks out of nowhere, her voice tight.

I step closer, looking down into her beautiful, flushed face. Her eyes fall on my lips as I ask her, "Why do you even care?"

"I–" she starts, but trails off, which is probably a good thing, considering that I'm stuck on her lips now too, and the way they are slightly parted. So full and tempting. If I could just taste them once…

Tentatively, she raises her hands up, and I just know she's going to touch me. I'm on fire with the anticipation of it, but I force myself not to move. She's like a fawn, and I know she'll flee if I frighten her.

Elise's fingertips brush the skin of my chest, just the ghost of a caress before she jerks them away and stumbles back. I catch her by the wrist, pulling her close to my body, not caring if she gets wet or not.

"Why do you care if Jessica comes?" I repeat in a growl, my eyes locked on hers. "Tell me."

Extricating her wrist from my grip, Elise moves toward the door, looking like she's both terrified and fascinated. "It's nothing," she tells me, not even looking me in the eye as she does so. "Have fun with Jessica."

"Wait," I say just as she shuts the door behind her, disappearing into the night, leaving me here desperate for her and alone.

Fuck, not alone. I left Jess on the damn patio!

Running, I push the glass doors open, but Jess is already pulling her clothes over her swimsuit. When she spots me, she whips around, angrier than I've ever seen her. "No need to make up excuses, Dan. I heard and saw everything! I'm done. Done!" She starts shoving her shoes on her feet. "Look, do everyone a favor next time and just invite Elise in the first place. You both aren't fooling anyone but yourselves here."

"I swear I was sending her away," I insist, moving toward her. "Jess, come on."

"Sorry, Dan," she says curtly, pushing past me.

Just like I did with Elise, I grab her wrist, stopping her in her tracks. She turns slowly, her shoulders slumped in sadness and defeat. "What excuse now?"

"What if next time I just book us a hotel room? A really nice one, just you and me?"

"Really?" she huffs, head shaking in disbelief. "Instead of setting some serious boundaries with Elise, you're just going to avoid being home?"

"She's unpredictable, but it's just because she's going through a rough time."

"Oh, sure she is. I saw her TV interview too, and she seemed pretty happy to talk shit about her brother and friend there. If she's having a rough time, it's her own doing. You're not her boyfriend, you know? Stop pandering to her."

"I'm just trying to be a good friend," I reply, thinking about Andries and correcting myself mentally. *Trying and failing to be a good friend.*

Jess tries to leave again, but I still hold her in place. "Look, next time we meet I'll have a brilliant place set up for us. Problem solved."

Having had enough, she jerks her hand away and starts walking toward the door again. "You're a fucking moron, I swear."

Watching the second woman of the night walk away from me, I yell, "See you soon, Jess!"

"Fuck you, Dan!" I hear her screaming back before she slams the door behind her.

Once she's gone, I feel lonelier than ever. I go back to the patio, and lower myself into a lounge chair, knowing I only have a few minutes before the chill of being soaking wet drives me inside. I decide to call Andries, just to make sure I have all sides of the story before I do anything else.

"Hey, man. Your sister just came here all mad because you uninvited her from the engagement party. You aren't really going to stick to that, are you?"

"Hello to you too, Dan," he says, sounding like he's walking at the same time. "Listen, don't you dare give her an invite, you hear me? She betrayed me, and Rome doesn't pay traitors."

I roll my eyes. "Dramatic as always I see. Can't you just admit that you and Elise are both victims here, and that maybe, *just maybe*, she didn't want to do what she did?"

"Even if that was the case, it's still nearly unforgivable."

"It was Sebastian who forced Elise to talk, and Patricia who told all your secrets within minutes of Elise going to visit her. Two people have wronged you here, but neither of them is Elise."

"Why are you defending her so much?" he asks suspiciously, but I already have the perfect, half-honest answer in mind.

"Andries, she showed up when I was *in the jacuzzi* with Jessica. And guess what? Jessica left, all because your sister ruined my fucking date. Had you kept your cool, that never would have happened." I pause, smiling at my next set of words. "Maybe I should just blame you for Jess leaving."

Andries grumbles on the other line, but I hear Roxanne yelling his name in the background, and he sighs. "I'll think about it, okay? I've got to go now. We'll talk later."

"Wait, what are you doing tonight? We could go get a drink."

"I'm headed out to dinner with Roxie. Sorry."

"Oh," I say, disappointed. "Well, have a good time."

As the wind starts to work its way into my bones, I think about how lonely I am now, and how my youngest friend is moving on with his life, getting married to the love of his life. I never would have thought Andries would settle down before me, but here we are.

Finally admitting defeat to the cold, I go back inside, flipping through my contacts until I find an old fencing friend that I'm positive is still single, sending him a text and hoping for at least some sort of company tonight.

Dan: *Hey Mark, what are you up to tonight?*

Mark: *Dan O'Brian! How are you, man? I'm at Bar Rouge, supposed to be waiting on a date but I think I'm being stood up. Want to take her place?*

I grin to myself. At least it's some consolation prize.

Dan: *I'll be right over.*

* * *

Just walking into Bar Rouge, with its low, red lights and sultry atmosphere makes me feel better. Scantily clad women move around the tables like gaudy little birds, stunning and fleeting. Mark is at a table waiting for me, grinning ear to ear.

"You're the last person I expected to see tonight," he admits, stroking his dark beard and looking around the cabaret. "But what good timing. It looks a little sad to be stood up in the Red-Light district, huh?"

"A little, yeah," I agree with a laugh, motioning a hostess over so I can order a drink.

The petite brunette looks down at me, and recognition registers on her face. "Dan?"

She looks familiar to me, too, and then it clicks into place. It's Heather, one of Roxanne's escorts that had worked at my Red-Light party.

"Wow, nice to see you, Heather," I tell her in surprise. "How come you're working here? I thought you were still escorting?"

She shrugs one small shoulder. "I wanted to quit, so Roxie got me this job instead. It doesn't pay as well, but I've got enough money saved for retirement."

"That's good, I didn't know Roxie knew the management of this club so well."

Heather gives me an odd look, tilting her head to the side. "Of course, she does, she's the freaking owner."

"The owner?"

"You didn't know that?" she asks, letting out a quick snort. "I thought you knew *everything*."

"His reputation precedes him," Mark pipes up, but I wave at him to be quiet.

I frown, wanting to make sure that I'm hearing her correctly. "What do you mean she's the owner? Like, of the whole cabaret?"

"Yes, Dan, the *whole cabaret*." Heather flips her hair, obviously becoming bored with the conversation. "She bought this place last year. Everyone knows that."

"Not everyone, apparently. I didn't know."

Heather rolls her eyes. "I mean, everyone who works in the district, you know. Did you want something to drink, or not?"

"Uh, sure. Whiskey, neat. Mark? I'll be right back."

My friend nods, and I rush outside, the perfect plan to hopefully fix this mess I've found myself in already solidifying in my mind. I pull up Elise's contact and call her.

Since she isn't picking up, I try once more, but nothing. So decidedly I type her a text:

I know how to get you an invitation to your brother's engagement. Give me a few days and I'll manage.

CHAPTER 14

Amsterdam, May 16, 2022
Elise

I wash my hands, looking at my reflection in the mirror as I do so, still not sure what exactly is going on or why I'm here. Still, I'm glad that Dan is talking to me without too much awkwardness, considering that I *almost* felt him up the other night. He's promised to have the coveted invite to Andries's engagement party for me, but he won't reveal how exactly he managed to get it yet.

All I know is that he's invited me to this cafe, and even after we order coffee and sit down, Dan won't broach the subject of the engagement invitation, no matter how hard I try. I go to the bathroom, confused and frustrated, and needing a moment alone to try and work out in my head what is going on.

Dan hugged me when we arrived, and while we might have lingered with each other a little bit too long, it wasn't anything out of line. I hope that our friendship can go back to normal. I can't handle the idea of pining after Dan while he fucks Jessica all over his condo, and I'm not sure I'll ever get the memory of her on his lap, sleek and wet like a seal in the jacuzzi, and the way his lips were moving on her neck, out of my mind. It made me feel ill and heartbroken, all in the same moment.

So considering the way we argued, and the tension between us over the last few days, what is this weird lunch about?

All I know is that I can't hide in the bathroom forever, and I have to go and face him sooner or later.

Exiting and heading back to our little table, Dan is waiting for me with a Cheshire grin. "Your surprise is almost here," he tells me, before plunging his phone back into his pocket.

"What surprise?" I ask, even more bewildered than before.

"If I told you, then it wouldn't be a surprise, silly. Now drink your cappuccino. How have you been the past few days?"

"Don't try to make small talk with me, Dan O'Brian!" I huff. "I know something is going on, but I just haven't figured it out yet."

"I thought you knew everything?" he says, his grin growing wider like he was waiting all morning to make that quip.

"Sometimes I really hate you," I snap back.

"But after today, you'll love me, I'm sure of it."

I already think I do, I say, but only in my mind, where admitting such things won't cause horrible consequences.

I don't want to make small talk, drink a cappuccino, or even have lunch. I want to figure out a way to get into the engagement party, and I have a scant few days to do it. If Dan is wasting my time with this asinine lunch, I swear—

I stop mid-thought as the cafe door opens and a familiar face walks in...one I absolutely did not expect. Roxanne Feng is dressed impeccably in a short black dress, her short blonde hair brushed behind, and her eyes are locked directly on Dan and me.

"Oh look, Elise," Dan says, sounding much too pleased with himself. "Your surprise is here."

"What the hell are you talking about? Why is Roxanne here!?" I ask as quietly as possible, but it's no use. Roxanne is already here at the table, and whatever nonsense Dan has set into motion is inevitable.

"Good morning, Elise," Roxanne says coolly, pulling a small envelope out of her purse and sitting it down in front of me. I flip it over, and to my shock, it has her and Andries's names emblazoned on it. "I hope to see you at the party on Saturday."

And then, as quickly as she had arrived, Roxanne departs, not even giving us a second glance. I'm speechless, opening the envelope to hold my honest-to-God invitation, right here in cardstock. I can barely believe it.

Dan waves our server over and orders champagne, even though it's just past noon, and refuses to answer my questions until both of us have a sparkling flute in front of us.

"Drink," he commands. "To my amazing success."

I take a tiny sip and set the flute aside. "Done. Now. How did you get Roxanne herself to deliver the invitation? I have to know."

Dan takes a much longer drink than I do before gracing me with an answer. "I just know how to be convincing."

"You're lying! Tell me the truth, Dan!"

He chuckles, swirling the champagne in his hand. "What's the magic word?"

"Fuck you."

He raises his eyebrows and lets out a quick snort in amusement. "Well, you're not wrong, but you're usually not the person that uses *that* magic word. I guess I can't disclose my secret to you."

"Dan…" Since he keeps quiet, I give in and use the magic word he wants to hear. "Please?"

"Fine. Fine. Do you know who the owner of Bar Rouge is? The cabaret I took you to once, where your brother lost his mind when he saw you there?"

I shake my head. "No, I have no idea. That was the only time I've ever been there."

Then, he drops the bombshell. "It's none other than Roxanne Feng herself."

"You're kidding," I gasp, leaning forward across the table. "Really?"

I can tell Dan is loving every minute of this, and to be honest, I am too. It feels like old times, gossiping and laughing while also poking fun at one another.

"Yes, and it looks like our favorite poet knows nothing about it."

My eyes go wide. "Uh-oh. That's insane. So you used that info against her to snag me an invite? That was powerful information, Dan. You could have saved it for another favor down the line."

"Yes, but I'll do almost anything to have you off my back. I was subtle about getting the invite, but Roxanne is sharp, and she figured it out pretty quickly. I also told her to make sure your brother speaks to you so you can smooth things out once and for all."

I can't help myself. I'm giddy, and I jump out of my chair, rushing to his side and leaning down to hug him in my excitement. I ignore the masculine smell of his skin, and the smoky sweetness of his cologne, focusing only on how happy I am right this second.

"This is absolutely brilliant. Thank you!"

He laughs, hugging me back, even from the awkward position. "You're welcome, but you're forbidden to use that info for your own gains, you hear me? You've caused enough trouble for your brother. If you try and pull a fast one, I'll do the same for you."

I squeeze him even harder. "Sure you will, Dan. Sure you will."

CHAPTER 15

Amsterdam, May 21, 2022
Elise

Standing on the lawn of the O'Brian's house, I can already hear everyone in the back part of the home enjoying the party. My heart is in my throat, but I know I can do this. It's what I've wanted this entire time.

When I got ready this morning, choosing a fitted white and blue dress and letting my hair fall loose around my face, I had been thinking of Dan and all that he had gone through to make this possible for me. I hope he likes my dress, and I doubly hope that he didn't invite Jessica along.

Even if he did, though, he's already proven that he'll choose me over her every time. I try not to be too smug about that, but it's hard not to when I recall how he's nearly kissed me twice already.

A butler comes to answer the door when I ring the bell, happily leading me to the festivities and announcing my arrival, once he successfully crosses my name off the guest list. There's so much to take in, but I force myself to look for reactions before anything else, and oh, is it worth it.

First and foremost, my brother looks incensed, glaring at me and moving toward me until his fiancée grabs him by the sleeve, pulling him back and talking to him quietly, no doubt telling him that she invited me for one reason or another. I don't care what lie she uses because I already have what I want. Andries looks bewildered, then angry again, and finally, resigned. An entire story in facial expressions in less than a minute. There's a reason Dan always calls him dramatic.

And speaking of Dan, his reaction is the one I seek out next. It had been hard to choose between looking as sexy and irresistible as possible in a skintight dress or dressing more like myself, but I had eventually chosen the latter with the elegant dress that makes my skin simply glow. Dan is enamored with me, I'm sure of it, so to get his attention I don't need to pretend to be someone else.

I know I make the right call when I see stars in his eyes as he watches me walk in, descending the small set of marble stairs that leads to the garden party, and had I not been so wrapped up in myself, he'd have probably taken my breath away equally. Dan looks incredible in his light gray suit, the shirt beneath unbuttoned to show that irresistible gold skin of his chest that I've been obsessing over ever since I saw him in his swim trunks.

There will be time for all those thoughts later, though, because Andries and Dan aren't the only ones that have taken notice of my arrival, and since my parents aren't with me, it's even more interesting that I still decided to come alone. Events like this are just a game of socialization and class, catching up with people you haven't seen in years all while spreading venomous rumors about one another when the conversation would grow quiet. I was born for this type of thing; it's almost as natural as breathing.

The party planners I had so rudely interrupted had done an incredible job with the place. Sunflowers and daisies nearly burst from every available vase and centerpiece, a large white tent erected with tables underneath, and what looks like an endless supply of champagne flowing from the open bar. There are small packs of guests everywhere, and when I scan the crowd, it's a pleasant surprise to see that my brother hadn't lied about the rest of the family coming to celebrate. Mom and Dad are the only holdouts, apparently, which makes me sad for him. He might be a dick to me any chance he gets lately, but I still love him, and no child should celebrate their nuptials without their parents there.

I approach Andries and Roxanne first. She's a vision in a white dress with large, red watercolor floral prints, her short blonde hair styled more softly than usual, and her normally dark makeup nearly natural looking. Roxanne is a true beauty without any extras, and she's proving that point today. I know Roxie hates it, but she leans in to hug me, and I do the same.

"Play it cool and don't make me regret this," she hisses into my ear before letting me go.

Andries watches the hug in confusion, considering she and I are supposed to be at each other's throats. After a moment, he says, "Roxie told me you reached out to her and apologized for everything you said to her and about her before. I don't know if you're being manipulative or not, but thank you either way. Since you're here, I'll choose to believe you're being genuine."

I choose not to answer his monologue, just smiling at them both and saying, "Congratulations to the beautiful couple."

With that out of the way, I can move on to something I actually have been looking forward to: talking to my extended family.

Grandmother Margaret presides over the entire gaggle of the family like the matriarch she is, white hair coiffed perfectly and the ever-present air of superiority surrounding her presence in full force. Her grin, which has always looked a bit predatory, grows the closer I get, and once I'm in grabbing distance, she embraces me and kisses both of my cheeks.

Predatory or not, I love her, and it feels wonderful to be held by my grandmother again.

"I'm so glad you came," Oma says, putting her hands on my cheeks as she looks me over. "It shows more emotional maturity than your parents, after all. My, my you have grown up to be stunning, little Elise."

"Thanks, Oma," I answer back.

She links her arm with mine as if claiming my whole attention for the time being. "How is school, love? Going well? And the internship?"

I hesitate before answering, and she chuckles knowingly. "Overwhelming, I take it?" she asks, always so curious. Since I just nod at her in return, she then, adds, "Understandable, but I have no doubt you'll emerge from the other side of all of this forged in fire, my dear."

I tell her about my classes, and how stressful yet rewarding working at Van den Bosch industries is. She's thrilled with me, and it's like a breath of fresh air to be just complimented and appreciated for once, without either being under Andries's shadow or only receiving the praise as the means to an end.

Aunt Maud, the more conservatively dressed of the group and also the quietest one, decides to speak up eventually when I'm in the middle of some story about my dad. "Tell me, Elise... is my sister really not coming?"

I shake my head. "No, sadly. Dad and Mom are... well, they heavily disapprove of this."

"If Andries and Roxanne have gone already to such lengths to be together, your parents will regret dying on that hill for the rest of their lives," Maud muses.

"I simply can't believe they'd spurn my poor grandson like that," Oma Margaret laments, before wetting her lips with some champagne.

"To be fair, I don't think Andries sent them a physical invitation," I tell them.

Oma shrugs one delicate shoulder. "Oh, but I did."

"Scheming around without me?" I hear a female voice I recognize well asking from behind me.

I pivot and my eyes land on another aunt that makes my lips twist into a big smile. "Just catching up on things," I say to Aunt Yara, before greeting her with a kiss on the cheek.

I rarely speak to Aunt Yara, who's known to keep a busy schedule due to her polo games, but of all of Margaret's children, I sometimes think I'm most like her. She's forged a path for herself, captaining internationally successful polo teams and even winning championships. She isn't in a dress and is wearing a sleek one-piece black romper instead, the muscles of her strong legs obvious through the fabric.

"Julia is only putting up a fuss because her husband is," Yara continues, giving large gulps of her champagne between thoughts. "Otherwise, I think she'd be weirded out by their age gap, but a slightly older escort is *not* the worst thing in this family." I see her slide a glance over to my Uncle Alex and his young wife Petra, free of their children for the night. "Definitely not the worst," she repeats, more to herself than anyone else.

Okay… I think, *Keep that in mind; no Yara and Petra seated together during any future events.*

I only have a second to wonder what the problem between the two women could be before Yara links her arm with mine. "Let's walk, niece, and have a chat. What do you say?"

Looking down at our linked arms, I rightly assume there really isn't another option. "Uh, sure."

We walk through the gardens, and Yara regales me with tales of winning her championship polo matches. "You ride too, from what I recall?"

I'm pleased she remembers. "Yes, actually, I do. But nothing like you do."

"Regardless, I'd love to go riding together next time I'm in town."

"I'd like that too."

Yara pauses for a minute or two before speaking again. "Elise… do you truly think Julia will spurn Andries if he goes through with this marriage? I'm concerned that my sister would behave that way, and it's also bothering me thinking about how it might harm the family image in unexpected ways."

I frown in confusion at her unexpected statement. "What do you mean?"

Yara heaves a sigh, before moving one step closer to me and, lowering her voice, she then says, "Once all the nonsense settles with Andries and this court case with your father's employee, I think the media will turn to Roxanne and Andries's private life. Most of the country is becoming more and more tolerant of prostitutes in general, and I can just see the headline, '*Van den Bosch family disowns eldest son for marrying sex worker.*'"

I contemplate it for a second. With the whole memoir Roxanne intends to publish and market around the country, this headline and others similar are way more plausible than I'd like to admit. "Huh. I never thought of that happening. As of right now, though, Mom and Dad want nothing to do with this whole thing. Dad called it a 'shit-show,' verbatim."

Yara sneers. "I guess we'll have to see how it all plays out, but I'll call your mom and try to talk to her in private. The last thing we need is more bad press right now." She leans over and hugs me quickly. "I mean it about that ride. I'm holding you to it, my little niece. After all, you're my favorite."

"I'll remember that!" I tell her with a laugh, watching my aunt walk back to the group of my family, and wishing I could just spend the rest of the evening with all of them. At least they understand the way things work in this crazy world we live in.

Unfortunately, there is still the rest of the party to get through, and many more people to greet. I look longingly at Dan, who is sitting with his parents, and wish he was making these rounds with me.

I take a flute of champagne from a passing server, take a bracing drink, and continue.

* * *

I'm actually tired by the time I'm able to sit down as dinner begins to be delivered, my assigned seat placing me with Andries, Dan, Roxie, Lili, and Robin. Possibly the most uncomfortable grouping Roxanne could have managed, but she probably did it on purpose, just as a way to get back at me for forcing her hand.

Little does she know I'm quite happy to be sitting with Dan, at least, and Lili and Robin are completely neutral parties as far as I'm concerned.

"What an amazing turnout," Lili comments happily, smiling at her date.

"I agree." Then looking at Roxanne, I add, "You two really have a lot of people who love you."

Roxie gives me a small thank you in return, and I send one back, really meaning it. There might be unfinished business between my brother and me, but even if our parents snubbed him, everyone else came to support him, and for that I'm happy.

The conversation is understandably stilted, but not as bad as I expected it to be, and Dan and I even find time to argue over whether toasts are appropriate at engagement parties, or if they need to be saved for the wedding itself. Everyone has had a good number of drinks at this point, and Dan is at the point where he wants more than anything to prove me wrong.

He stands, loudly clinking his fork against his glass until the gathering quiets.

"Good evening, everyone!" He has to all but yell to be heard over the whole yard. "I wanted to make a toast to the happy couple, and wish them all the best as we get closer and closer to the big day. Congratulations, Andries and Roxanne!"

Andries, drunk and not one to be left out of a chance to make a speech, follows suit. "And from me, a toast to the O'Brian's, who not only let us use their beautiful estate as a venue, but put everything together as well." He waves toward Dan's parents, Jake and Caroline, who come over to embrace the future groom warmly.

"How about you, Elise?" Roxanne says tartly. "Any speeches from you? I know you're so good at them."

Tipsy and feeling braver than I usually do, I only pause to think about it for a second before I stand. Dan and Andries, still on their feet, both turn and look at me in alarm. Dan, because he knows that I'm only here because he pulled a miracle at the eleventh hour, and Andries because I know he still doesn't truly trust me.

I clear my throat delicately, trying to think on the fly, and already regretting my decision. But everyone is looking at me, Roxanne included, and it's a little late for me to back down now.

How do I continue to put myself in these situations?

"Um… hi, everyone! I'm Elise, Andries's sister, and I wanted to also give a toast to the happy couple." I swallow, my mind racing. "Andries and Roxanne have the type of love that only comes around once in a while, almost like an eclipse, but when it does, it's an incredible thing to witness. Despite the obstacles they faced, and the way the world sometimes worked against them, their love prevailed over it all every single time."

I look into my brother's eyes, and from the depths of my heart, pull up a few words I really mean. I just hope they come out the right way. "I've looked up to you for never being afraid to take what you wanted, even when it shattered the expectations put on you. Seeing how far you and Roxanne have come, and the things you've done to stay by her side... I think that kind of struggle, and the conquering of it has to be the epitome of love." I look back at the crowd, which is eerily silent. "Don't you think, everyone?"

Raucous applause breaks out. I smile so wide that it hurts my cheeks, sitting back down, and I swear that Andries dabs his eyes with his napkin discreetly when he thinks I'm not looking. Even if he is drunk, I'll give him a pass, if my little speech was able to make him that emotional.

"Andries," I begin, much quieter this time, so we have some privacy. "I really am sorry for Mom and Dad not coming. I will do everything in my power to make sure the entire family is back together for the wedding."

Even inebriated, he doesn't completely forgive me, but he's closer than he has been in weeks. "I don't believe you, but I'm happy you went out of your way to put the past behind you and be kind to my fiancée so you could attend."

I turn my gaze to Dan, knowing that he's the one that has truly built this bridge between Andries and me, giving us a chance to reconnect and heal. I smile at him softly, thankful for his friendship even more than usual. Dan, though, looks at me as if he's never seen me before. He watches me like that through dessert, and when the course is over, reaches a hand across the table to touch my wrist.

"Can I have a moment with you in private?" he asks, the tone of his voice telling me that there will be no other answer he accepts but "yes."

My brother is distracted, so I give Dan a quick nod. "Lead the way. It's your house, after all."

He takes my hand, and we move through the party crowd. My pulse picks up, anticipation coiling through me thinking about why he wants me alone. There are so many options that it makes my head spin.

I think about my hands on his bare chest and shiver even in the warm evening air.

Dan takes me inside the home, leading me up a set of stairs and to a study, where he shuts the door behind him. "This is a spare room, so we won't be disturbed," he explains.

"I still don't know why you wanted me alone," I point out.

He inhales deeply. "I'm just not understanding how you, the same sister who was willing to throw her brother under the bus, is now telling the entire world how much she loves him and is happy for him. Are you being sincere or just faking it for the sake of the evening?"

This is not what I expected for our private moment, and my anticipation fades away rapidly. "I just don't want my brother to be hurt anymore. It's bad enough that our mom and dad didn't come."

"I don't believe you for one second," he says, raising his eyebrows and crossing his arms. "You are, at the center of your being, a selfish girl, who does selfish girl things. Tell me the truth, Elise."

"You're a lot soberer than I thought," I grumble, refusing to look him in the eye.

"Elise, I swear to God if you use that info of the cabaret as a way to blackmail your brother after I went to all that effort—"

"That's not it!" I insist. "If you must know, the only revenge plot I had in mind was to not invite him to my eighteenth birthday at our home estate. After making me jump through hoops like a dog to get invited to his party, he's definitely not getting an invitation to mine."

Dan looks shocked but quickly recovers. "That's a stupid plan because he won't go if your parents are there. Not when they're still convinced their future daughter-in-law is a whore."

"Who knows? My brother is a bit crazy sometimes." I shrug. "It doesn't matter, because he's not coming, but…" I look at him through my lashes, and with my lips curving into a smile, I say, "You are."

He makes an animalistic noise in his throat, walking toward me until the back of my knees hit the oak desk in the middle of the room. When he reaches me, he grabs me by the waist, lifting me until I'm sitting on the desk with him standing between my legs. "Don't play games with me." His voice is harsh and nearly threatening, definitely not what I was expecting.

"W-what are you talking about?"

"Looking back," Dan proceeds, his tone just as aggressive. "I see what you did that night on the dance floor. You were trying to flirt with me so you could have me under your thumb. You wanted to make sure I'd go to stupid lengths for you, huh?"

"Me?" I ask in total disbelief, before huffing. "You were just as guilty. In fact…" I loop one leg around his calf, pulling him forward with just the slightest pressure. "You're the one who sat me on a desk and has his groin pressed between my thighs."

Dan's laugh is dark as he lowers his eyes. "I'm not pressed against you. You're just fantasizing now." In one smooth movement, he moves forward and presses against me for real, the hard, hot length of him hitting me in all the places I've fantasized about having him for so long. I can't stop the moan of pure pleasure that comes out of me.

"Now, Elise… I'm pressed against you." He rubs his lips against my cheek and the shell of my ear, his breath warm, whispering, "How does it feel?"

There are no words for how good it feels, how *right*. It is everything I've been craving and didn't even know I wanted, but at the same time, not nearly enough. The feeling of him moving against me, only the thin slip of my panties protecting me, awakens a hunger in me like nothing I've ever experienced before.

Dan moves his lips from my ear down my jawline until he reaches my neck, and this sensation causes me to break out in full-body goosebumps. I moan again, shamelessly, and feel his cock jerk in his pants at the noise. He wants me just as badly, and this is all the proof that I've ever needed. The rough pads of his fingers make me shiver everywhere they touch, and the sundress is little protection. Dan slides his hands up my bare legs, then the back of his knuckles over my arms, all while he kisses and nips at my jaw and throat, sucking the tender spot where he can feel my pulse under his lips.

It's liquid ecstasy, pure and simple, and I'm drowning.

My body is burning hot, my eyes shut as I swim in pure bliss. I want his hands and mouth everywhere all at once. For now, though, I can think of only one thing to ask for.

"Kiss me," I breathe.

"Where, Elise?" he murmurs against my skin.

"My mouth."

He begins an agonizingly slow ascent from my neck to my lips, and when he's finally, *finally* about to kiss me in earnest, something happens.

We hear the horrible sound of the doorknob tuning, and the door being pushed open.

I have no idea who it is, but I jump down immediately, trying to straighten my clothes and hair all at the same time. I'm still quivering with need, but it's quickly being replaced by humiliation. The humiliation only grows tenfold when I get the courage to look up and see who caught us in the act.

It's Jake O'Brian, Dan's dad, and a handful of men I don't recognize. I want to sink into the floor and never be seen again. I've never been so embarrassed in my entire life, and I can feel my face practically glowing red.

Dan is flustered too, but not nearly as bad. "*Dad*," he grits out between his teeth. "Please get out of here."

Jake, who had been looking between the two of them with an expression that looked like amusement, suddenly comes back online. "Oh! Sorry, guys. You were here first. We'll go elsewhere." He motions his guests out with a waving motion. "Gentlemen, let's find another place to chat, shall we?"

The door clicks shut, leaving us alone for the second time, but now whatever spell of lust had fallen over us is long gone, and the only thing left in its place is awkwardness. And the ugly reality that I was about to kiss my brother's best friend at his own engagement party. What a fucking mess I am.

"Fuck, Elise, I'm so sorry," Dan starts, rubbing the back of his head uncomfortably. "I think... I think we should stay apart for a while to cool things off, you know?"

"Yeah, I um... think that's a good idea."

He reaches out like he wants to touch me again, but lets the hand fall limp at his side instead. "I'm so fucking sorry."

With a lump forming in my throat, and my face still burning with shame, I walk backward until I feel the doorknob beneath my hand. "I've got to go," I blurt out, desperate to be gone from the scene. Fortunately, Dan doesn't call after me, letting me go in peace.

I'm rushing down the stairs, already ordering an Uber, face fixed on my phone, when I run into my brother.

He is beyond drunk at this point, his usually frowny face relaxed and joyous. "Elise! My baby sister, whom I love very much. Have you seen Dan? He's my best friend, my best man, and I want to make a toast in his honor."

I pinch my nose between my thumb and forefinger, feeling a headache building rapidly behind my eyes. "I have no idea, Andries."

He frowns, leaning down to my height. "Are you alright? You look upset."

"I'm fine, don't worry. Why don't you, um... go find Roxanne. Maybe she knows where he is."

He agrees, leaving me alone once more, and I'm finally able to make my escape, taking a mess of emotions with me.

* * *

Once home, I strip out of my clothes as quickly as I can and run to the shower, cranking on the hot water, and letting it cover me. Washing away the feeling of Dan's lips and fingers along with all my makeup.

After I'm done, I don't even bother getting dressed; instead, towel drying and taking two acetaminophens for my head. Then, with a glass of water and a heart full of regrets, I climb between my sheets and try to find sleep, and hopefully hide away from the world.

It's then, lying there naked, the silky sheets rubbing my skin, that I come to the realization I can still feel the ghost of Dan's touch. The shower did nothing to banish it, and worse, I'm still burning for him.

Resigned, I close my eyes and give in to the memories of the way he touched me and how incredible it felt, tracing my own fingers over the path his took only hours before. Except I go further, and where I touch myself, the fantasy that I'm playing out in my head follows suit. If his dad hadn't walked in, Dan would have slid the straps of my dress down my shoulders, freeing my breasts for his eyes, hands, and mouth to feast on. I pinch them myself, wishing it was his mouth.

When I drag my hand down my entire body, I see Dan kneeling on the floor in front of me, working my wet panties down my legs, and then his dark head as he kisses up my leg, to my thigh, and finally, between my legs, pushing each one wide so he can taste me in full.

The imagery is so erotic, so taboo, that I can't stop thinking about Dan's tongue between my legs. I see him looking up at me, his mouth on my clit, while in reality my fingers work furiously on myself.

I don't even get to thinking about him fucking me, because the imagery of him eating me out is too much all on its own. I come with my own fingers and the orgasm is the strongest I've ever been able to give myself, and I'm able to drag it out longer and longer with my hands.

After I'm finally finished, all my muscles go limp, and I lay in bed panting, the quivers still shooting up and down my legs. I have just a few weeks to plan my eighteenth birthday, and I have to figure out how to force Dan to come. I'm afraid he'll be reluctant after our recent time alone. Not because he doesn't want me, though, but because he's too eager.

With contentment thrumming through me now, I close my eyes once more and drift off to sleep, my last conscious thought that I want Dan to be eager at my party. Just as much as I am for him.

CHAPTER 16

Amsterdam, May 22, 2022
Dan

Rolling over, I stretch my arms above my head and breathe out slowly. After the chaos of the previous night, my bed had felt like a welcome reprieve, an oasis all my own, where I could pretend that I hadn't made an enormous mistake just hours beforehand. That was last night though, and this morning, the reality of what Elise and I had done is hitting me full force once more.

Even scarier is what we *almost* did. The only saving grace of the whole ordeal was that we didn't go all the way. If we had, I don't know if I could forgive myself. Not because I don't want Elise, because I do—so intensely that I miss her even now—but because of the promise I made to my best friend, and the fact that his sister deserves more than someone like me who can never be more than a friend with benefits.

We aren't meant for each other. It's as simple as that.

Too bad staying away from her isn't going to be nearly as simple. Her insistence that I attend her birthday would be cute coming from anyone else, but from Elise, a girl that always has some sort of plan or machination in mind, the invite is dangerous. Combine that with how close she and I were last night, and it's a recipe for trouble. Big, big trouble.

There's one thought that bounces around in my head when it's quiet and there's nothing else on my mind: *Would it be different if it wasn't for Andries? Would I pursue Elise if there were no strings attached?*

She's gorgeous, of course, and she draws me in with little more than a look. Her mind is as sharp as a whip and she holds her intelligence close to her chest until she needs it, striking out like a snake and obliterating anyone or anything that stands in her way. As a more laid-back person, someone who likes to enjoy the finer things in life at a slower pace, Elise's ambitions should be a turnoff for me, but they are anything but. Maybe because she's my opposite in that way, and as the saying goes, opposites attract.

So, yeah… I think I would pursue her if there weren't so many chains holding us back if only to see where it could lead. One part of me thinks that a woman like Elise would be my endgame; the girl I settle down with forever, and I'm not sure if I am ready for that. The other part thinks that we might burn hot and bright for some time before our differences become too much and we fizzle out.

There's no reason to even think about those things, though. Andries is standing in our way, and my loyalty to him has to supersede everything else. Even if it means that I might miss out on my perfect match.

We could really be brothers one day if he would just get the stick out of his ass and let his sister make her own choices.

The idea of it makes my heart feel soft and vulnerable, and I'm considering just going back to bed to avoid how terrible it all makes me feel. I'm not a soft-hearted man when it comes to relationships. I want sex and opulent times with the women I choose from time to time, not love. At least, not usually.

There's no way I'm going to go back to sleep and avoid the day any longer. My stomach growls, and it's the last straw. With a groan, I throw the blanket off and sit on the edge of the mattress, rubbing my eyes and waiting for the inevitable dull pounding hangover headache. Spotting a few aspirins and a glass of water beside my bed, I mentally thank the butler and wash the pills down swiftly.

A hot shower and the avoidance of any more self-reflection does wonders for my mood, and by the time I'm walking out into the backyard to find my parents, I'm feeling much more like myself. No more mopey Dan today, not if I can help it.

Mom and Dad are taking breakfast outdoors, and even though it's still early, any evidence of the party has been cleaned up and done away with. I'm surprised at how quickly it can all disappear, and the world can go back to normal.

Then I lock eyes with my Dad, and the memory of why Elise and I stopped when we did hits me full force, and now I'm feeling anything but normal. More like I want to crawl under a table and hide away until the humiliation of being caught making out with a family friend by my own Dad can subside. But Mom is waving me over, and I can smell the coffee from here. Dad's favorite brew, no doubt, an impossibly dark Italian roast that has been painstakingly brewed by the pour-over method. It's not blooming tea, but it should get rid of the dregs of my headache. A small consolation for the embarrassment I'm about to endure.

I relax a little when I reach the table, because Mom greets me just as she normally would, which tells me that Dad hasn't informed her of my little escapades last night. I slide him a look and he nods once, sharply, reading my thoughts in the way that dads always can. I'm grateful for his secret-keeping, so the least I can do is be a good breakfast companion for them.

"You only look partially hungover, dear," Mom says, raising her eyebrows. "For such a big party, I didn't expect to see you up until well into the afternoon."

"We all have to grow up sometime," I reply, spearing a few pieces of sausage and moving them to my plate. "I hope all the youths didn't wear you two out."

"Nonsense." Mom laughs. "I can still keep up with the best of them."

Patting her knee, Dad smiles at her fondly. "I had to talk her out of breakfast mimosas, actually," he confesses.

I wince, pouring a mug of hot black coffee. "Oh no, that doesn't even sound good to me."

There is definitely an elephant in the room—well, in the yard—sitting next to Dad and acting like nothing had happened, but I have a sneaking suspicion that I haven't heard the last about my escapades with the Van den Bosch heiress.

Filling up on salty meat and life-giving caffeine, breakfast goes well, all things considered. Mom and Dad are both in good spirits, riding the high of having thrown one hell of a celebration for my best friend. Sometimes I think our family doesn't get the same respect in social circles because we aren't from old money and had to make our own way, but all three of us have proven over the years that we can keep up with the rest of the elite with no problem whatsoever. It's both a point of pride and an annoyance that we have to do it at all. The Van Den Bosches are the only group that hasn't treated us somewhat stiffly, but I can't help but wonder if that's why I was the perfect companion for grumpy, introverted Andries who always had his nose in a book. Strange that they would have rather he be a party boy in his youth instead of a bookworm, but I guess social skills rank above literary competence in some ways.

Then I think about if they would treat me differently if they knew I was off sticking my tongue down their daughter's throat. I wonder how good of a shot Sebastian really is?

Mom stands eventually, stretching her hands over her head. "Well boys, I'm off. I told Roxanne I'd treat her, her sister, and her mom to a spa day to recover from the raucous night we had all just lived through. Can you two get along okay without me?"

Standing briefly to kiss his wife on the cheek, Dad sighs dramatically before sitting back down. "If we must."

We both watch her go, me knowing that as soon as she's out of earshot it's going to be time to talk about all the uncomfortable things.

Once Mom starts to ascend the stairs to the house, Dad clears his throat, and I take an enormous swig of my coffee to stall and prepare myself.

"Son, I just want to say I'm sorry to have not knocked before entering the study," he begins, pushing eggs around his plate. "The door is never shut, and I should have known something was off just from that, but I was so distracted by guests, and I had a scotch or two at that point, so I didn't even stop to think."

"God, Dad," I groan, lowering my head to my hands. "Seriously, I shouldn't have gone to your study, not with any girl. I wasn't thinking either, and it was my mistake. Can we drop it now?"

"I'm not bothered by you taking a girl to my study, Dan," he points out. "I'm bothered that you took Elise Van den Bosch, and for... well, what you took her there for. That was no chat between friends."

"You don't think I know that?" I retort, snappier than I intend. When Dad winces, I immediately feel like shit.

"She's your best friend's sister, is all. I don't think that's a prudent move, and I'm sure you're aware of all the things it could change, maybe even ruin, in your personal life."

"I know..." I might be twenty-four, but I have the sudden strong need to get advice from my Dad, the wisest man I know. It's a punch to the gut to realize that even now, I'm not done learning from him. I feel like a kid at his knee again and think about how I don't always appreciate how lucky I am to have the parents I do. While Sebastian is playing Elise and Andries against each other like two pieces on a chess board, here is my dad gently trying to guide me in the right direction not just for my sake, but for the sake of my friends, too.

"I don't know what happened," I continue, swallowing past the tightness in my throat. "It was just... a moment of weakness."

He snorts, amused. "Just a moment, huh?"

Scrubbing my hands through my hair in frustration, I admit, "Maybe a few. And the thing is she even invited me to her eighteenth birthday at her family estate, but her brother, on the other hand, is not invited. Why the hell would she do that if she didn't want to be alone with me? She was so sweet to Andries and Roxie last night, so I don't think she has as much vitriol toward the two of them as she wants Sebastian, and maybe even herself, to think, so why not continue mending fences by inviting them? I can't help but think it's because *of me* that she's leaving them out. So Andries won't interfere, and I won't have the guilt of him skulking around while I snog his sister."

"Hm. That sounds to me like an opportunity for many, many more moments of weakness, don't you think?"

I chuckle, both at Dad's humor and the absolute nightmare of a situation I have waltzed myself into. "I just don't know what to do, Pops. Since the day I first saw her, she's always been on my mind. Even though she was too young for me then, I could see the woman she'd become, and it's been so tempting to see her come into her own. I've been struck by beautiful women before and had no problem pursuing the available ones and leaving the unavailable or troublesome ones behind, and Elise is both unavailable *and* troublesome. Yet, I almost feel obsessed with her sometimes." I feel like my words just keep coming and coming, unbidden, and I can't stop them. This is the first time I've spoken about it out loud to someone, and I haven't realized until now how much I need someone else's input. "I'm just... lost. I want what I can't have, but I also couldn't imagine hurting my best friend."

"If you are ready to lose your best friend for her, then the choice is clear."

"I can't," I snap back immediately. "Andries is so closed off from the world, he barely has anyone else but me as a friend. The fact that he is engaged to a living breathing woman is nothing short of a miracle." I blow out a breath. "I already told Elise we need some time apart. Maybe all this stuff can simmer down if I don't see her for some time."

Dad raises an eyebrow. "Until you meet her again for her birthday, you mean?"

"I can hear the judgment from your tone," I grumble. "I need to think about it. Maybe I should just decline, but boy, she will be so pissed if I do."

"And hurt," Pops interposes. "She's inviting you because you mean something to her. Whatever that thing may be— friend, companion, or even a potential romance. Regardless, you're important to Elise, and this denial might now be something she can easily bounce back from."

"So what do I do?"

"Risk assessment," he says simply, shrugging and leaning back in his chair. "Make sure that if you go ahead with her, it's worth losing her brother as a friend if he ever finds out. You can't really ask Andries to feel any differently about this, considering he's been on edge with you and her from the first day you met her."

"What kind of man would I be if I say that I'd trade Andries's friendship for his sister? After the oath I took? I don't even know what she feels for me. Maybe I'm just a game for her. She loves playing games and pulling strings."

"Hm. That's true. That whole family, Andries excluded, loves their complicated social games, don't they? You're going to have to figure her true intentions and feelings out first."

As Dad starts to gather his things, clearly finished with his fatherly advice, all I can think to say is, "That's an impossible task in and of itself. Sometimes I feel like she's an open book, but then I turn around and what I thought were her true and honest feelings were just another way for her to get ahead. She's a manipulative bitch. That's what she is."

"It sounds to me like you have her pretty figured out, all things considered. Use that familiarity to your advantage and try to discover what she's really feeling about you deep down inside. The only way you can make a decision that you're satisfied with is to know the full story." He claps me on the shoulder before heading to the house. "Good luck, kid."

Flustered and annoyed, I pull my phone out of my pocket just for a distraction, but I have a text from Andries waiting for me.

Andries: *You're the man! That party was absolutely fantastic! Yao was delighted, and she said she never had such a good time in her life. We need your help with the wedding too. Get your event designer and your team because we want something just as epic at Oma's estate.*

I can't even enjoy the thanks fully. My best friend wouldn't be thanking me like this if he knew what Elise and I had been doing right under his nose. I've already broken the oath I made to him by touching his sister in the first place, but at this point, it hasn't gone far enough that there is no turning back. Still, there's no way I can tell him about yesterday and forever taint the memory of his engagement party.

Trying to push guilt to the side for a second, I respond, *Good to know! Sure, we can schedule a meeting at Margaret's estate to check the place and get some inspiration.*

Andries: *Good idea! Next Saturday at 11 AM work for you?*

Absolutely, I text back, pocketing my phone with a sigh after setting the appointment in my calendar.

Housekeeping comes to clear everything from breakfast, refilling my mug, and I decide to savor the time alone with my thoughts. Last night when I was finally alone, my mind was still muddled from alcohol and lust, and my thoughts were anything but clear. I flip through all my socials, liking the pictures I got tagged in from the evening, and, for some reason, decide to go back to my inbox to check something else. The pictures of the gala are there marked as "important," and I can't help but click on the email, and pursue all the pictures again.

The photographer did a really good job. I just can't get enough of seeing Elise and me dancing. Her eyelids are lowered, her face softens as she leans toward me, and I seem to almost be welcoming her. Our bodies move so naturally together, so effortlessly, that I can't help but wonder if everything could be so seamless between us. If I really want to, I can find out on her eighteenth birthday. I'm almost positive that Elise wants me, and that's the reason for her insistence on my attendance. It would be all too easy; no Andries, plenty of empty rooms and little alcoves to hide away in, and no rush. We could take our time, really get to know each other... but I can't. Anger flares through me. It just isn't fair that I can't even have a chance to see what Elise and I could be. I'm a grown man, and by all accounts, I've been a good friend and confidant to Andries. I shouldn't have to choose between him and his sister. If I could have both, we may even get the chance to be a family, but Andries is too fucking stubborn.

Interrupting my daydreams, one of the maids comes over, giving me a little wave to get my attention. I snap back to reality, shaking myself out of all my useless thoughts. "Yes?"

"There's a woman waiting in the foyer for you, sir. I didn't catch her name, I apologize."

I hop up, hurrying past the maid and toward the home. What if it's Elise? How will I handle her after everything?

To my surprise—and disappointment—standing in the marble and white stone foyer is Jessica, her dark hair loose and wearing a matching violet crop top and yoga pants, one of my favorite looks on her. By the smile she gives me as I approach, the outfit choice, along with her presence altogether, was carefully planned to catch me off guard.

"How did you get my address?" I ask before she can say anything, annoyed that she would go out of her way to track down where my parents live.

"Don't look so pissed, Dan. A friend of mine was one of your waiters last night, and she gave it to me when I asked where she was going for the night. It's nothing nefarious."

"If you knew about the party last night, why not come then instead of this morning?"

She wraps her arms around herself, looking above her at the chandelier hanging above and the prismatic rainbows it casts on the walls. "I wasn't invited, so I didn't think it was appropriate to attend."

For the thousandth time today, the image of Elise under my hands in the study pops up again, and I'm infinitely glad Jessica had the social awareness to not show up at the engagement party. "Well, thanks for respecting that, at least. But why are you here now?"

"I…" She hesitates, and I notice there is something about this girl I thought I knew so well. There isn't any attitude in the way she's holding herself, no animosity. For weeks Jessica has been getting more and more frustrated with the time I've been spending with Elise, but apparently, she's put it aside for the time being. "I miss you, alright?" She pulls her eyes from the chandelier and looks me dead in the eyes. "Telling you over text isn't a cool move, and I wanted to say it to your face. Things aren't the same without you, Dan. I messed up, and I'm ready to admit it."

"So you acknowledge it's your fault, then? Because you wanted to leave me out of jealousy since I was spending time with Elise."

"Yeah, well… how could I not be a little jealous? She's beautiful, wealthy, and part of a family you're basically a part of. Elise seems like your perfect match, and then you leaving me alone all the time to cater to her really rubbed me the wrong way." She pauses, catching her breath back. "I can't lie and say I'm okay with the way you did that to me over and over, but I'm coming to terms with the fact that you care about her like you would a friend or sibling. So… I'd like to give this another shot if you'll have me."

She's hard to resist, all tan skin and willing eyes, but one thing she has said rings false. I don't like Elise like a sibling, or even a friend. I want her as a lover, and that's the lens I'll view her through the rest of my life I think. Looking at Jessica, and how her emotions are at play here, not just her physical wants and needs, I know that I can't keep leading her on. If there is anyone I only care about as a friend, it's Jessica. I take a deep breath, barely believing what I'm about to say. One single word and she'd be upstairs in bed with me, but I'm about to blow that all out of the water.

"I appreciate the apology, Jess, but I've moved on." She looks heartbroken at this news, but I push on. "You should too, okay? Find someone that will make you truly happy. You deserve it."

Jess purses her lips, looking away so I can't see the mist of tears in her eyes. It hurts my heart, because this woman has given me so much, and all I'm doing right now is telling her it was all for nothing. But what choice do I have?

In a world that Elise exists in, Jessica will never mean all that much to me. My perfect match is elsewhere.

Finally, she nods, her whole posture heavy with it. "I-I understand…" She walks to the door, and I take a last chance to look at her butt in the yoga pants as she does so. What a waste… I could be peeling them off her right now.

"Take care of yourself, Dan," she says, hand on the door handle.

"You too, Jess. You too."

CHAPTER 17

Elise

Class is dragging on impossibly, and I can't help but fidget, tapping my pencil on the desk as the professor drones on and on. I'm usually incredibly attentive because I could never deal with the shame of having bad marks, but something about today has my head in the clouds.

Oh, why even deny it? It's Dan that is occupying all the space in my head, and it doesn't look like he's going anywhere anytime soon.

He's like a song that has gotten stuck in my head, thoughts of him just repeating over and over again, leaving no room for much else. I just want to rush through the rest of today so I can go to bed. Hopefully, sleep will be a nice restart, and I'll wake up tomorrow morning feeling more like myself. It hasn't worked yet, but I guess I have to keep trying.

As much as I try to convince myself that I'm just using Dan for my own devices, the memories of our encounter in the study makes me doubt everything. Both my body and my heart were enraptured by him at that point, and as humiliating as it was to get caught, I can't help but wish we had gone further. I want more of him, like an addict. It's a real problem because getting involved with him when he's such a powerful tool when it comes to keeping tabs on my brother is a terrible idea.

Yet, if he was here right now, waiting for me outside the classroom door, I'd run to him. Let him shut us in an empty classroom and continue what we started, even. My self-control is almost nonexistent when it comes to him.

Maybe I need to let off some steam with someone else, and then Dan wouldn't seem so appealing. Is it possible I'm just obsessing because I need romantic, even sexually charged attention, not from Dan specifically?

I look around the classroom, trying to imagine myself with any of the other boys that are closer to my age. There are plenty that are attractive; fit, well-muscled, with bright smiles and expensive haircuts, but the idea of crawling into their laps and pressing my lips to theirs makes me feel nothing. Not disgust, excitement... just nothing.

Well, crap. Looks like Dan is the reason, then. Which leaves me in the same place I started. Grouchy, distracted, and stupidly needy.

Class lets out and I'm packing my bag so quickly that it has to be obvious how badly I want out of there. I quickly ask one of my classmates to send me her notes, making some paltry excuse about not feeling well, and escape.

Bursting out of the building and onto the concourse is a blessed relief. At least now I'm not feeling claustrophobic along with everything else.

"Elise!" someone calls from a small gaggle of girls hovering under a large tree. I look over and it's Tatianna, along with a few other girls I know in passing, all looking bright and excited to see me. I can't say I feel the same, but I put on the happy face I know is expected of me and head over.

Tati hugs me quickly. "It's been too long! How are you?"

"Getting by," I tell her honestly.

"Let's take a walk," she says, and we wave goodbye to the rest of the group as we start off on our circle of the concourse.

"Now that I've got you alone," Tatiana starts, her arm linked with mine. "I have to ask, and don't worry, I'm not feeling weird about it. How was the engagement party?"

Images of Dan try to float into my mind, but I shut them down just as fast. "It went well. Big. Extravagant. Everyone showed up but my parents."

She looks appropriately somber at that news. "Oh, how unfortunate. Your parents still don't approve of his choice of fiancée, huh?"

"I think we both know they don't."

"Well, as long as Andries is happy." Tatiana sounds wistful if a bit sad.

"Do you... uh... want to talk about it, Tati? Are you sad about their engagement?" I know I sound awkward, and honestly, I don't want to have the conversation, but I know it's what a good friend would do.

"Not sad exactly," she clarifies, shrugging one shoulder. "Andries will always be my first crush, and since our parents always thought we'd end up together, that expectation is a little hard to let go of, you know? Who I will marry is a big question mark in my life now, and I don't even know if it will be someone I like or not. At least Andries and I get along fine... but I can't deny him his happiness. It's not like we were in love, or even dating."

"I can totally relate," I fess out. "I too had a first crush years ago that I thought would be the love of my life. I guess that's what most teenagers think of their first crush."

"Oh, and what happened with him?"

"He was from England and was just here for summer camp. Don't worry about it, that was a long time ago." Tati just nods, smiling at me as we keep strolling through the concourse. "I have to admit, Tati, things would be a lot easier in all our lives if Andries had chosen you instead of Roxanne. But as we both know, my brother never makes anything easy."

Tatiana laughs, but it's clearly forced. I stop, grabbing her by the arm and pulling her into another hug, this one longer and more sincere. The other girl sighs but accepts the gesture and comfort.

When I pull back, I'm still feeling some guilt over it all, even if I had nothing to do with Andries's choices in women. How he could not feel anything for this sweet, beautiful girl is a mystery to me.

"Hey, Tati? What if after I finish work, we go and have a few drinks? I know a few places around here that have great happy hours."

She brightens, her lips twisting into a smile. "Really? That sounds fun."

I give her hands a final squeeze before letting go. "Great! I'll send you a message when I'm done, and we can meet up."

Maybe a few drinks before bed would help me sleep, anyway, and possibly give me that mind reset that I so desperately need.

* * *

Since my classes finish at one p.m. today, I spend the rest of the day at the company headquarters in order to get some work done. I try to slink to my office area, hoping to avoid talking to Dad about the engagement party, but I should have known better than to even attempt it. He's waiting in the break area when I pop in to get a bottle of water and immediately asks me to see him in his office.

I groan internally as I follow him, feeling like the only thing I've talked about, or even thought about since Saturday is the stupid engagement party. I really want to move on with my life and leave thoughts of it in the past. If I'm lucky, this will be the last time I have to recount all these events.

"So how was it?" Dad asks immediately, sitting in his leather computer chair and leaning back. "The engagement party?"

I take the seat across from him. "What exactly do you want to know?"

"Everything, but I know neither of us has the time for that. I guess it's too much for me to hope that something terrible happened and everyone was miserable, huh?"

I crack a reluctant smile. "Nope. No drama, Dad, sorry. Dan's family really did a stellar job hiring vendors and planners. It was a successful gathering all around. And the couple still seems very much in love, much to your displeasure I'm sure."

Dad pinches the bridge of his nose between his fingers. "Men fall for their mistresses all the time, but your brother would be the one to marry a woman that is, at best, mistress material. Roxanne Feng should have never been granted the possibility of becoming a Van den Bosch wife."

I must look slightly displeased because Dad waves me off. "I'm not saying I have a mistress," he clarifies. "Just that there is a place for women like Roxanne, and it's not at the altar, I'll tell you that much."

Even though I'm no fan of Roxanne, a flash of anger goes through me. I despise her career, but she's been kind to me lately, even after I've been an impossible thorn in both of their sides for quite a while now. Dad talks about her like she's trash, and it rubs me the wrong way, which takes me by surprise.

"You might be the only one that thinks that," I point out with more vitriol than I intended. "Everyone else was there. Oma Margaret, Aunt Yara, Maud, Uncle Alex… everyone. The only disapproval seems to be coming from you, Dad. Do you really plan on keeping this whole campaign of breaking them up going?"

"Your mother doesn't approve, either," he adds, but I shake my head.

"Do you really think Mom would have missed that party if you hadn't been boycotting it?"

He seems momentarily disturbed at the thought, but quickly redirects that negativity toward me. "That's enough, Elise. I'm trusting that you will find an adequate way of splitting the two of them up because that's the job I've given you."

"I'm just saying that it's going to be difficult, especially if the only opposition he's facing is coming from our side."

"Then maybe we need to change our tactics to get Roxanne to end the relationship first. After all, I'm sure you don't want an escort linked to you as your sister-in-law. Maybe she has some skeletons in her closet we just don't know about yet."

The cabaret, my mind offers, but I don't say it out loud. I don't want to give Dad something else to force me to focus my attention on, and if he knows Roxanne is hiding something that substantial from Andries he will fixate on it—pouncing on the chance to ruin their relationship.

My silence might also be related to the fact that I promised Dan that I would keep that secret no matter what. If I think about it too hard, I have to face the uncomfortable question of where my loyalties really lie.

After I finish telling Dad about the party, obviously skipping anything to do with Dan and I's alone moments, he tells me that I'm free to go back to work. He looks thoughtful but annoyed, and maybe just the smallest bit sad. I wonder if he regrets starting down this path and if he wishes he could have been there for his son last night after all.

I'm only at my desk for a short time when my landline rings. I'm only supposed to be in for a few hours today since it's also a school day, just to help catch up on some things for other employees around the office, but I shouldn't have any appointments to speak with clients. I frown, but after a few rings, pick the phone up.

"Elise, it's Karl," he says, causing me to roll my eyes upon hearing his name. "Why don't you come down to my office? There's something I want to discuss with you."

I get a chill, thinking about how much my brother and Dan have warned me not to spend any time with Karl alone, but he's been nothing but courteous and helpful with me, so what else am I supposed to do?

"What, exactly?" I ask.

"I know you had a meeting with your father an hour ago, and I wanted to see how that went. I have an idea to make that breakup you want so badly happen, but I'd really like to get your opinion on it before I set my plan into action. So, can you come down here?"

My interest is piqued, but I guess I shouldn't be surprised. Karl has every reason to hate Roxanne and want revenge on her, so it's easy to see why he would want to be involved in splitting up her engagement, too. It feels like I can't escape this topic, and it's driving me insane. First, Dan was on my mind all morning during class, and now I can't even get through a single email without someone wanting to talk about my brother and his fiancée.

"Fine, I'll be right down."

I don't hurry, taking the long walk through the open layout as a moment to breathe and collect my thoughts. I still haven't quite decided what I will do about Andries and Roxanne, but there's no harm in hearing Karl out, and if somehow he's figured out a way to separate them without it leading back to me, I might even consider it. I am torn because I want my brother to be happy, but I still think that Roxanne makes him happy *now*, but she can't possibly do so for the rest of his life. It's just too odd of a match, and those differences will have to make themselves unavoidable at some point.

I knock a few times before entering Karl's office and find myself once again annoyed at how lavish it is compared to my cramped little desk in the open layout. It will be different when I'm CEO. I indulge in a brief fantasy of moving Karl's office to a broom closet when I take over as I sit across from him and smile, my humorous thoughts completely my own.

He doesn't look like someone that has been drug through the dirt with the media for months now. Instead, he's relaxed and comfortable, clearly the king of this little corner of the world. It must be the confidence that comes with being so successful for decades.

"How can I help you, Karl?"

"Before we go any further, I need to ask you one thing: do you really want to separate your brother and Roxanne once and for all?"

Taken aback, I can't answer immediately. "That's—well, that's incredibly blunt."

"That's why I brought you here instead of talking over the phone, Elise. I want us to be able to be blunt, and not be eavesdropped on by some nosy employees. So, what's your answer?"

I exhale slowly, not able to avoid the question if I want to see what he has in mind. "Yes, I do want them to separate. They're getting married this summer, and I'm running out of time."

He grins, and it reminds me of a snake. "Wonderful. So, I'm thinking that the only way to get Andries to leave Roxanne for good is if he found out she was working as a madame again behind his back, and if we can provide him with concrete evidence that she's doing so."

"What!" I almost laugh. The idea is so absurd. "She will never work with you again, Karl, so I don't know why you're even considering this a valid plan of action."

"No, of course not, but maybe she will for you."

He drops the bomb so casually that it's believable. I sputter and then shake my head. "I don't care what I gain, I'm morally opposed to hiring prostitutes for any reason at all. Not even splitting them up could make me want to encourage sex work like that."

He waves my concerns off. "We aren't going to do anything with them. They'll be more like party decorations than anything else, but Andries won't care about the details. If he knows she's still acting like a pimp without him knowing, I think that will be more than enough."

It's bizarre, but it might work, even if I hate to admit it. The idea of hiring prostitutes still rubs me the wrong way, even if I'm not actually hiring them to do anything sexual, but I can live with it if Karl really thinks this plan is bulletproof.

"I don't know, Karl... I don't think she's going to buy it. She knows how staunchly I am against sex work."

"Just listen to what I have in mind, and you'll see how the request could be totally plausible. Remember the clients I introduced you to a few weeks ago? I plan on having a lavish dinner meeting with all of them, and I want you to hire the entertainment for the evening. That entertainment just so happens to be Roxanne's previous employees, and you'd really love her help on that."

"I mean... maybe, but I still don't think she'll believe me."

"Everyone can change their minds about things sometimes," he points out. "Can't you?"

I clasp my hands together in my lap, mulling it over. It will be catastrophic if this plan backfires, but it has all the necessary components to succeed. I just really, really don't want to play my assigned part. "What if she figures out that you're helping me?"

His mischievous grin disappears in an instant. "She *can't* find that out. If she asks about me, you have to make it clear that we don't talk to each other. Ever."

I draw in a shaky breath, knowing that despite the danger, I'm going to try. One last push to make my brother see the light and bring him back into the fold of the family—and a final attempt in securing my spot as the heir of Van den Bosch Industries. It feels selfish, but necessary.

"I don't think that will be enough for Andries. They are very committed to one another now. I think she needs to go and be at the dinner, too."

Karl strokes his chin and kicks his chair back, staring at the ceiling. "You want to hire her, too? Even better. Do it."

I blink. "Just like that?"

"I'm putting my trust in you, Elise. The less I'm involved, the smaller the chance all of this can be traced back to me, and I'm sure you realize the amount of bad press the company would receive if I was caught hiring sex workers again. This is your project now. Think it over."

The responsibility of it all settles over my shoulders like a weight. It will have to be pushed back to after my birthday, so there is no sort of retaliation at my party, but otherwise, I think I can do this. Let's just hope I don't blow everything out of the water and ruin it for us all.

CHAPTER 18

Elise

Arriving at the bar, I'm already questioning my decision to come, but I can't bail now. I know coming out to something like this is a huge deal for shy, introverted Tatiana, and I can't ruin that by ghosting her.

The talk with Karl has me on edge. Excited, because I have real hope that the plan might actually work, but also an enormous amount of anxiety. If I go about this wrong, not only will I lose Andries forever, but I'll probably lose my chance at taking over the company once Dad retires. Just one simple mistake and I could ruin my life in so many ways.

I try to put it at the back of my mind as I enter the bar, immediately overtaken by the sound of live jazz music playing and the rich, smoky smell in the air. The lights are low, and beneath the music, there is the constant buzz of conversation.

Tatiana is waiting at the bar counter for me, fidgeting with a cardboard coaster. She lights up when she sees me, and most of the reluctance I had coming out tonight dissipates.

"I ordered us margaritas!" she exclaims, motioning toward the two tall glasses filled with pale yellow liquid, white salt crusted on the rim.

Plucking my glass off the countertop, I take a drink, puckering my mouth at the sweet and sour taste of it, sharp tequila hitting on the back end. "Thanks! Let's go find a table."

There wasn't much left as far as private tables went, so we chose a longer eight-seater, hopping up onto the barstools.

"I'm so happy you suggested this." Tatiana sighs happily. "It's hard for me to make plans and all that. I usually just go along with whatever everyone else wants."

"That's no way to live your life," I tell her, taking a long pull on my straw. "Sometimes you have to take what you want."

"Most of the time, it's a quieter life, but this is still a nice change of pace." Tatiana looks around us as she sits. "Have you been here before?"

"Not here specifically, but it's been recommended to me a couple of times. So…" I lean forward so she can hear me better. "You're coming to my birthday party, right? I don't want any awkwardness about what went on with my brother, so he isn't coming."

She frowns. "W-why?"

"Nothing to do with you, I promise. I just wanted to make you aware that you wouldn't have to deal with any of that."

"I wouldn't miss it either way. Have you decided on a theme?"

I blow a stray piece of hair out of my face and shrug. "Not really. Maybe I just won't have one. I've had so much else on my mind I haven't even really stopped to think about it."

Tatiana finishes her drink, waving a server over and exchanging the empty glass for a new one. I hesitate, wondering how inebriated I really want to be tonight, but decide to let go a little and follow her example. The alcohol has me feeling warm, and is making some of those things weighing on me so much go fuzzy at the edges. It's a welcome change.

"What about a masquerade!?" she pipes up as if inspiration has just struck her. "Like the one we attended at Dan's house?"

Just the mention of his name makes a pulse of lust move through me. "Oh, w-well," I stutter, but my thoughts aren't even in the room anymore. They're back in the study at Dan's parents' estate, his pressing weight keeping me in place against the desk. He had barely even touched me, but I had been ready to risk it all just to feel his hands on my bare skin.

"Hellooo, Elise?" Tatiana says, breaking my reverie. I blush, hoping that she isn't able to determine what is on my mind.

"Sorry, these drinks are pretty strong I guess." I laugh, but she isn't buying it, grinning wide and narrowing her eyes.

"What are you thinking about, El? Or should I say, who?" she teases.

"Absolutely no one. Now. Let's go back to party planning." Tatiana tries to interject, but I barrel ahead. "What if I do a white night party since it will be during the summer?"

She looks like she wants to press the issue of my daydreaming, but the drinks are hitting her a little, too, and she's easily moved on to another topic. "That's a great idea. I didn't even think about how hot and stuffy costumes and masks would be during the heat of the summer. A white-themed party makes so much more sense."

We delve more into the details of the entire thing—catering, music, dinner, and entertainment. I'm shocked at myself because any other year I'd have all of these things arranged by now. But with my brother's engagement, and his best friend coming closer and closer to my orbit, I've let it all fall to the wayside, figuring Mom and her party planners would figure it all out. Talking to Tatiana, though, I can see that I actually do care about the minute details of the party, especially if Dan is going to be there.

As if he's summoned by just the mere thought of his name, I see Dan himself, flanked by another man and two girls, entering the bar. I turn away so he can't see my face, well aware that I'm blushing. Oh God, I hope he doesn't notice me!

My hopes of anonymity are dashed when Tatiana, comfortably drunk at this point, holds her arm up in the air and waves at the other group. Dan immediately spots her, right before I jerk her arm down for her.

"What are you doing?" I hiss.

"That's Dan! You two are friends, right? I'm just inviting him over."

"I don't know any of those people he's with," I say.

She just giggles. "Well, it looks like you're about to be introduced."

Through clenched teeth, I tell her, "I don't want to be introduced."

"Too late!" she chirps, giving the approaching group a brilliant smile. "Plus, his friend is really good looking. Help me rebound from the terrible heartbreak I'm feeling about losing your brother."

"You said you were fine," I groan, rubbing my temples.

Dan and his entourage reach our table, and Tatiana is almost bubbling over with excitement. She hops up and hugs him, and Dan introduces her to everyone he's with. The man he's with, a lanky but handsome man around Dan's age, is Mark, and the two girls they are with are just acquaintances whose names I don't even register. He doesn't say it out loud, but it's a tactic I've seen from him before. Provide beautiful girls both as a way to entertain guests and as a social buffer so he doesn't have to do all the hard work of keeping someone engaged the entire time. Still, seeing one of them hovering close behind his back, looking starry-eyed, has me pissed off.

When Dan is done introducing Tati, he turns to me. I'm still seated, not seeing any reason to jump up and simper over him like she is, but there's a tight, expectant look in his eyes that has me rising to my feet. Oh, this is very awkward.

"Everyone, this is my good friend Elise Van den Bosch," he says quickly, as if he doesn't want to pay much attention to my name or presence.

"A pleasure to meet you," Mark says, the complete opposite of the stiff and unhappy Dan. On a whim, I hold my hand out, and he plays his part, taking it, leaning over, and kissing the top. The touch of his lips makes me shiver in disgust. I hate contact with strangers like this. "You're almost royalty around these parts, aren't you?" he asks as he stands straight again. We're all taking our seats now, and he makes sure to get the one next to me. Dan, who was already in a black mood before the hand kiss greeting, looks ready to murder Mark when he has to sit across from me and next to Tatiana, who is blissfully unaware of all the undercurrents of emotion happening around her.

"Something like that," I admit with a small smile for Mark. I don't like him already, but it's worth the act to see Dan squirm.

"She's being modest," Tatiana pipes up. The girl sitting to her right winces from how loud she is. "Elise has one of the most powerful families around, and she's in line to inherit the family company soon, too. Isn't that amazing?"

"I thought there was an older Van den Bosch brother?" Mark inquires, looking at Dan.

"It's a long story…" he grumbles.

He turns his attention back to me. "You'll have to tell it to me sometime, Elise."

Not a chance, I think, but I just nod and smile instead. Tatiana is still rattling on about the last event she attended at my estate, and although she might be a bit over the top when she drinks, the extra confidence and lovely flush to her skin suits her. I was hoping Mark would turn his attention toward her; he seems well dressed and polished, and if he's hanging out with Dan, there has to be something impressive about him that I'm just not aware of. Probably not an endgame, but a pleasant distraction and a bit of practice for Tati.

Unfortunately, Mark seems to only have eyes for me.

"Regardless, let's celebrate new friends. What do you think?" He waves a server down and orders a round of tequila shots for all of us.

They come chilled, with a salt rim and a lime on the side. I squeeze the fruit into the crystal-clear liquid, following Dan's example.

"To this lovely happenstance meeting!" Mark cheers, holding his glass up.

"Whatever he says," Dan adds, deadpan.

We all tilt the shots back, and it burns down my throat, all citric acid and salt. There's enough margarita in my belly that it isn't too intense as it hits, but there's an immediate change in my perception of the space around me. Potent stuff, I guess.

I try to discreetly down a significant amount of my ice water, but I make the mistake of catching Dan's eye as I do. He looks disapproving, but also as if he's yearning for something.

"Don't drink too much," he warns me. "You've got class tomorrow. Plus, I don't need to be reprimanded by your brother any more than I already am."

"You're not my father, Dan," I rebuke instantly.

He huffs, turning his face away. He' was acting so strange and unlike himself, and while we had agreed to spend some time apart, it wasn't like I had orchestrated this stupid meetup. His behavior is annoying me.

After taking the shot, Tati makes a face, causing Mark to laugh. This gets the rest of the table, minus Dan and I, amused as well, and once it's all said and done Tatiana is wiping tears from her eyes, trying to stop herself from laughing anymore.

"You guys are such great company," she says, her words slightly slurred. "You should all come to Elise's eighteenth birthday party!"

I jolt, sitting up straight. "Tati–"

"I'd love to," Mark adds, talking over me. I open my mouth to tell him no, he's not coming to my party when I see how red in the face Dan has become. Could it be... jealousy I see in his eyes? Maybe I can still make this work in my favor, even if it means that Mark, a man I've just met, leaves with the idea he's attending my birthday.

"Don't feel obligated to attend, Mark," Dan says, his voice much more casual than his expression leads me to believe he's really feeling. "It's an eighteen-year-old's party, after all. I'm not sure that you share many interests with that crowd."

Mark tries to speak, but this time I talk over him. "I'm sure Mark is capable of making up his own mind."

I didn't think it was even possible, but Dan looks even more unhappy. Mark, on the other hand, turns to me with a surprised look on his face.

"Yes, Elise, I can. Thank you for saying that."

Both hating and loving every second of it, I lean closer to him, lowering my eyelids, "You're so welcome, Mark. I'd love to have you as a guest."

"I think," he says, his smile taking on a wicked edge, "that you and I might have much more in common than my friend Dan thinks."

"Oh, I'm sure of it," I continue, my gaze switching between Dan and Mark.

Mark orders us more drinks, strawberry margaritas for the four of us girls, and whiskey for him and Dan. When it arrives, Mark swirls the amber liquid in his glass and looks at me speculatively.

"Do you drink whiskey, El?"

"I don't drink much at all," I admit. "I'm fond of keeping my wits about me, but tonight is different. Tatiana and I haven't gotten to spend much time together lately."

"Sobriety is important, I agree, but so is letting loose once in a while." His gaze flicks to Tatiana, who is regaling a bored-looking Dan with a story about something that happened in one of her classes last week. "Would you like to try a sip of this at least? It's a barrel-aged whiskey. Very smoky and luxurious."

I take the glass, earning another glare from Dan before he's pulled back into Tatiana's story. It certainly doesn't smell luxurious. In fact, it smells astringent, just like every other hard liquor I've encountered. Having an appreciation for this sort of thing seems to be a must in a lot of social circles I'll be expected to move in as I get older, but I just don't know how I'm going to make that work.

Taking a deep breath, I sip the whiskey, suppressing the shudder that wants to run through me, and hand the glass back to Mark with a forced smile. "It's... okay, I guess. I still think I prefer mixed drinks, though."

"I get it. Sometimes it takes a little while to learn to enjoy the rougher things in life. You won't always want things to be so sweet, you know, eventually you'll crave—"

Glasses clink together, wobbling as Dan shoots up and out of his seat and slaps his hands down on the table. "Well, I'm tired of being here. Should we go check out another bar?"

Mark looks up at him, confused. "Uh, no thanks. I'm fine here, but you guys can go."

"Are you sure? You said you just wanted to pop in here for a drink. You've certainly had more than one at this point."

I'm secretly relieved that Dan interrupted whatever creepy point Mark had been getting at, but I'm still not done making him jealous. It's too much fun.

"What part of he's fine here are you not understanding, Dan?" I say.

He narrows his eyes at me, and I can see his jaw working. I've got him pretty annoyed now. Good. "Does your dad know you're here drinking tequila shots and margaritas? Don't forget, little girl, you're not even eighteen yet."

Now Mark is pissed, putting his arm around my shoulder, and pulling me close to him as if he's being protective. I don't like it at all. "Don't be a dick, man," he tells Dan. "Why do you care what her dad thinks, anyway?"

"Because I know Sebastian quite well..." he starts, but I'm already seeing red at his attitude. "And I'm pretty sure he wouldn't approve of his underage daughter being at a bar getting herself drunk with class the next day. It'd be a shame if he got to know about it." Things are spiraling out of my control, and it's no longer enjoyable making Dan uncomfortable. He's taking things too far with his lame threat and I'm ready to get out of his sight.

I throw Mark's arm off me, shouldering past Dan and aiming for the door. He grunts as I knock into him, and I feel his hand briefly try to grab my arm, but he doesn't manage to do it. Through the buzzing in my ears, I hear Tatiana yell, "Elise, come back!" but it's too late. I've already picked my course.

Out on the sidewalk in the night air, I open the Uber app and request a car. I hadn't realized quite how drunk I was until I stood, and it was taking everything in me not to sway in my heels. The streetlights are too bright, exploding into starbursts if I look at them too long.

Tatiana follows me out, which isn't a surprise. I'm sure she doesn't like being left with people who are essentially strangers, but she's also quite tipsy, stumbling as she reaches me.

"Hey, why don't you just come back inside?" she asks, her eyes wide. "I know Dan was being rude, but he was definitely just joking. You know how his sense of humor is."

"I don't care. He's being a dick, so I'm leaving." Tatiana's face falls, and she seems resigned to leaving with me, so I add, "You can stay, Tati. Talk to Mark, he seems nice enough. I know you're having a good time."

"Well…" She looks behind us and back at the bar. "You sure?"

"Positive," I assure her, giving her a quick hug and struggling not to pull us both down to the ground with the way everything is spinning. Tatiana squeezes me and then heads back inside with a bounce in her step.

The Uber arrives, and I'm so happy to be able to just sit down inside the cool interior and close my eyes. No more standing. It's quiet for about thirty-seconds, and then someone opens the other door beside me and climbs in. I'm offended until I realize it's Dan. Now I'm pissed off all over again.

"Get out," I say simply, but he closes the door and shakes his head.

"Either you let me go with you or I won't even bother coming to your birthday party."

I want to scream, but my head is pounding, and I don't want to engage him in an argument right now. I relent, sinking back into the seat, and closing my eyes once more. Maybe he'll be quiet, and I can pretend he's not there.

Wishful thinking...

The Uber pulls onto the road as Dan begins to talk. "First off, I'm sorry for having behaved the way I did. But Mark is total trash, okay? I was just trying to protect you."

"So why even hang out with him, then?" I ask, eyes still closed.

"Because he's an art collector and my family does business with him. That's it. I personally dislike him, but he's closer to my age than my fathers' and it's important to keep up appearances with him. Elise, he's not for you, and I don't want him around you ever again."

He sounds so adamant and firm that I can't help but smile. I open my eyes just enough to see him, his face in shadow. He's so close to me in this car, and I give in to the urge to scoot closer to him until we are hip to hip. I tilt my face up toward him, and after a second of hesitation, he looks down at me.

"Dan, were you jealous of Mark?"

"Ha," he huffs, shaking his head. "Don't be silly."

"I don't believe you for a second," I lay a hand on his upper leg, and he jumps. "So why don't you stop lying to me and tell me the truth? Were you jealous?"

He rolls his eyes to the sky, speaking as if he has to force every single word out individually. "You know the answer. Now go back to your seat, Elise. I'm not made of steel."

I snuggle closer. "What if I don't?"

He makes a sound almost like a growl, and it gives me goosebumps. "Elise... don't provoke me."

We lock eyes, and I feel like I can see the world in them, but more importantly, how powerful his need for me is. It takes my breath away, but I know I'm drunk and too exhausted to take this any further tonight, and I don't think Dan will ever forgive me if I make him touch me when I'm not sober. I see him swallow, his lips parting just slightly, and I know that if I don't pull away, we're going to kiss.

God, I want to, but he'll be angry at himself for taking advantage of a girl who has been drinking.

Pushing all my wants and needs aside, I sigh and lay my head on his shoulder instead. He's so warm, and he smells like evergreen forests and something spicy and masculine. I feel utterly safe.

Dan relaxes now that the almost-kiss moment has passed, and his body relaxes. I do as well, snuggling just a little closer to get more of that warmth and drift off into a quick slumber.

CHAPTER 19

Dan

Being around Elise is usually a test of my self-control when it comes to not kissing her senseless or ripping both our clothes off and giving into what we both desire so much. Having her asleep on my shoulder, cuddled close to me is a different sort of temptation altogether.

I want to brush her hair out of her face, and just watch her breathe. Like this, all her clever wit and irrepressible stubbornness is set to the wayside, and she's totally at peace. I think about what it would be like to wake up to her like this every morning, all warm and sleepy. It seems like a fantasy that won't ever come true for me.

She has been an enormous pain in the ass tonight. First, seeing her so soon after we had made declarations to get some space from each other was jarring, and seeing that she was out drinking with a friend, Tatiana of all people, also surprised me. Elise isn't an "unwind at the bar" sort of person, and I had to do a double take to convince myself she wasn't there. Part of me wanted to ignore her completely, but then Tatiana spotted us, and there was no such escape.

And then there was Mark, immediately smitten with her and dominating the conversation. He came on strong, leaving no question as to what his intentions were with Elise, and she had loved it, which was strange for her. I half expected her to tell him to leave her alone, but instead, she batted her eyelashes and leaned into him. I felt my blood boil.

All of that was worth this, though.

Intoxicated or not, I'm glad we didn't kiss a few minutes ago, either. As of right now, we haven't broken any rules or crossed any lines, so there is nothing about this time spent together that I can feel guilty about later. We could be any old pair of friends, going home after a night out. I'm protecting her, even, from getting lost or going home alone and getting sick.

We come to a stop in front of her apartment, and I tip the Uber driver before waking Elise.

"Hey, sleepyhead. We're home. Let's go."

It's difficult for her to rouse herself, and I have to help her out of the car with both hands. Once her feet are on the concrete, she wavers, holding onto me for dear life.

"I'm so dizzy," she mumbles, still half asleep.

"I bet. You drank way more than you're used to. Here, I'll help you upstairs."

It takes some effort, but I get her to the elevator and up into her flat, flipping the light on as quickly as possible so she doesn't crumble at my feet. It feels strange, being in her apartment this late, with everything darkened.

I know her flat well enough to find the bedroom, and I help her to sit on the edge of the bed. She's wobbly, but at least she complies easily, balancing herself with her hands on the mattress behind her.

I have to wrestle my mind to keep it in appropriate places as I lower myself to my knees and slip her heels off her feet. There are so many other things I would like to be doing in this position, but taking her shoes off was not on the wishlist. I have her rotate, so her head is on the pillow, and she gives me a soft smile. Seeing her in the bed in front of me is almost too much, but I keep my cool enough to gently kiss her forehead before backing up.

"Get some sleep, El. I'll call and check up on you in the morning."

"Wait," she calls, just as I reach the bedroom door. "Can you help me take my jeans off?"

My heart thumps hard in my chest. Why would she ask me that, now of all times, when I can't touch her no matter what? "I don't think you want me to do that."

"I can't get them off," she whines, as she tries to push them down. "And they're so uncomfortable."

I should still just leave, tell her no…but I wouldn't want to sleep in jeans either, and her voice dredges up some long-dead sympathy in me. With a groan, I return to her side and have her tilt her pelvis up so I can unbutton her jeans and slide them down her legs. They seem to go on forever, and I keep my eyes locked on the blanket beside her as I do so, not wanting to torture myself by watching inch after inch of her skin being exposed.

She wiggles the rest of the way out of the pants, and that little movement does me in. I *have* to look at her. Elise fumbles with her blouse, eventually throwing it aside, and now she's almost nude in front of me, and it would only take one movement to put my hands on her.

I guess I expected Elise to be the type of girl to wear black on black undergarments every day, so I'm surprised to see pale yellow lace panties and a matching bra covering her curves. She's so beautiful, so sexy, that it makes my mouth go dry. I can't possibly take this... why am I doing this to myself?

I screw my eyes shut and put all my focus into not getting an erection, clenching and unclenching my fists as I do so. I know she's watching me, there in her lacy, ridiculous panties, and that makes the task even harder.

"Dan..." she breathes. "How do I look to you right now?"

Irresistible. So delicious that I want to lick every inch of your skin.

I clear my throat, not opening my eyes until I can turn away from her. "Like a drunk, troublesome little girl. Now I'm going to go get you some water and aspirin."

"Hey!" she yells at my back, clearly annoyed that I didn't give in to her bid for attention. "I'm not drunk, just tired!"

"Yeah, right," I mumble, leaving her and all her temptation behind.

Like Elise herself—most of the time—her kitchen is perfectly organized and put together. I'm sure she has a house cleaner that comes by weekly and just walks a few circles around the place before leaving because I find it highly unlikely Elise ever lets it get anywhere near messy. This makes it exceedingly easy to find her medicine cabinet and to get her a bottle of Evian from her stainless-steel refrigerator. Even her food is organized in little clear bins inside of it. It looks exhausting.

When I return to her bedroom, I'm surprised to see that she isn't in bed anymore. Then I hear a retching noise coming from her en suite bathroom, and it all clicks into place. My little ice queen really is quite a bit drunker than she was letting on.

I set the aspirin and water on her bedside table and rush in to assist her. She's so pathetic, crumbled there in front of the toilet that I don't even register how nearly naked she is anymore. I rummage through her beauty box, finding a black hair tie and kneeling next to her slumped form.

"Well, I'm sure you're going to feel a lot better now," I murmur gently to her, gathering her long hair up and wrapping it on top of her head in a sloppy, but effective bun. Elise moans in pain from the pressure I'm putting on her head, but better a little headache than a head full of vomit-filled hair.

"That's it, love, get it all out." I rub her bare back as she heaves again, my heart breaking just the slightest bit at the sobs between the retches.

Once she's done, and there's nothing but bile coming up, I flush the toilet for her, close the lid, and help her to sit on it. Wetting a face cloth in warm water, I clean her face, neck, and give her a bundle of tissues to blow her nose into. Clearly miserable, her beautiful eyes ringed in red, she listens to everything I tell her to do for once. If she wasn't feeling so terrible, it might be a nice change of pace, but as of right now, it's just sad. Poor girl.

After squeezing some toothpaste onto her toothbrush, I hand it to her, telling her, "I did everything else, but I don't think I can brush your teeth for you. You're going to have to manage that one on your own."

She brushes them, eyes closed against the harsh bathroom light, and then I guide her to the faucet to rinse her mouth once she's done. Clean and with fresh breath and an empty stomach, Elise hobbles to her bed with me at her side, climbing into the thing so carefully, as if her world is spinning around her. Honestly, it probably is.

Against the headboard, she swallows the aspirin and polishes off the bottle of water, lazily pulling up the covers and crawling underneath. Her eyes are heavy, but she's looking right at me, a question in the depths of them.

"What, Elise?"

"Will you stay with me for a little while? I'm afraid of getting sick again and not being able to make it to the bathroom."

It's a terrible idea, but I also don't want to leave her in this state. She seems on the up and up now, but I feel like she could get incredibly ill again at any moment. With a resigned sigh, I crawl up to the headboard as well, kicking off my shoes and sitting against it. "Just for a little bit, okay? And I'm not going to get under the sheets."

She must truly be drained, because for once in her life, Elise doesn't argue with me. "That's okay… as long as you stay."

Now that she knows she isn't going to wake up alone, Elise falls into a deep slumber within minutes, one of her hands stretched out just enough to lay it on my leg. As beautiful as she is, the only thing I want to do is protect her, and make sure that she feels safe. Watching her breaths lengthen and slow, I can feel my own fatigue start to weigh on me. I'll just close my eyes for a few minutes, and once I've had a cat nap, I'll go home and leave her be. That should be long enough to ascertain that she isn't going to get ill again.

My eyelids shut just as I reach out to take her hand in mine. She sighs in her sleep, and then I too am unconscious.

* * *

I'm interrupted from floating in a sweet, dreamy nothingness by the harsh sound of a door buzzer. I ignore it at first, thinking that it's just part of my dream, or that whoever it is will eventually go away until I realize that the buzzer sounds off. Not like the one at my place at all.

I jump up in bed, not recognizing where I am for a second while the door continues to buzz and buzz. The night before slowly starts to filter back to me, and when I turn, there is Elise, sleeping so soundly beside me. How she can ignore that racket, I have no idea.

"Elise," I hiss, shaking her shoulder. "Get up. Someone is at your door."

She groans, pulling the blanket over her head and rolling over. I clench my teeth, but exhale slowly, crawling out of the soft bed and letting my feet hit the cold hard floor. I guess I'll have to greet the guest myself.

Thank God I check through the peephole to see who is waiting outside because had I just opened it without checking, Andries would have gotten the surprise of his life. He's loitering out in the hallway, holding a drink carrier and paper bag, getting more and more annoyed each time he has to ring the bell. I've been under the impression that the two of them weren't really on friendly terms, so seeing him here is a hell of a shock.

Shit. What am I going to do now?

As quietly as possible, I rush back to Elise's room, this time shaking her a little more forcibly. "*Elise*, your brother is here. You have to get up."

"Dan, plea—WHAT!?" The words finally permeate her slumber, and she jolts up into a sitting position, eyes wide as she clutches the blanket to her bra-clad chest. "Did you say my *brother* is here?"

"Yes, and he's been here for a while now, so you better hurry up if you don't want him calling your dad or something. Come on!"

"Scramble" isn't a word I would normally associate with Elise, but that's the only way to describe how she explodes out of her bed in a flurry of sheets, blankets, pillows, legs, and arms. I have zero time to appreciate how she's still in just lingerie, and completely sober and fair game to ogle this time, before she's wrapping herself in a floor length silver silk robe.

"I liked it better the other way," I gripe, and she narrows her eyes.

"Andries certainly wouldn't. Can you... go hide in the study or something? Until he leaves?"

"Am I your dirty little secret now, El?" I can't help but tease her, but it's cut off as soon as Andries buzzes the door again, and she looks out toward it with a hefty dose of anxiety.

"*Please* just go. I'll text you when it's safe, okay?"

"Fine, fine," I say as she pushes me out of her bedroom and onto another room in the hallway.

I close myself into her study, and as soon as I do she's gone, letting her brother in while I wait here like a teen boy sneaking into his first girlfriend's house. I'm a grown man, dammit, and this really shouldn't be necessary anymore.

I lean against the door and listen to the siblings as they talk. Andries sounds annoyed at being left in the hall for so long but overly friendly for the most part.

"I wanted to bring you breakfast and thank you for being so mature and coming to the engagement party when I was trying to keep you away."

There's a crinkling sound when Elise takes the bag from her brother. "It was nothing. I didn't want to miss it."

He chuckles. "You certainly made yourself known. But I want to say that you and Roxanne mending fences means the world to me." Andries pauses for a moment as if ruminating on something. "Elise, why are you still in a robe? Don't you have class in like, twenty minutes?"

"Yeah!" she replies sheepishly. "I overslept on accident. To my credit, I didn't think you'd want to see me so soon after the engagement party."

There's a vulnerable thread to Andries's voice that I haven't heard before. "I always love spending time with you. I just have Roxanne to think about now too, though."

"I understand. But it was a beautiful party."

There's another long pause, where I assume they are both shuffling their feet and feeling awkward before Elise makes an excuse to go change. Andries calls after her and tells her he'll walk her to class, and from where I am, I can hear Elise groan slightly. I chuckle under my breath, wishing that I was allowed to be part of this whole interaction. Any other time, I'd be welcome for coffee and croissants, too, but not when I've just slept over.

My first sleepover with Elise, and she was drunk while I passed out immediately. What a waste.

I listen to her change in the other room while I pace the study, bored out of my skull. All the niceties between the siblings seemed to take forever, and now it sounds like Elise is doing her best to get cleaned up enough for class after spending a lot of her evening puking. Her organization is a little less stringent here, and there are so many pictures hung on her wall that it's almost mind-boggling.

My favorite, though, is one I find of Andries, Elise, and I standing together, smiling like fools. Elise went through the effort of getting this specific picture framed, and it makes me happy inside. I was important enough to get space on her wall.

But she seems to have pictures of every other portion of her life, too. There are stunning shots of her horse, a brilliant chestnut mare, pictures of her and her parents, of her and her entire group of siblings, and all combinations of Van Den Bosches. She's captured everything on film, and each choice of picture is meaningful, and at first, this makes me feel utterly soft inside, but when I come across one last picture, my feelings change like the crack of a whip.

In this last 5x7 frame is a picture of a tall, blond young man, maybe in his late teens or early twenties, standing next to a younger Elise. Her arms are thrown around his neck, pulling him down, and they're both laughing. Their shirts match, and read *Summer Camp 2019*. My blood is boiling, and the longer I look at this picture of the two of them, a perfect fit for one another, standing in front of a scenic forest, the more nauseous I become. Even the idea of Elise thinking about being with another man makes me feel crazy.

I snap a quick picture of it, texting it to a hacker friend of mine and requesting an ID. He sends me a ridiculous number for a compensation payment, to which I reluctantly agree. Anything to see what other man was putting that smile on Elise's face.

Right as I'm considering taking the picture and burning it at home, I hear the door open and shut in the front room and the voices of Andries and Elise fading. She then texts me and says the coast is clear.

I take one more look at the photo, holding my hand to my churning stomach, and decide that I really do need to leave before I do something I regret. Like shattering the glass of that picture all over the ground.

CHAPTER 20

Elise

Walking next to my brother with my head ready to pound itself into a million pieces is harder than I thought it would be, but I manage to keep a neutral face on for him. The caffeine in the coffee he brought me is helping my hangover headache little by little, but I'm afraid not quickly enough that it will be gone before class starts.

I think the adrenaline surge and then fallout from Andries showing up while Dan was in my apartment has a lot to do with it, though, not just the alcohol. I had been so nervous the entire time my brother was in my home, acutely aware of his best friend milling around in my study just a single wall away from us, but somehow I pulled it off and got Andries out without him noticing what was going on. Now, my brother is going on and on about how much he enjoyed the engagement party and how happy he was that I came, but he's talking himself in circles, making it easy for me to just respond with noncommittal noises and single-word answers.

I wish I had time to stop at the campus corner store and grab some aspirin, but it looks like my brother isn't going to give me time to do anything at all. I can't cut and run because I'm too afraid of making him suspicious about being hungover or, God forbid, not being alone in my apartment earlier. I know I wasn't acting normal, but he seems oblivious thus far.

I check the time; I've got about five minutes until class starts, and the morning sun isn't doing my head any favors. Andries is bright-eyed and healthy looking, while I'm putting quite a lot of my faith in my oversized sunglasses to keep me from looking like the walking dead. I take another mouthful of coffee, and the tension in my head eases just the slightest bit more.

"So, yeah…" he finishes finally. "It was just really great to have all the family there together. I almost didn't notice that Mom and Dad didn't come."

I don't believe him fully, but whatever he has to tell himself to feel like this is all still going well is none of my business, so I just nod.

"I noticed you disappeared toward the end of the night, and I didn't see you until you were heading out. Was anything wrong?"

"Oh no," I say quickly, my heart rate kicking up. My own voice sounds squeaky to me. "I was just making my rounds to make sure I got to talk to everyone, is all."

He shrugs, apparently unconcerned with whatever I was doing that night. "I was pretty wasted, I'm not going to lie."

I can commiserate with him, considering how I'm feeling right now, but I'll never tell him so. "It was a long night. But…" I make a big show out of checking the time again. "I think we both have to be getting to class."

"You're right," he says after checking it himself. "Well, I guess we should get going, then."

In a moment of impulsiveness, I give my brother a quick hug. "Thank you for breakfast this morning. That was so thoughtful of you."

"Honestly, I brought it because I wanted to ask you something, but I was trying to gauge whether you would say no or not, but you've been a woman of few words this morning." He chuckles. "Studies must be getting to you. Anyway, I wanted to see if you would have dinner with Roxie and me at her place one of these days? I know you two haven't always gotten along, but she'd love to start fresh and put the past behind her. And so do I, honestly."

Guilt stabs at me, thinking of what Karl has asked me to do regarding Roxanne and my agreement to go along with his plan. Here is Andries, standing in front of me and telling me how much he and his fiancée want to mend fences and really have our families be a single unit. Andries wants to trust me again, but meanwhile, I'm scheming behind his back. I feel like a terrible sister.

I do need to get more information on what Roxanne is writing, though, and that kind of information is innocuous enough that she would probably tell me happily while also giving Dad and Karl some information to chew on while I stall on the whole escort thing.

"I'd love to. Just give me a heads up so I can make sure my schedule is clear with work and class stuff."

He grins, and he looks so young that it hurts my heart. Even though he's a year older than me, the last year has shown me that as the younger sibling, I can still be powerfully protective of my older brother. I don't want him to get hurt, and I want him to be happy… and I definitely don't want to be an agent in his misery in the future.

I hate being in the middle so much. How did I get here? I love all of my family, and I don't want to be pitted against anyone. Ugh…

"I'll shoot you a message when Roxanne and I pick out some options, but since you're the guest, you get the final say. Have a good day, El."

"You too," I say quietly, watching him leave for his own class through the dark tint of my sunglasses. Of course, Andries would start being the perfect brother as I start to scheme against his fiancée. Nothing is ever easy when it comes to this family.

I get to class with just enough time to spare so that I can interrogate my classmates for some ibuprofen. One girl I've only spoken to twice gives me one pill, but after a withering look, she drops two more into my hand.

"That time of the month?" she asks awkwardly, watching me swallow the pills one by one, dry.

"None of your business," I mutter, turning away. "Thanks for the pills."

She sneers in response, but I don't care. I've gotten what I needed.

I settle into my desk right as I feel my phone vibrate in my pocket. Pulling it out, I see there is a new message from Dan, and my body immediately feels warmer. Already starting to smile, I open it.

Dan: Managed to leave, but before doing so I snuck into your bedroom and stole your private diary.

Honestly, it wouldn't surprise me if Dan really did pull some trick like that, but I'm not exactly a diary type of girl.

Elise: Lol, I don't have a diary so good luck with that.

Dan: Oh crap. I hope it wasn't a notebook filled with classwork, then.

Elise: If it was, I'm sure you just took it so you would have an excuse to see me again soon.

Dan: Actually, just to piss you off.

Elise: Lucky for you, I'm the forgiving type. Hey… thanks again for last night. I shouldn't have drunk that much, and I'm embarrassed, but I really do appreciate you taking care of me.

Dan: It happens to the best of us, are you feeling any better?

My fingers hover over the phone screen as I consider my response, but just as I start to type something witty, my professor catches me unaware.

"Elise?" she asks, arms crossed and looking up at me from the lecture floor. My face burns with humiliation as the heads of all the other students turn in my direction, too. "Are you attending class today, or just wasting my time by catching up on your social life while I teach?"

"Sorry," I say, cringing at the embarrassment. "I'll focus."

The teacher harrumphs, but resumes teaching. I'm not usually a problem student, so I guess I'm allowed a slip up here or there without too much public shame.

Thinking about shame has my thoughts wandering back to my complicated feelings regarding the man I was just texting. Dan had cleaned me and comforted me, and made me feel a way that I'd never felt before. Sometimes, I'm ashamed that I am so affected by him, but other times I can't get the idea of what he and I can do at my party in a few weeks once we're alone out of my head.

It's so, so wrong for me to be so attracted to him, but I can't help it. It's such a strong, biological response that I couldn't stop it even if I wanted to. Truth be told, it's easy for me to savor the thoughts and phantom sensations he invokes in me, but much harder to think about bringing all of those things into the real world.

I put on a fake expression for the class to look like I'm paying attention, but behind my eyes all I'm thinking about is Dan, and all the trouble he's been causing me lately. Trouble, and pleasure, all rolled into the inconvenient package of my brother's best friend. What in the world am I going to do?

* * *

"Thanks for inviting me over," Tatiana says, wearing her own pair of dark glasses in a trendy tortoiseshell pattern to cover her bloodshot eyes. "I'd have just stayed in bed all day otherwise."

"You're most welcome, girl!" I wave for her to come in and we head to the kitchen where my Chinese takeout is waiting. "We need some junk food to beat this hangover."

"You bet," she answers, removing her big sunglasses.

It feels good to be finally home after a long day of classes, and I must say, I'm quite happy I didn't have to go to the office today; thank God, it was my day off.

I'm opening the paper bags of Chinese takeout and spreading the cardboard pagodas out on the counter table while Tati takes a seat on one of the stools.

"Considering how I'm feeling, I was sure that you must be feeling worse," I tell her. "I'm a lightweight, but you're on another level."

She laughs sardonically, pulling a bag of egg rolls toward her. "That's for sure. I know you're making fun of me but it's so true that it hurts. I've never been more hungover in my life."

"Have you ever even been drunk before?"

She shakes her head. "I've felt some tingles from drinks before, which I assumed meant I was drunk, but apparently I'm naïve because last night was something else altogether. I shouldn't have stayed with Mark and those girls for as long as I did."

"How long exactly?"

Tatiana bites into her egg roll, chews, and swallows before answering. "Two entire hours after you left."

I groan in sympathy, breaking my wooden chopsticks apart and rubbing them together. "I hope they were good company at least."

"I don't even remember the girls' names, but Mark was nice. He was more interested in you I think but once we got to talking about art we clicked. It was a good time, besides the hangover."

"I still feel bad for leaving you," I admit. "I wasn't in my right mind, either."

She shrugs, looking unbothered. "It's fine! We'll be more informed of our limits next time around."

"I hope so."

Between bites of fried rice, I get a text. I'm excited at the possibility that it might be Dan, and we could continue our casual flirtation from earlier today, but it's my brother instead.

Andries: *Hey! I talked to Roxanne, and she said to invite you over here for dinner this Thursday evening. Is that okay for you?*

I'm surprised because I was sure Roxanne didn't actually want to get together, but was instead doing it for Andries's sake.

Elise: *That should be fine, but I have to admit I feel a little awkward going to her place on my own. Can I bring someone?*

Andries: *Who did you have in mind?*

I know who I want to bring—Dan—but I have to bury the lead, so I don't make my brother suspicious at how quick I'm to suggest that his best friend accompany me. I look across the table at Tatiana, her glasses still on even though we are indoors, silently eating after applying a copious amount of soy sauce, and get an idea.

Elise: *The only two people who I know for sure are available that night are Tatiana and Dan.*

Andries: *Are you insane? Do NOT bring Tatiana to MY FIANCÉE'S FLAT. Just bring Dan so we avoid a diplomatic crisis, okay?*

I grin to myself at how easy he is to manipulate.

Elise: *Okay, okay! Dan it is. I'll text you to confirm after I ask him.*

I excuse myself, stepping out onto the patio and sinking into one of the chairs, calling Dan instead of texting him. The sun is down, and even though it's warm, the city is subdued on this lovely weeknight. I almost consider just inviting him over, but it's too much, too soon, so I settle for hearing his voice over the phone call instead.

"You are incorrigible," he says, picking up the call almost instantly. "A stalker, almost."

I wrinkle my nose. "Shut up, Dan. Come to dinner with me Thursday. Andries invited me to Roxanne's place, but I feel... weird."

"I don't solely exist to be your social buffer." He snorts. "Find someone else."

"Like who? Plus, he's your best friend. It will be fun."

Dan pauses, thinking it over no doubt. I wonder where he is, maybe lounging in bed, talking to me from the most private part of his home. It gives me a shiver of pleasure to think about.

"What part of '*we should stay away from each other for a while*' don't you understand? Last night was an accident, we were just in the same place by coincidence, but we shouldn't be purposefully making plans together."

I exhale, clos my eyes, and leaning back in my chair. "You know it's not a viable solution for us in the real world. Our lives and social circles are too entwined. We just have to learn how to deal with each other and keep our cool."

I can hear him laugh, holding the phone away from his face. Probably scraping a hand through his hair, frustrated by me. Oh well. "It's you that needs to keep your cool, not me. How typical for you to essay one thing and then change your mind the next day? The world doesn't revolve around you, you know."

"You sure act like it does when you're around me," I quip back, cool and casual. I hear him mutter something under his breath.

"Are you sure you wouldn't rather take Mark?"

"You told me to stay away from him. Plus, I think he and Tatiana hit it off. Are you going to be my plus one or not? I already told my brother I was going to ask you so I'm sure he'll want to know why you refused his generous invitation if you try to get out of it."

"Elise, you little—" He sighs, but mulls it over. "Fine. I'll go. But please restrain yourself from throwing yourself at me, okay? Have some class."

"Fuck you, Dan."

"Don't tempt me. I'll see you Thursday."

And with that, he hangs up, and I'm left with only the sound of chirping crickets and the city down below.

CHAPTER 21

Elise

I walk down the stairs of my building to greet Dan who is leaning against a vintage dark green BMW, one of the dozens of cars in the massive collection he shares with his father. He looks so good that it's almost obscene, in just a pair of dark wash jeans and a perfectly fitted olive shirt that makes his tan skin almost glow. With his hands in his pockets and the cocky smile on his face, I know he's in good spirits. Which is great because I'm uncommonly nervous.

I pull at my own clothes as I walk down to him; a simple pair of flowing beige pants and a fitted black sleeveless tank top, wondering if I'm either over or undressed. We're having dinner at their home, but Roxanne is still enough of a mystery to me that I can't pinpoint what exactly she considers dinner wear. Maybe I should grab a cardigan…?

"I can tell by your face that you're overthinking this," Dan tells me before I can even say a word. "We can still call it off if you want."

"No way. It's too late and I think you know how rude that would be."

Dan opens the passenger door for me, and I slide into the supple leather seat while he walks to the driver's side. The interior of the car smells like his cologne, something spicy and woodsy, and I take a huge breath of it before he's inside with me to notice.

"I've been thinking," I start as soon as he pulls out onto the road. "Do you think having dinner at their place is a power move on Roxanne's end? I can't help but think maybe she's doing it on purpose, so I'll be more on edge–"

"You're still way overthinking. Calm down. They're probably just more comfortable at home. It'll be a good time if you don't act as weird as you are right now."

"I am not acting weird."

"You are. Even weirder than normal, actually."

I slap his arm and he laughs, surprising me by grabbing the offending appendage and kissing my fingers lightly before letting go. I know my face flushes immediately, so I turn and face the window until it starts to subside. The energy in the car has changed, but I can't let it go in that direction anymore, no matter how much I want it to. There are a lot of things hinging on how well the evening goes.

"Listen, Dan… I didn't accept this invitation just out of some desire to mend fences or whatever."

He laughs, shaking his head. "I didn't figure you did. There's always something conniving going on in that pretty little head of yours. So, out with it."

"I'm really not trying to stir the pot," I insist. "I just want to get some more information from Roxanne on the memoir she's writing so I know how best to assist Dad with the fallout that the release will cause. I'm not going to try and stop her from writing it or anything like that. I just need to be prepared."

Dan rubs his chin with his hand, and it's then I notice his stubble, a shade darker than the hair on his head and grown in about a day's worth. I think about how it would feel against my skin and lips if I kissed him, but have to shut those thoughts away as soon as they appear to keep myself on track.

"That's understandable," he says finally. "As long as you aren't trying to interfere with her telling her story, then I suppose it's not the worst thing in the world for you to talk to her. It's none of my business, anyway."

"I didn't tell anyone about the cabaret, you know," I blurt out at the mention of "business". I feel guilty that I had almost told Dad what was going on with Roxanne still owning the cabaret, so I want to assure Dan that I'm not as much of a snake as people sometimes perceive me to be.

"I know, El," his voice softens and becomes comforting. "I think Roxanne actually respects that you're working so hard at your Dad's company and preparing for the future like you are. There really isn't a lot the two of you have in common, but being sharp and savvy when it comes to business and ambition is one of them. Lean into it."

"Into what exactly?"

He waves his hand in the air in front of him, trying to find the words. "Oh, you know. The boss babe stuff."

I laugh despite how anxious I am. "That sounds very stupid when you say it."

"You get the idea," he says in return, his tone humorous.

Dan doesn't know it, but his advice is helpful in other ways besides what he intends. I plan on leading with questions about the memoir, but the end game is to get Roxanne in the position where I can ask her about hiring escorts. If she thinks I commiserate with her about how hard it is to be a young woman in the corporate world, she might be more receptive to me.

We arrive and find parking, and I'm already surprised. It isn't the newest, most posh apartment building in Amsterdam, but it is one of the older, classic locations. Buildings are pressed up against each other, retaining their individual ity through color and different roof shapes. I didn't expect Roxanne to be able to afford somewhere like this, but it makes sense that she would want to live further away from the rowdier parts of the city. It overlooks the Dam square and must cost her a fortune.

Dan is holding a bottle of Malbec when he gets out of the car, a gift to add to dinner. I'm peeved that I didn't think of it, but glad that he's covering for us both. I link arms with him, and we enter, curiosity overcoming my nerves. I want to see what kind of place my brother and his unlikely fiancée now share, and if it's somewhere Andries can be comfortable for the long term. Somehow I doubt it, but I've been proven wrong multiple times before.

I guess this time is going to be another example of that because the penthouse is enormous. I don't even know Roxanne all that well, but I feel like if I had entered this place alone, I would have immediately been able to pinpoint it as her home. The penthouse glows in warm orange and yellow light, everything plush and unique in muted jewel tones. The carpet is soft beneath my shoes and looks to be an authentic Persian rug. There are scarves thrown over the brighter lights to filter everything through a more intimate lens. It's a home that has clearly been lived in for quite some time and carefully formed into the perfect sanctuary for its occupant.

There are touches of Andries, too. Newer, but no less obvious. Piles of books and poetry, bright tabs sticking out of the pages that he wants to return to later. His school bag is thrown haphazardly near the large velour sectional couch, looking slightly out of place. A humorous reminder that Roxanne is engaged to a college student. I suppress a snort of laughter.

As if summoned by my thoughts, the lady and gentleman of the house appear out of the kitchen, looking warm and happy to see us. I'm flummoxed by how relaxed Andries is; he doesn't hold any of that normal tension in his body that he usually has. No stiff, squared shoulders or perpetual frown. Instead, he's loose and comfortable in both his own skin and his new home. I feel another stab of guilt for all the ill things I've wished and worked for regarding this couple.

Roxanne looks equally happy, but there is some apprehension in her, and I get the feeling it isn't Dan making her feel that way. The only other guest in the home is me, and we don't have the best track record, so I can sort of see why she feels odd having me here. I need to make her feel otherwise, because she'll never open up to me if she still views me as some sort of threat or wildcard.

So, despite my desire to stay a few feet away, I come in to hug Andries quickly and then transition to doing the same with Roxanne. I can feel her jolt slightly when I go to embrace her, but her manners quickly take over and she does the same. We exchange air kisses above one another's cheeks, and I thank her for inviting me into her home.

"You have a really defined sense of style," I compliment her, motioning to the room around us. "It's very suited to you."

"Thanks. I've given Andries free range to add his own touches but that so far just seems to be a bunch of books and papers thrown all over the place," she jokes, smiling up at her fiancé. "He'll figure it out eventually, I'm sure."

They lead us into the dining area, which is connected right to the kitchen, and we sit around a wooden dinner table covered with a delicate lace tablecloth. When Andries tells us we're having homemade Italian pizza, I express concern about the tablecloth. Roxanne assures us it's washable and not to worry. A weird start to the evening, but empty of any negativity, so it's better than I could have asked for a week or so ago.

The pizza is even better than I could have ever expected. They had made the crust themselves. It's perfectly crispy and chewy, and the cheese and cured meats are wonderfully salty. I'm glad I didn't dress formally, laughing and dabbing at my mouth with my napkin for errant bits of sauce as we talk and eat.

We drink the wine that Dan has brought, but after a few nights ago, I keep my enjoyment of it to a minimum, sipping slowly only between large drinks of water. Andries and I talk about our classes while Dan and Roxanne look at each other, bemused.

"Enough about us, though. I'm sure your fiancée has heard more than enough about your schooling." My attention turns to Roxanne, and after taking a sip of my water, I ask, "What have you been up to?"

"Working on the memoir, mostly," she admits, and I cheer myself on internally at how easily she walks into the subject. "It's taking a lot more time than I expected. When you're living your life it goes by in a flash, but when you try and recall it all and put it to paper, you start to see how every little decision can mean so much. It's kind of exhausting to recall."

"I can imagine," I commiserate, nodding. "Is your publisher telling you what sort of things to include and what to leave out?"

I can see Dan looking over at me sharply as if he's trying to determine what my angle is exactly, but my brother is none the wiser. Roxanne shrugs one shoulder.

"They're giving me pretty much free rein right now. I'm sure that will change during the editing process, but I'm just trying to get it all down right now. I'm starting to see that things I find exciting are boring to readers and that the opposite is also true. So my current goal is to just actually write it all, and then parse through what is important and what isn't later on."

"Everything, huh? That must take forever," I say.

"Yeah, it does, but I have a good memory so at least I'm not struggling to remember everything." She smiles, somewhat self-consciously. "Sometimes I pretend to forget the more embarrassing things, though. No one needs to hear some of the more ridiculous things I did in my youth."

Dan snorts at this. "I feel you there."

I kick his ankle under the table for good measure, but he doesn't even flinch. Jerk. As if I need to be reminded how promiscuous he's been in the past. Even if it isn't any of my business, I'd rather not have to think about it.

Eventually, dinner ends, and Roxie has been completely vague about the contents of her novel up to this point. I understand her reluctance; she isn't sure about me yet, and she's probably been coached to not say much about it, so she doesn't give away all the juicy parts before publishing. Still, I need more information if this dinner is going to be worthwhile and provide me with enough tidbits to keep Dad and Karl quiet for a little while.

As Roxie and Andries take dishes away, insisting that Dan and I not lift a finger to help, I slide him a glance. "You're up. Go keep my brother busy."

He groans, rubbing his face. "She talked about the book plenty. Can't we just have a normal night with no weird scheming?"

"This is for my benefit *and* theirs, so just shut up and do your part, please."

He scowls at me, and I kick him under the table again. He snatches my ankle before I can connect, anticipating it, and my yelp of complaint silences when I feel his thumb make a small, lazy circle on the hollow of my ankle.

"I'm not going to take any more of that, Elise," he all but purrs, his hand traveling higher, fingers brushing the sensitive back of my knee. "Save that aggression for more appropriate places."

It's easy to get lost in his eyes when he's touching me, but I hear my brother's heavy footsteps not too far away, and I know I can't let myself get too caught up in Dan. I almost whimper in sadness when he drops my foot back to the ground, but after one more heated look, Dan pops up from his chair and greets Andries as he returns.

"Hey man, have you heard of this poet Robert Frost? I just read something of his recently and I really enjoyed it."

Andries stops and gives his friend a withering look. "Do you mean Robert Frost, one of the most famous poets of all time? Have *I* heard of Robert Frost?"

With a goofy, sort of empty look on his face, Dan nods. "Yeah. Something about gold and leaves."

Andries pinches the bridge of his nose and sighs. "Yes, Dan, I've heard of him. I did an entire set of poems myself based on his earlier work."

"Huh. You should show me sometime."

My brother jerks his head back toward the study. "Come on, then."

Roxanne joins me just as they turn the corner, and looks down at me where I'm still sitting, maybe unsure of what to do with her lone guest now. She sighs and turns to get back into the kitchen. "I'll get some dessert wine and we can go sit out on the terrace."

Unfortunately, this visit has ulterior motives, because otherwise, I might actually bond with Roxanne as we sit out and overlook the city, sipping sweet wine and simply enjoying the cool night air. My potential sister-in-law has a lovely home, great taste in wine, and seems to actually make my brother happy. I hate that things have to be the way they are, even if I don't really look forward to adding Roxanne to the family tree. This is all going to break Andries's heart in the end.

I take a deep breath to steady myself and get the courage to break the silence. "So about your memoir... is my brother helping much with that?"

She turns to me and seems to examine my face in profile, trying to discern what my angle is. "He is here and there, but some of the subject matter upsets him, as can be expected, so I work with an editor when I get really stuck."

"You don't think releasing it will upset Andries too?"

"I'm sure he doesn't love everything that I'm exposing, both about my own past and the state of the industry itself, but he's supporting me anyway."

Roxanne skates around the finer details that I need expertly, so I do the only thing that I'm sure will get me the answers I need. I ask her directly.

"I have been wondering... with the media still locked onto the case with Karl somewhat, will you mention his name and Patricia's name in your memoir, or use aliases?"

Now she narrows her eyes at me. "And why exactly do you want to know that?"

"Honestly Roxanne, Karl is still working at Van den Bosch industries, and you and I both know that it made my dad's company really take a hit both in the public eye and financially to deal with the accusations leveled against him. When your memoir is released, it's going to start that process all over again, and I don't want to have to deal with the same situation a second time."

"So you want me to cut parts of my own book out to make your workday easier?"

"No..." I tap my nails against the wine glass, looking for the right words. "Tell the story, just change the names. It will make things so much easier on me and it will prevent Dad from getting pissed about it all over again."

Roxanne exhales slowly, her gaze distant as she thinks it over. "You've been overly kind lately, and I can't help but wonder if this is some sort of trap that I'm falling into with you."

I shake my head. "No. I'm being direct with you," I tell her truthfully. "Dad won't fire Karl regardless, so your memoir will just cause another shit show for us lower-level interns. It's a big favor, I know, but clever readers will recognize who it is, anyway."

"Well…" She considers it, seeming to go back and forth again and again. "Only because you've been putting in the work to heal things with your brother. I'll change the names if it means that much to you."

I feel a surge of triumph, and I can't help the grin that comes over my face. "You're a lifesaver, Roxie, thank you. And… well, the secret about your cabaret is safe with me, too. I know it was kind of shady to use it against you to get an invite to the engagement party, but Dan—"

"It's fine," she says, cutting me off before taking another sip of her wine. "Thanks for keeping that secret, too. It will come up eventually, but I want it to be on my own terms. And technically I'm not escorting or running an escort business at all, so I don't think it's going to tank our relationship or anything like that. I just don't think your brother will like it much, and it actually means a lot to me to still have that minor connection to my old life."

This is my chance, and I know it. We're already on the subject and connections to her past, so asking about her old escort employees is a completely natural progression of the conversation. I could almost cheer at how perfectly it all worked out. I take in a breath, formulating my next words perfectly in my mind so I don't screw this up.

"I noticed a few of the girls that used to escort for you are working at the cabaret. Do you keep in contact with all the escorts you used to work with?"

"From time to time. I just want to make sure that the new manager is treating them right," Roxanne answers casually, not at all bothered by my question.

I open my mouth, heart pounding, to ask her if she could provide some girls for the event with Karl, but before I can say anything the patio door opens, and Andries and Dan come out. Their timing couldn't be worse, and I'm staring daggers at Dan, but no one seems to notice me. I was so damn close!

***

"How did it go? Your little talk with Roxanne?"

I glare at Dan across the car, but without any real vitriol. I hadn't expected to get everything accomplished tonight, and I definitely set up a good base to continue talking to Roxanne later. Even though it'd have been amazing to be done with it all right now.

"It'd have been better without your impeccable timing interrupting me, but at least I know that Roxanne isn't going to mention Karl or Patricia by name, so that's something," I say.

He whistles low in surprise. "Wow. That is an accomplishment. Have you told daddy dearest yet?"

"I texted him right before we started driving home," I tell him in a prim and proper tone, just to annoy him some more. "I haven't seen if he's replied yet."

I had planned on waiting until I was home to see what Dad has to say about the whole ordeal, but Dan bringing it up makes my curiosity spike, so I pull my phone out of my bag to check. As I had hoped, he responded, telling me that I'd done good work and that he's proud of me. I get that rush of pride from his response, but it's muted because I still don't feel great about my part in all of this. At least I'm on the way to being done with it all.

I read the message a few times before replying, keeping it vague and just telling him that I'm happy he approves. After tucking the phone away, I stay silent until Dan pulls up to the curb outside of my apartment, thinking over the night and what it all means.

On a whim, before we can bid farewell, I ask, "Do you want to come up?"

Dan chuckles. "Yes, but I can't. I'm determined to stay out of trouble when I can, for the next few months at least."

"Suit yourself." I shrug, planning on simply leaving and letting him watch me walk away and regret what he's missing out on, but on second thought, I sit forward and kiss him on the cheek.

Dan jumps, but his hand instinctively goes to my lower back to support me. I can feel the warmth of his skin through my shirt, and it makes me want to arch into him like a cat, but I resist, backing the rest of the way out of the car.

"What was that for?" he asks, voice husky.

"Thank you for keeping my brother distracted for me, is all. I'll see you at my birthday party."

He watches my every move with careful eyes. "I don't even know if I'm going to go yet."

"Don't you dare even think about not going!" I gasp.

"Why do you even care about me going if you have all your friends like Tatiana there? Plus, Mark's coming too, so you don't even need me."

Dan sounds annoyed when he mentions Mark's name, but I don't press him just to get a rise. Instead, I tell him the truth and leave him to mull it over all alone.

"Because," I start, giving him a little finger wave as I stand up straight on the curb outside the car. "You're the only person whose presence matters."

I hear him sputter my name as I walk away, and it takes all of my willpower not to turn around and go back to him. This time, I think he would accept me with open arms, or maybe even come inside with me, but I want him to really consider my words. They are from the heart.

CHAPTER 22

Dan

Andries isn't exactly the person I want to be driving through the countryside in my favorite convertible, but my best friend is happier than I've ever seen him, and his energy is infectious.

We're on the way to meet his grandmother and the wedding planners at her estate. Margaret Van Dieren is an intimidating woman, but no one can say she doesn't love her grandchildren, and I think she's looking forward to all of this just as much as Andries is. She likes me pretty well, too, so it should be a good time either way.

The Jaguar moves effortlessly down the road, cherry red and glinting in the sun. We're alone on the back country road, and the wind smells clean as it buffets us both.

"I could have driven," Andries comments, speaking loudly enough to be heard over the wind. "But I think I like your ride better."

"I always have better cars," I remind him. "There's nothing quite like the classics."

"I bet you don't say that in the dead of winter when I have heated seats and you don't." He laughs. "By the way, thanks for coming with Elise to dinner last night. I know she brought you as a buffer because she was uncomfortable, but it was nice to have you anyway."

"As if I'd turn up an opportunity to be wined and dined on someone else's tab."

"I know you're joking, but it really was amazing to have you both there. Elise and Roxanne started out roughly, and for a time there I didn't think they'd ever get along, but Elise really has been doing her best to fix things. I never expected that behavior from her, she's been so selfish in the past, but I have to admit I'm proud of her. So I just wanted to say thanks for playing your part, too, even if it is just to come and hang around so people don't feel as awkward."

It's so easy to just make a joke and keep things casual, but Andries is going through a transformation as we work our way toward his wedding, and I know he's being sincere. I clap him on the shoulder and squeeze. "Thank you, friend. I'm glad to be a part of everything, too, even if it is your sister learning that she can't be a straight-up brat anymore."

Andries chuckles. "She'll get there, eventually. Speaking of Elise, though, are you going to her birthday party next Saturday?"

I'm immediately transported back to the other night, listening to her telling me that I'm the only person that matters, and walking away from me. I had wanted to grab her back, make her explain what exactly she meant, but I just had to let her walk away, her confession ringing in my ears.

"Uh, well, she invited me, but I don't know if I'm going to go." Andries starts to ask why, but I cut him off, desperate to change the subject. "I guess now is as good of a time as ever to tell you that I'm planning a bachelor trip for you the first week of July, so don't book anything, okay?"

Andries sits up straighter. "What! You have to tell me more than that, Dan!"

I grin. "Nope. It's going to be a surprise, but I promise you that it will be the time of your life."

"Well…" He considers it. "Can I bring Roxanne?"

I glance at him quickly before returning my attention to the road. "You want to invite your fiancée to your bachelor trip?"

"Yeah. I'd want it to be the same if it was the other way around. Is that okay?"

"Uh, sure. I guess that's fine." It kind of ruins the vibe of it being a boys' trip to have her along, but whatever makes Andries happy. It's his wedding, after all. Knowing him as well as I do, he'll probably invite the whole Feng family to come over last minute, so better not to invite anyone until we get closer to our departure date.

Margaret's estate isn't too far from the city, but it's a long way up a winding driveway that has me working the gearshift overtime. Once we come around the last bend, the estate comes into view, and it's every bit as impressive as I would expect from a woman like Margaret. It's sprawling, multiple stories, and built out of pale, almost white stone. It's easy enough to miss the color of the stone, though, with all the windows that cover almost every inch of open space. Inside the whole place must be lit by natural light, and I'm sure it's stunning. Margaret isn't a woman that does anything by half measures, so it doesn't surprise me that her place is as lavish as it is.

There's a small pond in front of the house, and the water is crystal clear with a few moorhens lazily floating on the surface. Unlike a lot of the newer estates I've visited, there are clear signs that Margaret's property has had time to mature; ivy climbing up one corner, lily pads on the water, and a willow whose leaves droop nearly to the ground.

Margaret's valet meets us in the front as I pull around the circular driveway, a twinkle in his eye when he gets a look at what I'm driving and I hand him the keys.

"Don't get any wise ideas," I warn him, half joking.

"Of course not, sir."

Andries leads me through the home, which is every bit as sumptuous as I had imagined with artwork in heavy frames and vaulted ceilings, some even sporting murals themselves. All the natural light has the interior warm, and causes everything, including myself, to cast long lanky shadows. I follow my friend, wondering what it would be like to grow up in a place like this where it seems like nothing is ever out of place, and thinking about if Andries had any fond memories here or if it had just been a litany of adults telling him not to touch things over and over. My family has money now, but they are the first generation to be wealthy, so I was raised with a lot of the habits that my formerly middle-class grandparents had instilled into my parents. I've considered before that the stuffier upbringing that the Van den Bosch children have had might be a reason they've both grown to have such noticeable quirks. Introverted, overly serious Andries and Elise, a siren using every tool available to her in order to crawl her way to the top. What would they have been like if they hadn't been raised the way they had?

I close the lid on that train of thought as we exit onto the veranda, the glass walls wide open for the season allowing the breeze to blow through freely. Margaret is having tea, with two places set for Andries and me, and she happily waves us over when she spots us.

"Hello, boys! Come, come, sit with me. I have tea for us."

Andries leans down to give his grandmother a kiss on her cheek, and I follow suit, knowing that Margaret considers me part of the family at this point. Her sophisticated fragrance hits my nostril, and if I didn't know who she was, I wouldn't have guessed that she was any older than her mid-fifties. It's either that the Van Dieren women age gracefully, or Margaret is just too stubborn to get old.

Andries and I settle in, and the maid flits over to fill our cups and place orange cranberry scones on tiny ceramic plates in front of us. The tea is citrus ginger—not as fragrant as the blooming tea I prefer, but enjoyable, nonetheless. I've taught myself to navigate these careful social situations as if doing so has run in my family for generations, but I still feel like I'm acting sometimes.

"How are you two doing?" Margaret asks, sitting her cup down on her saucer. "That was quite the engagement party."

"Yes," Andries agrees, giving a quick smile in appreciation. "It took me a few days to get all the alcohol out of my system, but it was a brilliant event. I couldn't have asked for anything better."

"I have to say, I had never been to any sort of events at the O'Brian's before, but my grandson is right when he says it went brilliantly. I was very impressed with it all."

I smile at the compliment, but something inside me still cringes at the subtle "*you're not like us*" message buried in what Margaret had just said. I don't even think she meant it, but it just comes so naturally to these people to be aware when things just aren't quite up to par. Thankfully, the engagement party was so successful that I have a feeling it earned my parents and me quite a bit of respect we hadn't held before.

"The planners should be here shortly," I inform them after checking the new notification popping up on my phone.

"Andries," Margaret says, catching his attention once again. "Have you decided if you're going to invite your parents yet or not? Or are the three of you still at odds?"

He shakes his head. "No, I'm not inviting them. They've said some reprehensible things about my bride-to-be, and they refuse to give me their blessing. All of those things considered, I can't believe that inviting them to the wedding itself will be a good idea. They didn't even come to the engagement party."

"And, you're hurt, of course," Margaret adds.

Andries looks away, his expression tight. "I guess I am hurt, yes."

"You have every right to be," his grandmother points out. "They can't see past the expectations of what they wanted from your life, so much so that they can't accept the fact that it is indeed *your* life. Just keep an open mind in case they have a change of heart at the last minute. I do believe that as the date gets closer, your mother is going to wake up and realize how she's ostracizing her oldest child." I look at my best friend, nodding mindlessly as his grandmother speaks. "Your father, on the other hand…" She lets her words trail off, and lets out a breath, unsure whether to continue or not. "Well, I don't know about him, but we will see."

I'm ready to jump in and change the subject because my friend is looking sadder by the second, but the maid provides a welcome distraction by announcing the arrival of the wedding planners.

Andries stands and offers his grandmother his hand, letting her link her arm through his as we head out into the garden to meet everyone. Margaret's gardens are a sight to behold, full of prize-winning roses that are probably older than I am, their thorns long, stems thick, and petals bright.

The design team is *huge*, including the planners I had hired for the engagement party and Margaret's picks for additional help. There's enough of them to make a football team almost, but I can see Andries breathe a sigh of relief. It's one more thing off his shoulders. Well, one dozen things maybe, considering how many of them there are.

The chatter between them all becomes so quick-fire that I can't keep up, not that I want to anyway. My part has been done with the engagement party and the upcoming bachelor trip, so I happily shoulder this one over to Margaret. The older woman looks like she's glowing as she leads them around, giving expectations and ideas, and it's now that it hits me that this is her first grandchild to wed, and she gets to help mastermind the whole thing. Even more, the wedding will be at her estate. Margaret must be over the moon.

I fall back and give them some space, following at a bit of a distance but far enough away that I don't have to give my opinion on anything. It's a stellar day to just enjoy the sun and air, my hands shoved in my pockets and my face turned to the sky. Lately it's just been one thing after the other; temptation from Elise, guilt about hiding it from Andries, loneliness knowing that I'm going to be one of the only ones in my group of friends left single and living on my own... so it's nice to set it aside for a while and just stretch my legs.

After about thirty minutes, I feel my phone vibrate in my pocket. I consider ignoring it, but Andries, Margaret, and the design team have stopped to discuss something, so I go ahead and check it out. I have one message, and it's from the contact that I asked to get the identity of the man in the picture with Elise. Up until now, I'd almost forgotten that I'd even requested the identification, having been in a fit of emotion and just woken up when I did. But I'm still interested to see who she could be so casual and touchy with.

Hey! So the guy in the photo is none other than Johan from the House of Bentinck. Half-Dutch and Half-British, his family descends directly from the British royal family. He lives in England, though. That's everything I was able to find. He doesn't have much of an online presence.

I let the information sink in for a minute, considering what it means. Ahead of me, Margaret is holding court over the most sought-after and expensive wedding planners in the country while her grandson stands beside her, and it's easy to see how they were born into this world. Just like Johan Bentinck. Me, on the other hand... I'm a different story. Margaret, Andries, and most important to me, Elise, are all nobility. When she chooses a boyfriend, it won't be someone like me; an up-and-comer. It will be someone like this Johan, who is blue blood to his core. Royalty, even.

It's just another tidbit of information that makes me feel like an outsider, even though none of these people have ever treated me as such. It's all in my head, but I can't help that.

I resist the urge to look up Johan, simply pocketing my phone and staring ahead, wondering what my next move should be. Going to Elise's birthday will be a mistake, just like everything that happened in the study was a mistake. The question is, am I strong enough to tell her no?

Up ahead, Andries laughs loud enough that I can hear him, and I get the empty feeling of loneliness again. He has his wedding to the love of his life to look forward to, and what do I have? Because to me, it almost feels like nothing at all.

* * *

I get home late in the evening, tired even though I did little more than spectate the entire time. The few days after the engagement party have given me some time to relax, but now I have to shift into the next gear and start working on the bachelor trip. Tonight, though, I don't want to think about any of that. I just want to have a drink and unwind.

I'm barely inside when my maid scurries over, something clutched in her hand. I inhale slowly, trying to not get annoyed at being bothered the very second I enter my home. She holds out the envelope, thick and square, and I pluck it from her fingers.

"This was hand delivered today, sir. The deliverer stressed that it's important that you receive it as soon as possible."

"Thank you," I say absentmindedly, gingerly tearing the side of the envelope and letting the thick card-stock slide out into my hand.

Gold leaf filigree decorates the borders of the invitation, with the calligraphy words being handwritten in ink, not printed. Before I even begin to read it, I know who it's from. In fact, I feel like I can even smell her perfume, sweet and floral, wafting off of it.

You're cordially invited to celebrate the 18th birthday of Miss Elise Van den Bosch
June 14th at the Van den Bosch Estate, 8 pm sharp
Formal dress, all white

I run my fingers across the surface of the paper, feeling the gold leafing beneath my fingers and thinking about what the hell I'm going to do now. Still, holding this invite in my hands and thinking of all the things she and I could do together at this party makes me smile despite myself.

I hold it up, snapping a picture of the invite and sending it to Elise.

Dan: *Just received your invitation. Not sure that I can attend, though. Sorry.*

I pocket the phone and set the invitation on the console table, planning to go sit on the terrace and enjoy some tea. Maybe even a joint if I can't relax. But of course, Elise has other things in mind, no matter how many miles away she is. As soon as I step foot into my bedroom, my cell phone rings.

"Hello, Elise."

"What in the hell do you mean you aren't sure if you can attend? You *are* attending. I already spoke to my dad about it and we're planning on you spending the night in one of the guest rooms." She pauses, sounding thoughtful. "Or maybe another bedroom. I'll see. Either way, you're coming."

I don't point out the euphemism, sitting down on my bed for what I'm sure is going to be a drawn-out conversation. "Well, I'm still assessing whether it's the best way to spend my evening…"

"You better wrap that assessment up as soon as possible, then, because you're not getting out of it."

"What is with all the people in your family being so damn overbearing? I spent the afternoon with your grandmother, and I think she nearly had a few of the wedding designers near tears."

Elise laughs, and it's the sweetest sound I've heard all day. "I'm sure Oma Margaret would take that as a compliment, actually."

"I have no doubts about that…" I chuckle. "But Elise, you should have seen your brother. He's so excited about this wedding that it's almost humorous. I don't know what kind of conniving plans you still have in the works, but I hope you might reconsider. He's truly happy."

I hear her sigh as I kick up my feet and lie down. "I want him to be happy, too, you know. But not just happy now; happy for the rest of his life… I'm just not convinced Roxanne is the woman he's destined to spend his entire life with. It scares me that he's being impulsive."

"I know, I know… but you have to let him live his life, and we all have to work on trusting him a little to know what's best for himself. If I can do it, you can too."

"But you liked Roxanne from the beginning."

"You would have too," I point out, as I sit up against the headboard of my bed. "Had you just given her the chance and looked past her profession. I mean, the two of you are getting along swimmingly now that you've let bygones be bygones."

"Swimmingly is pushing it," she says, deadpan, and I can't help but laugh.

"Anyway… have you decided to give in and invite Andries to your birthday? You know he would love to be there for you."

"Actually, for the sake of politeness, I already did," she says haughtily. "But you know it doesn't matter because he won't want to come to the estate, and no one will let him in even if he does. So you can get off my back about it."

"You're trying to sound mean, but I know you love him, so you aren't fooling me anymore, Ice Princess."

I hear her exhale, and there is what I can only guess is real affection in her tone. "You know me so well, huh?"

"I do," I tell her sincerely, smiling.

Elise makes a sound like she wants to say something, but stops mid-breath. I can almost see her pursed lips in my mind when I close my eyes, wishing she was right in front of me instead of somewhere else much too distant.

"I've got some schoolwork to finish," she says finally. "But Dan, will you promise me that you're really coming to my party? No more second guesses?"

I chuckle, knowing how easy it would be to continue to tease her, but there is a note of vulnerability in the way she asks that stops me, so I give her an honest answer. The one I know she wants, and that I wasn't sure of until this very second. "Yes, Elise, I'll be there."

She sighs in relief. "Finally. I'll see you then, Dan."

"Bye, Elise."

I lay my now-silent phone on my chest and cross my arms behind my head, staring at the ceiling. She's been so insistent on my attendance that I can't help but wonder if she has something in mind. Especially since she's already planned for me to stay overnight at the Van den Bosch estate. Could she want to repeat what happened in my study? Or even more, maybe?

My cock swells at the very thought of it, but I close my eyes and bite the inside of my cheek to stop myself from getting too worked up. I want her. Of course, I want her. I have for years, but if we both give in to this thing between us, there will be no going back.

Rationally, I know I shouldn't let her pull me closer, but the more time I spend with Elise, the smaller and quieter the rational voice inside me becomes. For better or worse, I'm going to the damned party.

CHAPTER 23

Elise

"You've been back to check yourself like a dozen times now," Tatiana hisses. "You look incredible. Come on. It's your own birthday party you're missing!"

I thumb my bottom lip one more time, trying to even out the red lipstick that I can't help but feel self-conscious about. Tati has told me again and again that it looks perfect, and I'm just seeing flaws where there aren't any, but I just don't believe her. Everything has to be perfect. *I* have to be perfect because Dan promised that he'd be here. And just like I planned, my brother isn't.

I've spent so much of my life working toward the goals of my father, my brother, and everyone else in the world. This night is for me.

I take a step back and look myself over one more time, sucking in a breath and blowing it out slowly. I agonized over my dress all afternoon, going back and forth between the three options that I purchased, but finally, I'd settled on one that was both sexy but didn't scream "fuck me" so obviously as the other two. I keep having to resist the urge to run up to my room and change, but I still think I made the right selection.

The pure white silk flows in a shimmering curtain down my legs, looking almost demure until I walk, and the thigh high slits on each side of the skirt become apparent. My neckline is asymmetrical, with no sleeve on one shoulder, and the other arm covered by a bell-shaped gauzy sleeve that ends at my wrist. Everything fits perfectly, my bra working overtime to push my cleavage up so just a hint of it is visible. With my hair straightened and slicked back, minimal eye makeup, and a bold red lip, I look older than I ever have before. I barely recognize myself when I look in the mirror.

Tatiana, standing just behind me, puts her hands on my shoulders and squeezes. "I don't know who you're trying so desperately to impress, but their jaw is going to hit the floor when they see you. If you spend all night back here, they won't be able to check you out, so let's go."

"Okay, okay," I exhale, straightening my posture. "You're right. Let's go."

The night is glittering. There's really no other way to explain it. Lights have been strung through the trees and across every available pole and surface, giving the entire backyard and pool area an ethereal, unearthly feeling. Close to the house, there is a bar staffed to the max, constantly mixing my signature birthday drink, the Kir Royale, as well as whatever else anyone orders. There's a buffet of finger foods, but nothing too messy that might ruin everyone's white clothing, as well as servers floating through the crowd with trays full of food and drinks. Closer to the pool, which is full of floating, lit tea lights is the DJ booth—an area in the grass marked by thin, tall torches being used as the dancefloor. Everything, and everyone, looks spectacular. My parents have really outdone themselves, but my thanks to them will have to come later because there is only one person on my mind who I want to see right now.

Dan.

These past weeks I've shied away from admitting to myself why it was so important that he come to the party, but now that the night is here, I have to look the reasoning in the face. I want to continue what he and I started in that study. I want everything Dan has to offer me tonight, body and soul, and I've done everything I possibly can to ensure that we won't be interrupted this time. Every single person at this party could leave and it wouldn't matter to me, as long as he's here.

The idea of losing my virginity to him makes my pulse flutter and my chest feel tight with both nervousness and anticipation. I force myself to calm down, not wanting to get ahead of myself. I haven't even confirmed whether he's here or not, and I don't want it to be too obvious that I'm as excited to see him as I really am.

I pass the bar and buffet, snatching a Kir Royale from a passing server and plucking the raspberry out of it, popping it in my mouth and crushing it between my teeth. It's sweet and tart as I chase it with the drink itself. There's a table with towering white, silver, and gold gifts, and I make a mental note to have one of the staff make a list of gift givers so I can send out thank-you notes later. I certainly won't be sitting and opening them all in front of everyone like a child.

Once the first guest notices me, my discreteness goes out the window. I'm swarmed by friends and well-wishers, pulled from person to person to take pictures, chat, and even dance with. It's a whirlwind, and the drink in my hand continues to disappear and reappear as a full glass, but even though I'm still focused on finding Dan, I'm enjoying myself. There are people from school, family, friends of the family, and people my age that I've met through camps and trips throughout the years. Some faces are as familiar to me as the back of my hand, and others I haven't seen in years. I'm touched that so many people have made the trip here to celebrate me, and the embraces I exchange with everyone are real and full of affection.

I remain on the lookout for Dan the entire time I'm being passed through the crowd, but he's managed to elude me so far. Every once in a while I'll see a set of broad shoulders or a bright grin and think it's him, but he's like a phantom, and I can never pin him down.

Finally, after what seems like forever, I spot him standing next to the pool, a drink in hand as he chats with one of my classmates. My mouth goes dry as I rake my eyes over him. The moment has finally come, and now that it's here, I'm more nervous than I thought I'd be.

Dan is dressed in an ivory linen suit, the shirt underneath it unbuttoned to the third button so I can see the strong lines of his neck, where I'm dying to place my lips. Someone is talking to me at my side, but I can't hear a word they are saying. My head is buzzing.

I leave my current company behind, walking with slow, single-minded determination toward him. As if there is some sort of tether between us, he turns when I'm still far away, watching me approach like I'm a lioness and he's the lion. There is no one else around us once we lock eyes; we might as well be completely alone, we are so focused on one another. He drinks me in as I close the gap between us, and when I reach him, he takes me into his arms like a practiced dance.

If my head had been fuzzy from the drinks, it all becomes crystal clear now. There is the warmth of his skin, the smell of him; evergreen and spice, and the way he holds me against him as if I'm the most precious thing in the world. When he leans in, his lips brushing the shell of my ear, he whispers, "Happy birthday, El."

I shiver. It's a phrase I've heard hundreds of times tonight already, but from Dan it sounds like foreplay. Like pillow talk, almost. The words don't matter... it's the promise behind them.

"Thank you," I stutter as he pulls away, keeping his hands on my upper arms as he does so. "For a minute there I thought you didn't come."

"You made me promise, remember? You didn't really give me a choice, and I didn't want to hear your complaints if I didn't show."

"Have you ever been serious a day in your life?" I ask, wrinkling my nose.

"I can if you want me to be," he replies, lowering his voice to that seductive timbre again... the one that seems to race across my nerves every time he speaks.

"I do," I respond, swaying toward him. "There are so many empty rooms. Do you want—"

"Elise!" I hear from behind me. At the same time, Dan drops his hands, and I turn to shoo away whoever dares to bother me right now. I've been entertaining party guests this entire time; can't I have a moment to myself?

It's Tatiana calling for me, though, and she isn't going to take no for an answer. I can see it in her posture, and the harried way she grabs my hand and tries to pull me away. "There you are! Everyone is looking for you and they're driving me crazy. Come on, you need to address your *adoring* fans!"

"Tati," I say, trying to shake her hand off. "I don't want to right now. I'm busy."

"It's fine," Dan says, an annoyingly mischievous smirk on his face. "I'll catch up with you later."

My stomach drops, as he gives me a wave and starts to walk away. "No!" I protest. "I just found you!"

"Then it looks like you'll have to find me again, huh?" He shrugs. "I'll catch you around."

I could shove Tatiana in the pool, I'm so annoyed, but she seems completely oblivious to how upset I am, leading me to a group of our peers from school who all greet me enthusiastically. I don't even have time to feel bad for myself before I have to plaster on that fake smile again and thank everyone for coming to my party. At this rate, I'm beginning to think I shouldn't have had a party at all. It's almost more stressful than it is fun.

I break away for some time to talk to my Grandma Margaret and my aunts, who gush over how grown up I look and how much I resemble my mother, who also makes her way over to the small group of us. I can breathe here among family, even relax a little, but I still haven't gotten what I want most of all: Dan, alone.

Now that I've apparently said hello to every single person at the party, I can move through it unhindered without being pulled aside every five seconds. I break away from my family and begin the hunt, wanting to corner Dan before we have my cake because I'm too afraid he'll just leave during all the commotion. It's like when I'm not in front of him, he can leave me alone and be rational about everything, but when I'm with him, his walls crumble. Tonight, that's exactly what I want... Dan to crumble for me.

It's fully dark now, no more gloaming, and everything is lit by the lights overhead. It makes it harder to see faces, and I search for long minutes with no success. I'm becoming frustrated and even scared that he might have left the party early to get away from this chemistry between us. If he's still here, why is he so hard to find? Where could he be hiding?

I spot a group of guys that I recognize from college and parties that Dan has thrown before. I make my way to them, and after some small talk, I get right to the point.

"Have you all seen Dan anywhere?" I ask, trying to sound as innocent as possible. "He told my brother he was coming but I haven't seen him."

"I saw him playing billiards inside," one of the guys informs me. "That was just a few minutes ago. I bet he's still there. Do you want me to go and call him for you?"

I shake my head, just waving them off. "That's fine, I will head that way myself. Thanks!"

Inside, there are much fewer people. It figures Dan would be in the billiard room, since he knows the layout of the house, while everyone else was still outside. I almost feel bad because of all the effort he's putting into keeping distance between us, but he has to know why I wanted him here so badly. If he wants to reject me outright, he can, but something tells me that won't be the case.

Just like I was told, Dan and two other men are playing billiards. He's discarded his suit jacket, and the sleeves of his shirt are rolled up. When I enter, he's bent over the table, cue aimed, and a lock of hair falling over his forehead. He's concentrating, his brows drawn together, right before he shoots. The balls click together loudly, one solid color ricocheting into a hole, and he stands up straight. Then, he notices me standing in the doorway, and his casual, fun demeanor changes instantly.

"Hey guys," he says to the other two playing with him, "Why don't you get out of here? I'll catch up with you later. The birthday girl and I have something to discuss."

"But we're right in the middle of a game," one complains. "Can't you just wait?"

"Get out," Dan repeats between clenched teeth, his tone more threatening. "Before I throw you out physically."

There's some huffing and puffing, but both men gather their things and leave, giving me quick apologies as they pass by my side. Once we are left alone, I cross my arms and look at Dan, waiting to see what he has to say.

"So you've tracked me down." He sighs. "You're relentless."

I can't help but smile. "I know."

I move around the billiard table, and Dan does the same on the other side, both of us circling like sharks.

"Have you been avoiding me?" I snap.

To my astonishment, he goes to the door, but instead of leaving as I was afraid he would, he pulls it shut and locks it. And just like that, we're completely alone. "I have been...."

"Why?" I demand. Unlike the night I had drank too much, and he had put me to bed, we're both sober, and well aware of what we both feel for each other at this moment.

The tension in the air is so thick it could be cut with a knife. My body is already getting warm, preparing for his touch, and every inch of my skin feels needy and ready for him. Once the lock clicked over, it was like everything changed. Now those things that I've been dreaming about with Dan are right here at my fingertips.

He moves in until I have to take a step back, my calves hitting the billiard table. He puts his hands on either side of me, pressing against the wood and leaning his weight forward. Our bodies connect, and it's all I can do not to moan outright. It feels so much like the night in the study that if I close my eyes, it'd almost be like I am right there again.

"Because," he starts, breathing so close to my skin that I get goosebumps, "you have no idea how badly I want to kiss you right now."

His eyes are boring into mine, intense and fiery. "Then why don't you?" I ask, tilting my face up to him.

"Your brother will kill me."

"He isn't here," I point out, arching forward to press myself into him even further. He sucks in air between his teeth.

"I gave my word to him that I'd never touch you," he grits out, his hips unconsciously moving so the hard length of him is settled between my thighs. This time I do moan, but just softly.

"He's not even here, Dan," I complain, wrapping my arms around his neck.

Now, his face is next to mine. Into my ear, he growls. "Drop it."

I swallow hard, nearly shaking. I want him so much, but he's playing hard to get, so I search for another topic. Anything to keep him from pulling away from me. "Sorry to interrupt your game," I tell him, nodding toward the table as I drop my hands to my sides.

He follows my gaze, and then looks back up at me, one eyebrow raised. "You want to finish it?"

I frown in confusion. "What?"

"You want to finish the game with me? You can be stripes since I was solids."

I laugh. "Dan, I've maybe played twice in my entire life."

"It's okay…" I could scream when he backs away from me, heading to the cue rack. He pulls a cue down and tosses it to me. I catch it with both hands, still feeling unsure and way too turned on to be playing fucking billiards. "I'll teach you."

"That really isn't what I had in mind when I was looking for you," I admit, watching him chalk the end of his cue.

"Don't worry," he rumbles, looking at me with a hooded gaze. "You'll like it. I promise."

"Dan—"

"How about this? If you win, you can ask me to do whatever you want."

Now, my interest is piqued. My grip on the cue tightens. "Whatever I want?"

"That's what I said," he confirms.

"And if you win?"

"I get to do the same, of course." He gives me a Cheshire grin. Just like that, I'm on board. Either way, I think he will be touching me, and that's all I can think about.

"Fine," I say, tilting my chin up stubbornly. "Let's do it."

I don't know how to play billiards. Honestly, I don't even know the rules, but from the first play, it's clear Dan is throwing the game to let me win. This information makes me giddy because it means he'll give me whatever I want from him. Still, the game is more enjoyable than I would have thought, and after a moment of play, I'm no longer in any rush to end it.

Dan shoots wildly, missing most of the time and just shrugging it off as if it wasn't on purpose. When it's my turn to go, he comes up behind me, wrapping his body around mine as if he's my shadow, his arms outstretched and guiding each of my shots. Ball after ball sinks down into the holes.

"It's not fun if you're not actually playing," I tell him. His face is only inches from mine as he helps me make the shot. He grins, pulling back just enough to nip at my shoulder. I make a small noise of surprise.

"Are you saying this isn't fun?" he quips, and I can feel his lips moving against my skin.

"Maybe a little," I concede.

Once the last ball goes in, and I win officially, the already tense energy in the room becomes downright suffocating. We both know exactly what is going to happen next. Lust is so heavy in the air that I feel like I can reach out and touch it.

Dan is still embracing me from behind to help me with the last shot, but as soon as the last ball disappears I let the cue roll out of my hands and onto the table. Dan wraps his arms around my middle, his mouth going to the back of my neck, pulling my hair aside and peppering the skin there with kisses.

"So…" he says between the presses of his lips. "What do you want as your prize, Miss Elise?"

It'd be all too easy to stay just like this and let him touch me, kiss me, at his leisure, but I'm the winner. It's time for me to take what I want into my own hands. So I turn in his embrace, pressing my hands against his chest and locking eyes with him.

"I want you."

And, without wasting any more time, Dan closes the small gap between our lips and kisses me with such intensity that I gasp. His mouth is unforgiving, his arms around me so tight that I can barely breathe. It doesn't matter though. I need no air, food, or water. Just this kiss to sustain myself. I feel like I might die without it.

Dan's tongue sweeps across the seam of my lips, and I open for him without hesitation, letting him sweep into my mouth and claim me. I moan, hands pushing up the back of his shirt just to feel his skin in any way I can. His grip around my waist tightens, and he lifts me onto the billiard table. On instinct, I wrap my legs around him and pull him into me, until I can feel his erection through the thin fabric of my dress. If I had thought I felt out of control when I was drunk, it was nothing compared to this. Feeling him against me makes me almost frantic with need.

Moving with confidence, Dan runs his fingertips down my shoulders and arms, then back up again, leaving goosebumps in their wake. He gently cradles my head while his lips and tongue map out every inch of my lips, jawline, and neck, and when he sucks on the tender flesh behind my ear, it sends a surge of pleasure down my spine. My core is aching, and I feel drenched. Almost embarrassingly so, but I've been wanting this for *so long*.

"More," I moan, when he nips at my bottom lip again, refusing to touch me in the places where I need it most. "Please, Dan."

I've managed to undo the buttons of his shirt, and being able to feel the bare skin of his chest without him pushing my hands away is incredible. I want to kiss him all over, the same way he has been doing for me, but I won't stop at the neckline. No, I want to taste all of him.

Dan pinches my chin between his thumb and forefinger, looking deeply into my eyes. "We haven't done anything we can't come back from yet," he tells me, his tone stubbornly serious. "If we go any further, though, we've crossed a line."

"But you said if I win—" I wiggle against him, and he surges forward into me. "I can have anything I want. And I want you."

"You're going to be the death of me, you know that, right? Until this very moment, I have been a man of my word. A man my best friend could trust. But here I am ready to break any and every promise I've ever made just to have you."

"Then have me. I'm going to lose my mind if you don't do something, Dan," I say with a whimper.

He pulls away, but only enough to cup my breasts through my dress. My nipples are already hard, but when he thumbs them, it's enough to make me want to jump out of my skin. The pleasure from it is impossibly sharp. "Something like this?" he asks.

"Yesss," I respond, thrusting myself into his hands even more.

With slow, practiced caresses, Dan teases my nipples while he takes my mouth in a much slower, deep kiss. It feels so, so good, but as much as I want to continue on this pathway, I'm aching between my legs for him so much that it's almost painful.

Again, I say, "More. I need more."

Dan doesn't disappoint, one hand dipping between my legs, under the slit of my dress, until he can press the heel of his palm against my white lace panties. "You want me to touch you here?" he asks as if there is any doubt.

"You know I do," I whine.

"Right here…" his fingers push the damp fabric aside before grazing the swollen, sensitive flesh beneath. "On your pussy?"

Hearing that word on his lips is so taboo, that it leaves me breathless, and I can only nod. Dan pauses, as if there's any way we could stop now that we're on this path, but finally he curses under his breath right before his fingers part my folds and he touches me in earnest.

I cry out as his thumb finds my clit expertly, the pleasure from it short circuiting my brain. All the dull, throbbing pressure I've been feeling is nothing compared to this, and when his thumb begins to make small circles, I think my soul may leave my body.

"Damn, Elise," Dan grits out. "You're so wet for me."

My forehead falls against his shoulder, and all I can do is nod and moan in return.

His free hand lifts my face gently again, and he kisses my mouth one more time, slowly, before he sinks to his knees. I'm in such a haze of pleasure that it takes me a second to realize what he intends to do, and by the time I connect the dots, he's already pushing the curtain of skirt fabric aside and sliding his fingers beneath the waistband of my panties.

"Dan—"

"Hush," he snaps. "Not a word, El, or I'll have you on your back on this damned table, any control gone with the wind. Let me make you feel good, but know that I'm hanging on by a thread here."

I swallow. "Okay."

The panties come off, me lifting my hips to assist until they're hanging around one of my ankles. Dan puts his hands on the soft skin of my thighs and pushes my legs open, his hungry gaze raking over the puffy flesh of my pussy as if he's never seen anything more beautiful. His expression is one of reverence.

The fact that a party is still raging outside these doors slips in and out of my brain, but when he kisses my inner thighs, mouth moving toward the apex, the party slips away from my thoughts like water. Each arm wrapped around one leg, he pulls me forward just slightly, and then his mouth finally connects where I need him most.

I make a sound closer to a sob when he drags his tongue over my whole pussy for the first time, pausing to give my clit a quick but thorough suck, and then starting all over again. His tongue dips into my swell, tasting me, before returning to that bundle of nerves that makes my legs shake and my breath come in gasps.

I've been on edge for nearly an hour now, with all the foreplay in the form of billiards and the slow, unhurried make-out session. Dan's mouth on my pussy is the most exquisite pleasure I could have ever imagined, but it's almost too much. The sensations soar past any levels I've ever reached on my own, but it makes them harder for me to grab a hold of once more. It's too much, too fast.

"Easy," I beg, and he complies.

"Sorry," he murmurs. "I forget that this is all so new for you."

He takes his time now, kissing and licking and caressing me. There is no goal in mind for him it seems, just a hedonistic need to taste me over and over. This… this is exactly what I need.

I bury my hands in his hair, my hips grinding against him without me even having to think about it, showing him the rhythm of my pleasure. Dan picks up the pace slowly, spending longer and longer each time with his tongue and lips on my clit before backing off and going easy again. All the feeling builds slowly inside of me like a ticking time bomb, and his gentle pace makes it all grow larger than ever before. The tension inside of me is so overwhelming that I'm almost frightened of what is going to happen, but my body craves it like air, and nothing could stop me from taking what I want now.

And what I want is to come with Dan's mouth on me. The thought is so erotic that it's almost enough to send me over the edge.

Time slips away from me. I'm dazed, legs spread so wide that under any other circumstances I would be embarrassed, but I'm so far past that now. I'm almost there, so close, and whatever is about to happen to me feels like it's going to be life changing.

I hold myself up with shaking arms and look down where my hands are carding through Dan's hair, his mouth working over my pussy, his eyes closed and expression rapturous. The teasing is over, and now he's focused. Seeing what he's doing to me sends another rush of ecstasy coursing through my body, and it's the last drop in the bucket I need.

Dan sucks my clit between his lips now and doesn't let up, sucking my engorged flesh, and it makes me come so hard that all I see is white. I arch my back so far that I'm surprised my head doesn't touch the table, my hands fisted in his hair. It goes off like an explosion inside me, and it feels so good that it should be impossible. Thank God hardly anyone is in the house because the noise that comes from me is nothing short of obscene.

Bliss rolls over me in waves. It's like I can't get enough, holding Dan in place while I ride out my orgasm on his face. As I crest the wave of it, the unending pleasure morphs into oversensitivity, and my fingers finally unfurl from his scalp.

I can't believe what we just did. Still, I want more.

Dan, without a word, surges up and claims my mouth again. I can taste my own juices on him, and while I would have thought it would be unpleasant, knowing that the sharp taste on his lips is from me makes me feel almost feral. I can hear the clanking of his belt buckle, and in the back of my mind I know I don't want to lose my virginity on a billiards table when we're in a hurry, but it seems like he and I both are well past logical thought.

Then, someone bangs on the door—hard. He jumps back from me as if shocked, and I shut my legs with a snap, hopping off the table and tripping over myself trying to get my panties back on.

"Who the fuck—" he hisses, but then the pounding starts again, and this time it keeps going.

We straighten ourselves up, and my heart is racing so fast I think it might beat out of my chest. I'm panicking, thinking it might be my parents, or worse, my brother, but I relax a little as someone yells through the door.

"Elise!" Tatiana calls from the other side. "We're all out here waiting on you! It's time for cake!"

There's a cacophony of agreement from the other girls that are apparently with her. I exhale slowly, brushing my hair back into place and straightening my dress. Of anyone to catch me, this is the least problematic group. And maybe I can still hide what I've just been doing.

"Go stand in the back of the room," I tell Dan quickly while he's buttoning his shirt. "I'll lead them away and then you can come out after, so we aren't leaving together."

He searches my face as if there is more that he wants to say, but then he just nods. "Good idea. I'll meet you outside, then."

I hold my head high, even as the aftershocks of my climax are still rippling through me. I wish I had time to wash my hands, and I'm more glad than ever that I decided to go with the kiss-proof lipstick. Opening the door,

Tatiana and a few other girls grab me immediately, and I'm hauled out of the billiard room like a clandestine package.

"Your parents have been waiting for almost twenty minutes!" Tati informs me in a tizzy. "What the heck have you been doing? And don't try to tell me you've been playing *billiards*."

"We can talk later," I tell her under my breath, not wanting the pack of other girls to hear me. "But keep it down, okay? Don't go spilling my secrets everywhere."

"Alright... but you better keep your word and fill me in."

We exit onto the terrace, less than ten feet from the billiards room, and I'm about to tell Tati she can go get my parents when I see that Dad and Mom are already waiting for me. I'm overcome by a wave of humiliation, knowing what Dan and I were just doing with them only feet away. I can even feel my face turning red. I never would have guessed that my own dad would be up here mingling with my college-aged friends... I never considered he could be so close! Knowing I was maybe just minutes from getting caught having sex with Dan makes me want to run away and never come back, but the nearly one hundred expectant faces watching me make it impossible.

Mom draws me into a quick hug, talking about how beautiful I look and how she can't believe how grown I am, but I'm distracted, looking for Dan and feeling ridiculously awkward hearing her say these things after what Dan and I have just done.

"Thanks, Mom," I say, gently untangling myself from her arms.

I've read the party itinerary at least a dozen times, but since all my attention has been on getting Dan to the party, and then getting him alone, I guess I let a lot of it slip my mind. If I would have just checked the time, I would have known that there wasn't time for the long, drawn-out seduction and oral sex that just occurred. I don't regret it, not for a second, but my timing could definitely be better.

Everything is already set and ready for me; the cake is, of course, white, covered in areas of gold leaf to match the invitations that were sent out last week. The gold leaf is one hundred percent genuine, hand laid onto the icing just hours before so it wouldn't warp or become displaced before it was time to display the confection. It's two tiers, one vanilla and one chocolate, underneath the creamy buttercream icing, and there isn't much time before the entire thing starts to melt in the warm summer heat. *Where the hell is Dan?*

Surely he wouldn't leave me now, would he? I can just imagine him sneaking out the front, snatching his keys from the valet and disappearing into the night so he doesn't have to deal with what we've just done together. I'm not done with him yet, either. I'm so tired of being interrupted, and tonight we'll finally have the privacy we've been denied during our past two encounters.

I know that he's been hesitant about being with me in that way, but I took every precaution to make sure my brother doesn't catch us, and that we will have ample time to explore each other at our leisure tonight. I'm still buzzing from the orgasm he just gave me… I can only imagine what he'll do when given free rein. Plus, I really do want to return the favor.

Just as I start to really worry, Dan walks around the corner, only his slightly mussed hair giving away any hint of our indiscretions. He meets my eyes briefly, the emotions in them complicated, just before my dad approaches him and shakes his hand, pulling him in for a quick hug and pat on the back, as if he's greeting his own son. I really, really hope that at least Dan had time to wash his hands. Maybe swish his mouth with some booze.

He and Dad chat, but they're too far away to hear. I'm still reeling from the pace that everything has changed, going from nearly having sex to standing out here with my parents, family members, and friends ready to blow out candles. I watch Dan speak, entranced by the movement of his lips. That mouth was just between my legs, and now he's out here talking to my *dad* as if he's never done anything wrong in his entire life.

It's so bizarre, so absurd, that it's funny. A smile pulls at the corner of my mouth. Oh, life is about to get really, really interesting for Dan and me. I just know it.

CHAPTER 24

Dan

Never in my life have I felt a more complex mix of emotions than when I watched Elise blow out the candles on her birthday cake. It was like time slowed, the red and orange flames lighting her face, the cheers from all the people that love and adore her, and then right as the candles extinguish, an explosion of fireworks rose from above. Every single one of them crystalline white... of course.

If the white is to symbolize purity, then it is a mistake. Because there is very little purity here tonight, and I can't help but feel like it's all my fault.

Andries isn't here in person, and yet, his shadow still is. On this terrace, he and I have fenced, drank, and talked for hours. I've played pool with him on the same billiard table where I just defiled his sister. I'm full of shame, and at the same time, adrenaline about what has just occurred. Going down on Elise will be one of the things I will remember until the day I die, feeling her all around me, her legs against my ears and her hands in my hair... fuck. I'm a lost soul when it comes to this woman, and I just can't escape her. I have zero sense of self-preservation.

The fireworks continue, so loud that I can barely hear myself think. Elise meets my eyes from where she's standing behind the cake, a lazy, satisfied grin on her face. It makes my heart thump against the wall of my chest. I've thought this entire time if she and I hooked up, then I might be able to get this thing I feel for her out of my system. Then, I still would have betrayed Andries, but at least it'd only be one single time. After that, I could return to being the good, truthful friend I've always been. There would only be that one single secret between us. But everything Elise and I just did together has a heaviness to it that I didn't expect... and that heaviness was full of emotion. I *feel* something for Elise, something more than lust and sexual chemistry. Something more than just affection for my best friend's sister. I like her, cherish her even, above and independent of all of that.

I know the name of the feeling. I've never felt it for another woman, but I can't say it out loud. Hell, I can't even say it in my head. Because if I do, then it becomes real, and I'm well and truly fucked. Even more so than I already am.

The cake is cut as the fireworks wind down. Someone hands me a piece on a tiny golden plate. I take a single bite before sitting it down on a table and leaving it behind. I have no appetite.

Music is swelling and thumping from the DJ booth on the lawn. It feels like the crowd carries me there, all of them moving toward the same goal at once. Elise is already there when I arrive, her hands held to the sky and body moving to the music with reckless abandon. She's an athlete, an accomplished hunter, and rider, and when she moves like this, it's all too apparent how in control and in tune she is with her body. Every movement is practiced, precise, and intentional. I know without a doubt that she would apply that same focus in bed, using that beautiful form of hers to bring her partner the most pleasure possible, while also chasing down her own, not unlike the hunt that she is so good at. Right now, I would almost rather be the deer in her scope rather than the man she pursues... At least if I was the prey, then I wouldn't also be a traitor to my best friend.

Still, there's no escaping her, and all my self-doubt and misery dissipates as she slinks through the throngs of people and takes my hand, pulling me into the fray and against her body. The song is nameless, just some remix of popular songs on the radio, but I barely register it anyway. I can feel the bass in my bones, and it helps me dance with her, moving in tandem. I slot her against me, her back to my front, her sinfully round ass pressing against my groin. It's wrong, wrong, wrong, especially in light of the billiards room escapade, but no one gives us a second glance. Everyone is dancing close, sharing laughter and carefree smiles, and we blend in. Except, what is flowing between us is anything but carefree.

Elise's head leans back, her head on my shoulder, taking my hands in hers and guiding them to her hips. We sway together, and I'm harder than I've ever been in my life—the taste of her still on my lips and tongue. We were seconds... literal *seconds*, from fucking. Now, only the layers of our clothes separate us. A pair of linen pants and a silk dress. It isn't enough… but it's too much.

I don't know how long this goes on… through a few songs like this one and then one slow song that seems almost more intimate than the others, but eventually she grabs my hand and pulls me from the dancefloor, claiming she's thirsty. Like a loyal dog, I follow her without question, watching her drink chilled water from a server's tray until a single drop rolls down her throat. Every ounce of my willpower is focused on not licking it from her skin.

Elise returns the empty glass, but asks the server, "Are my parents still on the terrace?"

The server shakes his head. "No, ma'am. I believe they went to bed."

"Oh, alright." She turns to me, fire in her eyes. "Did you hear that, Dan? They've gone to bed."

When the server leaves, she's pulling me forward again, but I dig my heels in. "Where exactly are we going, Elise?"

"There's a guest bedroom next to the billiards room. We have some unfinished business to attend to, don't we?"

Yes! My body screams, but I shake my head. "Elise… we've already been too far tonight. Didn't I take care of you?"

"Well, yes, but I had more in mind than just that…."

"You know how guilty all this makes me feel. Everything is so incredible in the moment, but when that moment is overall I'm left with is the guilt for betraying your brother."

She huffs, rolling her eyes. "Andries isn't here, for the millionth time, and everyone is dancing and enjoying themselves. The party is winding down. No one will miss us. Come on, Dan."

She looks like heaven in this silk dress… like an angel, almost, but I feel like she's dragging me to hell at the same time. I just can't tell her no.

"Fine, but we *really* need to be discreet."

Elise almost jumps for joy; she's so excited to get her way. She laces her fingers through mine and then we walk toward the house. I can feel my pulse in my ears.

It's impossible to resist her enthusiasm, though, and before I know it I'm grinning along with her, pulling her to me and kissing her on the way to the bedroom. If I'm going to do all these morally wrong things, I might as well enjoy the process.

Just as her hand lands on the bedroom doorknob, my phone begins to ring. I frown, wondering who would be calling me so late, and pull it out to check.

It's Andries.

"What the fuck," I whisper, more to myself than her. "Does he have like a secret sense for when I'm messing around with his sister?"

"Ignore it," Elise insists, opening the door and coaxing me in. "Don't let him get in your head."

I hesitate, but do as she asks, silencing it and sitting it on the nightstand. Elise is on me instantly, her hands sliding up my chest and her lips on mine. She tastes like cake sugar and champagne. I cup her face in my hands… just as my phone rings again.

I give it one more shot, reaching behind me and silencing it, but as soon as the call ends it begins again. I have to pull my lips away from Elise's, knowing that Andries wouldn't blow up my phone unless he actually needed me.

"It could be an emergency," I say when she protests, trying to drag me back into the kiss. "I can't just ignore him."

"Fine," she huffs, crossing her arms and waiting for me to pick up the call.

"Hello?" I ask, guilt filling me up already.

"Hey, nice of you to finally answer! I'm outside the gate, can you let us in? My key doesn't work anymore."

My brain doesn't comprehend the words at first. "You're outside where?"

"My house, idiot. Can you let me in or what? Elise isn't answering. You are at the party, right?"

The room we're in is quiet enough that Elise can hear the conversation, and she blanches, mouthing, *He's here?*

I nod to her while telling Andries. "Uh… sure! I'll be right down."

I hang up, and Elise's first words are, "*What the fuck!?*"

"Enough," I tell her, readjusting my clothes for the second time tonight, "We have to let him in, let's go. He must have been waiting for your parents to go to bed too."

"Dad is going to freak out if he's still awake and catches Andries here!" she exclaims as we rush down the stairs and out to the front gate, trying our best to appear that we didn't just have our tongues down each other's throats. "Why couldn't he just wait until I got back to campus?"

"You made an effort to go to his party when you weren't invited. He's just returning the favor. It's a show of how much you mean to him, so don't be prissy about it," I warn her. "You're already driving me crazy tonight."

She sputters, but by now we've made it to the gate. Lo and behold, there is Andries's car, his driver at the wheel, and both Andries and Roxanne exiting out of the back. Andries is clutching an enormous horse plush, a red ribbon tied around the brown neck. Roxanne has a wrapped gift.

While he looks excited to be here, Roxanne looks much more nervous, her gaze flickering around to make sure that they aren't about to be interrogated by Sebastian or Julia, more than likely. Elise presses the code to open the gate, her antagonistic attitude gone now that she's seeing her brother in person, here at the home they've grown up in together.

She rushes out, running to hug Andries, the show of affection only hindered by the giant stuffed animal he's holding. Andries laughs, bowing his head and handing her the toy like he's presenting her with something much more lavish. He knows his sister well, though, because she clutches the horse to her chest happily.

"I can't believe you guys risked coming here," she says in awe.

"I had to convince him, but once he was on board, we swapped places," Roxanne admits, laughing nervously. "I've been scared to death, but he insisted that it would be alright. So far so good, I guess."

"Mom and Dad are in bed," Elise confirms.

"Good to know you both are still up, though," Andries observes humorously, letting out a quick chuckle.

This sets off alarm bells in my head. I've been wondering if he suspects she and I have been messing around, and now I'm almost sure a big part of the reason he showed up tonight is to keep an eye on Elise and me. I'm glad to see him, of course, and proud that he would risk an altercation with his father just to wish his sister a happy birthday, but him being here also sours my mood greatly. It is just a slap in the face to remind me how far out of control I've let my relationship with his sister get.

There is something I've been planning to give Elise, something more personal than anything I've ever gifted before, but now that Andries is here I just can't. It's too personal.

Elise invites them inside, and after a brief moment of consideration, Andries and Roxanne both agree. We lead them to the terrace, where the crowd has thinned out significantly, but the two of them can't go unnoticed. The prodigal Van den Bosch son and his ex-escort fiancée; all eyes are on them.

People whisper behind their hands to one another, but Andries and Roxanne just ignore it. I'm sure it's something they're unfortunately used to by now. Elise, on the other hand, sends withering glances around to anyone gossiping to make them fall silent.

She offers her brother and his fiancée cake and some of the signature champagne drinks, and we meander to an empty table a little ways away from the main portion of people still here.

Roxanne is on edge, and Andries must sense it because he grabs her hand in his and squeezes. "Thanks for inviting us in, Elise, but I don't want to push our luck. The last thing we need is some nosy housekeeper to go and wake Mom and Dad up and tattle on us, so we can't stay long."

"That's okay," she tells them, beaming. "The party is starting to wind down anyway. You guys coming out is a wonderful gift all on its own. Thank you."

"Are you guys driving all the way back to Amsterdam tonight?" I ask, surprised that they would drive this far just to hang out for five minutes and then bolt.

"Yeah, that's why I had the driver bring us instead of driving myself," Andries says, cutting off a forkful of cake and popping it into his mouth, "What about you, Dan? How does that old Jaguar handle in the dark?"

I glance over at Elise, who is looking at me expectantly, and I know that what I'm about to say is going to break her heart. Or piss her off. Or both.

"It handles fine, thank you very much. Which is why I'm also headed back to the city tonight."

Shocked, Elise opens her mouth but doesn't say anything at first. "Now wait a second, before Dad went to bed he said you should sleep in the guest room since you've been drinking so much and you're clearly tired."

"He can ride with us," Andries offers, patting me on the shoulder as he does so. "Just send one of our drivers here to bring his car back tomorrow."

"There's no need to be that complicated," she insists, visibly displeased at her brother's suggestion. "Dan can just stay overnight and tomorrow go back to Amsterdam with his car. We've already got it all planned out with Dad."

Now, a dark look falls over my friend's face, and he looks between Elise and me with no small amount of suspicion. "Oh, it sounds like Dad has a new son, then."

It's a gut punch, knowing that my best friend would think something like that. I'd never, ever want to take his place with his father. "It's not like that, man," I tell him. "Everyone just knows that I really enjoy parties, especially when there is an open bar. It's just for safety."

"Sure it is," Andries mutters, earning him an odd look from Roxanne and Elise.

We turn the conversation to the upcoming wedding, but the mood is spoiled, at least on Andries's end. He glowers at me between sips of champagne, and I'm becoming more and more certain that he thinks something is going on between me and his sister. What's worse is that he isn't wrong, but I can never tell him the truth. It's eating me up inside.

True to their word, the couple can't stay long. Plus, everyone else is beginning to leave, and this is the best time for them to depart unnoticed. We walk them back to the gate while the other guests leave through the main entryway to gather their cars from the valet. Roxanne and Elise exchange quick hugs, while Andries reaches out his hand to me so we can shake.

I accept, but instead he pulls me into an embrace as well, patting me roughly on the back and whispering into my ear, "Behave yourself, Dan. Just because she's eighteen doesn't mean you can fool around with her, understand? You made a promise."

Feeling sick, I let him go. "Of course, Andries."

He searches my face like he already knows I'm lying, but finally nods once and turns around to tell his sister goodbye. Roxanne glances at me from the car, right before she climbs in, a sympathetic look in her eye. It's too much… I don't deserve sympathy, trust, or anything else. I've betrayed my best friend, and there's no going back now.

While the sister and brother are busy with goodbyes, I make my exit, hurrying through the front yard and through the front door, past the people leaving. I'm so ashamed of myself, that all I can think to do is go to the guest bedroom alone, and hope that Elise catches the hint. I feel so strongly about her that it's almost a tangible pain that touches me, but I was her brother's friend first and foremost, and I don't want to lose that friendship. The problem is, I don't want to lose Elise and this thing we're discovering between us, either.

I take the world's quickest shower in the en suite bathroom, dutifully ignoring my raging erection that just can't seem to understand that we aren't getting laid tonight, and crawl into the bed in just my briefs. There is still music from outside, the last stragglers making their way home. I'm so tired, body and soul, but my broken oath is haunting me. The only thing I can fall back on is that Elise and I didn't go all the way and have sex. At least there's that, and I plan to keep it this way forever. If Andries never finds out what we've done so far, then everything will be okay.

I wish I'd have just driven home or gone with Andries and Roxanne. I toss and turn in the unfamiliar bed as the lights from outdoors slowly extinguish. The party is well and truly over, and I've managed to make an enormous fool of myself. Great.

It's not a surprise when, an hour later, the door creaks open slowly. In front of the dim light of the main part of the house, I can see Elise's silhouette in my doorway. Her hair is damp from the shower, curling just slightly at the ends, and her feet are bare. In an homage to her party dress, she's got on a short, simple white lingerie nightgown, the dark peaks of her nipples visible through the fabric. She's so beautiful like she's from another world. Angelic, almost, and oh so vulnerable standing there and waiting for me to acknowledge her, but I don't.

Undeterred, but clearly a little embarrassed, Elise approaches my bed and starts to climb in. I should continue to ignore her, or even feign sleep, but I can't. It must have taken a huge amount of bravery for her to come to me like this, and it's breaking my heart into pieces to have to turn her away. The least I can do is tell her to her face why she can't stay with me tonight.

"Elise," I whisper, sitting up and taking her bare shoulders into my hands. She freezes. "You can't be here. Go to bed."

"We have unfinished business, mister," she insists, clinging to her bravado from earlier in the night. Now, bare-faced and natural, it doesn't ring as true.

"Beautiful girl," I murmur, tucking one of those damp strands behind her ear, "I'd let you stay, but your brother is suspicious. He hasn't said it plainly yet, but he knows something is off with us. I can't lose my best friend over… whatever this is. A fling with you, I guess."

She rears back, offended. "A *fling*? Is that how you see me? Just a fling?"

No, I think to myself, *You are so much more to me than you will ever know.*

"Maybe, maybe not, but I still can't risk betraying Andries either way. I'm sorry, El. Really, I am."

There are tears in her eyes, but I know she hopes the darkness will hide them. I don't acknowledge her sadness, or the clear humiliation she feels when she ducks her head, cheeks flushed. I hate myself in this moment, but I'm stuck. There is no right answer.

"Fine," she says after collecting herself, all the hurt and unsaid things crammed in that one syllable. "I'll leave you alone, then."

I fist my hands in the sheets as I watch her go, my heart in my throat. I know I'm a real asshole, sending her away like this, but the alternative is impossible. What I feel for Elise is far more than a fling. It's more substantial than anything I've ever felt. It's lightyears beyond a crush. With Elise, it's... it's...

Fuck. I still can't face how much she means to me. Which, I guess it really doesn't matter if I ever do, because my best friend will never accept me dating his sister. Even if I care for her so, so much.

CHAPTER 25

Elise

Tap, tap, tap.

"Go away," I groan, pulling the blanket over my head.

Tap, tap, tap.

"Ma'am? Your mom is inquiring if you're coming down to breakfast."

"No."

The maid outside my bedroom door hesitates, before saying, "Well, it's more like she told me to bring you down for breakfast, rather than ask you to come. Your guest is waiting for you, as well."

Under the blanket, I cringe, wondering how long I can hide here before Mom comes up and drags me down to breakfast physically. I had hoped to stay away long enough that Dan would be long gone by the time I joined the rest of my family, but in her true, annoyingly polite fashion, it looks like Mom is forcing everyone to wait on me to eat. Which means I'm going to have to face Dan—just hours after he turned me down and sent me back to my room, face burning from humiliation.

"Fine," I call through the door, throwing the duvet aside and sitting up. "Give me ten minutes."

Looking at myself in the bathroom mirror, my silky white nightgown barely brushing the tops of my thighs, is the peak of embarrassment. I had picked this piece of lingerie specifically to wear for Dan, and as soon as he saw me, he sent me away. There was no soft seduction, no foreplay...nothing. Annoyed beyond reason, I jerk the nightgown over my head and throw it in the dirty laundry, hoping to never see it again.

Having showered last night, I simply drag a brush through my hair, wash my face, and get dressed. There's a dull ache in my skull from the drinking and lack of sleep the night before provided, not enough to count as a hangover but annoying, nonetheless. There is a sweet, gauzy yellow sundress hanging on the front of my closet, the outfit I had chosen for this morning when I thought I would be waking up next to Dan. Now that all of my carefully laid plans have come to naught, there's no reason to dress to impress. Instead, I grab a pair of black leggings and a matching tank top, putting in the least amount of effort possible. Still, it flatters my figure well enough, so Dan can get some sort of glimpse of what he's missing out on.

I finally exit my bedroom, slipping on a pair of sandals and brushing past my flustered maid, who follows behind me with worry. Through the tall windows, I can see remnants of the party being dismantled, and I'm glad I won't have to look at it much longer. As happy as the memories are, there are some hurtful ones, too.

In the dining room, the curtains have all been pulled aside and sunlight streams happily through the windows, illuminating cups of steaming coffee and tea as well as plates of food. Mom, Dad, and Dan are all there, dressed comfortably like I am, laughing together.

When they notice me, the laughter stops. I meet Dan's eyes for an instant before shifting my gaze away to my smiling mother, who is waving me over.

"There you are, sleepy head. Come and join the land of the living and have some breakfast!"

"Did you sleep well?" Dad asks when I lean over, and we exchange a quick kiss on the cheek.

I just nod in return, before scanning the table and trying to find a seat.

There's an empty chair next to Dan, but I pass it by, circling the table to sit next to my mother. Doting on me, she pours my coffee and loads my plate with fruit and sliced bread with appelstroop, asking question after question about the party last night.

"It was wonderful, Mom," I assure her, taking the offered mug and holding it tightly, letting the warmth absorb into my hands. "Really, it was."

She beams, still so beautiful even as she ages. I can only hope to age as gracefully as her. "I'm so glad, love. You only turn eighteen once, after all. I wanted it to be special for you."

Dan's looking at me, and I risk a quick look in his direction before turning back to Mom. I can feel heat crawling up my neck, thinking about how special the night really was, but also how much I missed out on. "It was the perfect celebration. I got nearly everything I wanted."

"You kids have always been a little spoiled." Dad chuckles. "But now that the party is behind us, let's move on to the next big event on the horizon; hunting season. Are you planning on attending the opening with me this year, Elise?"

"We have a trip to Lake Como in July though," Mom promptly interposes, looking at Dad with an ounce of annoyance on her face, which causes me to laugh. "Hunting season only starts in mid-August, right?"

"Of course!" I reply to Dad between bites of fruit, my excitement coming off a bit overboard, but the truth is it's the only activity we do together. "I've gone with you since I was, what, twelve? I wouldn't miss it for the world."

"Yes, it was the year after your brother had his first hunt and gave it up forever." Dad looks at Dan as if trying to discern whether Dan knew about it or not. "He takes after Julia in that way, I guess. Not much of a constitution when it comes to blood."

Mom shudders, wrinkling her nose. "I don't blame him one bit. There's no need to hunt nowadays, you can perfectly do another activity in the wild, like hiking."

"Nonsense," Dad tells her, looking incredulous. "It's the best way for us to reconnect with our most primal selves. If the world went to hell tomorrow, at least Elise and I would have the knowledge to hunt and survive. You and your overly sensitive, stubborn son though…"

"He's your son too," Mom points out, a bit pointedly, but Dad shakes his head.

"Not right now, he's not."

Tension rises in the air, and not the enjoyable kind that I've been feeling with Dan since yesterday. I know that disowning Andries weighs on Mom every day, but she won't go against Dad in this matter, and she definitely doesn't want him marrying Roxanne. Still, she'd rather still have him here at home with us right now, I'm sure of it. What is preventing that is Dad's pride and his concern for the image of his business. I need to change the subject, and fast, or things are going to get really messy.

"Dan, do you hunt?" I ask, speaking to him directly for the first time. Luckily, he knows me well enough that he can see the worry on my face and jumps right into the conversation.

"Yes, actually, but I don't get much of an opportunity to do it anymore. My dad goes occasionally, but it isn't something he goes out of his way to do."

This catches Dad's interest, and he looks swiftly at Dan as if he's sizing him up. "Why don't you join us for the opening of hunting season, then? The more the merrier."

I want to say no to him, but Dan doesn't give me the chance, telling Dad, "Really? Wow, thank you for the invitation! I'd be delighted to join you."

"Splendid! It will be a nice change of pace to have another man along. Elise and I start to wear on each other after a few days."

While Dad chuckles, looking rather amused at what he just said, his words find a way to hurt me more than I want to let on so I diligently eat my fruit, trying not to let them get the best of me. I focus on my plate, looking away from Dan even though I know he's watching me.

"Maybe having me along is just what you two need to shake things up a little," Dan adds, a smile in his tone as if he's mocking me.

I roll my eyes as the two of them start talking about the hunting season in detail. It's like Dad has latched on to Dan as his new son; someone to replace Andries now that he has disowned him. Even better, Dan doesn't mind participating in a lot of the things that Andries detests, like hunting and business talk. I've never seen Dan shoot a gun before, but the thought of him in his hunting attire, all his attention focused down the barrel of his rifle, is more attractive than I'd like to admit.

Mom and I chat about all the family members who attended the party last night, even though she seems reserved about the subject. Some of our relatives are giving both my parents the cold shoulder, knowing that they've shunned Andries and Roxanne and are basically boycotting the wedding. Family means a lot to my mother, and having them be mad at her must be painful. But Mom is her own person, and she doesn't need to follow Dad's lead on this if she doesn't want to, so it's hard to feel too bad for her. She's made her own bed, and now she has to lie in it.

She's going to break soon and reconnect with my brother; I can feel it. My only hope is that Dad and Andries come to an agreement beforehand, otherwise there won't just be tension between my parents and brother, but also between both parents themselves. It sounds like a terrible time all around.

Dan's phone vibrates on the table, and he lifts it to check the message, grinning his first real smile of today when he reads it. For one terrible moment, I think it might be some other woman texting him, but then he puts the phone down and looks around at us.

"That was my dad messaging me about his new car that he's added to the collection. I think I'm going to head out so I can stop by and see him and Mom both on the way home."

Mom gives him a polite smile. "Well, it was lovely to have you over, Dan. You're welcome anytime."

"Likewise," Dad says, standing to shake the younger man's hand. "And I will see you on August fifteenth for opening day."

"Absolutely. Can't wait."

"I'll walk you to the door," I pipe up impulsively, standing quickly.

Dan gives me an odd look. "Okay, then. Let me grab my things and I'll meet you at the bottom of the stairs."

Both my parents watch me as I finish my coffee and rush to go meet him once he's finished packing. "What are you guys looking at?" I snap, irritated.

"Oh, nothing, dear," Mom says, laughter apparent in her eyes. "Nothing at all."

Dan is waiting just like he said he would be, not looking very excited to see me. "I assume you offered this escort to my car as a way to interrogate me in private?"

I walk beside him as we head outside to his car. "No. Well, yes. Maybe…" I pause, biting my lower lip in thought. Finally, I decide to just go for it and get my answers once and for all. "Why did you reject me last night, Dan? I don't understand why you said the things you did…"

"Elise…," He sighs. "Honestly, why go through all this hassle? I've got a great friendship with your brother, your family likes me, and I don't want to ruin all of those good things just because of the lust between us, or whatever it is."

"There's no reason it would ruin—"

"Stop. You know I've always been attracted to you." He rakes his hand through his hair in frustration. "You fucking know it. Yet you still love playing this game to see how far you can push me, knowing that I'm so weak when it comes to you."

"It's not a game," I insist, but he isn't buying it.

Dan stops, turning to face me. We're alone outside, and he drops his mask of aloofness, looking both hurt and incredibly stressed out. "Really?" He takes a few steps in my direction and stands just a few inches from me. "So what is it, then, huh? If it isn't a game, tell me what it is."

The words are right there on the tip of my tongue, *I really care about you*, but I just can't say them. My pride won't let me do so. I look away, eyes misting over, refusing to meet his gaze.

Dan scoffs in return. "Yeah, that's what I thought," he says, shaking his head. "Look, I don't want us to repeat what happened in the billiards room. If your brother finds out… hell, if your Dad finds out, I'll be in serious trouble."

"But what if Dad is okay with it? With us?" I ask immediately.

He laughs, incredulous. "Your dad? Really? You think Sebastian Van den Bosch would be okay with his favorite daughter fooling around with a nobody like me? What world are you living in right now?"

"That's not fair…"

"Make no mistake, my family might have some money, but they aren't like yours. And we never will be…" He trails off, the emotions on his face almost too complicated to read.

Now it's my turn to be annoyed. My family has welcomed him with open arms, and now he wants to play the class card? "Oh, Dan, please. You know my family isn't like that. We just had breakfast with them."

"Tell that to Roxanne," he snaps, so sharply that I wince. "I've seen how they've treated her, and now your brother too. I have no interest in going down that path. I think we should just remain friends, okay?"

I clench my jaw, wanting to argue, to tell him that friends will never be enough for me, but I know he doesn't want to hear it. No matter what I say, he will never believe that my family will accept him just as he is. I simply nod in agreement, still not meeting his eyes.

Dan watches me for a few long moments as if he's waiting, almost anticipating that I will say something more, but I don't give him the satisfaction. His rejection hurts too much.

Finally, he sucks in a deep breath. "Well, I guess, on that note, I'll be going. Thanks for the hospitality, Elise… and happy birthday."

"Thanks," I mumble under my breath, watching him walk away in my peripherals. It hurts, a lot actually, but I'd rather let him go with my head held high than beg him to reconsider. At least now I still have my pride.

* * *

I flee to the terrace once Dan departs, wanting some fresh air and time to myself. Unfortunately, privacy isn't in the cards for me today, because Dad is there too, reading a book with his feet kicked up on an ottoman.

He smiles when he sees me, relaxed and in his element. So much different from how he is at work, I can't help but notice.

"Elise! Come sit with me and enjoy this fine weather."

I hesitate, but figure there really isn't much else for me to do, and go to sit on the loveseat with him. Dad watches me, frowning as I grow closer as if he can see how tortured my thoughts are just from the expression on my face.

"Is something wrong, dear?" he asks as I sit.

For a second, I almost consider telling him the truth about Dan and me. If I opened up about how hard things are for me right now, maybe he will ease up on all his demands from me at work and understand a little better how I'm feeling. Plus, just sharing what's going on with someone, anyone really, would be such an enormous relief.

But when I look at my father's face, and the genuine concern there, I can't do it. If by some chance Dan is right, and Dad wouldn't accept him, it will shatter my heart, and that's just something I can't handle today. So instead I search for the next biggest problem I'm dealing with, something I know he's going to discover anyway. After all, dozens of people witnessed it happening, so it's not like it can remain a secret.

"Dad… Andries and Roxanne showed up after you and Mom went to bed. I let them in the gate."

His face clears, and he waves dismissively. "Oh, I knew that already. We have cameras out there after all."

My mouth falls open. "Really? And you aren't mad?"

"Well, I'm not thrilled he thinks he can still just show up here whenever he wants, but I understand it was your birthday and you wanted to see your big brother. It's okay that you let them in, El. Just don't let it happen again."

Even though I wasn't overly concerned about what Dad thought about Andries's visit, I'm still relieved. It's one less argument between us in the future. "Thanks, Dad. It was just so nice to have him here, almost like everything was back to normal…"

"Except it's not," he scoffs, shutting his book. "Because he brought that prostitute with him, and everyone saw it. You're still working out a way to split them up, aren't you?"

Karl's plan passes through my mind, and it makes my stomach clench. I really, really don't want to get involved, but I know the answer that Dad wants, so I give it to him. "Y-yes. I've got a plan that I'm going to execute before we go on holiday."

He smiles proudly, but I don't feel like I've done something good at all. The only thing on my mind now is what Dan said earlier, that my dad will never approve of him, even though he literally just invited him to our hunting trip.

"If you want to invite Dan to Lake Como, I wouldn't oppose."

My eyes widen in surprise and I even suck in a breath. "Really?" And just like that, I knew that Dad wouldn't treat Dan like he did with Roxanne. Sure, Dan might have been a player in the past, but he's respected by my parents and has been accepted as part of this family for years now.

"Of course, I already invited him to the hunting trip, so if he wants to join us in July to go to Italy, why not?"

"Thank you so much for the offer, Dad. With Andries being so… occupied lately, Dan doesn't get to go out and do as much as he usually does. It will be a fun time I think."

"I think so, too," he agrees, nodding. "And feel free to share this news with your brother, as well. He needs to see that no one is missing him here."

With those words, Dad's real intentions become clear, and my face falls a little. He isn't inviting Dan because he enjoys his company, even if that is a little bit true. He's doing it to punish Andries. Fucking unbelievable… My chest tightens with the knowledge of that.

"Dad," I say in disbelief. "Please don't tell me you're trying to do all these things with Dan just to piss off Andries…"

Dad smirks, setting his book down on the table beside him and folding his hands behind his head. It's all the answer I need.

"That's really petty," I tell him, utterly disappointed.

"Maybe. But it's too satisfying to stop."

I have to turn my face away, just in case, he can see how disgusted I am with this entire thing. I continue to be manipulated into playing this part, making other people miserable, just to further my dad's interests. I don't want to do all this anymore. If it continues, I won't have any friends left by the end of it.

I'm saved by one of the maids coming out, telling me that Mom wants to speak to me. There's a pinch of apprehension in my gut, probably because everything has been bad news ever since Andries showed up last night, but at least it's an excuse to get away from my conniving father. Plus, Mom always handles things with a much gentler, yet equally effective, touch.

She's waiting for me in her office, answering emails or doing some other sort of computer work, but when I knock on the doorframe, she looks up with a welcoming smile.

"Come in, darling. Have a seat."

I almost feel like I'm being interviewed for a job, sitting across from her at her desk. Mom is usually in full control over everything happening in her sphere, but she has a flighty, unsettled air about her right now.

"I just wanted to check with you, one on one, to make sure that everything at the party went well. I know you wouldn't want to disappoint your dad by complaining, but are you sure everything was what you expected? The cake? The music?"

"Mom," I huff, knowing this isn't the reason she asked me to come over. "I already told you. It was *amazing*. I don't believe for one minute that you called me into your private office to rehash the birthday party conversation for the second time today, so get to whatever has you so flustered."

She blinks a few times, taken aback by how forward I am, but clears her throat and gathers herself. "Well, alright, then. I was trying to ease you into this subject, but apparently, you aren't going to give me the opportunity, so let's just cut right to the chase; I know we haven't spoken much about this subject before, but..." She pauses for a beat, her eyes studying my face for a moment as if to gauge my reaction. "Do you have a crush on a particular boy?"

"A crush? Mom, I'm not fourteen." My pulse starts to pound faster, unsure that her bringing up this subject is a coincidence, considering what Dan and I did last night. The only boy I've ever officially introduced to my parents was Johan. He was a boy I met from summer camp the year I turned fifteen. My parents had invited him over for a farewell dinner after the end of our summer camp and they had gotten along with him pretty well. I thought that Johan would be more than a summer crush back then but when he went back to England and only sent me a few vague texts afterward, I was heartbroken. After that, I didn't want to talk about him—or any other crushes—ever again. Mom seems to pick up on my thoughts immediately.

"Yes, you know… ever since Johan, you've never shown any interest in anyone. At least not outwardly. Don't tell me after three years you haven't moved on yet. You're a beautiful young woman."

I can feel a blush high on my cheekbones. "Mom… I'm just focused on my internship and my studies."

She stands, walking over to the office door, and locks it. I watch her as she moves to the loveseat situated in front of her bookshelf, patting the adjoining cushion for me to come and sit down. Breaking out in a cold sweat, I follow her to the loveseat, terrified that I know where this conversation is headed: Dan O'Brian.

"You don't have to lie to me, darling," Mom says, giving me a pointed look.

"I'm not lying," I insist, even though she's already caught my bluff.

"Oh, really? So... nothing happened between you and Dan in the billiard room last night?"

The room spins, and I feel like I'm going to vomit. I cannot talk about this with my mother! "No... no! Of course not! Who told you that?"

She checks her nails as she answers, "The security camera we have in there."

I blink twice, totally taken aback at her words. "...Y-you have security watching that room?"

"My love, we had over two hundred people as guests last night, most of them we know nothing about, so yes. We had security watching the cameras that we have in every room except for the bathrooms and our private bedrooms. Just to make sure no one is stealing."

I've never been more mortified in my life, but now that the subject has been breached, I need to see it through. "Dan isn't a stranger, though, so why was that specific footage reported to you?"

Mom looks at me, her expression blank. "Elise... you have to understand we just want to keep you safe, and the security that watched that feed reported to me because they were worried. That's all."

"Bullshit," I snipe, disgusted at the entire situation. "I'm sure you gave them clear instructions to watch me specially and report it to you if I was alone with anyone."

"Oh, Elise, don't be ridiculous," Mom huffs, but I don't believe her for a minute.

"I know you, Mom! I know just how controlling you and Dad are. Look what you have done to my brother!"

She slaps her hands down on the couch in a rare show of temper. "I'm not here to scold you, dammit! I'm here to help you." She inhales, and then exhales slowly, regaining her control. "I don't know everything that you and Dan are up to, but I just want to remind you to use protection, and if we need to get you on birth control—"

"Mom! Please stop!" I have to fight the urge to cover my ears. "I know how those things work, but you can rest assured that Dan has no interest in going any further with me, so I won't need any sort of protection, anyway."

She purses her lips, tilting her head to the side as she absorbs this information. "Oh, well… I, um, thought you and Dan were… you know…"

"Friends with benefits?" I offer.

"Yes, yes. Something like that."

Now that it's all out in the open, I find that I feel better not having to keep everything so secret. I lean back on the couch, looking at the ceiling and letting out a long, tired sigh. "No. He doesn't want anything like that to happen again, and I shouldn't either."

"But you sort of like him, huh?" Mom elbows me in the side, teasing, trying to lighten the mood.

"Yeah," I offer. "But when Andries showed up yesterday, everything changed. I think Dan is sure that he doesn't want anything more to do with me in a romantic… or physical… sense."

She reaches out and pats my leg. "Well, I want you to know that your dad and I like the O'Brian family very much and have no objection if you and him ever get together officially. Although, obviously, Johan Bentinck wouldn't be an unsuitable match either…"

"Ugh, Mom, that was a summer fling years ago. He lives in England."

"I know, I know. I just wanted you to know that either of them are fine with us."

"Thanks... but I need to escape this conversation before it gets any more uncomfortable. May I please be excused?"

She laughs softly and pulls me into a hug. "Of course, darling. I just want you to know I'm on your side, and that you can come to me for anything like this. I love you."

"I love you too, Mom. Thanks for being honest with me."

I'm desperate for a nap to reset my now frazzled brain, so I make my way back to my bedroom, relieved to be alone again. It's been a very strange day thus far. As I'm walking the halls, I hear my phone ping, and it's a message from Tatiana with a video attached.

Tatiana: *What an evening! It was amazing! By the way, I thought you might like this.*

I play the video, and it shows Dan and me on the dance floor, moving as if no one is watching. He's smiling down at me, looking with something like adoration in his eyes, and my own are closed in reckless abandon, just happy to be in that moment with him.

It makes me smile to myself, despite all the complicated emotions that he has made me feel in the last twenty-four hours. I really am starting to believe that there is something more between us than just lust. The real question is, is it just me that thinks that way, or does Dan too?

CHAPTER 26

Dan

The decision to pull off the highway and go to my parents' instead of my place was an easy one. I had already decided this morning to go and see the new car Dad has acquired, but now I just don't want to be alone with my own thoughts.

My thoughts are of nothing but Elise, as one might expect. Her sounds of ecstasy as I brought her pleasure, the eagerness of her kiss, and worst of all, the look of hurt when I turned her away from my bed are haunting me non-stop. No woman has ever affected me like she does, and it's turning into both a fantasy and a nightmare. She's the woman I want more than any other, while simultaneously being the only one I can't have.

Yeah, I definitely need a distraction.

Exiting the car, I let the valet take the Jaguar, just pulling it around to the enormous garage and hopping out in search of my dad and his newest jewel.

The emerald green '74 Porsche 911 was one of around one hundred cars found in an incredible barn find that had recently surfaced in the British countryside. As soon as the news broke that there would be an auction for the pristine, if dusty, classic cars that had been found there, Dad had been glued to the news about it. This 911 was the car he had his eyes on the most, and although it was the only auction he won out of the few he bid on, I'm confident he's more than happy with the results.

He has the hood up, digging around in the machinery to see what has held up all these years and what will need to be repaired. He's in cargo shorts and an old, dirty shirt, but he is completely and totally in his element.

"Son!" he exclaims, hearing my footsteps on the concrete floor. He raises himself out of the car's innards, wiping his hands on a red towel that is slung over his shoulder. "Have you come to see me, or is it my pride and joy that interests you?"

"I thought I was your pride and joy," I joke, meeting him in the middle for a careful half hug, not wanting to get an excessive amount of grease on my good clothes. I have things in my old room to change into if we're going to really get into working on the Porsche.

"Depends on the day," he teases back, stepping aside so I can get a good look at the 911. It really is pristine, and I let out a low whistle.

"She's a beauty," I say, walking a slow circle around it. "What a lucky acquisition."

"I still can't believe it myself," Dad says, smiling like a kid. "You think your mom will kill me if I were to keep this one instead of reselling it?"

"Depends on the day," I quip back, using his own logic against him. Dad laughs.

"I guess you're right. But speaking of beautiful ladies—"

"Dad, please don't…"

"How was the party for Miss Elise Van den Bosch? Opulent? Excessive?"

I roll my eyes, almost regretting having come here. "All the above, really. But we don't have to get into it."

"Why not? Did you have a bad time?"

Deciding that it isn't worth the trouble of lying, and honestly wanting some tried-and-true advice from my father, I bluntly announce, "I'm screwed." My shoulders sag.

He pauses in the act of wiping his hands, giving me an off look. "How so?"

I scrape my hand through my hair in frustration, feeling like I'm ready to burst. "I'm fucking in love with her, and I don't know how to keep her away without hurting myself in the process."

"Oh…" Dad leans against the Porsche, crossing his arms. "And what does she feel for you?"

"That's the thing; I have no idea. She swears that this isn't all a game, but when I ask her to elaborate, she always falls silent."

"Son, she is eighteen. That's not exactly an age known for its wisdom."

"I feel just as indecisive, honestly, even at my *advanced* age."

He chuckles. "So let me get this straight: you two have been seeing each other, quite a bit it sounds like, you like her, you think she likes you, but you're still afraid it might be a game?"

I just shrug. He doesn't know the manipulative Elise as I do. "Yeah, I guess."

"You know, the Dan I knew just wanted to be with women because he could make a game out of it. You loved the chase. Now you're upset because a girl might be playing a game with you?"

"It's different with her," I say honestly, seeing the irony in what he is saying. "But the stakes are too high. If I put my friendship with her brother on the line for her, then it can't be for a one-night stand. It has to be for something more meaningful, or it isn't worth the risk."

"Dan, you're a smart boy. Just tell her."

I throw my hands up. "Tell her what? That I have feelings for her? Or that I want to be more than just her friend?" I laugh, and it sounds cruel to my ears. "Yeah, she isn't like her romantic brother who is already engaged and planning his wedding. She's more cunning and calculated. An ice queen, even, plotting against everyone in her ivory tower."

Dad listens to me rant, a patient, if slightly amused look on his face, shutting the hood to the Porsche as he does so. "Don't you think you're being a little... dramatic?"

"I wish," I tell him. "I can't tell her what I feel for her or she will just freak out. You don't know Elise like I do."

"If you say so." He slaps the hood of the car with the flat of his hand. "Just think it over. The truth will set you free, as they always say. But for now, shall we take a test drive?"

The subject is nowhere near being closed, but like lancing a wound, getting it all out of my system has helped somewhat. My dad jingles the keys in the air in front of me, and I give in, snatching them out of his hand. "Fine, but only if I get to drive first."

* * *

"July is truly one of the most beautiful times to visit Capri. You've made a wonderful choice in dates, Mr. O'Brian. As you can see, the available villas—"

My phone rings, interrupting the travel agent and causing me to cringe. "Sorry, I have to take this."

"No worries," he says, voice chipper as he leans back on his desk chair. "I'll be right here when you're done."

In most cases, I wouldn't bother to answer a call during such an important meeting, but the name on the phone screen is Sebastian Van den Bosch. While I am on great terms with him and his wife, it isn't like we exchange phone calls often, and the fact that he's ringing me must mean there is something that he truly needs to talk to me about.

It's been a week since I've seen his daughter, and she's taken up space in my brain full time, rent-free. We haven't even exchanged text messages, something that we usually did every day, and I find myself missing her terribly. But this is what's best—staying as distant from her as possible. Eventually, she has to leave my thoughts… right?

I step outside the front door of the travel agency onto the sidewalk, answering Sebastian's call at the same time. "Hello, sir. How are you?"

"Good, Dan, thank you for asking. Listen, I know we talked about you joining us for the opening of hunting season, but I thought it might be a good practice run if you came with us to Lake Como on the first week of July, too. I know it's short notice, but I thought we could do some fishing and go over the plan for the hunt. We're taking Elise to celebrate the end of the semester and I know she would love for you to come as well."

His words shock me so much that I'm speechless, trying to think of how to answer. Andries and I have recently spoken about how he's going to miss spending the holidays with his family, and now his dad is inviting me to join them on one? I'm almost afraid that this is because he's discovered what happened between his daughter and me, and he's inviting me as some odd way to show me that I am indeed welcome into the family if I want to be with her.

The thing is, I've always sort of known that Sebastian and Julia wouldn't balk about Elise and I dating the way they do with Roxanne and Andries. I might not be old money, but I'm also still wealthy, and most importantly of all, not a former escort whose presence could taint their family name. I'm sure they have some royal in mind for Elise, like that Johan guy, but I'm not the worst possibility in the world. Still, going on that trip would be seen as a total betrayal for my best friend, and despite being quite tempted, I've got to decline.

Lucky for me, I don't have to tell Sebastian any of this to get out of joining them on vacation. One of my top choices for the Capri trip is the first week of July, and now that he's invited me to Lake Como that week as well, it cements the schedule for me. If I'm in Capri, and Elise is in Lake Como, there is no way we can run into each other and continue making the same mistakes we have been lately. He doesn't know it, but Sebastian just solved a problem for me.

The sad part is, I actually want to accept his offer. A week with Elise at Lake Como sounds like heaven, and if Andries wasn't standing in our way, I would love to go.

"Wow, thank you so much for the invite, but I'm otherwise occupied that week with another trip I've booked with friends. Maybe next time."

"That's too bad," Sebastian replies, and he honestly sounds like he's being genuine. "If you change your mind, call me anytime and we can add you on. The offer remains open."

"Thank you, sir. Have a good day."

"You too, Dan."

Not only does taking the bachelor trip the same week as the Van den Bosch family trip ensure that Elise and I won't have the opportunity to find ourselves conveniently alone somewhere, but it means Andries won't have to dwell on his family being on holiday without him. He'll be with me, his fiancée, and the rest of his friends, having the time of his life.

The travel agent is patiently waiting for me, and he beams when I take my seat across from him once more. I can see why he's so happy, knowing how much this is going to cost me, but it's a once in a lifetime trip. My best friend is getting married, and I'm more than happy to go all out.

I fill out all the necessary paperwork and billing information while the agent explains the itinerary and activities for each day. The five-bedroom villa we'll stay in overlooks the sea, which is a deep, dark blue, and the Faraglione di Mezzo poking above the water like some ancient ruins. He flips through the pictures of everything: the sailboat that will take us to Capri, the breathtaking views, and even the Blue Grotto, lit with an otherworldly glow.

There aren't many places I haven't traveled, but this is one I've yet to explore. My mind drifts as the agent shows me more and more shots, thinking about how amazing it would be to spend my time there with Elise instead of her brother. She would fit right in, her long hair drenched in salt water and only a bikini on her perfect body. I want to share it all with her, but of course, it's impossible, and I have to force myself to brush the thought away.

"Mr. O'Brian?" the agent asks, seeing that my mind is elsewhere. "Do you want to make the reservation?"

"Uh, sorry. Yes, check-in for the second of July. Go ahead and book it."

"Splendid! We will fly you to Napoli and from there, a private boat will pick you and your group up and take you to Capri. It's going to be like paradise on Earth, I assure you."

I simply nod, putting my last signature on the paperwork, trying as hard as I can not think of the only person I really want to be in paradise with, and how she will be just out of my reach.

* * *

With as worked up as I've been, fencing class with Andries is a welcome relief. Feeling my muscles stretch and warm up helps me clear my head, and by the time I break a sweat, I'm feeling more like myself.

Andries is as serious as he ever is at practice, all his movements tight and controlled. He lunges, weaves away, and lunges again, desperately trying to get a hit on me, but I'm full to the brim of pent-up energy. He's out of luck if he thinks he's going to win tonight. The happy-go-lucky Andries that I've seen the past few weeks isn't here today; not when he's so zeroed in on winning.

When I inevitably take the victory, Andries rips his face shield off and throws it down. "What is with you today?! It's like you're working on overdrive!"

I laugh, thinking about how his sister is a lot of the reason I've got so much built up inside of me. "Maybe you're just slow?"

"Dan, I swear—"

"I booked the trip," I interrupt, and his mouth snaps shut. "Your bachelor trip, I mean. We're leaving July second."

"That's in two weeks!" he exclaims, his grumpy attitude changing quickly into excitement. "Where exactly are we going?"

"Italy," I say simply, knowing that he's going to press me. "But that's all I'm telling you. It's a surprise."

He tucks his rapier under his arm, glowering at me. "You can't do that, Dan. I have to know what to pack, and what to tell Roxie to bring, too. She'll never accept 'it's a surprise' as an excuse. You know how she is."

I had hoped to hold the last little bit of the secret, which is the exact location of the trip, close to my chest until just a few days beforehand, but I'm almost as excited as Andries is. He's practically buzzing with it, and I can't hold it back from him any longer.

"Fine, you win, you impatient jerk. We're going to Capri."

Andries freezes, processing the information before his face splits into the widest grin I've ever seen on his face. He surges forward and hugs me, slapping me heartily on the back and causing me to drop my own rapier.

"Capri! I can't believe it! I've always wanted to go there." He grabs me by the shoulders and leans back to look at me. "You're the best best man ever, you know that?"

What I do know is that he wouldn't be saying that if he knew what I was thinking about his sister day in and day out, but there's no reason to share that with him now. "Anything for you, buddy. You deserve it."

CHAPTER 27

Elise

There's something about the last Monday before vacation that makes time slow to a crawl. It's been a week since my birthday, and all the tumultuous feelings that came along with my party and the attendance of one Mr. Dan O'Brian have now dulled to a manageable level... but I still miss him terribly.

Combined with the fact that I'm at work with very little to do has me bored nearly to tears. Since Dad is also leaving next week, work has been sparse at the company as we all wind down to close the office for a few days, and the amount of busy work has now become a trickle. I feel like I'm only here to stare at the computer screen and nothing else.

Tapping my fingernails on the table, I decide to check social media. As soon as my phone's in my hand, though, I get a message from Dad.

Dad: *Dan declined to join us at Lake Como. He most likely doesn't want to piss his best friend off, I'm sure. Why don't you try to convince him?*

My heart sinks a little, reading his words, but I can't say I'm surprised. He's avoided me like the plague this past week, so why would he want to go to Lake Como with my family and me? Still, it stings. There had been a little part of me that thought he might accept.

There's also the fact that Pops isn't inviting him because of some soft spot in his heart for Dan, or because he has any idea that Dan and I had hooked up. Instead, he's only trying to include him to get under Andries's skin, and that strikes me as so petty that I can't even stomach the thought of it. If Dad had really wanted Dan to go, I might be able to put my pride aside and ask him myself, but knowing that there is only a selfish reason for the invite, I'm not going to put myself out there to be hurt or embarrassed by being refused once more.

I shut my phone screen off and set it on the desk beside me, diving into what little work I have left with gusto, hoping to keep my mind busy. I look everything over three times at least, organizing and formatting just to have something to do.

I'm interrupted once more; this time, my desk phone is ringing, which means it's probably someone in the office. I fully expect Dad to be on the other line, reiterating his need for me to try to cajole Dan into the trip, but it's someone even worse... Karl.

"Elise, I'm just calling to get an update on the Roxanne situation. I overheard your father talking about her and your brother coming to your party late in the night, which leads me to believe that they're still going strong, and you haven't managed to drive a wedge into the relationship yet."

I pinch the bridge of my nose between my fingers, feeling a headache building. "You'd be correct."

"So you haven't hired any escorts yet?" He sounds annoyed, which pisses me off.

"No, I've been busy, Karl, and I'm not exactly well versed in hiring prostitutes like you. Give me some time, please."

His voice takes on a syrupy, sweet tone, talking to me as if I'm a child, and it makes me feel gross. "Listen, Miss Elise, this dinner is booked for Thursday, so you've got less than a week to get this ball rolling. Do you understand?"

I'm flabbergasted that he would book the dinner without telling me first. Karl has backed me into a corner, and he knows it. I'm deeply regretting collaborating with him on this plan. "Wow, thanks for giving me no choice, Karl. I really appreciate that," I tell him sarcastically.

"Your family is going on vacation and the wedding is looming closer and closer by the day. Time is of the essence, so if you ever want me to trust you again, I'm going to need you to do your part here." He sighs as if I've done something to disappoint him. "I'm not mad, okay? I just really want to get all of this over with and behind me. Behind us, really, since you're going to be the new CEO one day. I'm sure you don't want the shadow of this scandal still hanging around then."

I know he's right, and as much as I've grown to like Roxanne... well, *tolerate* Roxanne... there's still a big part of me that is sure she can't make my brother happy in the long run. Right now, they're blissful together, but in a few years, will it be the same? Or will they be tired of one another, Roxanne aging and Andries still so much younger?

It's nasty work, calling Roxanne to hire the escorts, but sometimes I have to get my hands dirty if I want to succeed. This seems like it's going to be one of those times, unfortunately.

"Okay, fine," I say, still reluctant and unsure if I'm doing the right thing. The memory of Roxanne handing me her little, carefully wrapped gift before hugging me goodbye stiffly the night of my birthday floats to the forefront of my mind, and it makes my chest tight with guilt. It had been a small bottle of perfume oil that smelled of night-blooming jasmine. She's really trying, so why am I being such a terrible person to her?

"Great," Karl says, his voice low, and it makes me feel slightly ill. "Let me know how it goes."

I hang up the phone without saying goodbye, staring at the receiver for some time, considering my next move. I snatch my iPhone off the desk and hurry to an empty meeting room, shutting the door and locking it behind me. I don't want to leave any trace of what I've done, or as little as possible at least, so instead of calling or texting I press the symbol for an audio message.

"Uh, hey, Roxanne! This is a weird request I know, but I've taken over some clients from other salespeople at the office and I've booked a dinner with them for next Thursday. One of them asked if any of your girls would be there, so I guess they've been hired for these business dinners before, and these clients would really love it if I could book them this time too. They're asking for the exact same girls from last time. Is there any way you can help me out with this?"

My heart is racing as I send it, my body full of adrenaline as if I've run a mile or more, but I'm proud of myself for actually going through with it. There is still that guilt sitting heavy inside of me, but if I manage to pull this off, it won't matter anymore.

As soon as I sit down at my own desk again, Roxanne replies with a short, curt text that takes the wind out of my sails immediately.

Roxanne: *Here's the number for my old agency. They can take care of your request.*

Attached is a screenshot of her previously owned agency's business page, and nothing else. I furrow my brow, confused about why she would be so short and cold with me. I send another audio message, trying to force myself to sound sheepish.

"I'm just not sure which are the escorts that used to go to these dinners. If I'm being honest, these are Karl's old clients, and I'm really nervous dealing with them since I'm so young and they're used to seasoned professionals. Can't you do this for me please, just this once?"

I send the audio message, followed by a text that just says, "*I'd really appreciate it, seriously. Xx.*"

I go back to tapping my nails on the desk, staring at my black phone screen, ridiculously impatient for her to answer. She takes much longer this time, to the point that I'm starting to get anxious, but finally, another message comes through.

Roxanne: *Is Li Chiu also attending this dinner?*

I have no idea who that is, but a quick search of Karl's clients reveals he's one of his wealthiest. I have no idea if he's attending the dinner, but if Roxanne needs me to bend the truth a little to get her involved, I'll do it.

Elise: *I think so, why?*

Roxanne: *Oh, well in that case maybe it's best if I go, too. He and I used to get along so well.*

I read the text over and over again, feeling like I'd won some incredible prize. I can't believe she's going to attend the dinner! Andries is going to be livid.

Livid, and then depressed beyond belief. I push that thought aside before it can sink its teeth in, not wanting to ruin my good mood from my great success. This is the final step in securing myself as the future CEO of Van den Bosch industries.

Roxanne: *Do you have the details of the evening?*

Elise: *Yes. Ciel Bleu at 8 pm on Thursday. Does that work for you?*

Roxanne: *I'll see what I can do. Karl isn't coming, right?*

Elise: *Of course not! Thank you so much for this!*

***

A storm is brewing outside, heavy gray clouds gathering over the canals and hanging low. I find myself staring out at the gathering rain, vacillating between being thrilled with myself for getting Roxanne to go along with the plan, and feeling off, almost sad because I pulled it off.

I had called Karl right after I finished texting with Roxanne, and he had been just as over the moon as I was.

"You are going to go so far in the company, Elise," he told me, that saccharine note still in his voice. "A woman that is so cutthroat that she will sabotage even her future sister-in-law to get ahead will conquer anything she comes across, I'm sure of it. Wonderful job."

His praise should have made me feel happy, but it did the exact opposite. Karl, accused rapist and guaranteed creep, was pleased with me. Meanwhile, Roxanne, a woman who I've dragged through the mud over and over again, was willing to go out of her comfort zone and even risk her relationship with my brother to help me. I can't help but think I've made a terrible mistake, and I start to weigh the CEO position over the happiness of Andries and Roxanne. I think back on their faces as they looked at each other during my toast at their engagement party, so in love, and I feel ill.

I had tried to push it from my mind, but now, hours later, it's still all I can think about. Rereading my messages with Roxanne, I get the feeling that even if she goes through with coming to the dinner, Andries won't be angry enough to leave. After all, she's only doing this to help me, his little sister, not because she wants to. All of this grief may be for nothing.

I want to take it back. Is it too late? I don't want to be part of this chaos anymore.

When my cell rings, a picture of Andries takes over the screen. I feel like ignoring the call and hiding from the world. I know it isn't a coincidence that he's calling me now, and that I've surely been caught in my deception.

I have to answer, though, or I'll look even guiltier.

"Hey, Andries," I say slowly.

His voice is overly cheery, and I close my eyes in dread hearing how false it is. "So, I heard you need Roxanne's help for a dinner with Dad's clients? How cool is that? Soon enough you two will be besties."

I cringe, now sure that Roxanne has shared the story I fabricated, and they've seen through my deception. "Andries..." I hurry to think up an excuse. "I'm handling Karl's clients now, and he worked with Roxanne so much a long time ago that those clients sort of expect her escorts to be at these dinners all the time."

"Huh, don't you think it's kind of odd that Dad is giving an intern the biggest company accounts? I mean, when you were defending Karl still working there, you said it was because he handled some of the most important clients."

This gets my hackles up. Calling me out is one thing, but insulting my work ethic is another. "I'm not just an intern, you know. Dad trusts me entirely."

"Whatever," he snaps, his real feelings starting to bleed through. "I don't get why you couldn't just call the agency. Why do you have to bring Roxanne back into this mess?"

"It's just an innocent favor, that's all. She's the only one that can help me."

"Yeah, right," he scoffs, unconvinced. "You're never innocent. There's always something going on beneath the surface. So tell me the truth, sister, why were you bothering my fiancée with your scheming instead of just calling the number she gave you?"

There's a lump forming in my throat, and I have to swallow past it to speak. "I told you the truth. I want to impress these clients, and Roxanne helping me is the only way I'm sure I can make this dinner perfect. That's it."

Andries lowers his voice, and it isn't just anger at me anymore. There's genuine rage, and it makes me want to cry. "Are you booking escorts on Karl's behalf, Elise?"

"What? No!"

"For some reason, I can't shake the idea that he's not involved. Think about it for a second. If you're lying, and this is Karl's idea, why would he ask it of you? What does he gain by doing it this way? If it was coming from Dad, I'd say it was to tarnish Roxie's name, but this reeks of Karl's involvement. Think, Elise."

Before he can even finish the thought, the truth hits me like a freight train. I've been such a fool. Karl booked the dinner with his clients, which means, despite what I told Roxanne, he could show up if he really wanted. Most importantly, Karl is banned from hiring escorts from all over the country, but he was just able to manipulate his boss's eighteen-year-old daughter into hiring them for him.

I clutch my stomach, nausea threatening to overwhelm me. "I… well… he might have given me the idea…"

Andries explodes on the other end of the line. "I can't believe it. Look at you! The fucking puppet of a nearly convicted rapist! What a new low, Elise. Congrats." From somewhere in the room with him, I can hear Roxanne protesting his harsh words, which makes me feel even worse because she's defending me. "Don't bother coming to Italy with us," Andries sneers.

I pause. "Wait, what? Italy? You're coming to Lake Como with Mom and Pops too?"

Andries also hesitates, the anger falling out of his voice. "Huh? I'm talking about the trip Dan is preparing for us to go to Capri. It's for my bachelor party."

If I thought I had been upset before, it was nothing compared to what I feel right now. Tears roll down my cheeks, and I'm infinitely glad my brother can't see me. "Holy shit, he's taking you to Capri?"

"Wait—he didn't tell you? Fuck! I thought you were among the group of friends he's bringing. You know, given how close the two of you are." Andries puts his hand over the phone receiver, and it sounds like he's talking to someone. Roxanne, I assume.

"No!" I say when he returns. "I thought you were talking about the Lake Como trip Mom and Dad have planned. Our family vacation…" My words trail off.

Andries stutters and then goes silent before sighing. "Ah, hell, Elise. I'm sorry. I thought you knew. Damn. Looks like we are both heading to Italy with very different people."

"Yeah… have fun in Capri."

It takes him a second to answer, and if there's one good thing about finding out that Dan has excluded me from my dream vacation it's that Andries is definitely feeling more pity than anger for me now. "Have fun in Lake Como, sis."

The line goes dead. I drag my hands across my face, clearing it of any tears, before rushing to my dad's office. I knock once but don't wait for a response. He's on a call, but when he sees the look on my face, he hangs up immediately.

"Did you know Dan and Andries were going to Capri at the same time we are going to Lake Como?" I demand.

His expression goes blank with surprise. "I had no idea. Dan just told me he had another trip with friends."

"Of course he did." I cross my arms around myself, clenching my teeth so I don't appear as upset as I really am, but Dad sees through me easily.

"Hey, dear, why don't you sit down with me," he says comfortingly, rising from his desk and walking over to the leather couch on the other side of the office. His tone reminds me of how he used to speak to me when I was little, soft and kind. So different from the harsh, scheming voice that he uses at work.

I sit, and he puts an arm around me, pulling me in for a side hug. I sniffle but don't cry, trying to get my emotions under control.

"I–I wasn't even invited," I say shakily. "I thought Dan was my friend. I'm heartbroken, Dad. I've told him so many times how much I've always wanted to go to Capri."

Dad is quiet for some time, just holding me. I know he's putting the pieces together, realizing why this upsets me so much. It isn't just that he's going to Capri without me... it's that Dan knows it's someplace I've longed to go to, and he wants to avoid me so badly and cares about me so little, that he left me out completely.

That, and the fact that I think I have genuine feelings for Dan, and now I don't get to go with him.

"Elise, why don't we cancel the Lake Como trip and go to Capri instead? I know you want to go, and we probably won't see the other group. Would that make you feel better?"

I shake my head. "No. It's okay. The island isn't big enough to completely avoid them, and I don't want my summer vacation to be ruined even more by running into Dan."

"Have you ever considered just telling him how you feel?"

I know he doesn't just mean about Capri, but I don't acknowledge it. "No. I'm not going after him and begging for an invitation. He knows what he's doing."

Dad sighs. "Maybe he doesn't. Something tells me that this young man truly has no idea what he's actually doing... or at least he doesn't fully understand."

I don't say anything, just soak in the comfort of this moment with my usually brusque father, watching out his floor-to-ceiling office window as the sky opens up once and for all, and the rain comes.

* * *

When I leave for the night, the storm has abated, and everything smells like fresh earth. I start to order an Uber, but stop. Maybe I'll walk the canals instead and try to clear my head.

The first thing I have to do is the easiest: piss off Karl. I gleefully pull his contact information up and text him: *Ask your PA to book the girls. Roxanne is out.*

He tries to call immediately, but I simply block his number and take a deep breath of the fresh air, glad to be free of him for the moment at least.

I'm one of the only ones out after the rain, and it's so soothing, just the sound of the water in the canals and the city starting to come back to life after the storm. I pass the Astoria hotel and pause, looking through the windows at the cafe bar inside. On a whim, I enter, knowing how much Dan loves this place and wanting to be close to him in some way, even if I hate him right now. He's still heavy on my mind and heart.

As I expected, he isn't here, but I take a seat anyway, ordering the Hibiscus blooming tea off the secret menu like I've heard him do before. The bartender raises her eyebrows, but nods, disappearing into the back.

She returns, setting the tea service in front of me. The scarlet flower is already starting to open, tendrils of the essence rising through the water.

"Will Mr. O'Brian be joining you?" the server asks. "I brought another cup, just in case."

It takes me by surprise, but I laugh it off. "Oh, no. I wish, but no. Not tonight."

Shrugging, the server disappears, and I pour the tea into the clear glass mug. I thought I would be disappointed with how bitter it is, or wish for sugar, but the fragrant tea is perfect for my melancholic mood.

I think about what Dad said, and consider texting Dan, turning my phone over in my hand again and again. I know it won't change his mind, though, and I don't want him to know how much he's hurt me.

Instead, I pull up the contact of the person who I do want to mend fences with, my brother.

Elise: *I'm sorry for what I did. I blocked Karl's number and told him to take care of his own dinner. I won't bother you or your fiancée anymore. Enjoy Capri. X.*

CHAPTER 28

Dan

Andries reads the text from Elise out loud to Roxanne and me, then stares down at the phone in his hand for a long moment, clearly conflicted.

The three of us are in Roxanne's living room, having digestifs after a large dinner. Mine is a sweet limoncello, but after hearing what Andries has just read, it tastes bitter on my tongue. I may have really, really fucked up not inviting Elise.

"What do I do now?" Andries asks, looking forlorn. "She sounds so... sad."

"Maybe she genuinely regrets what she did?" I offer, not really sure whether I believe it or not. If someone would have asked me yesterday if Elise could feel remorse, I would have laughed, but now, I think something may have snapped inside of her, and she's crumbling under the weight of her choices.

"I don't know, man," Andries groans, scrubbing his hands over his face. "She's been acting so weird lately. Sweet and caring one minute, and then shady and underhanded the next."

"Well, consider this: she works for your dad, so she has no choice but to be cutthroat in the office so she can prove herself to him. I bet it's hard for her to snap out of it. It's not easy."

Andries turns to his fiancée, still not sure what to do about his wayward sister. "What do you think, Roxie?"

She shrugs one shoulder. "You two have never been an eighteen-year-old girl, so there are a lot of things you don't understand. She's right between who she was as a teenager, and who she is going to become as a woman. Elise is so young. It's obvious she wants to prove herself to Sebastian, but at the same time, she loves you, Andries. She's been stuck between the two, but that text shows that she's chosen you once and for all."

"You aren't even mad that she tried to drag you into this mess with Karl?" I ask, incredulous.

"I didn't say that." Roxie laughs. "I'm pissed. Elise can be a little bit of a bitch sometimes, but like I said, she's so, so young. And I think there is a good heart in there. I won't hold a grudge against her."

Andries leans back on the chaise, swirling the snifter of Grand Marnier as he ponders his choices. I have a suspicion about what he's going to say, and I'm dreading it. At the same time, my heart is aching for Elise, wondering what she's doing out there all alone tonight, having to sort through all this mess she's found herself in. I know she has to learn these things and grow from them, but I still wish I could save her the heartache.

"What if…" Andries starts but pauses as he ponders a bit further. "We invite her to Capri with us? If she comes instead of joining Dad's trip to Lake Como, it will show him that she would rather be with us than him, right?" He grins now, thinking about the revenge of it all. "It'd be like switching teams and Dad would be so pissed."

Roxanne rolls her eyes, but I'm much more animated in my dissent. Spending ten days with Elise in a bikini—lounging by the villa pool and swimming in the sea—will be the most difficult temptation I've ever faced in my life.

"I don't know, man. Even you said she's been acting erratic lately. Do you really want that at your bachelor party?"

With a hum, Roxanne interjects. "Actually, I think Andries is right. She's your sister, after all," she points out, looking over at him. "A lot of how she's acting is this cold facade she's trying to master. She loves you, and I think she'd want to be with all of us. Like I said, I think she has a heart, just hidden maybe."

"If she has one, it's made of stone. Unless she can get something from us, it isn't going to happen."

"Dan!" Roxie gasps. "Why are you being so rude?! I thought the two of you were friends."

"At the end of the day, Dan planned the trip, so he can decide who can or cannot go," Andries interposes, before looking at me. "If you don't want to invite her, that's fine by me."

Sitting forward, Roxanne narrows her eyes at me. "Dan, I *really* think Andries would appreciate having his sister there. And as he said, it'd show Sebastian that his daughter is willing to switch sides."

"Laying the pressure on a little hard, aren't you, Roxie?"

"No pressure!" she responds, holding her hands up. "Just my honest, humble opinion."

Andries laughs at this, leaning over to kiss his fiancée on the temple. "My love, you are many things but never humble."

"Okay, fine," she sniffs, tilting her chin up. "But still, that's what I think we should do. Invite her, Dan."

I toss back the rest of my limoncello, puckering my lips at the taste before relenting. "I'll think about it."

* * *

Once I'm sure the rain is done, I take the top down in the Mercedes and proceed to take the long way home. I need a long, lonesome drive to parse through my thoughts, and the cool, humid night air is absolutely perfect for some deep contemplation.

The roads wind back and forth, back and forth, around the canals and finally a small cliff side. It's a maze, just like my mind. Should I invite Elise, and make her happy, or should I ignore her, and end this thing between us once and for all? One thing is for certain: if I leave her out of the Capri trip, she will never forgive me.

Andries had her on speakerphone over dinner when he confronted her about Karl and the escort situation. I tried to motion to him not to mention our trip, but he wasn't paying me any mind and spilled the secret about Capri wide open to Elise. The heartbreak in her voice when she responded was so tangible that I could feel it stabbing into my heart. I had purposely not invited her, but I've never felt more like an asshole in my entire life than I did right then.

I think I made her cry. Fuck. *Fuck*. I hate myself.

My best friend played it cool when we spoke about inviting her, but I know deep down, he'd be over the moon to have her along. Both he and Elise crave the chance to fix their once-unbreakable bond, and Capri would be the perfect time for that. Sure, at first it was supposed to be a boys' trip, but with Roxanne already coming along, what does it even matter if we add Elise too?

Reconnecting in beautiful Capri will be a memory Andries and Elise will cherish forever. How can I think of denying them that?

The answer is simple. I want Elise with every atom of my being, and having her there, in one of the most stunning places on the planet, nearly alone, will be too much for me to handle. My desire for her burns inside me like an eternal flame, and if I can't keep my distance from her, it will never go out, haunting me forever.

A twisted part of me wants that, though. If I can't have Elise herself, at least I can cling to this feeling I have for her, so strongly that I can feel it like a physical thing in my chest.

Elise being in Capri means trouble for me. Even if she's turned a new leaf and is ready to fix things between her, Roxanne, and Andries, she's still the type of girl that loves games, and she seems to have a special fondness for those that involve me. Elise knows her power over me, and even if it makes me a coward, I have to admit that I'm scared of what she can do.

My tires hydroplane, skidding across the road and dangerously close to the guardrail. I get the car back under control, breathing out a shaky sigh of relief. I had been going much too fast, maybe trying to outrun these thoughts about my best friend's sister, but even now, with my adrenaline coursing through my veins, she's right there at the back of my mind, waiting to pounce.

I'm well and truly fucked.

* * *

As I awake the next morning, I have finally made up my mind. Or at least sort of. For better or worse, I'll have to talk to Elise face to face. And eventually invite her on the trip. I know if I do that it will make Andries happy and given the fact I don't want her to cut me out of her life forever, I'm left with no other choice. I text Elise asking where she is, but she doesn't answer me, so I call Tatiana and she tells me where her friend is without a fuss. Heading to one of the cafeterias on campus, I pass the entrance door and notice Tatiana walking in my direction, leaving her friend alone at the table.

Tatiana stands next to me, looking me up and down, her eyes catching on the bouquet of fresh sunflowers in my hand. "You brought her flowers, huh?"

I brush my hair back with my hand, unnaturally stressed. "Yeah. I don't know what the hell I'm doing. There was this vendor outside the campus, and—"

"You don't have to explain yourself." Tatiana giggles. "Just go talk to her. You two have a lot to figure out, I think."

I look at Elise, eating her salad and scrolling through something on her phone, completely oblivious to my presence in the doorway of the cafeteria. "Yeah, we sure do."

It's Tuesday—the last week of classes for all the college kids—and we're leaving for Capri on Saturday. I've been agonizing over what to do about Elise, finally deciding just to come see her, figuring once I'll be face to face with her the answer will come to me. Now that I'm here, though, there is still a thread of uncertainty in me. Although, when it comes to her, it's almost impossible to deny her.

There is hardly anyone else here, so I bid Tatiana farewell and make my approach. It doesn't take long for her to notice me, and when she does, her eyes go wide as saucers and her fork goes limp in her hand. Elise's eyes travel from my face to the sunflowers and back again.

I sit beside her, plopping the bouquet right in front of her face on the table. "Here. A little sun to melt all that ice."

She ignores me, taking another bite of her salad and keeping her eyes fixed on her phone.

"So you're pissed because I didn't invite you to Capri, huh?"

Elise continues to eat, not giving me the time of day. I sigh dramatically. "Very well, then. Guess you aren't interested in coming along after all."

I stand, but she stops me, not looking up but simply asking in a small, hurt voice, "Why didn't you invite me?"

I fall back into the seat, my eyes meeting hers. "You know why. Because I'm trying to keep my distance from you. If you come to Capri, that isn't going to help our situation."

A small smile tugs at the corners of her mouth. "Am I too irresistible for you to handle?"

A wave of annoyance whips through me, which is apparently evident on my face, because her smile blooms into full-blown laughter. For the first time in my adult life, I feel my face going red from embarrassment, having just basically admitted that Elise was too hot for me to handle.

"Fine!" I snap, throwing my hands in the air. I've completely lost control of this situation. "Fine, you know what? We fly this Saturday at one pm. Now I'm warning you–" I point at her to emphasize my point, and she just laughs harder. "Listen to me, dammit! You will be invisible to me. Do you understand? Not irresistible, in-vi-si-ble! You can strip naked in front of me, and I won't give two fucks about it."

She raises her eyebrows, leaning back on her chair, her arms crossed over her chest. "Is that a challenge?"

"Fuck no, it isn't," I grumble. "I'm only inviting you because your brother truly seems to like you, no matter how much terrible shit you do. Hell, even Roxanne seems to be warming up to you. I have no idea how these people keep forgiving you after everything you do to them."

"Because that's what good people do," she says simply.

It stops me in my tracks. She's right, but I can't admit it. "Yeah, but you aren't one."

She looks hurt, and I curse myself internally for being so petty, but I've said my piece. I walk away, and I'm almost out of earshot when I hear her say.

"Thank you for the flowers, Dan. They're beautiful."

I pause, close my eyes, and prepare to say something to her. Nothing comes to mind, though, so I just continue on until I'm out of her sight, and finally, out of the cafeteria itself.

Afterward, I go meet her brother at another campus cafe, this one located near the English department, right as he finishes class. I try to put her out of my mind, but as soon as I see Andries, I'm reminded all over again why I'm here to speak with him. Everything is about Elise. She is all over my life, and in every nook and cranny of it.

My friend walks in and sits down, not even bothering to stop and order anything from the counter. He seems tired from class but glad to see me, nonetheless. Lucky for him, I already ordered for both of us, and slide his cappuccino in a cardboard cup across the table.

"Here you go. Now, I'm here to tell you that I invited that harpy you call a sister, and she's officially coming to Capri as far as I know."

Andries grins, standing halfway and slapping me on the shoulder a few times affectionately. "I knew you'd make the right call."

I scowl. "If you wanted me to invite her, why not just say so?"

"Because if I made the decision for you, you'd be pissed the whole time. Now, if she gets on your nerves, you only have yourself to blame."

"Oh, fuck off Andries," I huff, and he laughs.

"One more question. Can Lili and Robin come too? Roxanne mentioned it and Lili got all starry-eyed. She'd love it, I know."

I sigh, sliding down in my chair. I fucking knew it. I'm glad I held off on the invitations for the guys I had in mind.

"If you wanted a family vacation, you should have warned me. But yes, that's fine. We have plenty of room."

I inform him of the itinerary and the delicate process that will get us to our eventual destination of Capri. I'm mentally switching things around to fit the more family-oriented style that the trip has now taken on, annoyed but amused. Leave it to Andries to make things as complicated as possible.

"We will have a private jet waiting at 1 pm, and we'll be arriving at Napoli around 3 pm. Then things are a little rushed from there, unloading everything onto the private boat that will get us to Capri, which is forty-five minutes away."

Andries listens intently, becoming more visibly excited by the minute. Despite how much his sister drives me crazy, in more ways than one, I'm so happy I can do all of this for my best friend. I know it must be hard for him to be disowned just because he's marrying who he loves, but I'm determined to make up for what he's lost, and then some.

I know it's near to impossible, but maybe showing him how far I'm willing to go for people I love, like him, will change his mind on how he feels about Elise and me dating. A far-fetched fantasy, but one I hang on to, nonetheless.

"Should we invite Yao, too? Maybe we can do some knitting on the coastline?" I joke, but I half expect him to agree. Thankfully, he shakes his head.

"Yao hates the heat, so she's out."

"Perfect. Now, one more thing," I lean forward across the table, a mischievous smile creeping across my face. "I'm also organizing a party to celebrate the end of the semester

Friday. Something chill, but with plenty of herbs, if you catch my drift."

He groans. "Come on, man. That's so much."

"I don't care. It's on."

He rolls his eyes, not at all fond of my idea of a pre-trip party. "Okay, well… we'll see on Friday how I feel about it."

CHAPTER 28

Elise

The rest of the week has seemed to drag on forever, but at the same time, there aren't enough minutes in the universe to make sense of everything going on in my life right now.

After Dan had left me in the cafeteria with a bouquet and an invitation to Capri, I had felt every possible emotion —excitement about being allowed to come along, annoyance at how clear it was that Dan didn't want me to come, and nervousness about how I was going to tell Dad that I had to cancel our plans.

He had been annoyed at first, of course—because who wouldn't be—but Dad is business-minded, and he's had his eyes set on the goal of splitting Andries and Roxanne up for so long now that any extra scrap of information is invaluable to him. Therefore, he was fine with me going to Capri if it meant that I could get closer to my brother and his fiancée, still thinking that I was going to be able to break them up before the wedding. The more time that passes, though, the more unsure I am that I'll be able to cause the break. Also, the more unsure I become that it's actually something I want to do.

Andries and Roxanne love each other, and while, at first, I had been sure it was just a case of mistaking lust for real affection, my opinion is changing the more I see the two of them together. Each time I find myself smiling softly as I watch them happily living their lives together, the yawning pit in my stomach about how wrong it is for me to try to split them up continues to grow.

It isn't just Andries and Roxie on my mind this last week of school, either. After inviting me to Capri, Dan seems to have disappeared off the face of the earth. I'm becoming nervous that his threat of pretending that I don't exist in Capri is actually something he plans to do, not just empty words meant to make me regret coming. I miss him…miss the easy way things used to be between us when we were just friends skating the line of flirtation. Now that we have acted on the mutual attraction burning between us, it feels like nothing will ever be the same again. I want him—want to feel his touch, and hear his voice, but at the same time I hate that he continues to just leave me hanging like this. As if I'm just any other girl he's hooked up with, and I didn't even get the full hook up experience!

Dan heats me up in every possible way imaginable. He makes me hot and furious with anger but also leaves my body burning for him. I'm bordering on obsession at this point, and I hate it.

My last class before break finally lets out, and I breathe a sigh of relief as I pack my things up and haul my bag over my shoulder. School hasn't been my main focus these last few months, but as a bit of a perfectionist, I still managed to do exceedingly well in most of my classes. Tatiana is waiting for me outside, as happy and bubbly as ever. Maybe even more so, considering that it's finally summer break.

"Hey!" she greets me, her face beaming with joy. "I know we said we were going to get a drink together, but with the party tonight, I don't think I'll have time to get ready if we do. Can we reschedule?"

"Sure," I say before her words catch up with me. "Wait, what party?"

Tatiana looks like a deer in headlights. "Um. Dan's party?"

I feel heat creeping up the back of my neck. How dare he invite innocent little Tati and not me? Oh, that man is going to drive me insane. "I had no idea Dan was having a party."

She cringes. "Geez, Elise, I'm sorry. I just automatically figured you'd been invited since you guys are close."

"Apparently not that close," I seethe.

My friend pulls at the strings of her jumper, looking anywhere but at my face, clearly feeling awkward. "Maybe it was a mistake, and he just forgot to invite you?"

"No. Dan has been on a crusade to avoid me lately, and I'm sure this is just another manifestation of that." I'm pissed, but I can see Tati is getting more uncomfortable by the minute. I sigh. "It's fine, Tati. Just go and have fun. I don't want to be somewhere I'm not welcome."

She thinks it over, nibbling her bottom lip, before getting a look of bravery I don't often see on her. "Just come with me, then. Who cares about an invite? If Dan is too much of a chicken to invite you himself, then we'll just fix that problem for him."

Considering her words, I shift my weight from hip to hip, thinking. On one hand, I don't want to humiliate myself by crashing a party somewhere that I'm clearly not wanted, but on the other hand, seeing Dan's face when I walk in with Tati will be such delicious revenge for how he's been ignoring me lately. It isn't the ladylike thing to do, but then again, most things I do these days are far from ladylike.

I have to quickly push the memory of the billiards room aside before I blush. "Are you sure? I don't want him to take it out on you by not inviting you to anything after this."

"You know Dan. He just sends out invites to every acquaintance he's ever made. It's all about how many bodies he can get at his parties, so I'm sure he'll get over me bringing you. Plus," she leans toward me, a mischievous smile on her face, "maybe you and Dan will have such a good time that he'll end up thanking me instead."

And there's the blush I've been trying to avoid. "Oh, hush. But yes, I'd love to be your plus one."

"Great!" She moves to flounce away, in a hurry to get ready for the party. "Wear something nice since you're going to be my hot date tonight!"

I grin to myself, thinking of all the things I can wear to drive Dan mad. "You've got it!"

* * *

Before I decided to go with something slightly scandalous, I had to confirm that my brother wasn't also coming to the party. Nothing ruins a good time like your brother getting in the middle of your secret friends-with-benefits situation.

Andries doesn't even know Dan and I are interested in each other that way, so having to walk on eggshells all night regarding it was not something I was interested in.

Thankfully, when I messaged Andries to see what he was up to, he let me know that he and Roxanne were staying in for the evening to celebrate the end of school together. I made some small talk with him so he wouldn't get suspicious, but on the inside, I was elated.

When I asked Tatianna what the dress code was, all she could tell me was that Dan suggested jewel tones, and while I don't own a lot of things that bright, I did have a ruby red, low cut jumpsuit that moved with the breeze as I walked. Shimmery and silky, I think it gives just the right feeling for the evening.

Tatiana and I take an Uber together, her dressed in aubergine purple, and I try to get some information out of her about what exactly this party entails.

"I really don't know," she insists. "I'm pretty sure he invited me at the last minute because we ran into each other a few days back, so it's not like I got a formal invitation or anything."

"He's so hard to read," I groan in displeasure. "This could be just like any other get-together, or it could be something over the top that I'm completely unprepared for."

"I'm sure he'd have at least told me if it was something crazy," she tries to convince me, but her voice betrays her. She's unsure, too. "It will be fun though, right?"

"Fun, I'm sure. It's all the other adjectives that I'm worried about."

My first warning sign that tonight is going to be different from his usual parties is that, when the Uber pulls up to the curb to let us out, the lights in Dan's townhouse are low enough that if I didn't know better, I might assume no one was home. I look at Tati, who just shrugs.

When the housekeeper opens the front door and we step inside the hallway, there's a slight haze that rolls out around me, smelling of smoke and cloves. We head to the living room where everything is lit only by soft shades of pink and orange light, scarves of diaphanous material thrown over the lamps throughout the home. The music playing is thrumming and exotic.

There aren't the usual crowds of people vying for space or gathering together in groups. Instead, there are low tables scattered about the floor on top of woven carpets, ringed by soft, puffy pillows. The guests sit around these tables, which are dominated by huge, intricately designed hookahs, each one more detailed than the last. I recognize a few faces from school and other parties I've attended, but this is lower key than I imagined, with everyone taking deep inhales from the hookah mouthpieces and blowing the smoke into the air above them. Everything feels intimate and hedonistic. I look at Tatiana again, who is glancing around the space, goggle-eyed.

At first, I think it was just servers moving amongst the small groups of smokers, but I quickly see there are a number of belly dancers, too, their bodies moving in graceful waves. They're stunning, leaning forward and even sometimes bending backward in front of the partygoers, close enough to be tantalizing but never close enough to touch. It's entrancing.

We walk across the floor, smoke billowing around us. Tatiana appears to be looking for someone, but I can also tell that she doesn't want to leave me behind. She's become so brave, my shy friend, and I don't want to hold her back.

Plus, there is someone I'm interested in finding myself, and something tells me that it will be better for me to confront him without Tatiana there to witness it all.

"You can go, if you're meeting people," I tell her, taking her hand and giving it a quick squeeze. "I know you didn't plan on bringing me."

"Oh," she says, flustered but happy with my statement. "I thought I might see Mark here, so…"

"Go ahead." I give her a little push in the right direction. She deserves to hang out with someone who makes her happy. "If we don't catch back up with each other, don't worry about me, okay? But if you need anything, just call."

Tati only hesitates for a moment more before nodding and disappearing into the darkness of the party. Standing alone, I take a few deep breaths to find my courage and begin to search for the man that has been eluding me for too long.

Dan, of course, is at the biggest table, surrounded by beautiful women, and too few men for my taste. As one of the only guys, and the party host, he's getting a plethora of adoring attention, and it pisses me off. He has time for all these people, but not for me? Every time I think that we are at least close friends, he does something that makes me think that maybe he doesn't think of me the same way. Still, I'm here, and I'm not going to let this chance go.

He doesn't notice me at first, and I take the time to watch him, taking long draws from the hookah and blowing streams of shisha smoke into the air above him. He laughs with the other girls, even letting them lean on him somewhat, but I also notice how he subtly shrugs them off, disguising it as movements to reach for something or turn to speak to someone else. I hate to see them touch him, but I do get a distinct feeling of satisfaction watching him brush them off. It gives me a glimmer of hope that he's doing it all for me. Maybe the fuckboy lifestyle doesn't appeal to him quite so much anymore.

When he places the mouthpiece between his lips again, I make my move, obscured by the dimness of the room. Dan doesn't even see me until I'm next to him, pulling the mouthpiece away with a gentle tug and placing it in my own mouth.

He watches me, eyes going wide with surprise, and then narrowing with annoyance as I draw in a deep breath. The smoke tastes heavy and complicated, like molasses and patchouli—slightly burnt but deliciously bitter. Still, I fight the urge to cough, not wanting to make a fool out of myself in front of everyone, and blow the mouthful of smoke at Dan with my eyes watering, watching it cascade around his face like a gust of wind.

While he's still speechless, I say, "Damn…first you don't want me to come to Capri, and now you're not even inviting me to your parties. You're really cutting me out of your life, huh?"

"What the fuck are you doing here?" he finally manages to ask, low and dangerous. "This party isn't for you. Hence why you weren't invited."

I ignore him, drawing in another mouthful of shisha before Dan stands and makes a lunge for the mouthpiece, and takes it from me. I try to grab it back, but if his expression is anything to go by, he isn't messing around.

He grabs me by the upper arm, pulling me close so only I can hear him. "Knock it off. Some of these people know your brother, and they might tell him you're here smoking. Is that what you want?"

"Like who?" I say mockingly, my eyes briefly checking the guests at his table before they fall on him again. "You're his best friend, right? Are *you* going to tell him? Plus, it's just shisha, no?"

He flicks his eyes to the hookah table, and I follow his glance where it lands on a large, suspiciously full bag. Dan tries to reach for it casually, but I snake my arms past him and pluck it off the surface quicker than he can. Holding it up to my face, I can smell it through the plastic, pungent and ripe. Marijuana.

"Oh, I get it now! You're going to smoke weed too, right? Is that why you didn't invite me?"

His expression darkens. "Elise, I'm not joking. Give it to me right now."

Everyone is watching us, but what do I care? My feelings are hurt that he wouldn't invite me and that he's getting up to such debauchery while I sit at home wishing we were spending time together. I hate that he can just go on and live his life without ever thinking of me while I borderline obsess over him.

In one movement, I pivot and flee, walking quickly through the maze of tables and smoke hanging in the air, dodging servers and belly dancers, and heading for where I know the stairs are. Thankfully I'm familiar with Dan's house because otherwise I'd be lost.

I can hear him behind me, and it gives me a thrill, knowing that he's giving chase. I fly up the stairs, grabbing the handle of the first door I see and hiding inside, the bag of weed still clutched in my hand.

It doesn't take him long to find me, pressed against the wall in the dark room. I try to hide when I see the door begin to open, but it's so dark I can't make out anything around me, and before I know it he's flipped the lights on.

It's a bedroom; one that has clearly been lived in, meaning that it must be Dan's. This gives me another little shiver of delight, knowing I'm in his most private space. Taking advantage of his surprise at finding me here I kick my heels off and hop up onto the bed, using the added height to my advantage in keeping it away from him.

I wish I had more time to look around and really absorb what his bedroom is like. Dan has been free and open with women in the past but never letting them into his real personal life. I have to keep my eyes locked on him, so the only thing I get is the impression of forest greens and black, the mattress under my feet soft and luxurious.

"Get down, Elise," he tells me, looking annoyed and exasperated. "Quit being immature."

"Oh, I'm the one being immature? Not the guy avoiding me just because he can't handle the fact we sort of hooked up? At least I can face you!"

"This is all so much more complicated than you're making it out to be, and you know it. Get down, give me the weed, and get out of my fucking house."

I smirk. "Make me."

Dan doesn't waste any time after I issue my challenge, jumping up onto the bed with me. I try to hold my hand above my head in one last attempt to keep the bag of weed away from him, but he's got the height advantage now, and easily snatches it from my grasp. With a well-aimed toss, he throws the sealed bag on his bedside table before grabbing my wrists in his own. I try to pull away, but he pushes me backward. The bed is so soft that my feet are immediately tangled, and I fall back onto the mattress, but Dan is there too, still holding my wrists with his body now covering mine.

He looks triumphant, for a moment at least. That is, before he realizes the position he's put us in.

I feel his body tense, either to pull away or just out of instinct at how close we are. He's warm, and the weight of his body on mine is addicting. Afraid that he's going to jump away, I shake my wrists free from his now-loose grasp and lock my arms around him. He's staring at my lips, and almost unconsciously, I purse them, wetting them with my tongue. There's an answering jolt that goes through his frame, pelvis tilting into mine without him even realizing it.

"Well," I whisper, our eyes locked on each other. "Are you going to kiss me now?"

"Do you want me to?" His voice is husky.

Instead of answering him with words, I tighten my grip on him, pulling him down until I can slant my mouth over his. Dan lets out a breath, his guard against me evaporating as we deepen the kiss. I like to think that I am still in control when we come together like this, but I can feel my rational thought melting away like snow on the mountaintop with each sweep of his tongue against mine, and when he pulls away enough to bite my lip, a sharp nanosecond of pain that he sucks away immediately, I'm lost.

He moves down my body as if in a trance, his lips grazing my jawline, teeth and tongue moving around my neck and collarbone. We don't speak, knowing it will break the spell, but the sounds coming from him tell me more than any conversation ever could. As his control grows shorter and shorter, he covers the tops of my breasts and the line of my cleavage with love bites, his hands moving from where they were resting on my waist to my chest. Once Dan realizes that I'm braless under the jumpsuit, my tits only separated from his mouth by a thin layer of silky fabric and two flimsy straps, he grinds his pelvis into mine, his cock a hard burning line that presses exactly where I need it most.

I moan. I can't help it.

"Tell me to stop," he begs, fingers already pinching my nipples through the cloth despite his words.

Too much talking, I think, grabbing Dan's head between my hands and pulling it back down to my flesh. He groans, aroused and helpless, but acquiesces to my silent demands. I raise my shoulders just enough so he can pull the straps down my shoulder, pulling the top part of the bodysuit to my waist, and I am bare from there up. I can hear my heartbeat in my ears when Dan starts to kiss a slow line from my sternum to one of my nipples, but he's too heated for such a slow buildup. It only takes moments for his mouth to find my already hard nipples, and he sucks them, one after the other, to hard peaks while his busy hands continue to pull my bodysuit down. The rush of pleasure from his tongue and teeth on my tits is intense, and it makes me crave his touch even more. I just want my skin against his, wherever possible, and for him to ease the hollow ache growing in my core.

I know Dan can take his time when he wants to, but we're both desperate for one another, and I don't complain when he gives my nipples a final nibble and his mouth continues down my body, over my ribs and fluttering stomach, and finally to my now-bare thighs. The red panties I'm wearing are the only thing left on my body, but with Dan between my legs now, I suddenly feel bereft. He's not touching me enough, even if the possibility of his mouth landing on my core is tempting as hell. I don't want just a repeat of the billiards room, or for Dan to just get me off and then leave me alone again. I want all of him that he is willing to give.

I push up, and he raises too, giving me a questioning look as I almost jump toward him, working at the buttons of his white, oxford shirt as quickly as I can. In the chill air of the bedroom, the wetness still on my nipples is making them cold, and I want us to be chest to chest, soaking in the warmth of him. Dan is quick to help me, expertly unbuttoning his shirt and shrugging it off so I can run my hands over the hard planes of his chest. Looping my arms around his neck, I give into my darkest desires, pressing against him and kissing his mouth with abandon. Grabbing my hips forcefully, he grinds against me again, the press of his erection rubbing over my aching clit through my panties. I can't take it anymore. I want to touch him, so badly that it's almost maddening.

My hands are on his belt, pulling it open, while I look up and into his eyes, wanting to see if he's watching me undress him. But when our eyes meet, it's like Dan remembers who I am, and what we're doing, and the first threads of doubt start to manifest within him. Carefully, doing his best not to touch his own hard length, he pushes my hands away from him.

"Elise, we can't fucking do this," he forces out, every syllable sounding difficult.

"Relax," I reply in a purr. "My brother isn't here. It's only us."

I go to continue my work, but he pulls away again. "Are you sure about this?"

"Yes," I huff, growing annoyed. "I messaged him to make sure before I came."

"I don't just mean about Andries not coming. Are you sure *this* is something you want to do? This is going too far, I think."

I won't let him back down now that we are so close. "If I'm going to be invisible to you in Capri, I better get your full attention now."

Pulling me close again, he doesn't touch me the way I want so badly but instead looks deep into my eyes with a serious gaze, completely different from the hazy look of lust he was wearing before. "If we do this, we take this secret to the grave, okay?" It's a big declaration, but I nod anyway, eager to get on with it. Dan doesn't quite believe me, though, doubling down. "Elise. To *our graves*. Do you swear?"

Knowing that he's taking this oath solemnly, I cup his face in my hands, feeling his stubble under my hands. Even though I'm trying to match his serious mood, I can't help but sweep my thumb over his full bottom lip as I tell him, "I promise."

When he kisses me now, it's sweeter, the frantic pace between us slowing down now that we've both acknowledged the truth about what is going to happen. It's all out in the open, and this kiss is freer than any others we've ever shared.

Dan helps me remove his pants until he's just in his boxers. We're both on our knees, facing each other, and the excitement between us is palpable. We take turns touching each other slowly, learning what makes each of us jump or shiver in pleasure. As his thumbs hook under my panties and I rise up so he can remove them completely, Dan looks almost reverent.

He doesn't even wait for me now, shucking his own boxers and tossing them somewhere off to the side. His erection is truly something to behold, longer and thicker than I expected even after having felt him against me so many times now. His skin is paler there than the rest of his body, but the tip of his member is darker and wet with a drop of precum, but he's completely and undeniably as erect as he can possibly get. I don't think I will even be able to close my fingers around the width of him, and stirrings of anxiousness rise up in me. How am I going to be able to take that inside of me?

My body, on the other hand, celebrates at the sight of him completely nude for me. My pussy pulses and aches now that I can finally see what I need inside of me so badly, and even my heart is gearing up to be fucked. I'm hot, needy, and nervous. Not the best combination.

Seeing the worry on my face, he pauses, suddenly uneasy as well. "Are you on the pill or something? If not, I can grab a condom–"

I do quick mental math, and figuring that my period just ended, I say, "I'm good." Dan looks uncertain, and his expression combined with the sight of his hand now holding his hard cock, makes me laugh. My anxiety eases. "Don't worry, Dan, I'm good." Leaning forward, I grip his shoulders and whisper in his ear, feeling more wanton than I ever have in my life. "I want to do it raw."

He makes a noise akin to a growl, his control snapping. He's stroking his cock now with one hand, the other grasping my chin and kissing me punishingly. I'm on my back again now, him nibbling at my nipples while his fingers part my folds and run quick circles around my clit. I'm undeniably wet and ready for him, already losing my concentration over how good this all feels.

He seems to confirm everything he needs to know—that I'm wet enough, so he places one hand on the bed beside my head while the other maneuvers his cock outside of my opening.

It's really happening! I think, still scared but so desperate for Dan that it doesn't even matter.

"Are you okay?" he asks one last time, and I nod quickly. Even if I wasn't, I'm not going to back down now.

He holds my eyes as he thrusts into me for the very first time. I'm almost unbearably tight, and Dan hisses through his teeth, pausing before pushing again, even slower this time. Every millimeter is a struggle, and I'm starting to get nervous. Really nervous. What if he doesn't fit inside me?

Once it becomes almost impossible for him to push any further, the pain starts. It's a stretching, burning feeling, and I have to blink rapidly to clear away the tears that prick at the corner of my eyes. Dan stops then, looking down at me with worried affection, his gaze searching for mine.

"Elise, can I ask you something?"

"Yes," I breathe, no air in my lungs.

"Am I going to be your first?"

I can't look him in the eye anymore, turning my head away and nodding, embarrassed beyond belief. I didn't want him to know until afterward, afraid that he wouldn't sleep with me if he knew I was a virgin. But now, halfway inside of me, surely he won't leave now?

"Is that a problem?" I ask, looking back into his eyes, afraid of what I'll find there, but I shouldn't even have worried. Dan might be silent, but at least he doesn't look unhappy. In fact, his eyes are glowing with some unnamed emotion. The smile that blooms over his face is beautiful.

Kissing me gently, taking ample time as he does so, he continues working his cock inside of me. The pace is achingly slow but welcome. Knowing that he doesn't care about my virginity relaxes tension that I didn't even know I was holding, and it goes much easier than before.

"You will be the death of me," he whispers against my lips, just as the head of his cock hits home inside of me, his hips meeting mine. He continues thrusting, this time back and forward, gently enough not to hurt me, and yet, I can't help but gasp at the tearing feeling between my thighs.

We are really fucking. Holy shit. The truth of it pulses through me, leaving me breathless.

"I'm going to make this good for you," he promises me, his tone just above a whisper. "Unforgettable."

I don't tell him that the experience is already unforgettable, and we've barely started. Instead, I just return his kiss, my eyes fluttering closed.

Dan's first few thrusts still burn with how much he's stretching me out, but within minutes, the pain fades away and leaves something else in its place; a delicious fullness I've never felt before. We're so connected, legs tangled together, Dan deep inside of me and his tongue in my mouth. It's incredible.

When he notices that I'm not hurting anymore and that his movements are making me sigh and breathe harder, his smile takes on a feral edge. He raises himself up on his elbows, coaxing me to lift my knees so he's thrusting into me at an angle. Deep in my channel, the head of his cock hits some bundle of nerves that makes me shake against him. It feels just like when he caresses my clit, except the pleasure is so much more intense and concentrated that I can't help the way I arch into him. The noise I make is low and desperate.

"Oh my God," I breathe. "Just like that. Please."

He's more than happy to comply, but Dan keeps his pace even and just slow enough to make me feel crazy. The feeling of him stretching my walls and then hitting that secret spot is building a pool of pleasure in me, deep and filling up fast. Even as he fills me relentlessly, the way he kisses and touches me is sweet and careful. I stroke his body, running my fingers over his smooth, tanned chest and sweeping my tongue over the hollow of his collarbone when he's close enough. But I feel closest and most connected to him when we kiss, tongues dancing, as he continues to fill me again and again.

There's a line of concentration forming between his eyebrows, showing me that he's holding back. I'm both thankful, knowing I'm already going to be sore tomorrow, but also curious about what it would be like if he truly unleashed himself on me. There will be time for that in the future, I'm sure, but I decide I still want a little taste of it right now.

I start to pepper in little nips and bites in with the loving kisses we're exchanging, meeting him thrust for thrust as he fucks me. Dan's jaw is clenched, his control slipping, which is exactly what I want. It feels so, so good, but I'm greedy. I want more.

Dan raises himself up off me, grabbing my hips and holding me in place as he continues to thrust, harder now than before, his body snapping against mine. Like this, he touches me everywhere, and when his fingers land between my legs, right over my clit, I see stars. He strokes it gently with his thumb, adding sharp, bright pleasure to the deep, rolling sensation that his cock in my pussy is providing. These sensations meet, and unconsciously, my legs start to shake. Dan laughs low in his throat.

"Like that, huh?" He rubs my clit quicker now, and it feels so good that I can feel the pleasure filling me from my pussy all the way up my spine. I cry out his name, head thrashing from side to side. It's too much, and yet, everything that I need.

"Elise," Dan commands. "Come for me."

I'm close, but not quite there yet. Back arched off the bed, I'm teetering right on the edge of the most mind-shattering orgasm of my entire life, but I want him closer. I need to feel his body against mine when I come apart... need to cry out my climax against his lips.

"Kiss me," I beg.

He complies, moving his body forward until he's entering me at an even steeper angle so he can capture my mouth with his. Somehow, his hand stays between us, stroking my clit relentlessly, just as he's fucking me. Connected through his cock, fingers, and now tongue, I finally have everything I'm looking for. It fills that pool of pleasure in me to the brim, and as I writhed beneath him with the intensity of it, I come.

I'm speechless, but even if I could describe it, my mouth would be busy. Dan drinks down my cries of pleasure, savoring them. My entire body is covered in goosebumps, every nerve alight with how good it feels. Since he continues to fuck me, the orgasm doesn't seem to end, even when he finally takes his hand from between us and has to brace himself, fucking me hard and unhinged.

Dan breaks the kiss, a vulnerable noise escaping him as he orgasms too, painting the inside of my walls with his seed. I can feel how hot it is, my pussy still spasming around his cock with the aftershocks of my orgasm and a feeling of satisfaction coming over me like the tide. This was worth it all. It's all so perfect. How can anything ever compare to this moment?

Collapsing beside me, Dan pulls me into his arms. I whimper softly as he pulls out of me. Not wanting this to end, I tangle my legs with his, pressing our sweaty foreheads together. Thankfully, he wants to keep me just as close and starts cuddling me.

We don't speak, just listen to each other's breaths and heartbeats. I could stay here forever in his embrace, warm and safe, but I can already feel fluids from our encounter going cold and drying on my thighs. I slowly pull away from him, intending to clean up in the shower, preferably with him, but Dan watches me rise with trepidation.

"Where are you going?"

He sounds so stiff that I can't help but think that he wants me to stay. Good, because that's what I want too, but I can't help but tease him a little. "Showering so I can go home."

He looks offended and, in the blink of an eye, reaches out for my hand. "No way. You're staying here."

I tilt my head to the side, fighting the growing smirk on my face. "Why?"

"Because I'm not done with you yet."

Dan rolls to the edge of the bed and grabs me by the hips. As tired as I am, I still squeal as he lifts me back onto the bed on top of him, locking his arms in legs around me to stop me from leaving. I giggle right before he kisses me again, with all the same passion as before, and in seconds I'm sighing against him, returning his kisses happily.

We make out unhurriedly in the afterglow, Dan's hands carding through my hair as I lazily trace the muscles of his arms and shoulders with my fingers. This newfound access to each other's naked bodies is addicting, and I can now see why people will sometimes spend all day in bed together.

It takes some time, but the energy changes, going from indulgent and slow to heated. Dan's hands grip me more forcefully, palming my ass as he ducks his head to suck a nipple into his mouth. I moan, grinding against him when I feel his erection start to grow once more.

When he's hard, I reposition myself, lifting my hips until my pussy is hovering over the head of his cock, balancing with my hands on his shoulders. All thoughts of teasing and showers have left me, and I'm ready to watch the expressions on his face change as I ride him.

With agonizing carefulness, I lower myself onto him, hissing as my walls are forced to stretch again so soon. It stings but in a good way. Dan watches me as if I'm something holy, gaze going from where we are connected, to my eyes, and then back again.

"You're so fucking beautiful," he tells me, voice thick with emotion.

I take him into me fully, rocking forward to find my rhythm, just the right way so he's rubbing against my inner walls. Once I find my pace, I ride him in earnest, clumsy at times but eager to please. Dan holds my hips, stroking my ribs, stomach, and pinching my nipples as I do. My whole body is still vibrating from how hard I had come the first time, and it's happy to rise to the occasion again.

My second climax feels like a natural continuation of the first, hitting me hard but then washing over me like a wave of wonderful sensations. I ride with abandon, tits bouncing and moans echoing off the bedroom walls. Dan grips my hips again, this time so hard that his fingertips leave little indentations in my skin, thrusting up just as I roll my body forward, again and again, until he too is orgasming. Teeth clenched, he takes over fully as I have to stop, exhausted, pushing up into me until he's spilled the last drop of his cum deep inside me.

This time, when I fall forward and we snuggle close, Dan is quick to pull me against his body and cover us with the duvet. I know I need to shower; we both do, but I'm still twitching with the aftershocks of coming so hard, twice. Dan is nearly boneless beside me, eyelids heavy.

With a soft smile, I press my lips against his, heart swelling when he sighs in contentment. The shower can come later. For now, I don't want to leave this space or the man beside me.

CHAPTER 30

Dan

Last night, I had every intention of getting high enough that I would be able to pass out and forget my fate for the upcoming week, but of course, Elise had to show up and ruin my carefully laid ideas yet again. This time, though, she managed to do it in the best way possible.

I'd like to think I'd have never slept with her, had she not tricked me into rolling on the bed with her and just being so damned tempting all at the same time, but at this point, what does it even matter? We had sex. I took her virginity, and there is no going back now. The cat is decidedly not getting back in the bag.

Do I even want to? If I'm honest with myself, no… no I don't. There is something so cathartic about having given into the whole thing between Elise and me. No more trying to hold myself back, no more denying the burning attraction I feel for her… it's done. Now I feel like I can breathe again.

As I wake up, there is a strange mixture of self-loathing and hedonistic happiness flowing through me. Stretching my muscles out, I brush away the loathing, planning to deal with it later, when there isn't a beautiful, willing woman in my bed.

Except, she's not.

I reach over for Elise, planning to pull her body against mine and try to coax her into another round of lovemaking before we have to face the real world. Here in this bed, we're in our own little world, and all the consequences of this choice we've made are far away on the other side of my bedroom door. My stomach sinks as I find her side of the bed cold and empty, nothing but messed up sheets even hinting that she had been there at all.

I sit up, brows drawn together in concern, ready to call out for her when I hear the sound of the sink from my en suite bathroom. Breathing a sigh of relief, I slip out of the bed, putting on a pair of boxers in a display of some sort of modesty, and pad my way across the room to find her. I feel jilted out of my romantic morning wake up and how much I had looked forward to cuddling her warm body in my arms, but maybe she'll still join me for an encore of the previous night's performance.

In the bathroom, Elise is already dressed once more in her scarlet romper from the party, finger-combing her hair as she leans close to the lighted mirror. She spares me a glance and a small, secret smile before returning to her grooming.

"Good morning," I tell her, feeling slightly unsettled that she doesn't even speak to me.

"Morning," she bursts out, her eyes still pinned on the mirror in front of the sink.

I make my way to her, planning to step behind her and kiss her long, graceful neck, but she doesn't move a single inch to greet me, and I know her body language well enough to see that she doesn't want me to touch her. My heart jumps into my throat. What have I done wrong?

"Um… it's pretty early…" I start lamely. "Are you alright?"

Like me, I'm sure she's still in disbelief that we had even slept together, let alone spent the entire night in bed with one another. Losing her virginity must have been a big deal for her, and it's hard to imagine how she's feeling right now. Still, the stiffness of her frame has me on edge.

"I'm fine," she responds, her voice as neutral as possible.

"Oh. Good." I watch her check her face once she's done with her hair, wetting a finger under the faucet, and using it to wipe away an errant smear of mascara from the night before. I don't want to pressure her, but the idea of Elise shutting me out now is almost too much to bear. It might not be the best idea, but I decide to see if I can get anything else out of her. Maybe she just needs to process what we shared. "I think we might want to talk about what happened yesterday…"

She makes eye contact with me through the mirror and shrugs one shoulder. "Nothing happened yesterday."

Her words strike me like an arrow in the chest, and a million thoughts race through my mind. Does she regret last night? Is she having second thoughts? I have finally given in to the desire I had for her, physically and emotionally, and all I want right now is to kiss her and assure myself that I haven't lost her for good. I've never let my heart get involved with anything like that, never let my emotions get the best of me when it comes to a girl, and this is exactly why. Losing Elise means losing so much more than just losing a silly hookup.

I've been falling for her for weeks now. Hell, years. After last night, I'm fully in love with Elise. So why is she now pulling away from me? Surely she couldn't have just used me for sex...

I swallow the hurt I'm feeling, and nod. "Okay, I see... do you need anything like a toothbrush?"

Elise straightens, shaking her head and she brushes her hands down her clothes in an attempt to knock out any wrinkles. She doesn't look at me, but she also seems unbothered by everything. It isn't like she's mad, just... like she doesn't care at all. I think I'd almost prefer the anger.

"No, I'm okay. Actually, I'm about to head home if you want to walk me to the door?"

This just twists me up inside even more. Not only did she not want to wake up with me, but she also just wants to bolt as soon as she possibly can. "What, why? You don't have to go. Why don't you stay a while?"

She doesn't respond, just continues gathering the few things she came with, face devoid of any emotion.

"You don't want to even stay for breakfast?"

Elise finally glances up at me with a sad smile. "No, I have... things to do. See you later, Dan."

It's all I can do not to grab her arm and force her to talk to me, but I know that will just drive her farther and farther away. "What's wrong? Please talk to me, El."

"It's nothing. I'm just heading home. It's almost ten a.m. and I've got to pack my things for the trip."

I follow her out of the bathroom where she is putting her shoes on. "Are you sure? If there's anything you didn't like–"

Sliding her second heel on, she stands up straight, finally coming close enough to give me a chaste peck on the lips, but when I go in for the second kiss, she turns her head with a small laugh.

"Everything was great. I've got to go now, though. See you later."

Elise exits my room in a flash of bright, impossible to ignore red, just like she had entered last night. I can't pinpoint exactly why the exchange we just had makes me feel so horrible, but I think it all boils down to our failure to communicate. Well, her failure to communicate. I really did try to get her to open up.

With nothing left to do, I start to prepare for my own day. We're leaving for Capri this afternoon, which seems unreal, considering the night I just had with Elise. There is a feeling of guilt about how things will be when I see Andries, but I can't dwell on it. We're going to spend quite a bit of time together, and if all I can think about is my broken vow to him, I'm going to be miserable.

A flash of our evening travels down my mind, and I can't help but sigh at the sweet memory. As I come to think of it, there are two things I'm sure of: one that I'm completely and madly in love with the sister of my best friend, and two, that I totally screwed up. In a few hours, I'll be flying to Italy to spend ten days in a villa with not only the woman I love but with her brother casting a watchful eye on us. Yeah, inviting Elise was a big mistake. I should've stuck with my gut feeling.

I try to set the thoughts of her aside so I can finish my last bits of preparation before we leave for Capri, but I can't. She's stuck in my head like glue. The more I think about it, the more I'm sure she at least enjoyed the physical aspect of what we did. I took my time to make it as pleasurable as I could for her, and even if she didn't say so out loud, her body told me all I needed to know about how much she was enjoying what I was doing to her. Which means it wasn't anything physical that drove her off. It had to be something mental.

I wash my face and brush my teeth, trying to figure out a way to see the night before through Elise's eyes. Maybe she sensed how deep my feelings really are toward her, and she didn't like that. It could have even frightened her, learning how much I really cared. Elise has never given me any indication that she was looking for love or a relationship, always keeping her true intentions so guarded. I guess it's possible that she really just wanted to have sex with me, but didn't expect all the emotional ties that would come along with it. I've come to terms with the fact that I'm in love with her, but maybe she was blindsided.

I almost want to laugh at how stupid I've been. Of course, an ice queen like Elise wouldn't be able to fall in love or have romantic feelings toward me. Something like that would make her too vulnerable, and vulnerability is one of the things that she hates most of all.

When I exit the bathroom, I can hear the murmur of voices from downstairs. One is Elise, but the other two are speaking more quietly, and I can't quite make out who it is.

Curious, I tug my clothes on and head down to the foyer, where I find Elise talking to my parents. I groan internally, knowing that they must recognize that Elise is wearing party clothes from the night before and is leaving early in the morning. It looks like a walk of shame.

Mom and Dad look up at me as I descend the stairs, both of them looking particularly smug. After Dad and I had talked about Elise before, they both undoubtedly see what's going on, and probably can't wait to tell me that they knew all along that she and I had a thing for each other.

"Hello, darling," Mom says cheerily. "We were just talking to Elise here and seeing if she's excited about the trip."

Elise meets my eyes and looks extremely uncomfortable. Oh, well… I guess that's her karma for leaving me without any sort of explanation.

"We wanted to surprise you with breakfast before you left," Dad explains. "But at this point, it will be more like brunch."

"I have a great idea!" Mom exclaims, and I already know what's coming from a mile away. "Elise, you should join us! We have a reservation at the Astoria, doesn't that sound lovely?"

She blushes high on her cheeks. "Ah… no thank you. I still have some packing to do."

"Don't you have someone that can do it for you?" Dad interjects. "I'm sure Dan would love it if you came along—"

"*Mom, Pops*," I grate out. "She said she's busy, don't be pushy."

"Oh, fine." My mother sighs. "I guess I was just hoping for some female company among all these men, but I'm sure we'll see you soon, Elise."

"Uh-huh," she answers, already starting to slip out the door before she can get caught in another conversation. "Can't wait."

After she shuts the door behind her, leaving me with just my parents, I fix them both with a glare. "Don't. Say. Anything."

Mom titters, holding her hand to her mouth as she slides a look over to my dad. They exchange a knowing look with one another, and I scoff, turning on my heel and going back upstairs.

"I'm going to shower!" I call behind me. "If you two nosy people are still here when I'm done I guess I'll join you for brunch."

"Good call on the shower, son!" Pops responds behind me. "You've still got some red lipstick on your neck!"

* * *

At the Astoria, I ignore the desire to get hard liquor before eleven a.m. and order my usual blooming tea instead. The colors of it curl and dance in the water as the flowers inside open their delicate petals, and I'm too busy watching it, lost in thought, to hear my parents when they ask me a question.

I look up at my dad, who seems to be waiting for me to say something. "Could you repeat that?"

Pops sighs in annoyance. "I said it's news to me that Elise is going to Capri too. I thought this was a bachelors' trip?"

I'm not happy to be back on the subject of Elise, but maybe they just have one or two questions, and we can move on. "I invited her at the last minute. I'm already beginning to regret that decision."

Mom blinks, looking bewildered. "But why? You seem very fond of her."

I exhale slowly, pouring my tea into the glass mug with practiced ease. "It's complicated... I'd rather just think about what Capri is going to be like instead of her. Elise has been interjecting herself into my life plenty as it is."

"You're going to love it," Dad assures me. "The sailing there is second to none. The entire island seems like a perfect paradise. What kind of activities are you planning on doing while you're there?"

Happy to be on any other subject but Elise Van den Bosch, I launch into my itinerary with Pops, going into minute detail to keep the conversation rolling. Mom's eyes seem to glaze over, and soon enough she's swirling her mimosa in her glass and looking around the restaurant. She seems to spot someone she knows, and excuses herself, leaving Pops and me alone, chatting about the best dining options on the Amalfi coast.

As soon as Mom is gone, Dad lets the topic of restaurants die, and levels a serious look at me. "Now that we're alone... what's on your mind, son?"

I wave my hands in the air. "Nothing."

He sighs, clearly already knowing what's on my mind. "I'm going to cut straight to the point. I know you and

Elise have some sort of thing going on. That was made abundantly clear when we ran into her leaving your house this morning in last night's clothes. I also know how worried you are about her brother finding out, but if you really like her, he's just going to have to understand."

Scoffing, I reply, "You have no idea what you're talking about, Dad. I might have some sort of feelings for her, but I highly doubt she likes me in the way I like her. It isn't worth ruining my friendship with Andries over."

He takes a drink of his coffee, looking thoughtful. "Well, there's only one way to find out…"

"Absolutely not." I can't help but laugh. "I'm not going to admit my feelings for her. No. Fucking. Way."

It feels strange, having one of the most serious adult conversations I've ever had with my father while the world goes on around us; other people are talking, laughing, eating, and enjoying their lives while I live in turmoil over my feelings for the only woman in the world who is off limits to me.

I know Pops is just trying to help, but the more he pries, the less I want to say. Speaking out loud about how I'm in an unrequited romantic tangle just makes me feel stupid. I'm older than Elise… more worldly. I should know better than to fall for her, but apparently, she's the blind spot in my logical intelligence.

Mom comes back eventually, and we finish brunch, the terse atmosphere never dissipating. All of a sudden, I'm actually dreading Capri, and I need to find a way to salvage this trip for Andries while also keeping myself sane around Elise.

I bid my parents farewell in the parking lot, and Dad hugs me, thumping me on the back and telling me quietly, "Call me if you need any advice at all, son. I'll pick up any time, day or night."

I promise him that it won't come to that, but knowing he at least understands what I'm going through—because I'll be damned if I share it with anyone else—eases my stress somewhat. If I need to vent, I can always call Dad. It's not much, but it's something.

CHAPTER 31

Elise

"I will do my best, Dad. I can only spend so much time with them, you know."

"I know, I know." Pops lets out a sigh on the other side of the line. Despite everything going on in my mind today, I'm happy he at least gave me a call before I catch my flight. "Honestly, dear, I will miss you on our summer trip this year. I hope whatever you're doing in Capri is worth your time."

I think of Dan poised above me last night, and blush furiously, glad that Dad is miles away at our home estate and not here in person. "I think it will be. Just... give me some time to work on it."

"Well, try to have a good time, yes? I know you're all work all the time, but you can squeeze in some time for fun."

More mental images of Dan flash through me, and I drag my hand over my face. "Yeah, yeah, Dad, I get it. I'll send you and Mom a message when we land."

"Have a good flight, dear. Keep an eye on your brother."

With an exhausted laugh, I hang the phone up and cram it into the pocket of my leggings. With everything going on in my life, especially the last twenty-four hours, I had almost completely forgotten that my excuse for skipping the family trip with my dad was to try and split Andries and Roxanne up. At this point, I find myself thinking of them as a permanent couple more and more before I catch myself and remember that I'm supposed to hate the idea of them together. Truth is, seeing my brother happy makes me happy, even though he infuriates me to tears at times.

There is no denying that the biggest reason I'm going to Capri is for my own personal gain. I want to spend time with Dan, and see if I can get under his skin and between his sheets, all while not getting caught by Andries. We're basically going to be in paradise, and I want to make the most of it.

So why did you act so distant with him this morning?

I can't help but wonder what caused me to behave like that. The truth is when I looked over at him in the morning light, it felt like panic and exaltation combined, and I had fought with the desire to lean forward and press my lips all over his adored face and flee his bed with all the speed my legs could manage.

With all the conflicting feelings churning inside me, I had frozen. I can't let Dan know how much he means to me, how much I've wanted for him to do the things he did to me yesterday; it'd make me look like a complete fool. And yet, his signature is written all over my body; in the soreness between my legs, my swollen lips, and the warm areas where his stubble had rasped against my neck, making it more sensitive than ever. I became a coward in the face of it all, pulling on my clothes and running to the bathroom, hoping to get home and sort through my feelings before he woke up. Unfortunately, Dan was up almost immediately after me, and I had still been in that frozen mindset. I know I upset him, but there was no help for it. I'd messed up, so now I have to figure out my next move.

The rest of the morning is a blur, gathering my things and finishing up all my preparations for the trip. The schedule had been so tight when Dan finally invited me that I had hired a personal shopper to pick up my new things for Capri, giving her a few inspirational images and just hoping for the best. When the packages were delivered and I parsed through what was bought, some of the items were so skimpy or out of my comfort zone that they made me feel prematurely embarrassed, but I shook it off and at this point, I'm excited to show myself off for Dan. I want to show him an entirely new side of myself. No more workaholic, underhanded Elise. He was going to be dealing with Elise, the woman, and all her varied desires.

For the flight, I pull on a pair of bike shorts that leave nothing to the imagination and a breezy, taupe button-up shirt that ties under my ribs, exposing just enough of the skin of my stomach to catch the eye. With one last look around my apartment, I text the driver to come get my luggage, and I'm ready.

It's strangely lonely, riding over to the airport on my own, with only my phone to keep me company. Once we arrive, it's even stranger to arrive and ascend the steps onto the jet alone, because once I'm inside, it's readily obvious that I'm the odd one out.

Andries and Roxanne are glowing with happiness, Roxie with her legs draped over my brother's as they talk quietly, probably about all the beautiful, private little moments they plan on having once we arrive. Roxie's sister Lili and her boyfriend Robin are sitting across from them, less touchy with one another but still clearly excited. A trip to Capri can be a once-in-a-lifetime thing for a lot of couples, and I wonder if Dan knows how special this whole thing really is.

Speaking of Dan, the only other person who has arrived as a singleton, he's lounging in a seat of his own, hair slicked back, wearing a lightweight summer suit unbuttoned to display the tan skin of his upper chest. I think about how my lips have kissed his throat, and heat ripples through me. He isn't looking at me, but something tells me that it's a struggle for him not to. It's bizarre to think that we were just a mess of tangled limbs just the night before and now we have to pretend to be antagonistic almost-friends again. We're lovers, or at least we were, and I want to sit close to him like Roxie is with my brother so much that it almost hurts. I'm used to putting on a brave face, though, and this will be no exception.

There is no way he can ignore me the entire ten days we're there. I've got a bag full of the sexiest outfits I've ever owned, and a body he's proven he can't resist. It's just a matter of time before his walls crumble.

I greet everyone as we make our way on board, hugging my brother and exchanging happy greetings with everyone else, taking a seat across from Dan so he's forced to acknowledge me at least a little bit. The nod he gives me is tight, but his frown holds a lot of secrets that I can't quite decipher yet. There's a lot going on in that handsome head of his, but I have plenty of time to figure out what it is.

There is a touch of awkwardness among us all. I'm sure everyone knows that I didn't get invited until the last minute and that Dan didn't want me to come for whatever reason. Certainly, Andries and Roxanne do, since they broke the news of the Capri trip in the first place. All I can hope is that Robin and Lili don't know so I can keep my embarrassment to a minimum. Not that I'm ashamed about having scored an invite at the last minute... especially after last night... but I know everyone expects me to be.

"I'm glad you're joining us," Roxanne says, addressing the elephant in the room so no one else has to.

"Me too," I respond, telling her with my eyes a silent *thank you* for having gotten that out of the way.

"You know, this was supposed to be a guys' trip, not a family vacation," Dan mutters, but Roxanne and Lili just laugh.

"We all know that isn't Andries's sort of thing anyway. He likes to be around all us ladies," Roxanne quips.

Andries rolls his eyes but then turns to his fiancée with an affectionate look.

"One of them at least," he tells the group, receiving more laughter.

Dan is back to looking out the window as the plane begins to taxi and take off. Conversation is quickly moving on to other subjects, so I take a second to shoot him a quick message.

Elise: *You can't ignore me forever.*

I watch him pick up his phone, read the message, and put it away once more without even an ounce of recognition. I narrow my eyes at him, but it's not like he's looking anyway, so, resigned to my boring fate for the trip to Capri, I settle back into my seat with a huff.

The flight is relatively short, a little over two hours, and after requesting a blanket from the single flight attendant, I recline my chair and catch a quick nap to make up for all the time I was awake late last night. It's bright and loud on the plane from all the chatter, but I manage to sneak in a little more than an hour of sleep before we've landed in Napoli.

Already, it feels like we're in a different world, the air hotter and the sun warmer on my skin as I step off the plane. There is a distinct feeling of relaxation that is coming over the entire group of us, the constraints of our normal daily lives falling to the wayside. My brother and Roxanne are even more enamored with each other than usual, acting like smitten teenagers as they lean their heads close together to share secret words and what I assume are declarations of their undying love. The other couple, Lili and Robin, are equally attached, but more excited about the trip than anything else, talking endlessly about all the things they want to do in the next ten days.

Dan has made himself the de facto go-between with the drivers and other professionals we'll be dealing with, probably to have something to keep him busy in his quest to avoid me. Placing my oversized sunglasses over my face, I go to talk to the rest of the group while we wait, shooting Dan looks every now and then to see if he's looking at me. Most of the time he's otherwise occupied, but I do catch him staring in my direction once or twice. Each time is a boost to my ego.

The yacht Dan has booked will take us to Capri in just an hour, and the excitement in the group is palpable. Even Dan, who has been as standoffish as possible, relaxes and accepts a drink as we board the boat, lounging in the leather seats and waiting for all our things to be loaded. As the vessel bobs in the water, I look over the city resting in the shadow of Mt. Vesuvius, letting my thoughts wander. It's been so long since I've had some time to really let all the worries of my life slip away for a little while that I'm having a hard time letting go of some of my die-hard habits. I find myself wanting to be more involved with the planning of everything, to know where exactly we are staying and what, if any, events have been pre-planned for the week. Giving up control isn't something I usually enjoy, but at the end of the day, this trip is for my brother, and I know he doesn't want me sticking my nose in everything. If he trusts Dan to have planned everything out, I should too.

All those thoughts bring me back to the fact that I'm supposed to be finding a fault line between my brother and his fiancée. To look at them, most people would think that there is no separating the happy couple. I tell myself that I still believe they're wrong for each other and that the shame Andries marrying a former prostitute who's seventeen years older than him will bring our family isn't worth whatever temporary joy she gives him, but when I let my guard down and think with my heart, I find myself glad for them. Roxanne has proven time and time again to be savvy, responsible, and even forgiving toward me when I went so far as not to ruin just her relationship, but her reputation, too. I want to return that grace, but every time I consider it, I think of Dad and how pissed he will be if I give up. All the hard work I've put into Van den Bosch Industries weighs heavily on me every minute of every day. The question of whether I'm ready to give it all up for the sake of my brother has been haunting me. I just hope it doesn't ruin everything else during my time in Capri.

When the boat departs across the deep, sapphire blue water, I give up on Dan and try to connect with my brother, hoping to ease the nebulous guilt I'm feeling, revolving around him and Roxie.

"So you really don't feel like you're losing out on your bachelor vacation?" I ask, speaking loudly enough to be heard over the engine.

He shakes his head, expression completely earnest. "No, I don't want anything like that. I just want to celebrate spending the rest of my life with Roxanne." He looks at me, seeming to consider something, before speaking again. "I'm glad to be able to spend it with my best friend and my sister, too. I really am happy you came… as long as you stay out of my business, that is."

I feel a stab of panic that he might know what Dad has asked of me, but Andries is just teasing. I relax and roll my eyes. "You don't have to worry about that. I don't want to interrupt you two gross lovebirds."

"I can't wait till you're in love with someone, Elise, so I can rub it in your face like you're doing to me."

I resist the urge to look at Dan at the mention of love, and after giving him a quick smirk, I say, "You'll probably never have to worry about that with me."

"I don't know…" He smiles, looking like the teasing brother that I've grown up with for the first time in a long time. "I think you've got a romantic streak in you somewhere, sister. You just need to embrace it."

Soon enough, Capri rises out of the ocean ahead of us, looking craggy and intimidating from a distance but quickly clearing up into the gorgeous formation that it really is. The boat captain slows to a near crawl as we pass a few of the Faraglioni shooting out of the sea like huge teeth protecting the island. It's easy to see why the small island has been an irresistible destination even since the times of ancient Rome, and it does feel a little bit like going back in time as the boat maneuvers us into Marina Grande. The town of Capri stretches over the coast and up the cliff sides in some places in waves of cream and sunny yellow structures interspersed with small explosions of red and burnt orange buildings.

Gulls are crying amidst the sound of waves hitting the rocky shore, they cry alongside different street sellers battling to be heard at the busy port. Curving in a rough C-shape, the marina itself looks like a second, smaller cover welcoming us in with open arms. From here there are a few little hints of the other secret parts of the island–caves carved into the rock walls, shimmering deep grottos, and paths leading deeper into the island where it only takes a few moments to be completely alone. The charm of Italy is there, but condensed down into something wholly unique to Capri itself; the ancient history of the island, the generations of lovers that have frequented its shores, the mystery of its hidden places… it all comes together to form the paradise where we will be spending our next ten days.

Romance is in the air here, and we're breathing it into our lungs already. I see Dan looking at the view, unease on his face before he looks back at me. The smile that blooms over my face is slow and knowing. Our collision is inevitable, it's just a matter of when it will happen.

We disembark and head for the funicular railway that will take us to the center of Capri Town and from there we can make our way up to our villa on Belvedere of Tragara overlooking the sea. We could take a private car, Dan tells us, but as a group, everyone decides they want the full Capri experience. Instead, we send our luggage on its way and walk through the streets on the way to the small train. I start to balk at the crowded station, wanting to forget the quaint travel option and opt for the longer car ride instead, but after some cajoling, we board our third method of transport. It's only a four-minute ride, so I guess it won't be the end of the world.

The funicular is cramped, but as it exits the station tunnel and into the open air, we pass through stunning lemon groves and watch Marina Grande retreat beneath us. The island is covered in greenery wherever the town hasn't taken over; the aforementioned lemon trees, Italian stone pines looking like oversized bonsais, and myrtles. When we step off the train just minutes later, I suck in a deep breath of the clean, fresh air, and it smells to me like citrus and salt. My eyes flutter closed, and I soak in the moment all on my own. We've finally arrived, Dan and I haven't been at each other's throats yet, and the island is more beautiful than I could have dreamed.

Stone and stucco homes and businesses line the walkways and streets in all colors of neutrals, yellows, brick reds, and corals. Most have small balconies facing the roads, many covered with creeping and trailing vines of greenery.

On the opposite side facing the sea, the terraces and overlooks are much more splendid, taking full advantage of the magnificent view of the Tyrrhenian Sea.

Finally, after what seems like an entire day of travel, we reach our villa. I have to say, it was worth the wait.

The exterior is snow white with turquoise shutters that almost perfectly match the water below. Built right into the side of the cliff, the terrace takes up nearly as much space as the house itself, bordered by a waist-high stone fence everywhere except the infinity pool that occupies the center, overlooking everywhere below with just glass, making it appear as if the liquid was held there by magic alone.

Inside, everything is open, airy, and light, done up in shades of sand and sage. The house staff welcomes us, and after a brief tour of the villa, we all peel off to go and choose our own rooms.

Well, everyone else does. I take a moment to ask the maid for a glass of water, drinking it while exploring the bottom floor and the pool terrace, dotted with luxurious lounge chairs and private corner cabanas with breezy curtains that could be pulled for extra privacy.

Once I'm sure everyone has had time to choose their rooms, I go in search of Dan, breaking an ice cube between my teeth as I congratulate myself on my plan. My idea is, if I had rushed to get the room next to Dan, my brother might have had some suspicions. This way, everyone else has already chosen, and if I'm right, the couples surely chose more secluded bedroom suites so they could have all the privacy they need for their nighttime activities without having to worry about being heard by the rest of the house.

As I expected, Dan had chosen the master bedroom on the East wing, and the smaller suite next to it was blessedly empty. I drop my purse on the bed as a way to mark the space as my own, and make my way to Dan's doorway, leaning on the doorframe and watching him unpack.

He's taken off his jacket and the thin white button that was beneath it has the sleeves rolled up to display his forearms. I know he senses me in his space, but he's still trying to act like I'm a ghost, so it becomes a weird standoff to see who is going to speak first.

Looking at the master suite, I have a brief moment of regret that I didn't fight for this space myself. Like the other rooms, the floor is ivory marble interspersed with veins of gold and emerald green, but behind the bed, there is a stone staircase with recessed sconces that leads down to what I can only assume is a private indoor pool. I can only catch a glimpse of the reflection of the water from here, but it figures that Dan would choose the second most sumptuous room for himself.

Finally, Dan runs a hand through his hair in an annoyed gesture, his eyes closed. "What do you want, Elise?"

I take a few steps in his direction, standing inches beside him. "I just wanted to tell you that I love the room you picked out. Did you choose this one specifically for us to share later?"

The seductive edge I put in my voice doesn't change how frustrated he looks. "I explained this to you already. Here in Capri, you're invisible to me. Completely, utterly, *invisible*."

"True, but you said that before everything that happened back home," I point out, but he just shrugs.

"That doesn't change anything that I promised. I want nothing to do with you while we're here. In fact, I'm considering inviting someone else to stay with me here tonight for company, so you're just going to have to get over yourself and whatever you think is going on between you and me."

His words are like a knife twisting in my heart. "Don't you dare!"

He huffs a sarcastic laugh. "The more you sit here and bother me, the more likely I am to need another woman here to make sure you leave me alone. So go ahead, keep needling me."

Shocked, I stare at him, wide eyed, while he just crosses his arms and raises a single eyebrow. Pissed beyond reason, I consider throwing my water at him, but just storm off to my own suite instead, depositing my glass on the side table and falling into the overstuffed mattress, staring up at the diaphanous material draped over the four-poster frame as it blows in the wind from the open balcony doors. It felt like a good idea to get the room right next to Dan, but not if he is going to be bringing other women over! Our balconies are less than a single foot apart... that's way too close to know he's entertaining someone else.

I grab a pillow, holding it over my face and screaming into it, feeling overwhelmed. Surely he wouldn't actually sleep with someone else while we're here? There's no way...

I'm considering stomping back to his room and giving him a piece of my mind when my phone pings. I scramble for it, hoping that it's Dan with some sort of apology, but instead it's my brother, just letting me know that there are a few of his college friends on the island too and they're all going for a swim in the villa pool here shortly. I don't really want to go, but I can hear people outside already, laughing and having a good time, and I know I can't just hide away the whole trip because things are confusing between Dan and me. If I want things to change and to get his attention, I'm going to have to be around. Otherwise, I'm afraid his gaze will wander.

In my luggage, I pull out my first bikini for the trip. It's a solid olive, the sides sitting high on my hips while dipping down low in the front. As a cover up, I throw on a tunic that falls just above my knees and covers my arms to my hands, but it's made of such a gauzy, transparent material that it's basically nothing at all, only accentuating the even tone of my skin.

Barefoot and with my hair loose around my shoulders, I follow the sound of happy shouting and splashing out to the terrace to see everyone else has already arrived. I wear my diplomatic expression at first, seeing the two couples and a few of the vaguely familiar faces from college, but my attention is almost immediately drawn to the three figures in the pool. Even in the baking summer sun, I feel myself go cold.

There, in the water, is Dan, leaning against the wall with his elbows bracing him, looking relaxed and smug as two girls float in front of him, giggling and looking as if they've known him forever. One has darker hair and an olive complexion while the other is paler with ginger hair. They seem to be strangers to everyone but Dan. Seeing Dan bringing random girls into his circle wouldn't be strange at all to me before, but now, after what we've shared... I'm in shock. I know I'm staring too long for it to be courteous, and it isn't until the server working at the villa comes and hovers next to me that I snap out of my stupor.

"Can I get you a drink, ma'am?"

"Ah… a gin and tonic. I'll be over in the lounge chairs."

The server bobs his head in acknowledgement and leaves. Dan is flirting with them, it's all too obvious, and for the first time I start to think that maybe he was serious about having someone else stay with him tonight. Or, if the two random girls he's entertaining are any indication, *two* girls to sleep over. My stomach churns, and when the server reappears to hand me the drink, all I can do is hold it, too sick to my stomach to partake.

Andries and Roxanne are slipping into the pool, posing together near the infinity edge while Lili takes photos of them. As much as I hate everything else going on here right now, I've never seen my brother so happy as he looks at his wife-to-be, relaxed and happy in paradise. It's all he's wanted for so long, and despite the strife with the rest of the family, it's clear that she means everything to him.

Will I ever find a love like that? Glancing at Dan, playfully splashing the darker-haired girl, I doubt that I will. The first time I even consider anything romantic, I get it thrown back in my face.

In a huff, I ignore the pool and take my gin and tonic to the lounge chairs. I'll just bide my time until I can slip away and go unnoticed. The idea of sitting out here and watching Dan flirt it up makes me want to scream.

He hasn't looked over at me a single time, that asshole. The gin and tonic burns down my throat like icy fire, but it does nothing to cool my temper or the jealousy growing in my belly. I'm in a place I have dreamed about for years. How can I feel this crappy already?

Angry thoughts boiling through my brain, I watch Robin and Andries set up the volleyball net across the enormous pool while Lili and Roxanne float together, talking quietly and watching as their men work. Maybe coming to Capri was a bad idea... maybe this is why Dan was so against bringing me in the first place–because he wanted to spend time with random women.

As if he can sense me thinking hateful, murderous things about him, Dan finally graces me with his attention, looking me over head to toe before pulling himself out of the water by his arms. I wave the server down for another drink, but there is no distracting myself from what I'm seeing. Now that I've seen Dan naked, I thought that his body wouldn't have such an effect on me anymore, but seeing him glistening with water—muscles flexing as he pulls himself upwards—is something different altogether. There are no blankets or lowlights to mask the absolute perfection of him and the shape he has kept himself in, and having the knowledge of how his skin feels under my fingers makes it even worse. I'm itching to touch him, to lick those droplets off the side of his neck, or push my hands through his wet hair to kiss him. Clenching my jaw, I turn away and face the other side of the overlook even as lust washes over me. Lust and anger, all for the same man, all at the same time. It's a lot for me to handle.

Of course, he won't let me suffer in solitude, either. In seconds, Dan plops down into the lounge chair next to me, stretching his arms above his head like a contented cat ready to lay in the sun.

"Nice day, huh?" the asshole asks smugly.

The server brings me my next gin and tonic, and I make sure to swallow at least a fourth of it before answering a brief, "Sure."

"Oh, don't have such a sour face in such a beautiful place!" he teases, and for the second time in an hour, I have the almost irresistible urge to throw a drink on him. Again, I resist, sipping the libation and glaring at him over the rim of the glass.

"Why are you even over here talking to me, Dan? It looks like you have some new friends to entertain. Who are they, anyway?"

He shrugs, and it infuriates me. "I actually don't even know. Their names are Tiffany and Mia and I just met them about fifteen minutes ago as I was walking outside the villa. They asked me directions to a bar and after we got to talking, I invited them in to come swim."

"You invited strangers to swim with us? We haven't even been here an hour!" I can't hide the incredulousness in my voice.

"Why not? It's vacation, after all." He folds his arms behind his head, lays back, and closes his eyes. "I have to have something to keep me busy."

I open my mouth to reprimand him more, but just then, the darker-haired girl saunters over. Her walk is slow and sultry, but what shocks me most is how she bypasses all the empty lounge chairs so she can perch on Dan's lap as if she's known him for ages. I'm seeing red, but at the same time, I can't look away.

Dan jolts up when the girl sits on him, but after a moment of what looks like annoyance at her, he schools his expression. "Well, hello again, Mia."

She tilts her head to the side, walking her fingers up his bare chest. "Why'd you leave the water?"

"Just having a chat with my friend Elise here," he tells her, and Mia doesn't even bother to look in my direction. Hurt and annoyed, I jump up from my seat, more than ready to retreat to my room even if everyone sees me doing it. I'm absolutely sure now that coming here was a mistake. I can feel a lump growing in my throat and tears pricking the corners of my eyes behind my sunglasses when I hear my brother calling for me. With a heavy sigh, I turn around, glad that my face is mostly covered by the frames.

"What, Andries?"

"Don't go! Come play volleyball with us! We're a person short." He motions to the area in the pool next to him. He and Roxanne are making up a team, while Lili and Robin have paired themselves with the other new girl, Tiffany.

I consider ignoring him and going to hide away, but I have to remember that this is a trip for him, and even if I start to get information from him for Dad, it's imperative he thinks I'm just here to celebrate his engagement. Plus, when I let Dan slip from my brain for even a second, I'm once again happy to be here, and the thought of the cool water on my sun and anger-heated skin sounds divine.

"Fine," I relent, pulling my tunic over my head, and depositing it on one of the lounge chairs as I pass. I sneak a look over at Dan, who has taken an interest in my now nearly bare form right before Mia demands his attention again. At least he isn't totally shut off from me, even if he's trying to replace me with some random woman off the street. Mia might be beautiful, but something tells me Dan is done with the part of his life where he only chooses partners based on looks alone.

I perch on the edge of the water and slide in, sighing at the warmth of the water, just cool enough to be refreshing but not frigid enough to make me shiver. I wade over to my brother and his fiancée, both of them looking like they've never had a better time in their entire lives, and take my position. Roxie looks over at me, an amused expression dancing on her face.

"Sooo did you expect to ever play in an aquatic volleyball game with me? I have to say, it's not something I ever expected to be doing."

Thinking back on my not so stellar history with Roxanne, I have to agree and laugh. "Yeah, you're right. This is so weird."

"Only as weird as we make it, I guess," she quips.

I'm in good shape from all the riding and hunting I do, but volleyball, especially the water-logged variety, isn't exactly my forte. The difficulty does take my attention away from Dan, and how I've basically come to Capri to watch him be his usual playboy self right in front of my face. It wouldn't sting so much if he hadn't touched me so tenderly, and if I hadn't seen real emotion in his eyes when we slept together.

Focus, I tell myself. *Focus on the game.*

So I do, surging through the water and jumping to hit the ball when it comes to me. It's a mess of splashing water and shrieking bodies, but even I'm laughing along with everyone else in a few minutes time. Then, there is another feminine laugh coming from over near the lounge chairs, and my curiosity gets the better of me. Andries has just hit the ball over the net, and I figure I have a second to look over… but I instantly regret it.

Dan is still on his back with his arms behind his head again, but now Mia is laying on top of him, kicking her feet in the air happily while she touches him in all the same places I want to so very badly, taking advantage of his damp muscles on display. I hate myself for it, but watching the scene unfold makes me feel like crying. This isn't what I expected, or what I wanted at all. If I had just gone with my parents on their trip, none of this would be happening. I'd be none the wiser that Dan was out cruising for hookups.

My reverie is rudely shattered when, coming from the other side of the net with an overly intense speed, the volleyball comes directly for me and smacks me in my distracted face, hard. I yelp, seeing stars. There are a few awkward laughs, but everyone goes silent rather quickly.

There is a moment of nothingness where I think I'm fine, but like a delayed reaction, the pain comes soaring in, making tears come to my eyes.

"*Fuck*," I gasp, vision still fuzzy.

Andries is rushing over, pulling my hands away and looking at my face for himself. His concern and quick action makes me think of all the times he would come to my rescue, even when I didn't need it, when we were kids. He's moving my head side to side, frowning and brow furrowed, and I have the bizarre thought that I'd like him to hug me and tell me everything is going to be okay, but it's a childish desire that passes quickly enough.

"Are you okay?" he asks, and I simply shake my head. *No.*

Roxanne shoulders him out of the way gently and grabs my shoulders. "Let's go in and get an ice pack," she tells me, her voice low as she leads me out of the water by my elbow. "I've got this, Andries, don't worry," she tells my brother over her shoulder.

The maid hovers around as soon as we're out of the water, but Roxanne waves her off, asking for towels and ice instead of assistance. We go into the kitchen where she has me sit on one of the tall bar stools so she can check my forehead and nose out without the craziness going on outside. It's aching, but the maid is quick with the ice pack, which I hold to my face with a sigh of relief.

"You've got a tiny nosebleed," Roxanne informs me, her eyes inspecting the damage intently. "But I think it's already finished. Does it feel like you've broken any cartilage or anything?"

I squeeze my nose gently, wincing. It hurts, but there are no suspect, out-of-place pieces, thank goodness. "I don't think so. It just made me see stars."

"The ball was probably waterlogged. It made it heavier." She sits on one of the other stools, watching me like she's afraid I'll run away. "Are you positive you don't want to go get it looked at?"

"No," I assure her. "I'm just being a baby, I guess."

She scoffs. "If I had gotten hit, my entire afternoon would have been spent at the emergency room. You're doing better than I would have." Peering closely at me again, she purses her lips. "Although, and if I'm prying, feel free to ignore me, but I think there is more bothering you than just a potentially broken nose."

I can see Dan and Mia in the lounge chair from here through the glass walls that give unobstructed views to the terrace, but there is no way in hell I'm telling Roxanne that's what is bothering me. It doesn't matter, though, because she follows my gaze and makes a knowing sound.

"Uh-huh. Just like I thought," Roxanne says, amused. "It's about that girl all over Dan, right? It pisses you off?"

Flustered, I shake my head in denial. "No, why would I care? He's always been a fuckboy."

"Hmm…" she mutters, her eyes pinned on the area I got hit, while she takes the ice pack from my hand and presses it against my skin a bit higher. "You're going to get a bruise on your forehead…"

My hand goes up to reach for the ice pack and I hold it against my skin, letting her know that I can do it myself.

With her hands now free, Roxanne leans back on her stool and watches me with a pensive air. "Look, I'm sure I'm the last person you want to be getting relationship advice from, but… you can do better than Dan." My eyes widen at the unexpected nature of her comment, but Roxie goes to clarify. "Don't get me wrong, Andries and I love Dan, but no one on earth would think the two of you would make a good match. Dan isn't going to just suddenly stop taking interest in all these girls and settle down out of nowhere. That's not how this works, and if you're anything like your brother, you're going to take stuff like love and sex really seriously. I don't think Dan ever will." Roxanne sighs, pausing for a beat. "There are more fitting people out there for you, is all I'm saying."

I watch her as she walks across the Mediterranean decorated kitchen, taking a small, folded towel from one of the drawers and wetting it in the sink.

"Why are you so sure I have something going on with Dan?" I ask her, my voice low enough so that only she can hear it.

Roxanne returns to me, blotting at the blood underneath my nose with the towel as she speaks. Up close, she really is stunning... I can see why Andries was drawn to her in the first place. "Now, remember, for a long time my job was one of gauging lust between a man and a woman, so it might be easier for me to see, but it's pretty obvious that something is up between the two of you. Andries has already mentioned how he thinks you and Dan are mad at each other, and when I asked why, he said that there is no way the two of you would have spent so much time together today without arguing, so even he is getting suspicious."

My brows frown instantly. "Andries is suspicious that Dan and I are messing around... because we *aren't* fighting?" My voice is doubtful. "Shouldn't it be the other way around?"

She sets the wet towel on the counter and washes her hands, chuckling, "Elise, you're young, so take my advice. Passion that is denied romantically must come out some other way. You and Dan were so fiery toward one another because there was no other way for you to express your attraction to each other. Andries might not be aware of that fact like I am, but he can tell something is different between you guys. Combine that with the longing looks coming from you both and…" She holds out her hands, her eyes meeting mine. "The conclusion is pretty easy to come to."

A flush of embarrassment is creeping up my neck, knowing that no matter how much I try to hide how I'm feeling, people are picking up on it. "Please don't confirm it with Andries. Even if he has his suspicions, I don't want him to know for sure. He'll be so angry. I'll find a way to keep it under wraps or whatever—"

She sighs heavily, slicking her wet hair out of her face and rolling her eyes to the ceiling in exasperation. "I knew you were going to ask that. I'm not going to outright lie to him, we promised not to do that to each other ever again, but I won't say anything if he doesn't ask."

"Thank you." My shoulders sag in relief, even as my face continues to pulse with pain.

"But, Elise, I'm going to give you my honest opinion here." Roxanne dries her hands, leveling a serious stare at me. "Fucking around with your brother's best friend, especially knowing how Andries feels about it, is selfish." I open my mouth to object, but she holds up her hand to stop me and continues. "I don't care how good the sex is, either. It's selfish. There are literally hundreds of guys out there that you can choose from, so there's no reason that Dan has to be the one you pick. You're putting Andries and Dan's relationship on the line, and their friendship supersedes your little fling. So… knock it off."

In the heat of the moment, there are a million curse words I want to throw at her, and yet, all I can say is, "Okay, Roxanne." I drag my hands over my face in frustration, being careful not to hit my abused nose. "Whatever you say."

She raises her eyebrows, considering me for a moment as if something has just occurred to her. "But if this is something more than just a hookup—"

"We should get back out there," I blurt, shooting to my feet. "Before anyone starts to worry."

My pulse quickens, I'm terrified to have this conversation with my brother's fiancée, or at the idea that she might have figured out how I really feel about Dan. Andries finding out that he and I had hooked up is one thing, but if he knows that I actually care for Dan on more than just a physical level… their friendship will be over for sure, and I can't stomach the idea of being the reason for that.

Back outside, I walk past Dan and Mia still sitting on the lounge chairs, her beside him with her arm around his neck while she takes a number of selfies of them. It annoys me even more, though, that he doesn't even take the time to ask how I am, all of his attention being given to this new girl.

Feeling jilted, I walk back to the pool where the volleyball game is still going strong. I'm not going to play anymore after my accident, but I decide to perch on the side of the pool and dip my legs in, watching everyone compete while being safely out of the way. Roxanne gives me one last knowing glance before sliding back into the water as the players redistribute again to form more even teams.

They play for twenty minutes more, and the entire time Dan refuses to even look to see how I am, even after my brother swam over to make sure I was actually okay. Once the game is done, Lili herds everyone, including me, into a group photo and sends it to all of us. I'm still angry, but the fact that Dan and his new female friend aren't in the first group pictures from the vacation he paid for makes me feel a little better in a petty sort of way. Oh well, if he wants to be immature about all of this, I can too.

I grab a fresh, fluffy white towel and throw it down on a lounge chair that isn't anywhere near Dan and Mia, but I can't help but notice that once I lay down to dry off, he stands and offers his hand to the other woman and the two of them leave and head inside the villa. I watch them, my chest feeling tight, and the urge to cry coming on again… hard. I guess this is the end of whatever romantic affair Dan and I were having, because where else would he be taking her inside but his bedroom?

Damn. I really feel something for him. Apparently, that means I'm a fool because if he can move on so easily, I must have meant nothing at all to Dan.

To distract myself, I dig my phone out of the small beach bag I had brought out with me, wanting to see the group photo Lili had taken. Annoyingly, it looks like Andries has already posted it to Instagram and tagged my account without asking me, but luckily it's a great photo of all of us. No one would know the turmoil going on inside of me from how happy I look in the photo.

There are a few comments even though it was just posted minutes ago, so out of curiosity, I open them to see who could be so interested. I sit up straighter when I see who the commenter is, pulling down my sunglasses to make sure I'm seeing things right.

Johan Bentinck—the only other man who I've ever been interested in—commented under Andries's post saying, *Having fun in Capri without me?*

My brother had responded, *Come over here then!* But there was nothing else after that. I turn the screen off and sit the phone down beside me, feeling apprehensive. While Johan coming here would be a wonderful distraction from Dan going off and messing around with other girls, if there is any chance I'm reading Dan's intentions wrong, and he does still want to spend time with me, having Johan here would ruin that before it even starts.

I bite my lip, flip my glasses back up, and lay back down to finish drying in the sun. Maybe Johan joining us would be the better outcome either way. Just because Dan might take notice of me again doesn't mean I should reciprocate. After all, he's already treated me like shit. Why would I give in so easily? Johan might have left me high and dry when I was younger, but I was way too young to really be considering a relationship anyway. It isn't like he left me for another woman right in front of my face like someone else who is close to me…

My parents may approve of Dan for the most part, but there's no denying that Johan is the better match for me on paper. He's rich, attractive, part of the royal family, and a good man all around. Now that I'm an adult, it could be the best chance I'll have to give Johan a second chance.

Considering Johan, or anyone for that matter, as my next partner makes me feel even more horrible about sleeping with Dan. When it happened, and earlier this morning, there hadn't been any regret. I was happy with what had happened. But now that he's going through with the whole "pretending I'm invisible" thing, I really am starting to hate myself for going so far with him right before we left. I consider texting him and asking him to come talk it out with me, but then like a slap in the face, I remember that he's inside doing God knows what with his new friend!

What if everyone is right and there are way better men for me out there? If even Roxanne, a former escort, thinks that I'm doing myself a disservice by spending my energy on Dan, well…

I have a lot to think about. And not a lot of time to do it.

* * *

I doze off outside for a little while, glad I'd applied enough sunscreen that I didn't fry, but my nap doesn't last long. Andries comes outside and shakes me awake, telling me to go get dressed for dinner, which I do reluctantly.

There's a lovely tan coming to life on my face, so I just sweep on some mascara and highlighter, dragging my hair into a low ponytail and pulling some curling pieces around my face to frame it before pulling on a pale-yellow crop top and a swingy coral handkerchief skirt. Paired with some slip-on sandals, it gives off the casual, lazily sensuous beach vibe I'm going for. The effect is dampened for me knowing that it's probably wasted now that Dan has someone else to keep him company, but I can't dwell on that the entire trip. There is still the entire island of Capri for me to enjoy, I can't just let the whole experience be ruined by one asshole.

I go out to the terrace again where dinner will be served and make it to the table before Dan anyway, so I don't get to experience him seeing my entrance, but Andries and Roxie stand to greet me, nonetheless. The server pops by and I agree to have a glass of the dry, fresh white wine that everyone else at the table is already enjoying, settling into the comfortable dining chair with a sigh. Looking around, I notice how I'm facing the ocean. The sea breeze blows over us like a welcomed friend, the sun kissing the horizon in shades of pink and orange.

I wish I had continued to watch the sunset instead of being distracted by motion coming from the other side of the terrace, but when I hear my brother say Dan's name, I turn my head to see him walking in with Mia. She's wearing the same blue maxi dress I had seen draped over a lounge chair outside, which makes me clench my teeth. That dress being the same one from earlier tells me she hasn't left since swimming, and her dark, still-damp hair is braided back from her face. I bet they showered together, and that's why she's still here, and why her hair is still wet.

Swallowing hard, I turn my attention to Dan. Ironically, his lightweight button-down is the same coral as my skirt, almost like we matched on purpose, with fitted white Bermudas and boat shoes. To my vast annoyance, he takes his seat next to me, and Mia sits beside him, tittering and hanging all over him like she must be touching him at all moments, or he'll disappear. I jerk my face away from him as he lowers himself next to me, even though I can feel his gaze moving over my face, neck, and body.

Go ahead and look at what you've given up, asshole, I think to myself bitterly.

Then, to my shock, I feel one finger trailing up my knee, dragging the skirt with it. I jerk away reflexively, glaring at him and hissing under my breath, "How dare you sit next to me, let alone touch me!?"

He gives me a Cheshire grin. "Why wouldn't I?"

I have a million things to say to him, and the words all burn on my tongue and fill up my mouth until I can barely breathe, but I don't let them spill out. I can't give him the satisfaction. Plus, my brother is right in front of me, and it would raise suspicion if we start a fight right now, so I just lean discreetly toward Dan's ear and simply whisper, "Get lost, Dan."

He doesn't reply but proceeds to leave me in peace, turning his attention to the other guests at the table.

There's a salad course and then a lightly dressed olive oil pasta with sun-gold tomatoes. Conversation is simple and easy, made even more so by the delicious, freely flowing Italian wine. Andries is the happiest I've ever seen him, and while I would normally reserve the compliment for another woman, he's basically glowing from inside with joy. I tamp down any thoughts of manipulating him for Dad, wanting to at least soak up this first day without any sneaky undercurrents.

Everything falls to the wayside in my mind, though, because Dan just can't keep his hands to himself. He's single-handedly put me on a rollercoaster of every emotion possible today and I want nothing more than to shove him as hard as I can and give him a piece of my mind, but surrounded by all these people whose opinions I value, I can't give into my most base desires.

It starts with another one-finger caress on my knee, under the fabric of my skirt, making my skin rise in goosebumps. I dutifully ignore this, but it doesn't take long for the touches to get more personal and intimate. There is no indication from either of us about what is happening under the table as we hold full conversations with the others and barely acknowledge each other, but when Dan starts to work his way up my inner thigh, I can feel my face heating, unbidden. I almost slap him away, figuring that he's touching Mia with his other hand, but a quick visual check shows me that he's holding his wine with his other hand, which means I'm the only one getting his attention right now. That knowledge is heady... I like it more than I should. The combination of his longed-for touch and the alcohol has me turning redder than any normal blush, but thankfully there are paper fans on the right of each place setting. I discreetly try to fan my blush away even as Dan gets bolder and bolder with his hand while displaying nothing on his face while talking to my brother as if he isn't feeling me up at the same time.

As plates are being cleared, Dan grazes the edge of my panties with his thumb, and I break out in a full body shiver. Finally, he glances at me, and the need in his eyes is so strong it's almost physically palpable. I open my mouth to say something to him, anything, but I'm interrupted when my brother stands and clinks his knife against his wine glass. The sound silences the table, and Andries, eyes bright with the alcohol, starts his heartfelt toast to none other than the man next to me with his hand between my legs.

But of course, as soon as Andries opens his mouth, Dan puts both hands on the tabletop, cutting off our contact and leaving me feeling bereft. I miss his touch already, the ghost of it still lighting up my nerves with wishes of what could have been. Looking completely innocent, Dan grins at my brother, his best friend, and listens to the praise being heaped on him.

"I just want to say thank you to Dan O'Brian, who has been beside Roxanne and me from the beginning and through all the hard times without hesitation. He planned this incredible trip for us and didn't even blink when I wanted to bring my beautiful fiancée and her family along as well—for which I will never be able to thank him enough. From the bottom of my heart, Dan, thank you."

If I'm not mistaken, Dan's eyes look misty. It makes me feel even worse, knowing that Andries and Dan are so close, because the disappointment I felt when Dan stopped touching me makes one thing crystal clear: I can't stop lusting after him, even when I want to. Roxanne was right, I should leave him alone, but I can't help myself. It's like I'm out of control.

I'm a terrible sister. For more things than just this, but still…

Everyone else raises their glasses to Dan as well, who bows his head graciously. Andries is soon caught back up in conversation with some of his college friends, and I can't help but take the opportunity to needle at my former lover in the lull.

"So, I'm just wondering, since the two of you arrived together…" I start, causing Dan to finally give me his full attention. "Where did that girl get ready for dinner? And why is she here?" I say it quietly enough that Mia can't hear me, but Dan can. He chuckles knowingly, setting his wine glass down, his eyes holding a glint of amusement.

"Her name is Mia."

"I don't give a damn what her name is. Answer my question," I fume.

He tilts his head to the side, searching my face with his penetrating gaze, and crosses his arms while a smug smile tugs at the corner of his mouth. "Elise Van den Bosch... are you jealous?"

I sniff haughtily. "No."

"Then yeah, maybe we showered together." Observing my face attentively, he leans in, that infuriating smile fully on his lips now. "Why do you ask?"

"You know why." I try to keep the quiver out of my voice, but don't quite succeed. Maybe it's the wine.

"No, I don't, actually." He leans back into his seat nonchalantly. "Last time I checked, we weren't mutually exclusive."

I can't read him, which makes me angry. There is no hint in his posture or expression telling me if he's just messing with me, or if he actually shared the shower with Mia. Dan patiently waits for my reply, but he offers me no kindness or reassurance that he hasn't moved on already. Hurt is swelling in me—real, fierce heartbreak, and I hate that I'm giving him the satisfaction of being able to witness it.

"Fuck you, Dan," I whisper, standing so quickly that my chair scrapes across the floor. I don't know if he reaches for me or tries to quietly call me back, because I rush away, giving Andries a quick excuse about the sun and the drinks having made me exhausted enough to go to bed early, and then I'm gone from that damned dinner, the man I'm falling for, and his new girl.

Once I'm sure no one can see me, I let the hot tears roll down my face, slamming my bedroom door behind me and sliding down the inside of it until I'm sitting on the floor. I give in and have myself a heavy, cathartic cry, even though it hurts my bruised nose. I just need to bleed some of the anguish off so I can function. I'm so over all of this already. Capri has been nothing but an enormous mistake, and I wish I was with my father and the rest of the family in Lake Como. No Dan, no Mia, no visions of them beneath his steamy shower head—all bare limbs and tan skin. Fuck them both.

I hate him. I'm falling in love with him, and I hate him.

I can't stomach a shower of my own, the images in my mind too sickening to handle tonight, so after a quick, sad bath, I crawl into bed naked and with my hair unbrushed. As an afterthought, I pad to the locked balcony door and unlock it. Just in case.

There is no light coming from Dan's suite, and the night beyond is dark.

I fall into a restless sleep with my hand holding my phone, waiting for even a single message from that asshole; anything would be better than the radio silence between us. But, throughout the entire night, the silence endures. I spend my first night on the beautiful island of Capri miserable and lonely, just feet away from my heart's greatest desire, but feeling somehow miles apart.

CHAPTER 32

Dan

We take breakfast at the same dining table as last night, and when I arrive at the terrace it's just Lili, Robin, and Elise present. There's no formal time for this meal, and I can only assume the soon-to-be newlyweds are having a late lie-in and taking their time. Which I'm happy about because it means I can see how annoyed Elise is without interruption.

Normally, I wouldn't try to upset her, but after she gave me the cold shoulder once we had our night together, I was determined to stick with my previous plan of icing her out the entire trip to Capri. It's been damned hard, especially seeing her prance about in a bikini that barely covers her, but on a whim I had invited Tiffany and Mia into the villa, and they had ended up being my secret weapon. Especially Mia, who took a quick liking to me.

I had no intentions of doing anything other than just flirting with Mia, but she had been all too willing to play the part of a smitten new flame, and I had loved watching Elise get angrier and angrier as the day went on. Except for when she got her nose bloodied, of course, but she hadn't been seriously hurt so there was no reason for me to break character and let her know that I really am still into her.

Now she glares at me as I approach the table in nothing but my black swimming trunks, sitting across from her and pouring myself a cup of the provided coffee with a smile.

Breakfast is being served family style so everyone can come and go as they please, but Elise seems to only be having coffee, pale brown with extra cream and no doubt sweetened excessively. When she raises her face to me, there are subtle dark circles under her beautiful eyes. Either she's bruised more than I expected from the volleyball hit, or her sleep had been restless. I'm betting on the latter.

"Rough night?" I venture.

"Shut up."

"Well, I for one, had a great sleep. Those beds are so comfortable, don't you agree? The mattresses are so soft."

"I don't want to talk to you right now," she grumbles. I see Lili look at Robin, and then back at Elise and me, her brow furrowed, but she doesn't say anything.

"But I so want to talk to you," I remark, eyes drifting to where her beige silk robe gapes open, but she jerks the garment shut before I can look my fill. "You're being awfully grouchy, El."

"I wonder why?" she hisses, standing so quickly that her coffee cup rattles on the table. "Did Mia enjoy your nice soft mattress last night, too? I bet she did."

"Frankly, it's none of your business, but if you really want to know—"

She turns in a huff, still holding her robe closed as she stomps back to her room. I watch her go, appreciating the length of her long, bare, tan legs. Elise is clearly pissed, but oddly enough, I'm happy about it, because she's displaying an emotion I've seen in many women who have been involved with me over the years: jealousy.

Elise is jealous of Mia. After how aloof she had behaved after we had sex, I can barely believe it.

The other two at the table are clearly uncomfortable, but I'm suddenly feeling a lot better about the day to come. Elise is so fun to tease that it's almost too easy to push her to the edge of blowing up, but since we're all set to go on a sailing tour of the islands and its many rock formations, I won't pick on her too much. I was rather harsh on her yesterday, and I have to admit that it has been hard not to treat her like I normally would. Before we were lovers, we were friends, albeit contentious ones.

I guess it's time to make nice with Elise. I just have to be careful not to cross the line into flirtation territory and tip off her brother, or we're all going to have a terrible time.

* * *

The original plan had been to take a smaller, quicker boat around Capri so we could all be close together and experience the sights together, but after everything going on between Elise and me, I decided to call and change our tour to a bigger sailing yacht so there would be enough room for me to get her alone. Not for anything nefarious... at least not yet. I just want to talk.

Being four hours long, the tour will take us around the Faraglioni—up close and personal—and is complete with refreshments. The captain of the boat has years of experience, so it should be a relaxing day for us all out on the water. It's a stunning day, and as we all make our way to the private cars that will take us to Marina Grande, the anticipation in the air is palpable.

Andries and Roxanne are both relaxed and loose-limbed, no doubt having made good use of their suite's jacuzzi. They had slept in so late that the housekeeper had to rouse them, lest they'd miss the time of the tour. Roxie, who is usually clothed in darker reds, forest greens, and black, looks like she belongs right at Andries's side today in her nautical getup. She and Lili are dressed alike, in white and blue striped shorts and white button-downs tied above their belly buttons. Andries, as always, looks like the perfect heir to the Van den Bosch empire in his perfectly tailored vacation wear, but his sister is a different story.

Elise arrives at the boat last, a beach bag on her shoulder. She's irresistible in a sunset orange floral romper that has the shortest shorts I've ever seen on her, and a sweetheart neckline that I can almost see down when she leans over to deposit her things on the floor of the yacht. It would take the smallest effort to strip her bare. How am I supposed to concentrate on anything else with her around, looking like heaven on Earth?

She has her long hair loosely braided in two braids, her skin shimmering in the sun with whatever tanning oil she's applied. As she passes me, not even sparing me a glance, I can smell her flowery perfume and a tropical note from whatever she's wearing to protect herself from the sun. It makes my mouth water.

Oh, I'm really in deep with this girl. Damn.

All these surface level games we're playing are all well and good, but there is something deeper going on here that is going to be even more problematic than the physical stuff. Andries might try to fight me over sleeping with Elise, but I have to think he'd forgive me for breaking my promise to him all those years ago when Elise was still a teenager. But if I break her heart? He'll either try to kill me, shut me out, never speak to me again or all of the above. I'm so torn. I care about them both, in vastly different ways.

Elise goes to sit on the back side of the yacht while Andries and I go talk to the captain. We aren't going to the Blue Grotto today; I want that to be an entire day all on its own, but we couldn't have asked for a better day to tour the exterior of Capri. With the sails extended, the boat pivots out toward open water, and we're off.

"We should rent a smaller sailing boat to take out on our own," Andries suggests. "I've done it a time or two."

"Yeah, a time or two…" I laugh. "Nothing more fun on a pre-wedding trip than to have the groom drown or be lost at sea. How about we skip that idea for now?"

The wind picks up the sails and carries us across the glassy water. It's so clear that when we look over the sides, jellyfish are visible floating below the waves. The girls' strip to their bathing suits, and of course Elise is wearing something white and barely there that makes my eyes want to bug out of their sockets. It's only held on by strings tied at her back and on each hip bone. I have the wildest urge to undo those tiny knots with my teeth and lick the skin beneath.

Scrubbing my hands over my face, I excuse myself from the tour as the guide explains the history of the Faraglioni formations towering above us like fingers reaching toward the heavens. There's a bar in the hold of the boat, and I pour myself two fingers of Scotch and throw it back, ignoring the burn of it in my throat and sinuses. I've got to get myself together if I'm going to have any sort of reasonable conversation with Elise.

After a second shot, I make my way back to the deck and see the object of my desires once more separated from the group and lounging on the padded, bench-like seats toward the back part of the yacht. She's put a large, floppy hat on to protect her scalp from the sun, her legs stretched out in front of her while she looks out into the ocean in deep thought. A quick glance behind me shows Andries busy learning all the local legends about the different sights around the island, no doubt for inspiration for his work, which means I have at least a few minutes to talk to Elise on her own.

She doesn't acknowledge me when I first join her, sitting close enough that her floral scent fills my nostrils once more. I think about how I bet the scent is even more concentrated on her neck, right below her ear, and how much I want to feel her pulse beneath my lips. Elise seems content to ignore me, so after a few minutes of sitting in silence, I finally give in and address her first.

"Fine. You're not invisible anymore. Happy?"

She tilts her sunglasses down so she can look at me unhindered, raising her eyebrows. "Convenient," she mutters, not a trace of a smile to be seen. "You managed to sleep with a random woman, and now that you've got that out of your system, you're ready to come sniffing around me again. Do I only merit your time when you've got nothing better to do?"

I think I can hear a note of pain in her voice, and all the glee I had felt from getting on her nerves with Mia begins to fade fast. I never meant to actually hurt her. "Come on, El. You have to know I didn't do anything with that girl."

"Oh she's just 'that girl' now? Yesterday you insisted I call her Mia."

"I was just trying to ease any suspicion your brother and his fiancée might have about us, okay? Even if she was Aphrodite come to life, I've only got eyes for you, for better or for worse. It's causing me endless grief, but I can't shake it. I didn't touch her."

Elise is quiet, closing into herself. "You didn't even check when I got hurt."

"Only because Andries and Roxie already were."

"I don't know…" she seems unconvinced, heaving a long sigh pensively. "I figured you just didn't see it because you had Mia on your lap."

I cringe. Maybe I did take things too far, letting her crawl all over me… "Fuck. I made a mistake, okay? But I swear nothing happened between us. She showered alone in a guest bathroom before dinner, not with me."

"And after dinner?" she asks, sounding dubious, her eyes searching for the answer in my gaze. "Where did she sleep?"

She knows damn well the answer, but I tell it out loud, nevertheless. "In her hotel room, El. Just like her friend."

Silently, Elise looks away from me, gathering herself. It's becoming more apparent by the second that my little trick with Mia has caused her real emotional distress, and me apologizing is throwing her through a loop. A soft breeze stirs the loose piece of hair around her face when she concludes whatever decision she has been making in her own mind, and just sighs.

"If you want me to trust you, Dan, then you can't pull that shit ever again. Knowing that you would trick me like that really makes me second guess whether you're being real with me or not."

"I am. I swear I am." I have to clamp my mouth closed because the urge to tell her that I love her and want her to be my girlfriend legitimately is so strong I'm afraid the words will sneak out on their own. Everyone else is right at the front of the boat, and we're already taking too much of a chance talking in private like this. Confessing to her here would make me an absolute fool... well, more of one than I already am.

Elise's shoulders relax, and she exhales a long breath, the tension she had been holding close flowing away. "You really owe me one, you know that?"

Out of the corner of my eye, I see Andries looking at us for a prolonged moment, so instead of teasing Elise like I really want to, I just nod. "Oh, I know. And I'm sure you're going to make me pay in full sooner rather than later."

She smiles then, the first real one I've seen since we arrived at the villa, wrinkling her nose adorably. I want to remember this moment forever; Elise, with one of the monumental Faraglioni rocks behind her and the deep, sapphire ocean stretching out beyond. She's an island goddess, and I'm just some idiot here to pray at her altar.

I have to have her alone. Even if it's just for a few minutes, I can't go another entire day without having her to myself. I feel like I'm addicted, but it's an enjoyable vice. Right as her brother, suspicious as always, peels away from the main crowd, I slide Elise a quick glance and tell her, "Make some time for me this evening."

"What do you—" she starts, but I'm already up, heading to meet Andries halfway. I don't have any plans for her and I yet, but by the time we're back on dry land, I will have figured it out.

* * *

Once we get back to the villa, everyone heads inside and back to their suites for a quick nap after the hours in the sun and on the water. I had anticipated everyone would be exhausted, and now that I've had some time to think, I know exactly what I want to take Elise to do. It's going to be difficult to figure out "dates" with her since Andries seems to be around every corner watching us, but being here in Capri with her is too precious of an opportunity to let slide by.

Speaking of the eldest Van den Bosch sibling, I pass the terrace on my way to Elise's suite and see Andries leaning on the stone fence and looking out over the ocean. I sigh heavily, knowing that there is no way I'll be able to sneak his sister past him and out of the villa, so I have to confront him now.

It turns out he isn't waiting on me to grill me about his sister, but instead wanted a private moment to thank me for the tour. I feel immense satisfaction, knowing that Andries is having such a wonderful time. His parents might have abandoned him over this wedding to Roxanne, but I promised myself that I would pick up the slack that they left for my best friend.

"That was a fantastic tour," he tells me, slapping me affectionately on the back as I join him on the terrace. "I never knew you were such an accomplished travel planner."

"You're giving me too much credit." I laugh. "It's almost impossible to choose a bad activity here. Everything is a good time."

"Just take the thanks, man." Andries chuckles, but when his jovial expression dims, I know what's coming next. "Hey, I'm not trying to suggest anything, but why were you and Elise talking alone for so long on the yacht today? She hasn't been acting like herself, but she seemed in better spirits once we got back."

The lie flows so naturally from my mouth, even though I know the truth will have to come out, eventually. "I think she's just feeling left out since everyone else is busy with their significant others. She just needed someone to give her some attention. That's all."

"Hmmm." Andries examines me out of the corner of his eye. "As long as you're not giving her *too much* attention, if you catch my drift."

"Shouldn't you be spending time with Roxanne instead of worrying about what I'm doing, anyway?" I can't help but snap back at him.

I know he wants to question me more, but Andries is reluctant for these small inquiries to turn into a full-blown argument, just like I am. He glances back toward the inside and makes his decision. "Yeah. I told her I'd be right in to shower. But seriously Dan, you and Elise—"

"Are nothing!" I insist, growing tired of his fucking, nosy behavior. "Now go find your lovely lady and stop spending time around me. You already forfeited the chance for this to be a bachelor's only trip."

He finally leaves, and while I know I should find Elise to discuss our next moves when it comes to owning up to Andries, there are much more pleasurable pursuits that are occupying my mind at the moment.

I knock on her door as quietly as I can, and she opens it wearing a white sundress that seems sheer enough that I should be able to see everything, but by some magic of fashion, I can't. How many outfits did this girl bring?

She's gotten some color from the sun, gracing her lovely cheekbones in dusky pink. Her face is bare of any makeup, her hair loose and wavy, freshly unbraided. I take a chance, unable to resist, and step just slightly into her room, kissing her sweet mouth for just an instant before returning to my spot in the hallway. She blinks, touching her mouth with her fingers.

"Let's go get some sorbet and walk through the *Giardini di Augusto*," I say putting my best Italian accent on.

"I haven't even showered yet," she complains, but I couldn't care less. The idea of tasting the sweat on her skin has me half-hard.

"Me either, but we've only got a few hours before dinner. Let's go!"

She pokes her head out and looks around, but once she confirms the coast is clear, she shuts her door, returning a few seconds later with her strappy saddles on and sunglasses sitting on top of her head. "Alright. Let's go, then."

We hurry up like two thieves out of the villa and to the public road. Adrenaline rushes over us as we pass the arched metal gate and hit the sidewalk.

As soon as we're outside, the villa finally behind us, I can't help but link my hand with hers, and she lets me, watching me with a soft look on her face as we walk away.

Like everywhere else on the island, there are lemon trees everywhere, filling the air with the scent of ripe citrus. It's fitting because the sorbet shop I've picked out for us specializes in what else but lemon sorbet. It's a quaint little shop, but we don't stay, getting our cups to go and walking through the bustling downtown together. I have a destination in mind; Giardini di Augusto—also known as the Gardens of Augustus—where we can have some time alone on the paved switchback trails that lead down the cliff side of the island, shaded by palm and Italian stone pine trees.

"I feel like we're two teenagers sneaking out of the house after dark," she confesses as we enter the gardens, sucking the sorbet off her spoon.

"Well technically you're still–"

"Don't you dare!" she laughs, bumping me with her shoulder. "You know what I mean. Two *really young teenagers*. Aren't you afraid my brother is going to catch us?"

"It's not like I'm taking you somewhere to steal your virtue." I sigh dramatically. "Alas, I've already done that back in Amsterdam."

"Ugh," Elise groans, before putting a spoon full of lemon sorbet into her mouth. "Don't say it like that. But seriously… you're not afraid of him catching on to what's happening here?"

"I'm counting on him being so wrapped up in his fiancée that he won't have much time to look outside of their relationship. It seems to be working for the most part, but I think we made him a little suspicious on the yacht."

"I wish he'd just mind his own business," she laments.

The sun is close to setting, hovering over the horizon and painting everything in gold. Even the blue of the sea can't escape its rays, shimmering with flashes of sunlight as the waves roll into shore over and over again. There are only a few other tourists on the winding path with us, and after finishing her sorbet and depositing it in a trash can, Elise leans on the stone balustrade to look out at the natural beauty coming to life right in front of us. Me, on the other hand… she's all I can see.

I come behind her, resting a hand on either side of her body and leaning my weight in just slightly. "That's the problem," I murmur, kissing her neck and reveling in her scent. "He thinks everything is his business. Andries is a certified busybody."

Elise snorts, but her laughter turns to a sigh of pleasure when I take her earlobe gently between my teeth. "If you're still trying to pretend I'm invisible, I think you're failing miserably."

"I already told you. I've decided I can see you once more." Her body is soft and willing as she leans back into my embrace. "You're lucky, though. I could have just kept you invisible for the rest of the trip."

"You kind of ruined that for yourself, having me sleep over with you the night before we left," she points out.

"I wasn't counting on having sex with you before coming here, you know?" I slide my hands over her ribs, making her squirm. "That kinda ruined the entire plan before it even started."

There is more to be said about our one night together, but there are other things on Elise's agenda. She leans her entire weight into me. "Speaking of sex, maybe we could go somewhere quieter…"

I freeze before exhaling in amusement. "So you really liked it?"

"Of course I did, why? You don't think so?" Elise sounds incredulous. "I thought it was very clear that I was having a good time."

"I don't know, you just left so abruptly the next day. I was so fucking confused."

"And that," she whispers, heaving a long sigh, "is where I fucked up. So… I'm sorry, Dan."

Turning her body to face me, she bumps her nose against mine before we meet in a gentle, but thorough kiss. It heats me up from the inside, slow and steady, like embers on coals. The kiss is a lot of things all wrapped into one; us re-familiarizing ourselves with one another, the sweet relief of finally being alone together, and most importantly of all… an apology.

I'm sorry, I tell her without words, using my lips and tongue to express myself instead. *Don't leave.*

When the kiss breaks, I take her hand again, leading her past a curve in the stone wall that takes us down a hidden dirt path to an older, forgotten part of the gardens. The balustrade here is showing its age, but otherwise, it's just as beautiful as the rest, just a little wilder. Which is fitting, because I feel nearly wild right now. My need for Elise is almost out of control.

"We're alone here," I tell her, voice low. "This is too off the path for most tourists, so we should be good."

Looking at me from under her lashes, Elise doesn't need any coaxing, intrinsically knowing what I want as she turns to face the sunset. From behind her, I curl a hand around to cup her jaw, turning her face so she and I can kiss in this magical, somehow private spot. We could stop here, exchanging indulgent, wet kisses, but I know that isn't what is going to happen.

The catharsis of finding out that I hadn't been messing around with any of those other women spun Elise apart, and I'm almost giddy with relief now that I've given in to being with her again, telling her with my teeth and tongue how much I've missed this thing we share, whatever it is.

Elise smells like her floral perfume and the faint coconut scent of suntan lotion. When she first presses her lips to mine, they're still cold from the sorbet, as are mine, but we quickly warm each other. Tasting the sorbet on her tongue makes it even sweeter.

I want to stay in this moment forever, even as she pulls away from my mouth and kisses my jaw and neck, but if we don't hurry, then the sun's going to go down and we'll end up half naked with each other in the dark. It sounds like a good time, really, but I don't think we know our way around Capri well enough for all that.

My hands itch to turn her around and touch her skin, push them under her dress and feel the soft round curves of her, but I tell her to keep her fingers locked around the balustrade. I'll do all the work right now to make her feel good… I've got a lot of lost time and bad behavior to make up for. Later, I will take my time, reacquainting myself with her body at leisure.

I want her to feel how hard I am as I press my pelvis against her ass, and sense Elise's frustration that we can't hook up the way we both want—naked and unrushed.

"I don't want to be too rough with you," I rasp in her ear. "I don't trust myself to stay calm once I'm finally inside you."

I kiss her mouth again briefly, hands moving up her legs and under her skirt. She lets out a shivery exhale when I touch her pussy through her white silk panties, peeking out at me as I throw her skirt up and over her perfectly round ass.

"Rough is fine," Elise pants. "Rough is wonderful actually."

Despite what she says, I stroke her folds softly through the damp fabric, before pulling the panties down until they fall around her knees. Skirt still on, it feels even more taboo to be standing here, her pussy bare to the sea breeze and my searching hands. Palming her ass cheeks, before letting go with one hand. I undo my belt buckle and pull my painfully hard cock out of my boxers. I don't undress at all besides pushing my shorts down my thighs enough to free myself. I take half a step back, stroking my dick with my hand as I take in the impossibly erotic sight of Elise's naked ass and pussy arched up for me with the sun setting out in front of us. We're just steps from being in public, but she's still so willing to be taken by me. What have I done to deserve this?

"I can't make love to you the way I want," I murmur, heart aching for how much I care for this girl. "But I promise that you'll enjoy yourself."

She throws me a sultry look over her shoulder. "I already am."

It's a demonstration of my control, the way I manage to slowly feed my entire length into her. Elise is hot and tighter than I would have thought possible, and even though it has to be a challenge for her, she still wiggles and moves backward toward me, disoriented with arousal. Want for her courses through me like my own blood, even as she grasps the balustrade for dear life. Below us the city stretches and moves, climbing upwards so that some of the higher houses might even be level with us. Thankfully, the brick wall obscures our actions, and Elise and I are alone to fuck in the most frantic way possible.

That we even have the time to escape the rest of our group is amazing, and I'm not going to waste such an opportunity. It's almost a dreamlike experience, the sun glowing off the jewel-toned sea in little embers of orange and gold. Salty air blows Elise's hair as I brush it off her neck, leaning forward to map all the skin I can reach with my mouth in sucking kisses. I still have to go as slow as possible in and out, Elise's body both protesting and welcoming the intrusion of my dick.

"Does it hurt?" I ask.

She shakes her head quickly. "No… no. It's good. Just frustrating." I see her lick her lips. "I want it so bad."

I couldn't agree more. I want this fast and hard, gazing upon the city and the people there without having any idea what we're doing above them.

I gently kick Elise's feet further apart, hand skimming down her back and between her shoulders, pushing her lower and widening her stance.

"There you go," I grate out. "Open up for me, baby."

Now when I grip her and sink home, it's easier, and I feel the head of my cock kissing the mouth of her womb with each thrust. Elise gasps, letting her head fall forward until her forehead touches the stone railing. She's trying to keep her knees locked and upright as I fuck her in intense, even strokes.

The perfect angle, the illicit nature of the location and the act itself, and the sweet relief of finally being with Elise again makes the entire experience feel like a whirlwind inside of me. I'm focused on bringing her closer and closer to the precipice of climax relentlessly, but the squeezing and fluttering of her inner walls adding to the tension inside of me. Her skin is so damned soft, raised in goosebumps from how over-sensitized she is. I caress her ass cheeks, up her spine under the dress, and on the sensitive spots on the flesh of her graceful neck. Reaching forward and cupping her throat gently I step forward so I can hold her through the final strokes, feeling her pulse fluttering under my palm and the vibration of her voice as she moans.

Elise keens my name quietly, both of us hearing the hushed sounds of the people on the streets behind us but unable to stay silent. The way the feeling of her spasming inner walls is making the pressure inside of me build and build is incredible, but I have to make sure she comes first. No matter how easy it would be for me to just let go right here, right now.

Just as the sun starts to dip below the horizon in earnest, I feel the wave of her orgasm beginning to crest, pulling my cock deeper. I'm breathing hard, breath fanning over her neck and shoulders in ragged huffs. My fingers flex on her throat, not exerting any pressure but just keeping Elise right where I want her. As her legs start to shake and she cries out in ecstasy, I move my palm to gently cover her mouth so she can scream to her heart's content, muffled by me.

"That's right, Elise. Come for me," I growl, balls drawing up and tightening as the orgasm starts to build at the base of my spine, ready to explode. "I'm going to fill you up, baby. Are you ready?"

She can't answer me, still being rocked by pleasure, but I don't need her verbal approval. Elise's body is telling me everything I need to know. With an animalistic noise, I start to come, our flesh clapping together, until I go silent and still, whispering a single, "Fuck," as I come inside her. I feel the heat of her pussy grabbing me like a vice and the quivering of her thighs against me. It's perfect, all of it. A moment I'll never forget for as long as I live.

CHAPTER 33

Dan

After our interlude in the gardens, I helped Elise fix her dress, and we stayed there to watch the sun fully set while I held her in my arms. It wasn't the usual afterglow I'd enjoy, naked in bed with a woman, but it was unbearably meaningful to me to just be able to spend those moments with her. I buried my nose in her hair and just breathed her in, the woman in my arms a million times more beautiful to me than the sunset happening in front of us.

Taking that extra time to be together is biting us in the ass now, though, because as we approach the villa, it's readily apparent that everyone else is already sitting down for dinner in the dining room, the French windows wide open and giving us a full view of everyone. In fact, we can see the warm glow from the candlelit dining table from the road, and I'm all too aware that they are watching us come up the walkway and into the house.

"We're fucked," Elise whispers.

"Just play it cool. We're friends, remember? Friends spend time together."

"Oh, yeah? When was the last time you and Andries went and watched a sunset on a paradise island and snuggled?"

I glare down at her, and she returns the look. "Point taken. But what else can we do? Let's just get through dinner. I'll try and get your brother drunk and then maybe he'll forget about it."

"Ha," she scoffs, head shaking. "This is Andries we're talking about. He's going to go back to his suite and write an angry journal entry about this, so he'll remember it forever."

"You're such a pessimist."

"Better than a foolish optimist."

We stop in front of the dining room entryway, quickly checking each other's clothes to make sure they're not messed up in any sort of way, and with a nod to each other, we enter to join the rest of the group.

"Welcome back," Roxanne greets with a broad smile.

Her fiancé, though, is not so welcoming. "And where have the two of you been for two and a half hours?"

"Just to get some sorbet," Elise chirps, taking a seat and happily accepting the crisp white wine the server offers. She's coming off too positive, but it's too late now.

"Sure." My friend laughs sarcastically, everyone else at the table looking uneasy. "Since when do the two of you hang out together so much?"

"What are you even talking about?" Elise counters in that tone that can only come from siblings that have spent their lives arguing with one another. "Dan and I hang out all the time in Amsterdam. You know that."

"There's a difference between a bagel before class and disappearing for two hours during a family trip," Andries snaps. Roxanne lays a hand on his shoulder, and he sucks in a huge breath, letting it out slowly as he composes himself. "But you're telling me nothing weird is going on between the two of you, right?"

"Right," Elise and I both say at the same time.

In the main portion of the house, the doorbell rings, and we all hear the butler opening the door to let whoever has shown up in. Andries smiles now, looking smug, and I have a terrible feeling that I know what he's done.

"That's a relief because if not, it would be really awkward for the guests that I've invited." He makes a show of taking a long drink of his wine while Elise slowly realizes what's going on.

"Who did you invite, Andries?" she hisses.

"Just Tiffany and Mia." He shrugs. "Mia was going on and on about how much she liked Dan, and since I know he's into her too, I went ahead and told her that he found her attractive but was just too shy to say so." He chuckles, looking at me. "We all know you have never been shy, but I just wanted to make it easier for you, man. You do find her attractive, right? That's what you told me yesterday."

I want to throttle my best friend right then and there, upcoming wedding or not. With my jaw clenched, I tell him, "Yeah, I guess I did."

Elise's eyes shoot up to look at me for a second, hurt, before glancing back down at the kale salad in front of her. She's giving no indication that what Andries just said is bothering her, but I know better, and I feel like an idiot for lying yesterday just to get Andries off my back. Mia was a pretty enough woman, but she had just been a pawn to make Elise feel a little bit jealous, but now…

She and Tiffany walk into the dining room, Mia immediately rushing over to me and giving me a quick hug before sitting. Elise had taken the seat across from me, and now Mia is on my left. What a disaster.

"Thanks so much for inviting us," Mia crows happily. "I was worried you weren't into me," she tells me, lowering her voice so only I can hear her. "But I think it's cute that you're shy."

I fight the urge to roll my eyes. "Uh. Sure."

Dinner continues on as normally as it can after the earlier outburst, with Mia being an unabashed flirt the entire time. Her hands are constantly stroking my arm or landing on my knee, no matter how many times I shift away. Elise has taken the only avenue left to her and is pretending that Mia and I don't exist, talking animatedly with Roxanne about the other attractions they want to see on the island, and making plans to go shopping. Roxie looks confused that Elise is being so overly friendly, but I know she's just doing it to distract herself from the nonsense that her brother has caused.

It's just one dinner, I keep telling myself. *One dinner and then I'll tell this poor girl that I'm not interested and that will be that.*

The worst part is that whenever Andries looks over at Mia and me, I'm forced to give in to her overbearing affection just to maintain the image that it's her I'm interested in, and not his sister. Hell, if I had never met Elise, I probably would have already slept with Mia, so Andries inviting her to dinner wasn't completely out of the realm of the possibility of things I would have done on my own. Something tells me he knows more than he's letting on about Elise and me though, and he's using Mia as a wedge to get between us.

Midway through the meal, I get a text. I hope it's Elise, but instead, it's from Roxie, and simply says, *Sorry, I had no idea.* I give her a discrete shrug from across the table, noticing that she kicks the attention she's giving her fiancé into high gear. It tells me that Roxanne has picked up on what is going on between Elise and me, and while I had hoped to keep it secret until we were ready to tell Andries, at least I know Roxanne will be on our side if she thinks whatever is between us is genuine.

Dinner finally ends, and I'm more than ready to flee Mia's grabbing hands and go to my room until I'm sure she's left, but Andries asks the butler for music and digestives out on the terrace once the meal is finished. Mia's eyes glow as we all shift outdoors where soft songs are being piped in over the surround sound speakers, but all I can do is look at Elise, leaning against the railing by herself and watching as all the couples join together in gentle dancing embraces.

There's no help for it. I put my hands stiffly on Mia's hips, and she watches me, eyes hooded. I try to catch Elise's eye, just so she knows that this isn't what I want, but she's turned to glance out over the cliffside—anywhere but where Mia and I are stiffly turning together to the music… I can't blame her, either.

After a moment, Elise stands, a frown fixed on her face, and walks silently past the makeshift dance floor back into the villa. I want to call out to her, but I just can't. Not here, not now. Andries, Roxanne, Robin, and Lili are all tipsy, laughing and twirling across the tile floor, and I can tell Mia is getting frustrated with my reluctance to do anything but the most unenthusiastic slow dance known to man. Once Elise is gone from my view, I come to the conclusion that I have to let this girl down gently because I'm dying to follow the woman that I'm actually falling for. Mia might be handsy, but it's not like she's to blame for any of this. I was even the one to invite her in yesterday, showing her false interest just to further my own desires. But I can't feel overly guilty for her because every ounce of my concern is now on Elise, who is gone, thinking god knows what about this terrible turn of events.

"You seem distracted." Mia sighs as if she's finally catching on to my disinterest.

"What?" I wince, realizing I've just proved her point. "...Yeah, you're not wrong. I guess my mind is elsewhere."

"Maybe there's something I can do to bring it back to the present," she purrs, leaning in and trying to press her lips to mine.

Disgust rolls through me, and I push her back by the shoulders, breaking our embrace. Mia freezes, looking distraught.

"Sorry. I'm not feeling right," I babble, looking for a way to get off the terrace without being confronted by anyone else. The sweet, slow music is almost a mockery of how chaotic I'm feeling. "I'm just going to bed. I guess you can… uh… see yourself out or whatever."

Eyes fixed forward, I take no notice of everyone looking at me as I make a beeline for the doors leading back inside.

As soon as I'm in, I feel a hand grab my arm; Andries, looking pissed. *Fuck.*

"What do you think you're doing? I brought that girl over here for you and now you're just going to bail?"

"I'm just tired man," I tell him honestly because I'm suddenly exhausted from all of this.

"Bullshit. It's barely ten pm. Are you sick or something? I've never known you to refuse a beautiful woman like that."

"Shouldn't you be more worried about your fiancée than my sex life, Andries?" I gripe, shaking his hand off me. "Just because I took your sister out for sorbet doesn't mean anything is going on, and it certainly doesn't mean I need you to set me up on blind fucking dates without telling me."

Stunned, Andries just blinks at me before responding. "I just didn't want you to be alone when everyone else has a significant other here—well, except—"

"Yeah, except your sister. Did you ever think I was hanging out with her because she doesn't have anyone else to spend time with here?" The temptation just to tell him the truth about everything hovers on the edge of my mind, but I know I can't take such a drastic step without Elise here to make the decision with me. "If I spend the entire time with some random girl like Mia, what is Elise going to do? I'm just being a good friend."

My friend looks like he can't decide if I'm telling the truth or not, but before I have to remind him that I footed the bill for this entire trip, he sighs and nods. "Okay, Dan. Sorry, I might have overreacted. It's good to know you haven't broken your oath. Let's just forget this and talk tomorrow, okay?"

"Sounds good to me."

I watch him go back outside to find Roxanne, and once he's shut the door behind him, I go back to my suite, intending to spend the rest of the night alone. There is nothing good that can come of me trying to speak to Elise tonight, not while her brother is on high alert, so I keep telling myself it will just be a shower and bed for me.

That is, until I hear her moving around in her own room, and the sound of her shower kicking on. Thinking about her showering, just one wall away from me is almost painful. I retreat to my own en suite bathroom and hide under the nearly scalding water, hoping the sound of it will drown out the matching sound of Elise's shower from across the way, but the knowledge supersedes everything else.

After the fastest shower of my entire life, I throw my clothes back on, intending to knock on her door and force her to talk to me. I can't live like this for nine more days, with her occupying my every thought.

Since I can't talk to her face to face, I settle for sending her a text.

Dan: *Are you awake? Still in your room?*

Elise: *Yes. You still slow dancing in the dark with the love of your life, Mia?*

I start to type out a sarcastic response, but then I have another idea. A stupid one, but if it works, there is no way anyone will see me going into her room, which is what I want to avoid.

Out on the balcony, lit only by the moon and stars, I try to judge the distance between my balcony and Elise's—it's less than a foot. I can jump it, no problem. So, like the love-struck teenager sneaking out that Elise had accused me of being earlier tonight, I climb over the railing of my balcony and hop to hers.

I make it, thank God, because had I fallen it probably would have been to my death down the jagged cliff that the villa is perched on. I'm nimble enough, though, and the surge of adrenaline I get from the dumb decision makes me laugh out loud. Still feeling giddy, I knock on the glass door into her room.

The sounds of her moving around in her room pause, and then hesitantly, she pulls the curtains aside and sees me through the glass. She looks shocked for a second, and then laughs, opening the curtains fully and then the door, pulling me inside by the collar of my shirt. She doesn't shut the door behind us, letting the salty, lemony air cascade around us.

"You moron," she gasps, head shaking in amusement. "Did you really *jump*?!"

"Anything for you, fair Juliet."

"I think Juliet left Romeo outside, but either way… what are you doing here?"

"I needed to talk to you." I slide my hands down her bare arms, trying not to get distracted by the criminally small negligee she's wearing. Her skin is damp and warm from the shower. "I can't sleep knowing you're so close, but all alone over here…"

"You're being ridiculous," she chides but doesn't pull away either.

"Obviously I didn't know Mia was going to be at dinner. I'm sorry I didn't tell her to leave earlier, but it's so hard with Andries right on our heels, I didn't know what to do. But when I saw you leaving, you looked hurt, and... fuck, Elise. I feel like we just figured out that we want to be in each other's lives, at least for now, and I don't want to mess things up again already."

"It's not messed up," she whispers, her eyes locked on mine. "I promise it's not, but you and I both know that we have to end this soon. If my brother finds out, your friendship–"

I put my finger on her lips to make her stop talking, sliding the pad of it over the seam of her mouth. Her eyes close as if in a trance when I lean forward to kiss her, but at the first hint of touch, she jolts back to the present. "We can't." Her voice agonizes. "If we continue this affair, then Andries is sure to find out, and it will ruin your friendship forever. I know how much it means to you both."

"I don't care," I tell her, and as soon as the words leave my mouth, I know they're true. Of course, I care about Andries, and love him like a brother, but what I feel for Elise eclipses anything else.

My head is spinning. The confession, the truth, and the depth of my feelings for her are lodged in my throat. I don't think I can hold them back any longer, even though confessing now would be a fool's errand. I've already fucked her in a nearly public space and jumped across the space between our two balconies, so foolish behavior where Elise is concerned is nothing new for me. So why are these few simple words the most terrifying, intimidating thing in the world for me?

And if I'm so frightened of them, why can't I just hold them down and never tell her?

Moonlight is reflecting in her wide, round eyes, shimmering off of the creamy white silk of her scandalously short nightgown, and I want to see what it looks like falling over the peaks and valleys of her naked body beneath mine. I want that *every night* for the rest of my life. Why do I feel this way, feverish and thunderstruck?

You love her! My heart chants inside me, seeming to have a mind of its own. *You love Elise Van den Bosch. Admit it!*

Her body language is guarded, hands still raised in case I try to gather her up and kiss her again. Part of me wants to grab her and slam my mouth over hers until she relents and gives in to what I know is between us, but I simply can't. She has to come to me of her own volition, or not at all.

Am I really going to do this? Am I really going to confess my love to her?

"What do you mean you don't care?" she demands, blinking twice in confusion, her mouth slightly agape. "He's your best friend."

"If he really is my best friend, then he'll understand what I'm about to do, and forgive me one day." I take a deep breath, teetering on the edge of proclaiming something that will change my life forever. I'm scared, unbelievably so, but above all else, enlivened by the possibilities of it all. Once I tell her, it will all be out in the open, and I'll be able to live honestly for the first time in so, so long.

"Elise," I begin, slowly and confidently, "I love you. I'm *in love* with you. I have been for weeks now. Months... hell, probably even years. I love you and I don't give a damn how Andries feels about it."

If I thought her eyes were wide before, it's nothing compared to now. She gapes at me, eyes like saucers, shining suspiciously bright in the darkened room. For maybe the first time in her entire life, my fiery, opinionated, pushy Elise is speechless.

"Say something," I beg softly. "Anything. Don't shut me out."

She licks her lips, her mind searching for words while her gaze evades mine. "I... Dan... I..."

"You don't have to say it back," I amend quickly. "I don't care what you feel for me. But I love you. And I'd rather lose my friendship with your brother than lose you."

Elise gathers herself with a shake of her head. "You would do that for me? Seriously?"

Feeling an odd combination of grimness and elation, I nod. "I hope it never comes to that, but if it comes down to it... I know what choice I'll make. All I can do is pray that Andries never tries to force that decision on me, but..." I trail off.

She exhales, turning around in a flash of fabric and pacing the length of her suite, unable to stand still and hold onto the confession I've just let out into the world. "Dan, I don't want to hurt you," she pleas, stopping in her tracks and holding her hands out to me in supplication.

"What do you mean?"

"I like you, but..." Her eyes flutter closed.

"El," I step forward and take her out-held hands, brushing my lips over both sets of her knuckles. She opens her beautiful eyes, and it feels like she's staring into my soul. "I'm okay with that. I don't need you to love me back, I just..." I pause, my heart thundering hard inside my chest. "I just want to continue whatever is going on between us."

"What if one day I want to stop?" she asks, her voice nearly quivering at the end. "Are you going to seek out revenge or something?"

I laugh sadly, shaking my head. "Of course not. I've just given up on denying what I feel for you. All I want to do is soak up all this time with you without any of the things that have stood in our way thus far. I want to love you and be with you, freely. I'm so tired of lying to myself… and the world."

"So even if this is just a short, temporary thing, you'd still risk your friendship with Andries for it?" She sounds skeptical, but underneath it all, hopeful.

"It's crazy. I know it is, but I would—even for just these few minutes I've shared with you. To be fair, if Andries wants to end our friendship over this, that's on him. I still want to be his friend, and will still care about him even if he cuts me off forever, but we're both grown men. I'm not going to hold myself back because he doesn't approve. If our friendship ends, that's his choice. Not mine. But this…" I release one of her hands and stroke her soft cheek. "This thing between us… well. I'll take whatever you give me."

She blinks swiftly, and if I didn't know her better, I'd think she was blinking tears away. "Even if I want to stop right now because of my brother?"

"Yes, even then," I promise. "But I don't think you should stop because of him. Not if this is something you want."

Elise crosses her arms over her chest, hugging herself and looking over my shoulder at the night sky outside. I don't rush her, knowing that she's taking her time thinking over everything that just happened. Part of me knew that she wouldn't return my confession of love, but there had been a little naïve part of me that had hoped she would. Still, I'm sure she feels *something* for me, and maybe whatever it is, I can coax it from affection to real love.

I have to clench my fists to stop rushing forward to touch her. She's so used to going through things alone, that I'm afraid if I push her right now, she'll shut me out. I have to let her make up her own mind, no matter how much I want to comfort her.

Time seems to stretch on endlessly, but finally, she closes her eyes, tilting her head back and taking a bracing breath. "Okay. I want to continue this thing, too. But we have to be on the same page about how there might be an expiration date on it."

I have no plans of letting her go, but for her peace of mind, I nod. "Whatever you want, Elise. I will respect your choice no matter what."

Walking to me as if in a trance, Elise is soon in front of me looking up into my face with what looks like awe. I don't need any more hints, cupping her face in my hands and leaning down to kiss her. She exhales shakily into my mouth, and I agree with the sentiment. It's a sweet relief to be able to have her again, even if we had just hooked up not too long ago. It's different now that the truth is out.

We walk backward together until her calves bump into the edge of her bed. I push her gently down, and Elise holds her hands in the air, a clear sign for me to remove her negligee. I obey happily, kneeling between her legs and covering her full, naked breasts with small, circling kisses. I take my time getting to the peaks of her nipples, waiting until she's panting to suck one into my mouth, and then the other. She makes a breathy noise of approval, grabbing my head and holding it in place as I lick and nibble at her tits until her nipples are hard and peaked. Elise spreads her legs, letting me move in closer and take her panties off in one swift motion.

I take the time to kiss her again, this time slowly and passionately, mapping the inside of her mouth with my tongue. She makes small noises of contentment as I do so, and I drink them down like wine. Even completely naked in front of me, I want to show her that I truly do love her. Not just her body, or the sex that we have, but everything else too. Her entire being is priceless to me.

It isn't long until the sweet kisses go heated again, though, and I can feel how hard I am. It's also becoming increasingly obvious that Elise wants more from the way she presses against me and writhes beneath my touch. I move my mouth from hers, along her jawbone, down her neck, and over her collarbone. With my fingers, I find the apex of her thighs, testing how wet she is for me, and find her soaked. It's always amazing how much she wants me, and I don't think I'll ever get tired of it.

Feeling her wetness sends a surge of arousal straight to my cock, and it strains even harder against the zipper of my shorts. Elise watches me with heated eyes as I duck my head between her legs and replace my fingers with my tongue, carefully parting her folds and lying claim to every bit of her. Her taste is heady and sharp on my tongue, and the need to possess her fully surges through me, unstoppable.

Hitching her legs over my shoulders, I dip my tongue deep into her channel while my thumb circles her clit, which swells at my touch. Elise covers her mouth with the back of her hand to control herself and the noises she's making. The balcony doors are still open, and all of our rooms are so close together that the risk that we'll be heard is all too real.

Seeing how out of control I make her spurs me on even more. I suck her clit between my lips, fingers sliding deep into her pussy and arching up until I feel her shudder when I hit her g-spot. Smiling against her flesh, I set to work with the single-minded intention of making her come. I see her sit up, looking down at what I'm doing to her, before moaning again quietly and rolling her eyes to the ceiling. She can barely take it, and that's exactly what I want.

"I'm the only one who can make you feel this way," I tell her, pulling away just long enough to speak. "Remember that when I make you come, Elise."

"God, Dan," she keens, gripping the bedding in her fists when I put my mouth back on her pussy.

When I feel her walls fluttering around my fingers, I grip her thighs to hold her still as the orgasm rolls over her. I can taste the rush of fresh wetness as she grinds against my face, sucking on her clit until she's gripping her hands in my hair to ride it all out.

Elise manages to keep the volume down until she hits the very peak of her climax, and I have to surge upwards, keeping my fingers inside her but claiming her mouth with my own to muffle the sounds of her ecstasy. She claws at my shoulders desperately but finally goes limp in my arms. I chuckle, giving her one last kiss and letting her fall back onto the bed while I strip my own clothes off.

"You've got to keep quiet," I tell her. "Or you're going to get us both into big trouble."

"I thought you said you didn't care if people found out?" she asks, sounding spent.

"I mean, if they do, then so be it, but I'd rather it not be right in the middle of me fucking you."

Once my clothes have joined her things on the floor, I crawl over her on the bed where she had scooted up to the headboard. Elise reaches out to grip my cock, stroking it a few times, her eyes hooded. Letting her take her time with me sounds extremely tempting, but I really, really want to come with my cock buried deep inside her, not all over her hand.

"Let me take care of you," she purrs, resting her head against the pile of pillows at the head of the bed while she touches me so carefully.

"Another time," I respond, lifting one of her legs and kissing from the hollow of her ankle all the way up. "I didn't get your pussy all ready for me just to not fuck it."

Her eyes go wide at the filthy words, and I laugh darkly. She wants to meet me beat for beat in the bedroom, but sometimes it's so apparent how inexperienced she really is. I look forward to teaching her everything.

For now, though, I want to make love to Elise. I've just confessed my feelings for her, and I want to show her without words how utterly serious I am. Just like I did kneeling between her legs, I lift each of her ankles over my shoulders so I can enter her at an angle. Bracketing my elbows on either side of her head, I position myself and start to slowly sink into her. She seems unsure about how I have her nearly bent in half at first, but when I thrust fully for the first time, stroking her deeper than ever before, her mind quickly changes.

"Oh, wow," she whispers. "That feels amazing."

"Tell me what feels amazing, baby," I demand.

Her eyes flash. "Y-your cock, Dan. Your cock feels amazing."

With a rumbling noise of approval, I give her everything she needs then, fucking her with long, even strokes that hit her g-spot relentlessly. She arches her back, throwing an arm around my neck to force me to kiss her, but I go along with her happily, using my tongue to mimic the motions of my hips, in and out, in and out.

I know it must be intense for her because the heat and tightness of her channel is driving me insane. She feels so good, every time, that it's unreal. Hearing the sounds of our bodies coming together combined with her breathy sighs and muffled moans is enough to make me come right then, but I control myself. What I'm doing to Elise is making her spin apart more and more with each thrust.

First she tries to cover her moans by kissing me, and then when that doesn't work, she bites the meat of her own palm, body tense and shaking, but when I snap my hips forward just the right way, her hands fly to the sheets and fists them in her hands, losing control. One overly loud note leaves her throat before I'm able to cover her mouth with my hand, feeling the vibration of her cry against my palm.

"Shhh," I tell her, but she just shakes her head, as if to say I can't.

I give in, covering her mouth softly while I piston into her the last few times. Elise strokes my chest and arms now that she doesn't have to control her own volume, and her touch leaves fire and goosebumps in its wake. Her hips are moving in time with me, helplessly chasing her peak that I'm driving her toward.

I can't hold back any longer, not with the way she's moving beneath me, but it doesn't matter, because Elise comes apart right at the same moment I do, her pussy contracting around my cock just as I come deep inside of her. A groan escapes me even though I try to stay silent, but I manage to keep my hand over Elise's mouth, even as she arches and writhes. The pleasure is so intense that it feels like my soul is leaving my body, melding with hers. The second I feel her start to relax, I take my hand off her lips and kiss her hard, letting her legs fall off my shoulders so I can press myself flush against her body. We're connected, skin to skin, head to toe, shivering through the last bits of our shared orgasms with my cock still seated within her. The things I whisper into her ear then would have embarrassed me a month ago, but now there is no shame. I mean every sweet, sappy word, and while she still doesn't tell me that she loves me, the things she says back as we lay in the afterglow, pretty close to love in my opinion. Still, I won't ever expect it from her, just valuing her being with me now.

As the sweat on our bodies cools and we come back to ourselves, minds clearing of the haze of lust, I start to think that maybe I pushed her too hard, too fast, with the love confession and the soul-shattering sex. Elise is still in my arms, her only movement the beating of her heart and her breath fanning over my cheek. I don't regret any of what happened tonight, but maybe I need to give her some space to process everything. Plus, I'm not sure how safe it will be for me to climb balconies in the early morning when anyone could see me. I also don't want to push my luck in trying to sneak out the front door when Andries could be anywhere in the villa.

I press a chaste kiss to her temple. "I'm going to go back to my room and get some sleep," I tell her quietly, and she stiffens, looking into my eyes.

"What? Why are you leaving?"

"So we can both get some actual rest."

Elise looks hurt, frowning. "No. Just stay here until the morning. It will be nice."

"It's too dangerous. We'll get caught if we keep pushing our boundaries around here, and you know that as well as I do."

Instead of protesting again, she rolls out from underneath me and lays her head on my chest, sighing. "Now you can't leave."

It's my turn to frown, but even as I start to push her off, my heart tightens at how beautiful and sweet she looks, slotted against the side of me so perfectly. It feels warm and domestic. And if she really wants me to stay, what kind of monster would I be to leave her all alone?

I push a finger under her chin until she lifts her face, her expression questioning. I give her a gentle kiss on each corner of her mouth and then her forehead. "Fine. I'll stay."

Her smile is like the sun, bright and warm. I want to bask in it forever. Elise snuggles back down, head on my chest again, and I stroke her arm with my free hand. It strikes me that lying together like this, cuddling with no expectations of anything else sexual, almost makes us seem like a real couple. I squeeze her closer, closing my eyes. I wish I could spend every one of my nights like this, holding her, feeling her heartbeat, cherishing her.

Loving her.

The idea that I actually confessed my love to her is so bizarre that it almost feels like a dream. I might not have her love back quite yet, but she cares for me, I'm sure of it. Maybe I'm a fool for thinking that a girl like Elise, one of the heirs to the Van den Bosch fortune and business, could ever fall in love with me, but with the way she's tracing small circles on my chest with her fingers, eyes closed and a small smile pulling at her lips, it's impossible not to have hope.

I love her. Soon, I think I might be lucky enough to be loved by her too.

CHAPTER 34

Well, last night I had sworn to myself that I was going to figure out a way to end this thing with Dan, and now he's sleeping next to me, his scent all over my body and his confession of love bouncing around in my mind.

Waking up with him is one thing, but turning to the side and seeing Dan laying there in the light of the rising sun, his messy hair and the stubble on his cheeks glowing bronze, makes me feel invincible. This man, this beautiful, fit, incredible man confessed his love to me and swore multiple times that he would choose me over my brother. For the first time in my life, I feel like someone sees my worth for *who I am*, not because I'm Sebastian's daughter or Andries's sister. Dan loves me, not the potential of who I could be, and that's so meaningful that it's almost incomprehensible. Dan really sees me, and for that, I could almost love him.

And there is the problem. Sometimes I think I love Dan just like he loves me; powerfully, romantically, but other times I think he just believes he loves me because I'm the one girl he can't easily have. That leads me to be conflicted on whether I feel the way I do about him out of lust, or if I really am falling for him. When he confessed last night, I wanted to respond in kind, but something stopped me.

I shake my head, trying to clear the thoughts, and just admire him lying next to me. The little bit of color he's picked up on the trip suits him, making him look tan and healthy. I love the extra warmth of his body after he's been in the sun and the taste of salt on his skin. Our comforter is at his waist, exposing his toned chest, arms thrown over his head and muscles naturally flexed. Looking at him like this makes me feel oddly possessive. I've already come to terms with not wanting any other woman to touch him, but with him sleeping in my bed, that emotion is even more intense. Something deep in my brain is chanting *Mine, mine, mine.*

So. Lust or love? I think I know the answer, but I'm not ready to face it in full yet, so instead, I turn to lust.

I slowly push the comforter down until it uncovers him to his knees. Dan's manhood is already standing, erect and proud, even though he's still sleeping. Seeing him hard gives me a warm feeling in my belly. I wish he would wake up, so I could touch him, but then I have an idea...

Starting from his neck, I kiss him, moving downwards. The presses of my lips are feather light, only briefly sweeping my tongue over a single nipple as I go, following with equally soft touches of my fingertips. He's so warm that I want to just lay my cheek on the planes of his chest, but I'm on a mission, and if I snuggle back up with him again, I'm afraid I'll fall asleep.

Dan's skin smells spicy and salty, an addicting combination. He stays asleep until I reach his hip bones, and even then he doesn't snap awake. I feel his hand stroking my hair at first, and then my cheek wordlessly. He makes a rumbling noise in his chest as my lips and tongue slide over his strong, muscled thighs, flexing under my touch, but it isn't until I gently lick the head of his erect cock for the first time that he quietly moans.

It's a deep, wholly masculine sound that settles in my bones and makes me shiver. Oh, I really, really liked that noise. I lick him again in exactly the same way and receive the same groan, his fingers burying in my slightly tangled hair.

Still, he doesn't speak, and it makes the whole thing feel even more intimate. I continue to lick him, eventually taking the entire thick head in my mouth, licking the salty bead of precum off as I do so. Dan hisses between his teeth, hips instinctively thrusting upwards before he gets control of himself. I could almost sigh in relief, knowing that his entire length would be too much for me, but I'm happy to slowly try to take more and more of him into my mouth. Here, his skin is even hotter and softer than everywhere else, and the noises he makes as I lick and suck at him are turning me on more than I thought they would. I can feel his fingers tighten in my hair and his thighs tense when I do something he really likes, so I file away the information for later.

Somehow, Dan gets even harder when I make a satisfied noise with my lips around his manhood.

"Elise…" he breathes, voice strained. "You've got to stop, baby, or I'm not going to be able to stay quiet."

I take that as a challenge, gripping the base of his erection in my hand and stroking him as I continue to suck him off. He strains against me, a shiver running up his spine and a growl building in his throat.

"Fuck, Elise—" he starts, louder than he should, but just then a ringtone comes from somewhere near us. We both look over at the bedside table accusingly, only to see that someone is calling him on his iPhone.

Worse, it's my brother's contact picture on the screen. I pull away from Dan quickly, sitting on my ass and tucking my legs under myself as I watch him sit up shakily and silence the call. Dan lets out a shaky breath and shakes his head.

"This is bad news. He's probably looking for me. I have to go." He runs his hands through his hair, clearly stressed. "Shit. What if he went to my room, and I wasn't there? What if—"

I can't help but laugh at his stress, and his mouth clicks shut before he glares at me. "You're a fucking bitch, you know that?"

I laugh again, and with a sigh, he chuckles too, leaning forward to kiss me quickly. "I'll get a hold of you later, okay? I want to see you."

"Okay, Dan," I say quietly, watching him dress, affection blooming in my heart. "I want to see you too."

* * *

As the shower water soaks me, carrying away all the evidence of what Dan and I did last night, he's still the only thing on my mind. I close my eyes, imagining that he's here with me, holding me close.

This trip started as a mess, but like two opposed stars caught in each other's gravitational pull, we came together again, and it's been even better than I could have imagined. His smile, his kiss, the way he looks when he finishes inside me...

All of it makes my heart race. Every single bit of it. I'm smitten, and as much as I should hate it, I can't bring myself to.

Feeling happier than I have in weeks, I pull on a short sundress covered in bright yellow sunflowers and go to find breakfast. It's being served just like it was yesterday on the terrace, and everyone but Lili and Robin are already present. Dan has managed to convince the villa staff to source him some blooming tea, and without even asking, he pours me a cup and holds it out, not even pausing in his conversation with my brother.

I take the clear mug and pluck an orange cranberry scone from the tower of pastries balanced in the center of the table, taking off my oversized sun hat and sitting it on the empty chair next to me, content to listen to the boys talk while I eat. I'm famished, having only angrily picked at dinner last night and then partaking in strenuous physical activities.

"Roxanne is dying to go visit Positano," Andries announces, looking at Dan. "Her and Lili both. So we're going to take a boat ride to Positano in the afternoon. Do you want to go?"

Dan sips his tea, looking unconvinced. "...Am I allowed to say no?"

"I'd love to go," I chime in. "If there's room, that is."

Andries looks at me, and there is a hint of apology in his gaze that I suspect has to do with how he acted out last night. "Of course there is. You're always welcome, El."

Once I voice my approval, I know Dan will come too, and I love the idea of spending the day with him there. Sure, we'll be with the other couples, so we can't be romantic, but like Dan has reminded me time and time again, everyone expects us to be friendly to each other. I can keep my hands to myself because in my heart, I know that he and I are really much more than friends.

"That settles it then I guess." Dan sighs, before shooting me a glance. "I'll go tell the captain to prepare the yacht."

* * *

Tucked into a valley on the Amalfi Coast, the city of Positano looks like it was placed right where a giant ax had cut a piece of the land out. The city crawls up the sides of the steep coastline, full of ancient architecture and newer, posh shops that draw the wealthy elite in droves during the summer.

Once just a small fishing village, the oddly shaped town thrives now, and the busy energy of it is apparent as soon as we step off the yacht once it drops us off. There is so much to do and see, but we don't have any set schedule, which makes the excursion even more exciting.

Our end goal is to make it to the top of the city where we can look down at the unbelievable view of the city, but there are a bunch of other stops I want to make first. I insist on stopping by Antica Sartoria to get my mother a hand-embroidered silk scarf, and the maximalist style appeals to Roxie right away.

There is a bead shop where we stop so I can grab something for my younger sister, Aleida, and even find a stationery store for Lili to peruse. Roxanne stays outside at this one, dragging me to the side of the building with her before pulling a cigarette out of her bag and lighting it up after checking to make sure my brother isn't nearby.

"Don't tell Andries. He wants me to quit," she tells me hastily before taking a drag and blowing the smoke into the air in curling wisps. "We keep a lot of secrets from each other for two girls that supposedly don't even like each other, huh?"

She offers me a cigarette, but I shake my head. "No thanks. But…times are changing, I guess." I look her up and down and cross my arms. "Do we still not like each other, Roxanne?"

"I think you're a snake in the grass," she admits without hesitation. "But in your line of work I think that's necessary, so I can't exactly blame you. Otherwise… you're growing on me, kid."

"Kid!?" I gasp, offended.

Roxanne laughs her low, sultry laugh. "Maybe it's the whole star-crossed lovers thing you and Dan have going on, but I think I've got a soft spot for you at this point."

"I want to revisit this conversation later," I tell her, both unamused and secretly happy that we're mending things. I push all thoughts of my dad and his plans far to the back of my mind.

Dan, Andries, and Robin have disappeared, but we find them at a wine bar higher up in the city. Once the group is back up, we stroll through the narrow sidewalk, gifts in hand, and visit some of the must-see sights.

In the rush of it all, with Andries and Roxie far ahead of us taking pictures of the Santa Maria Assunta, Dan slips his hand into mine and squeezes lightly. He doesn't look down at me, wanting to keep the attention on us to a minimum, but he says, "You look beautiful today."

"You're not so bad yourself," I reply, my tone just as low. Our little secret moments warm my heart.

We finally make it to the top of the city, and the view takes my breath away. I didn't think that, after Capri, anything could strike me so much, but it almost looks unreal from up here gazing down at the city spreading out in shades of red, yellow, white, and tans, green trees and climbing vines peppering the vista among the rough gray rocks. My brother joins me at the lookout, bumping me with his shoulder to get my attention.

"You feeling any better?"

I frown. "Fine. Why do you ask?"

"You seemed grumpy on the yacht yesterday, and then understandably mad at dinner. Which I'm sorry for overreacting, by the way. But Dan pointed out that you might be feeling left out with all the couple things going on and…" He clears his throat, looking sincere yet struggling to find the right words. "Well, I'm glad you're here, and I want you to enjoy yourself too."

"I'm having a great time," I tell him honestly, laying my head on his shoulder. "I'm happy to be here with you and Roxanne… to be a part of all of this."

We're both silent for some time, before my brother quietly adds, "I'm glad you are too."

***

After our sightseeing, we head to *il Tridente,* a posh restaurant where Dan got us a table, not too far from where we were. With its beautiful terrace perched high enough to offer picturesque views to the city, the beach with its brown sand and sea stretching to the horizon, we eat a light lunch and drink too much limoncello. The bright yellow libation pours over my tongue like liquid sunshine, sour and sweet, making my head feel buzzy and lifting my mood.

We toast to, well… everything. Dan to Andries, then Andries to Dan. Lili toasts her sister with tears in her eyes, and then the two women hug and weep happily in each other's arms while Robin and Andries look on awkwardly.

Finally, Dan raises his glass a final time in my direction, and my heart soars before he even says anything. "And last but not least, I want to raise a toast to everyone's favorite last-minute addition to the trip, Elise. You started out as kind of a brat, but you've grown on me over the years—"

"Hey, I told her the same thing earlier!" Roxanne interjects, but Dan continues.

"You've grown on me over the years, and I'm glad to call you my… friend. To Elise!"

"To Elise!" the table echoes and this last drink of limoncello tastes even sweeter than all the ones before.

That is until I lower my glass and see Andries looking between Dan and me with his brow furrowed suspiciously again. Great.

"I want to go to a few more shops," Roxie announces when we're done, leaning heavily on her fiancé as they stand. "But you have to come with me, love. I'm dizzy."

"Of course you are," he tells her fondly, kissing the top of her head. "Don't worry, I won't let you fall."

The two couples all gather around a map that Robin has acquired, looking at the array of shops and deciding what else still needs to be visited. I hang back while Dan pays the bill for the meal when I feel my phone vibrate in my purse. Blinking away the haziness in my vision, I tap the screen on and read the message there waiting for me.

Dan: *Wanna go to a private bay?*

A little thrill runs through me. What does he have in mind now?

Elise: *My brother is already suspicious... Did you see him when we toasted? He was watching us like a hawk. If we disappear now, it's only gonna get worse.*

Dan: *Are you hearing them right now? They're planning to go on like ten other errands. We've got plenty of time for the yacht to take us there and bring us back.*

Elise: *You're crazy!*

I look up at him, standing right outside the doorway of the restaurant, a Cheshire grin on his face, and I can't resist any longer. Any hesitations I have melt away, and while my brother is distracted with Roxanne and her sister, I hurry over to him and take his outstretched hand, and then we're free.

I feel like a kid again running through the cobblestone streets with Dan, holding his hand and giggling as we hurry through the city to the waiting boat. Limoncello and the adrenaline rush of what we are doing makes me feel blissfully lightheaded, and when we reach the pier where we can step onto the yacht, I'm laughing so hard that I can barely stand.

Dan lifts me onto the boat with his hands around my waist, his hair mussed from the run and hanging on his forehead. I brush it back as he sits me on my feet, leaning in to kiss me on the corner of my mouth.

"Look at you, rule-breaker," he tells me. "You're going to get us in so much trouble."

"This was your idea," I point out, still laughing at the whole thing.

"I'll never admit it," he quips as the boat starts finally heading off the pier. "Now, come sit with me. I've got a surprise for you when we get there."

The wind starts blowing softly on my face and the sun beams on my skin but it's rather a comforting feeling. I lay my head against Dan's shoulder and after intertwining my hand with his, I shut my eyes, savoring the present moment. This is too perfect to even be real, and yet, here I'm going to a secret bay with my brother's best friend. I can only hope Andries will never find out.

After just ten minutes, I hear the engine stop, and the boat coming to a halt. Without so much of a breeze, the sunlight on my face intensifies to a point that it makes it unbearable.

"Here we are," Dan whispers in my ear, before kissing the top of my head.

Opening my eyes wide, I straighten myself and stand in awe at the beautiful bay in front of me.

Our secluded little cove is cut deep into the cliff, so it's surrounded on almost all sides by towering black rocks. Despite that, when we step off the yacht and into the sand, it's sugary, white, and soft on my feet. Palm trees ring the beach, and the cove is far enough back that the waves are small and placid. It's truly a secret paradise just for the two of us.

A few staff members are setting up a lounge area for us farther back in the sand, with a huge beach blanket, towels, and what looks like champagne. It's shaded by an enormous umbrella, and I can even spot crystal flutes waiting on us.

"What is this!?" I gasp, whipping around to face Dan, who looks obnoxiously proud of himself.

"A date."

"Dan…" I turn in a circle, kicking my sandals off as I do so. "This is more than just a date. This is…this is…"

"All for you," he murmurs, wrapping his arms around me from behind and kissing my hair. I lean back into his embrace with a happy exhale.

"No one has ever done anything like this for me. Ever." My heart feels like it's swelling in my chest, emotions swirling in me so strongly that if I had any doubt whether I was falling in love with Dan or not, there is no question at this point. I'm absolutely smitten.

I turn in his arms, ready to tell him that I love him, but he looks playful, mischievous even, and it gives me pause.

"What exactly is it you are thinking about right now…?" I ask as he backs away from me and toward the crystal-clear turquoise water.

Cut off on all sides by the towering, jagged rocks of the bay, it feels like Dan and I are completely alone, even as the staff members bustle around the sand putting together our beach picnic.

"Get in the water with me," he coaxes, already pulling his shirt over his head.

Dan shoots a brilliant smile at me over his shoulder, looking so tan and handsome that it makes my heart skip a beat. "What are you staring at? Let's go."

Nervously, I glance back at the five or so staff members still putting our things together. "I didn't bring my bikini."

Right as I'm speaking, Dan shimmies his linen shorts down his muscular legs, standing near the surf in only his black briefs. He looks back at me again, laughing, "Yeah me either. Let's go!"

Hesitating once more, I finally give in, pulling my sundress over my head and letting it fall to the sand. I had only put on a white lace bralette this morning, with matching panties, wanting to be comfortable, but as I follow Dan at almost a run, I'm wishing for just a little more support.

Just as I catch up to him, Dan turns quickly and grabs me by the waist, spinning me around and growling playfully. I squeal, and he lowers me just enough to kiss me on the mouth before sitting my feet back in the sand. I blink up at him, lips curling in a smile, but as quickly as he had grabbed me, Dan is off again, running into the water, arching his arms over his head, and diving, as slick and graceful as a seal, beneath the placid waves.

Huffing, I contemplate waiting on the shore and refusing to play his game, but I can't help but be charmed and amused by him. Dan seems to feel so free in his exuberance, and here in this private cove, it feels like we're a normal couple. The hindrance of having to pretend like we're only friends is gone, and it makes me understand why he's so playful and makes me want to join him, even if he is being silly.

Resigned, I follow him into the water. It's as warm as ever, and I cut through the salty water without anything slowing me down. Having swam out far enough that the water is to his waist, Dan is waiting on me, beads of water sparkling in his hair.

"Took you long enough," he says as I finally reach him.

"I didn't know it was a race," I counter.

He's so much taller than I am that the water is nearly to my shoulders. Dan takes me by the waist once more, pulling me toward him. "Less about it being a race, and more about how badly I know you wanted to get to me and put your greedy hands all over me."

I try to wiggle out of his grasp, pretending to be offended, but he holds fast. Just like he had said, the staff back on the beach completely ignores us, and at this distance, it'd be hard for them to see what we're doing, anyway.

"Keep acting like this and I'll never touch you again!" I threaten, even as he runs his hands up my back soothingly.

"I don't believe that for one minute." Dan has got me flush against his body now, and I go limp. Even the playful fight is gone out of me once we're skin to skin. "I think that you want to touch me every chance you get."

"How do you even remember to breathe with that big ego taking up all the space your brain should occupy?" I tease, reaching up to run my thumb over his full bottom lip. "I've never met a man so self-obsessed."

"It's why we get along so well. Your ego suits mine, you know?" He's spinning us in a lazy circle, and I instinctually wrap my legs around him. "We could rule the world, you and I, Ms. Elise Van den Bosch, if we ever had the initiative to leave the bed."

"We're not in bed right now," I point out.

"That's true." His voice lowers seductively, making me shiver. "But even now, I've got bedroom things on my mind."

He emphasizes his words by pressing his body into mine, the hard line of his erection telling me everything I need to know about his current feelings for me, bedroom or not. My cheeks heat, even in the warmth of the summer sun.

"Can't you control yourself even for a few hours?"

He chuckles. "Elise, you're nearly naked, soaking wet, with your legs wrapped around me. I'd have to be a dead man not to be hard right now."

I grind myself against him experimentally and hum in approval at how firm he is already, and the frustrated noise he makes. "Well, you're certainly not dead, then."

"I will be soon if you don't stop," he rumbles in my ear, brushing my damp hair out of the way so he can kiss my neck. When he moves back to my mouth, his lips taste like salt.

I don't take his warning, wrapping my arms around his neck and pushing my pelvis against his again. Dan makes a strangled noise, lowering his hands until he's supporting my weight by holding my ass, fingers clenching and unclenching.

"Still not dead," I point out with a wicked smile, and when he kisses me this time, it's deep and intense, our teeth clicking together. Even though there are people on the beach behind us, Dan manages to make this moment feel so intimate and personal. When we're together, it's like the world shrinks down to just him and me.

"If you're going to continue to tease me, I'm going to finish what you've started," he murmurs against my lips, his fingers starting to work under the waistband of my panties under the water.

"We can't!" I hiss. "There are people right over there!"

"It won't look any different to them whether I am inside you or not," he assures me, palming my ass a few times before giving up on removing the offending garment fully. Inside, he pulls them aside so his fingers can graze my bare pussy and I jump.

"And you'd be okay fucking me out here knowing that other people can see us?!"

His touch grows more demanding, fingers sliding between my folds as my breath shudders out of me. "It will just look like we're swimming together." He runs a thumb around my clit, and I make a helpless sound at how good it feels. "It will just be our little secret, El. What do you say?"

I know that I should deny him, and how wrong this is, but the temptation is too strong. I can't resist Dan, and he knows it. Biting my lip, I try to come up with a good reason to say no, but finally, I nod. "Okay. If you really think no one will notice."

Dan grins fiercely, pushing me so I float away just enough for him to jerk his briefs off. I know that out here in the sea, under the open sky, there can't be much foreplay, but he still takes his time touching and caressing my pussy with a practiced ease, using his thumb to tease my clit until it's swollen and I'm bumping my mound against his hand. I'm anxious to have him inside of me, taking this rare chance to admire his tanned chest and arms while he works to pleasure me. Dan seems to enjoy my touch just as much as I do his, and it doesn't take us long to reposition ourselves once more; this time, for him to sink home into me.

The warm sea water makes our movements slower than they would usually be, everything deliberate and slick. He's finally gotten my panties off, but I keep them around one ankle, so they don't float away as I wrap my legs around his waist once more. We're so perfectly made for each other than when I do, it's like we're perfectly lined up for him to enter me without even having to try.

Cupping my ass again, he pulls me forward until the head of his erection is pushing between my folds and into my core. I'm still sensitive from last night and exhale shakily as he fills me, having to go in small increments because of how snug the fit is. He can't look away from where he's entering me, transfixed by the sight of his cock disappearing into my body, but for me, watching the expression on his face turns me on even more. I love watching how good my body can make him feel, especially since he's such a generous lover with me. This time is no exception.

"This is going to be quicker than I wanted," he tells me as I trace his pecs with my fingertips. "It's just you… all wet… so tight…"

I kiss him, hard, before pulling back, "Just fuck me, Dan. Please."

With a groan, he captures my mouth once more, surging into me until he's sheathed to the hilt. I suck in a shocked breath at how quick it was, my body is forced to accommodate his impressive size, but after the surprise comes a sharp pleasure. Dan doesn't waste any time, pulling out and slamming home again, finding a rhythm in this strange, aquatic position that doesn't make what we're doing too obvious.

I hold myself as close as I can to him, just riding out his pace and enjoying every second of it. Once Dan is settled into a tempo, he goes back to gently stroking my clit in tighter and tighter circles until his thumb presses against it in earnest before starting the process over. I can't keep my hips still at this, jerking spasmodically against him, dropping my forehead to his shoulder when he breaks our kiss. Surely the people on the beach can't still be in the dark about what we're up to, but at this point, I'm feeling so good that I don't care.

Pressure is building at the base of my spine, and Dan doesn't slow down his pace at all, feet firmly planted in the sand. He's driving us both toward a steep, fast, satisfying peak, and all I can do is hold on.

"You're mine," he growls into my ear. "Tell me, Elise, tell me you are."

"I-I'm yours."

"And who is about to make you come?" he demands.

"You!" I cry, quieting the sound against the flesh of his shoulder, biting down. Dan exhales in a rush at the nip, his thumb never ceasing on my clit and his cock filling up my pussy again and again, relentlessly.

I come with another near-yell, burying my face in his neck and holding on for dear life as my world crashes around me. It bursts out from my center, setting all my nerves on fire, hot and fast as a firebrand.

Dan isn't far behind, and when he spills himself deep in my pussy, all he can say is my name, over and over. "Elise," he groans. "Elise, Elise, what did you do to me?"

It sounds like music to my ears.

Thank goodness he's still holding me up, because I'm not sure there is any way I can swim back to shore now, and from the exhausted sound Dan makes as he lowers me back to my feet in the water, I can't help but think we both might be stuck out there now. Oh well. At least we'd be together.

"I can't swim," I tell him in earnest, tightening my leg's grip on his waist.

"What, ever? Or just now that I've fucked your brains out?"

"Now, jerk." Despite the bite of my words, I snuggle my face into his neck. "Carry me to shore."

"Yes, princess Elise," he groans, using one hand to pull his briefs up. "Anything for you. It's not like my legs are jelly right now or anything."

I can't help but giggle as he carries me back onto the dry land once the staff is gone, maneuvering me into a fireman's carry once we're close. I kick my legs, unhappy with the change in position, but Dan just slaps my ass with an open hand hard enough to sting, laughing uproariously the entire time.

It's all silly. Stupid even. And I love every minute of it.

I love him. I really do… which is a problem for another day. Looking around at everything Dan has organized once he gently deposits me on the beach blanket, there is no way in hell I'm going to ruin this all right now.

We drink the champagne, crisp and dry, out of the crystal flutes, kissing between sips until Dan takes it upon himself to pour a splash down my chest and lick it off. I yelp, and we wrestle until I'm on top of him and repeat the action. When I take my turn licking the alcohol from his skin, he tastes like sea salt and sunshine.

Have I ever been this happy before? If I have, I can't remember it.

He wraps his arms tightly around me then, until every inch of our available skin is pressed together, and once that's done he completes the circuit with his lips on mine. We're lazy and redolent, limbs tangling up and hands caressing anywhere they can reach. Here we are alone and can be whoever we want. Do whatever we want. I hope we never have to leave.

When Dan rolls me onto my back, bracketing my head with his forearms and gazing deep into my eyes, I know this is the moment I've been waiting for. We're so close now that I feel our souls reaching out for one another. I'm going to tell him that I'm in love with him, damn the consequences. I'm tired of playing by the rules... tired of being prim and proper Elise. Above anything else—I want Dan.

I open my mouth to form the words, and yet, nothing comes out.

If you say it, then you're vulnerable, the frightened part of me says. *You're giving him a weapon to use against you. Right now, you still have the power. Once you say those words, you hand it over to him, and you're never getting it back.*

"What is it?" Dan says, confused at why I'm staring at him with my mouth open, but silent.

"Just that…" I have to look away, so utterly disappointed in myself but in a way relieved that I didn't tell him. "I really like this."

"This?" he echoes.

"Yeah, whatever is happening between us." I rub my thumb over his bottom lip. "I like it."

Dan chuckles, nipping at the shell of my ear and whispering, "I like it too."

Of course, we can't stay in this perfect moment forever, and it isn't too much longer before my phone rings. Neither of us says anything as I untangle myself from Dan's embrace, and it's no surprise to see that it's my brother calling.

With a heavy sigh, feeling like a dark cloud is starting to form over me, I answer. "Hello?"

"What a shock that you and Dan are gone again," my brother gripes. "Where the hell are you?"

"We just went to walk the beach. We were tired of the city and all the shopping. What do you need?"

Andries makes a disbelieving noise but continues. "We're ready to go back to Capri. Should we wait on you?"

I glance at Dan, who shakes his head no. "Don't worry about us. We'll meet you at the villa."

My brother's tone changes then, and he sounds almost cajoling. "If I were you, I'd hurry up. I have a surprise waiting at the villa for you."

Something about his words makes my blood run cold. "A surprise? What is it?"

"I'm not going to ruin it. See you back in Capri."

When he hangs up, I pull the phone away from my ear and stare at the now-blank screen in disbelief. "Oh. This can't be good."

"What do you mean? He just said he had a surprise. That doesn't sound bad."

"There's no way he wouldn't argue with me about being alone with you again unless he was about to pull a fast one on us. Mark my words, there is something unpleasant waiting back at the villa for us." Even in the summer heat, I shiver. "I just feel it."

"Well… should we head back then? Face the music, so they say?"

I take in the cove and our private beach around us. Still in our underwear, covered in sand and salt, I don't want to let go of this. I'm not ready to reenter the real world just yet.

"Can we stay a few minutes longer?" I ask. Dan's smile is sad, but he nods.

"Of course we can, love."

He holds me as we listen to the waves, drinking the rest of the champagne out of the bottle, passing it back and forth. The magic is gone now that Andries has interrupted us, but he can't erase the wonderful memories we made beforehand. I try to keep myself here in the present, not in the future back at the villa, worrying about my brother's shenanigans, but it's impossible.

After another thirty minutes, I take a long sip of champagne and set the dark bottle back on the beach blanket. "I guess we should go."

"Yeah…" Dan brushes my now dry hair to the side and kisses the back of my neck tenderly. "I guess we should."

With the sun low on the horizon, we dress, board the yacht and head back to Capri. Dan and I stay attached to one another, him sitting so I can rest my head in his lap. He gently runs his fingers through my knotted hair, working the tangles out with patience and loving touches. I keep my eyes closed, trying desperately to decipher what my brother could mean by a surprise. Unless he has been following us around every minute of every day, I can't figure out a time when he could have confirmed that Dan and I were hooking up. It seems very unlikely to me, though, that he has an actual, fun surprise for me. Instead, I know it's going to be some sort of double-edged sword. Nice on the outside, but made to make me miserable. After we've reconnected lately, I was sure that Andries would be able to accept Dan and me together, eventually. But now I'm beginning to think this is one pill he will never be able to swallow. Being in love with Dan might cost him his best friend, and me my brother.

I swallow hard, and Dan senses the rising tension in me. "What's wrong, El?"

"I've just got this gut feeling that Andries is about to mess everything up for us in a big way. I can't figure out how, but I just know he is."

Taking my hand in his, Dan brushes my knuckles with his lips. "There is nothing your brother could say or do to separate us now. I've already told you—if I have to choose, I'm going to choose you, baby."

Struck by his loyalty, I pull myself up, cupping his face in my hands and kissing him soundly. This man... I can't believe he's been right next to me all this time and I've only just noticed how incredible he is. I can't lose him. And I won't.

Dan pulls back, resting his forehead against mine and closing his eyes. We share breaths, the only sounds around us being the noise from the yacht's sails in the wind. Again, a confession of love is waiting right there on the tip of my tongue. I'm sure that I mean it, but still, I'm too much of a coward to tell him.

"No matter what happens," I say instead, "I really liked this adventure between the two of us."

Dan opens his eyes, as deep as the ocean around us, and in their depths, I see disappointment as well as love. He wants more from me, and I just can't give it. At least not yet.

We embrace, and I'm not sure why, but it feels like a goodbye.

CHAPTER 35

Elise

Once we have cleaned ourselves up in the small yacht bathroom, Dan and I kiss one last time below deck, before we have to emerge and take the private car to the villa, where we get to pretend that we're nothing but rivalrous friends once more.

The atmosphere in the car between us is tense, but once we arrive back at the villa, the energy is lighter and happier than I expected. Maybe Andries isn't about to fuck things up... maybe he genuinely went out of his way to make me happy. Is that even possible?

Everyone is gathered on the terrace, and we follow their laughter to join them. At first, nothing seems amiss, just a group of people standing in a circle, but when Andries hears us approaching, he pivots quickly and steps to the side. Next to him is a man, even taller than my brother, who I don't recognize from behind. But something about his silhouette is oddly familiar.

"Who is that?" Dan asks in a whisper, just as confused as I am.

That question is quickly answered when none other than *Johan Bentinck* turns around, his smile as bright as the sun.

"Fuck," Dan spits, his pace slowing down. "This guy? Seriously?"

No one seems to hear him, especially not Johan.

"It's good to see you, El," Johan greets, his tone laced with genuine excitement, while we pad slowly but surely toward my brother and his new acquaintance.

I'm not sure if I've ever been in shock before, but I am now. My hands and lips are cold as I take in the impossible sight of my crush from all those years ago, now an even more attractive twenty-two-year-old man. Johan's jaw is chiseled, his dark blond hair perfectly cropped, and just like it was at equestrian camp, he has the most handsome smile. He's grown taller, his shoulders broader, but his face is still so open and kind that I almost feel bad that I'm so taken aback.

Johan broke my heart when I was fifteen. Until Dan came along, I had never trusted a man since Johan had all but ghosted me. At camp, I had fallen almost instantly in love with the older boy who seemed to have some sort of supernatural connection with the horses. He had made me laugh like no one ever had, and he was clearly the most handsome guy in the whole camp. Johan made it clear from the start that he was leaving for Oxford in the fall, but that didn't stop fifteen-year-old me from falling head over heels, and being ultimately crushed when he left that September. He had promised to visit me the following summer, but as the calendar days in June, then July, and finally August ticked by, it became clear that Johan was never coming.

But now... now he's here. Did he finally come back for me after all this time?

What a stupid thought, I chide myself.

"What's the matter?" Andries laughs, looking triumphant that his plan to come between Dan and me has worked so instantly. "You can't say hi, El?"

Amused, Johan breaks from the group and approaches me, his arms open for an embrace. I look from him to Dan, and then back again, heart in my throat. I never, ever wanted something like this to happen. Beside me, the man I'm currently in love with, and in front of me, my very first love.

Time moves in slow motion as Johan comes to hug me in greeting, but before he can touch me, Dan is there, not pushing or being belligerent in any way, but simply standing in Johan's way, an unreadable look on his face. Johan stutters to a stop and raises an eyebrow.

"Is there a problem?"

"I'm not sure," Dan deadpans, holding out his hand for a handshake. "I'm Dan O'Brian. Welcome to my villa."

Johan's lips twist into a smile of relief, and he reaches out to shake Dan's hand, although very briefly, before Dan leans closer to him and says, "Now, get the fuck out."

"Dan, please," I say, stepping in, quite shocked at his lack of manners, and I grasp his arm so he can back down. "Johan is a friend of the family."

Dan remains just as serious, glaring at Johan as if his stare could shoot daggers. He seems to know exactly who Johan is, which is strange since I never told Dan about him.

"I'm sorry, man," Johan starts, his tone laced with genuine humility. "I didn't know it was your villa, Andries invited me over and I took a plane over from England and —"

"Is everything alright?" Andries has come over and is now standing beside Johan, looking inquisitively at both Dan and me. "Dan, this is Johan, a longtime family friend. Since we have a spare bedroom, I figured he could come over and stay with us."

Despite their respectful and polite tones, Dan doesn't seem convinced by either of them, and the air between the four of us grows thicker by each passing second.

Dan finally turns to my brother and says, "We need to talk. Only the two of us. Can we go back inside?"

Oh no! What the heck are they going to talk about? My eyes are pleading with Dan for him not to reveal our affair to my brother out of revenge or something, but Dan pays it no mind.

"Sure." Andries just shrugs and the two of them leave Johan and me alone as they walk back to the villa.

My heartbeat is racing as I watch the two silhouettes getting farther and farther from us and then disappearing inside the house.

"It's been such a long time," Johan says, his tone joyful, breaking the uncomfortable silence that had settled between us. He takes a step back, making a show of looking at me with pride in his gaze. "Look at you, you are all grown up now."

I chuckle, wishing I could have a glass of wine or something in my hand to ease the awkwardness of the moment. "You too," I say simply, my eyes already scanning through the terrace in desperate need of a server to bring me an alcoholic beverage.

"Excuse me!" Johan seems to have understood the situation because as soon as I pivot to follow his gaze, he's actually calling the server that is behind me, who's holding a tray of bubbles, and takes two glasses.

"Here," he says, handing me one. "Looks like you might need it."

"Thank you, I really needed to have a drink." Before I can bring the bubbly to my lips, though, Johan raises his glass.

"Well, cheers, to our little reunion here in Capri."

I reply with nothing but a smile as we clink our glasses and quietly take our first sip. Despite his cheerful tone, I have felt rather uneasy to see him again. After all, this guy ghosted me for three damn years and then shows up here like nothing happened.

"If you don't mind me asking..." Johan lets his words trail, as if he's still contemplating whether to go ahead or not. "Is Dan your boyfriend or something?"

I nearly spit out my drink at his question, a wave of shock taking over me. "Uh, no," I manage to blurt out. "He's just a good friend." My eyes travel up to meet his and I study his face more attentively. "Why are you asking me that, though?"

Johan takes another sip of champagne, answering with a shrug. "It's just the impression I got. That's all."

Not interested in dwelling further into my private life, I turn the subject of the question to him. "And you? Any woman waiting for you back in England?"

Instantly, his lips twist into a smile I haven't seen before and there's even some sort of twinkle in his eyes as he says, "Nope, the only one I want is here."

"Oh, stop it." I roll my eyes, shaking my head in total disbelief at his bullshit. "You've ghosted me for the past three years."

To my astonishment, there's a frown forming on his forehead. "I'm sorry—what?" His tone becomes overly serious and confused. "You told me to never text you again or your dad would get me arrested. I just respected your wish and figured you had moved on or something."

I stop immediately in my tracks, my mouth gaping in shock at his words. "What are you talking about?" I ask, my gaze facing his again. "Me?" Shaking my head, I take another gulp of my bubbly, trying to tame all this mix of emotions surging through me, while a thought suddenly forms in the back of my mind. "When did I say that?"

He seems to mull over the question before saying, "When I moved to Oxford and asked you how you were doing."

"That's impossible," I tell him, my puzzlement growing at every passing second. "I never said anything like that!"

Despite my louder and shakier voice, Johan keeps his calm and composure, reaching for his back pocket to take his iPhone out. "You definitely did. It was a message that came from your number, and I even tried to call you, and then you blocked me."

"Johan, that's not possible," I repeat, this time slower but still in disbelief. "I'd have never blocked you."

He shows me his screen, and more precisely, the text message he was just talking about. I check the number of the sender and I instantly gasp as I realize it's definitely mine.

"What the hell!" Adrenaline kicks in as I reach for my own iPhone inside my purse, ready to show him all the unanswered texts I'd sent him and his unblocked contact. To my surprise, my heartbeat is speeding up as I unlock my screen and start scrolling down through the Messages app.

Then I stop at the texts exchanged with *Johan Bentinck*, back in 2019, and start searching for the one I just saw on his phone. As I expected, after searching for a while, I don't find it, so I turn the screen to him, and say, "I didn't find that text, but I did find all the ones you didn't reply to."

Johan takes my phone in his hand and starts clicking around, until he heaves a long sigh, as if finding out something. Something even worse than he thought. He turns the screen back at me, pointing his finger right under his contact details and says, "El, that's not even my number."

My mouth hangs open as I try to process his statement. "Wha—what do you mean that's not your number?"

"The person who blocked me also changed the number on your phone, most likely to receive your texts themselves and make it seem like I'm the one who ghosted you. Look." He reaches back for his phone, and then sends me a test message and, just like we predicted, I don't receive it.

I immediately try calling the number I have been texting all this time, hoping somehow to find out who it belongs to, but I land on an automatic voice message saying the number is no longer valid.

"Dammit!" I snap out of frustration. My mind starts fuming in realization that someone made it a point to screw my relationship with Johan. And all I want to do is scream from anger!

But now at least everything makes sense. Johan never ghosted me, he truly cared for me just as I thought! Someone close to me made sure I wouldn't talk to him until now, though. Could it be my brother? My overbearing and nosy brother blocking my crush in an act of revenge for whatever conflict was going on between us back then? And what about Dan? Could it have been him who helped my brother achieve it? Fuck, fuck, and fuck!

"El, it's okay…" Johan reaches out and holds me in an embrace to ease the rage I have inside me. "I'm here now."

Yes, Johan is here, the English boy with his dark blond hair, his beautiful blue eyes, his sharp jawline, and his supernatural gift for horses and equestrianism. But Dan is here too. What am I supposed to do now?

If only I had reached out to his family and tried to check on him before assuming the worst out of him. But I was just too prideful, too hurt to even give it a try.

With my head lying on Johan's shoulder, his arms around me, I should feel much better, but the truth is I'm lost, torn, and I don't know what my heart wants anymore.

Johan was my first crush, the man I thought I would lose my virginity to, but now I'm in love with my brother's best friend. Confronting my past is leaving a sour taste in my mouth. I release myself from his embrace, unable to look him in the eye for the time being. There's so much to process, so much to think about.

"Is it too late for us?" he asks trying to look me in the eye, his gaze filled with hope.

I don't think I have ever had such a difficult question to answer in my entire life. "What are Dan and Andries still doing inside? I'm gonna go check on them."

When I'm about to leave his side, his question unanswered, Johan reaches out and holds my hand before I can even walk away. "El, wait—"

"I can't answer you now, Johan," I tell him, my tone coming off more aggressive than I expected. "After three years without any news from you, maybe it's too late for us. I don't know. It's just all too sudden to answer you."

There's some silence between us while I catch my breath and try to calm myself down.

"I still have the shirt you gave me, you know," he says out of nowhere, causing my eyes to widen in surprise again. Memories of our time together at summer camp start flashing through me and the moment I bought him a shirt because I had accidentally ruined his makes me laugh. "I took it with me to Oxford. It became kind of my lucky charm."

I remain too moved to talk. Johan, on the other hand, takes a few steps forward, his hand reaching out and tucking a small lock of hair behind my ear like he used to.

"I missed you," he says, his tone just above a whisper. "Did you miss me?"

He's dangerously close to me now, but I can't help looking him in the eye, wanting nothing more than to see how sincere he is.

"I've missed you too." My eyes are locked on his for a moment, and in silence, I can hear our heartbeats louder than before, while his gaze starts lingering down to my lips —an indication of what he wants.

I can't do this!

I take a step back, breaking the spell between us. And, in the heat of the moment, say, "I, um, I've got to go and check on them." Johan can't hide his disappointment at seeing me walking away, but it's for the better. I truly need to go and fix whatever damage Dan and Andries's quarrel has already caused. "See you around."

THEIR STORY CONTINUES WITH

BOOK 4, DAN.

Don't have the sequel yet?

Enjoy 10% off on your next purchase using the code FLYER10 at melaniemartins.com (code has to be manually entered at checkout).